MW00721310

SPINDRIFT

A CANADIAN BOOK OF THE SEA

SPINDRIFT

Edited & Introduced by

MICHAEL L. HADLEY & ANITA HADLEY

Douglas & McIntyre

Douglas and McIntyre (2013) Ltd.
P.O. Box 219, Madeira Park, BC, V0N 2H0
www.douglas-mcintyre.com

Cover and frontispiece: David Blackwood, *Flora S. Nickerson Down on the Labrador*, 1978, etching and aquatint on wove paper, final wp 50.5 x 40.2 cm (imp.) All other illustrations by Matthew Wolferstan
Dustjacket design by Anna Comfort O'Keeffe
Text design by Mary White
Printed and bound in Canada
Printed on 100% PCW paper

Douglas and McIntyre (2013) Ltd. acknowledges the support of the Canada Council for the Arts, which last year invested $153 million to bring the arts to Canadians throughout the country. We also gratefully acknowledge financial support from the Government of Canada through the Canada Book Fund and from the Province of British Columbia through the BC Arts Council and the Book Publishing Tax Credit.

Library and Archives Canada Cataloguing in Publication

Spindrift (2017)
    Spindrift : a Canadian book of the sea / edited, with introduction and commentary, by Michael L. Hadley & Anita Hadley.

Includes bibliographical references.
Issued in print and electronic formats.
ISBN 978-1-77162-173-1 (hardcover).—ISBN 978-1-77162-174-8 (HTML)

    1. Seas—Literary collections. 2. Canada—Literary collections.
I. Hadley, Michael L., editor II. Hadley, Anita, 1938–, editor III. Title.

PS8251.S43S65 2017   C810.8'032162   C2017-902727-1
                                                    C2017-902728-X

Dedicated to the memory of
Norman Borradaile Hadley (1964–2016).

"Bon matelot."

"I never could have lived away from the salt water or the salt air, because the sea runs in my blood."
—Captain Andy Publicover (1877–1960),
captain of the Lunenburg schooner *W.N. Zwicker*

CONTENTS

CHAPTER III   **VESSELS**

CHAPTER IV   PASSAGES

BEGINNINGS

The inspiration for this book arose from an evening of nautical readings held at the Maritime Museum of British Columbia, Victoria. Entitled "Master and Commander," the presentation offered an entertaining selection describing daring exploits upon the high seas. While passages were largely drawn from the adventures of Patrick O'Brian's swashbuckling hero, Captain Jack Aubrey, other works from around the world were also represented. We were enthralled—and our seagoing imaginations tweaked. As we walked home past the vessels moored in Victoria's Inner Harbour, we began to imagine a similar evening based on *Canadian* nautical writings. What would it include? Who would be the writers? How varied the experiences? How deep the emotions?

So began a five-year quest for Canadian nautical writings. It was a time of joyful discovery. Casting a wide net, we began with literature—novels, poetry, short stories, plays—but soon moved beyond this rich source to include non-fictional writing: journals, histories, biographies, memoirs, even articles. And sometimes we found that they all seemed to be rolled into one. Ship's logs, myths, stories of quiet exaltation and wrenching lamentations can all become poetry when the experience resonates deeply with the rhythm of the human heart.

What we discovered has changed forever the way I think and feel about my country. I once had an image of Canada—narrowly populated from east to west along its southern reaches, then stretching endlessly northward towards limitless, unrelenting ice. It was the *land*—not the sea—that defined my country. But reading about the Canadian experience of the sea has reconfigured my image. From the

Atlantic to the Arctic to the Pacific—yes, also to the Great Lakes—this land of heroic proportions is, as writer and novelist Rudy Wiebe has discovered, shaped and defined by water. Whether we live close to the sea, or far from its shores, it is the oceans that bind our destiny and inform who and what we are as a nation.

The ten sections of *Spindrift* attest to the breadth—and sometimes contradictions—of our relationship as a nation to the sea. How our oceans encompass us, defining the limits of our vast land mass—at once connecting, separating, nourishing, threatening, bestowing, destroying, enthralling, betraying, inspiring...

A whole community of seafarers inhabits these pages: Inuit, First Nations, explorers, navigators, immigrants, refugees, fishers, whalers, crabbers and squid-jiggers, hunters, boat builders, traders, scientists, adventurers, former slaves, lepers, missionaries, lighthouse keepers, divers, salvagers, travellers and pleasure boaters, poets, surveyors, rescuers, survivors and victims... and those who wait silently in solitude. The stories they tell—or that are told about them—are, in fact, our stories, for they broaden our experience of who we are as a nation. I can no longer remain detached from events occurring on one of our distant shores. From shore to shore to shore, we are bound to one another by a surging in our veins awakening some primordial memory deep within our common experience.

In his book, *The Idea of Canada: Letters to a Nation* (2016), Governor General David Johnston challenges Canadians to give their country a gift to celebrate Canada's 150th anniversary of Confederation. In celebration of our nation's unique relationship to the three great oceans that bind us, we offer as our gift, *Spindrift: A Canadian Book of the Sea.*

—ANITA HADLEY

WAYPOINTS

Spindrift *n.* i. Blown sea-spray; ii. Spume; iii. Wisps of spray curling off the crests of waves in extreme winds.

—Nautical lore

The sea is a powerful archetype. It strikes unique emotional resonances when we experience it. This is also true when we experience it second-hand through the words of others. As captured in various cultural and literary traditions, the sea conjures up sublime images of power and majesty, of hazard and daunting challenge. The sea reveals undercurrents of myth, memory and imagination. It inspires haunting poetry. Just what this means for the Canadian experience of the sea is the subject of this book.

Our collection gathers responses to a fundamental question: what is the recorded *relationship* of Canadians to the sea? More pointedly, how has the sea—as a medium, and as an experience— shaped the Canadian consciousness? By contextualizing passages drawn from a wide selection of authors—seafarers and non-seafarers among them—we have let each voice speak for itself. Each witness brings a unique perspective and flavour to what emerges as a compelling mosaic. The authentic tones and moods of these stories and reflections embrace all modes of expression from lyrical to dramatic. Canadian maritime experience—whether in home or foreign waters—is central to the nation's cultural tradition and lore.

Our principle of selection from among this rich diversity is clear: memorable writing that is brief, representative and engaging. Had we included everything that we had wished, this volume would have run to well over six hundred pages of revealing testimony. Clearly, we have had to adjust our sails to weather and wind: trimming, shortening and even bare-poling to complete the voyage. We have therefore restricted ourselves to those cultural documents which—taken together—reflect the spirit of what Canadians have experienced. What we now offer is "spindrift—wisps of spray curling back off waves." While we have always sought intrinsically good writing, we have not hesitated on rare occasion to dip into the local and popular. But we do so only if it illuminates some dimension of the Canadian experience.

Of course, other published collections have addressed the topic of Canada and the sea, each one with different emphases and focus. One thinks, for instance, of Allan Anderson's compilation of interviews with seafaring workers in *Salt Water, Fresh Water* (1979); or of the regional perspectives in George Nicholson's self-published *Vancouver Island's West Coast, 1762–1962* (1966) and Meddy Stanton's *We Belong to the Sea: A Nova Scotia Anthology* (2002). Rainer K. Baehre's *Outrageous Seas: Shipwreck and Survival in the Waters off Newfoundland, 1583–1893* (1999) provides yet another graphic regional focus. Reflecting on Newfoundland's historical record, he writes that the "influence of the sea has been pervasive, and it has left a deep cultural imprint, particularly in Newfoundland and Labrador." By casting our net even wider, we have found such cultural imprints wherever Canadians have put to sea.

Writers who envision this broader canvas tend to argue for a particular seabound, geopolitical view of Canada. We see this, for example, in Victor Suthren's edited work *Canadian Stories of the Sea* (1993), or in his historical survey *The Island of Canada: How Three Oceans Shaped Our Nation* (2009). Here he tacitly endorses the perspectives so often repeated in naval and nautical journals. "There is no nation with a greater physical connection to the sea than Canada," he explains, "and yet there are few people with such a stunning wealth of seacoast who are as unaware, or unknowing, of that connection as Canadians." His point is well taken.

The written record projects "the sea" as a predominantly male domain: visceral, aggressive, challenging and subject to mastery by commanding figures. By contrast, it portrays women in their traditional roles as the supporters and mourners of male endeavour, and as the strength in family and community. Significantly, however, the actual Canadian experience of the sea has been gradually changing that image. For with the engagement of women in leading marine roles from deckhands to skippers, a new reality has emerged. Strikingly, however, the written lore of the sea has not yet caught up with these contemporary social changes. Our collection necessarily reflects this conventional reality. Ultimately, "the sea" sets the scene for a world of self-realization, beauty and tragedy, which embraces the experience of both women and men alike.

The geographical context of Canada explains just how important such experience actually is. The nation lies gripped on three lengthy and rugged sides by the Pacific, the Atlantic and—by far the smallest of the world's oceans—the Arctic. These form the primary focus of our exploration. They constitute a natural three-ocean frontier. Together they form a realm of maritime endeavour that has, since the earliest days of Canadian history, inspired the major share of nautical reflection. They bear the burden of proof for what the sea means to Canada.

Yet we recognize that Canada has also been shaped by the Great Lakes, a remarkable inland sea. The largest body of fresh water on earth, it has been the scene of human endeavour matching anything the world's oceans could offer: enterprise, migration and war among them. Mariners on these lakes have experienced all the weather conditions they could find deep-sea. The completion of the St. Lawrence Seaway in 1959 opened this maritime heartland to ocean-going vessels. With its fifteen locks, the seaway now takes ships over two thousand nautical miles from the Atlantic into all five of the Great Lakes. Embracing over one hundred ports, it carries over 160 million tons of cargo. Fifty percent of the cargo runs between international ports in Europe, the Middle East and Africa. Like the sea, the Great Lakes have also engaged the creative imagination. In the final analysis, however, we recognized with regret that traveller and poet Henry James got it right in 1871 when he observed: the Great Lakes are "the sea and yet just not the sea." Their written heritage belongs in a separate volume.

Significantly, Canadian heraldry has long proclaimed the centrality of the sea for Canadian identity. Certainly, the Latin motto *A Mare usque ad Mare*—From Sea to Sea—on the Canadian coat of arms expresses both a political and strategic vision. The motto is taken from the biblical proclamation of God's all-encompassing grasp as expressed in Psalm 72:8, "He shall have Dominion from sea to sea." Drawing on this, one might well argue for an overarching metaphysical vision of nationhood. One nation under God. Indeed, we owe that insight to Sir Samuel Leonard Tilley, one of the thirty-three Fathers of Confederation who gathered in Charlottetown in September 1864 to discuss the draft British North America Act. It was the devout Tilley who suggested the name "the Dominion of Canada" for the new nation, a concept which the other Fathers endorsed. The sea, at this point, would seem to have been a boundary marker. In this light, all that lay between the Pacific and the Atlantic was an immense land to be bound together and, where necessary, mastered.

Nor does the heraldry end there. Chiselled over the front entrance of the Parliament buildings in Ottawa stand the words "The wholesome sea is at her gates... Her gates both East and West." Carved in stone in 1920 when the Peace Tower was being built, they evoke yet another range of possible meanings for the national motto. Though still regarded as a bounded land, Canada now has "gates"—like those of a fortress—encompassed by a single, "wholesome sea." The author of this poetic insight was Ottawa lawyer and occasional poet John Almon Ritchie (1863–1935), remembered now perhaps solely for these words set in stone. Yet many have found the words both stirring and prescient. Take, for example, the reflections in Jeffrey V. Brock's naval memoirs *The Dark Broad Seas* (1981): "Thrilling in their simplicity, they awaken the imagination and speak eloquently of a land that is not bound by physical horizons. Any pride and satisfaction that may result from contemplating Canada's future should be tempered by the reminder that gates remain but prison bars unless the roads beyond are free." This assertion about the freedom of the seas has particular significance for Canadian strategic thinkers and naval historians. In short, the phrase is a plea for navalism, national security and national defence. Here the sea has become a moat. Or perhaps a bridge for commercial and economic—or military—power projection.

Our *Spindrift: A Canadian Book of the Sea*, by contrast, illustrates a much more multifaceted and nuanced experience than this. It reveals our human relationships to the oceanic environment, and how that environment fascinates and forms those who encounter it. The collection explores the interfaces between sea and shore, and evokes reflection on the meaning of human endeavour and purpose in great waters. While localized in expression, the themes are timeless: survival and isolation, loneliness and restoration, hope and despair, awe and dread, steadfastness and mastery. Beneath the surface of the experience "sea" runs an undertow and rip current marked by adventure and exhilaration, and by reflection on the sea as the setting for rites of passage. Always poignant, sometimes passionate—and even pacific—the sea emerges in these witnesses to Canadian experience as a key to understanding this vast three-ocean land.

A diversity of experience—immediate and personal, or vicarious and national—invests the sea with meaning. Indeed, writers have shown how local experience can develop into a national tradition. Like the Atlantic schooner *Bluenose*, which is celebrated not only in song, postage stamps and popular lore, but also on the obverse of the Canadian dime, their writing projects a national vision.

Within these pages, Canadians—with occasional foreign writers among them—celebrate the unique ties that bind us intimately to the sea. Out of the nautical diversity of their accounts emerges a striking unity. Like the eighteenth-century understanding of "wit"—a cast of mind that brings together objects that are normally kept separate and apart—our book presents a new kind of Canadian mosaic. Here the "wholesome sea" is not merely "at our gates." It is an intrinsic part of our national identity.

—MICHAEL L. HADLEY

The sea
Pouring
Harmlessly
Past the port
Is yet the
Menacing
Tyrant of old
That the
Drowned
Know.

—Malcolm Lowry, "Injured Choriant or Paeonic"
from *The Collected Poetry of Malcolm Lowry*

CHAPTER I
THE FACE OF THE DEEP

The expression "the face of the deep" is an ancient, biblical term that conjures up a primordial, re-creative phenomenon. Endowed by mariners with human moods and emotions, this face conjures up equally ancient notions: might, majesty, dominion and power. Indeed, writers who have actually experienced the phenomenon themselves, or whose creative imagination is alive to it, turn repeatedly to evocative language to express it. They speak of the sea as menacing, beckoning, mothering, creating, shifting, hungering—and awe-inspiring. This sense of awe captures what the face of the deep ultimately means: a synergy of fascination and attraction, mystery and invitation, and a reverential fear mixed with dread and delight. Venturing upon the deep invites one on a two-fold voyage: one, a journey into an untamed external world of the senses, and another into the human soul.

THE CALL OF THE SEA
L.M. Montgomery (1874–1942)

"I understand now why some men must go to sea," said Anne. "That desire which comes to us all at times—'to sail beyond the bourne of sunset'—must be very imperious when it is born in you. I don't wonder Captain Jim ran away because of it. I never see a ship sailing out of the channel, or a gull soaring over the sand-bar, without wishing I were on board the ship or had wings, not like a dove 'to fly away and be at rest,' but like a gull to sweep out into the very heart of a storm."

—from *Anne's House of Dreams* (1920)

SEA MAGIC
Theodore Goodridge Roberts (1877–1953)

Who has not heard the call of the sea? Many of us can respond only with yearning hearts, in our dreams. It is heard in the markets and offices of inland cities; in vineyards and orchards; in sloping forests, upland farms, prairie kitchens and mountain fastnesses.

Those who go to her are the lucky ones—in the opinion of the rest of us. Yet of those who go to her, many curse her; and yet again many of the defamers return to her.

We know that salt is in our blood, for chemists have found it there—but that fact is a small part of the truth of the allure of salt water for the children of men. Salt is present in the flame of the human spirit and the tissues of our imaginations. Salt of the Seven Seas is the very stuff of our ancestral dreams. In our origins pulse the urge and zest of the turns and tumults of dark and flashing tides, sea winds, sea coasts, sea triumphs and sea-bred fears are native to our souls as to our blood. Of sea salt and sea magic are we fashioned and sprung.

One, two or many generations ago, your ancestors and mine were seafarers and dwellers beside salt water. Swing of flow and ebb of salty tides is the primal rhythm of life in us. Adam was not of an inland garden, but of a sea beach and a seaward facing cave; and not of fig leaves was Man's first dress, but of kelp and dulce and pearly shells.

Man's first tales were of sea adventure—if the truth were known! And Man's first pictures were of great fish and flippered sea beasts, drawn on sand and scratched on soft rock; and the sea rubbed them out and scrubbed them away. Do you think that the first pictures were of elk and bison? Those pictures are the work of the great-great-great-grandchildren of the first artists—if only the truth were known!

When mountain or plain or any inland place breeds a poet, does that poet sing only of inland life and scenes? Not in one case in ten. The chances are that he sings early and often of salt waters, beginning his spiritual seafaring and salty rhyming before even so little as the frothy edge of the least of weedy landwashes becomes known to his physical eye. Soon or later, his feet follow his dreams down to the sea, by sloping valleys and swift rivers, down and seaward to tidal marshes and ringing beaches; for to the sea his mind must go for its creative salt, even as his ancestors went to it to take their daily food from its gleaming shoals and mysterious depths. The business dearest to the poet's heart (after those of romantic love and heroic death) has to do with islands, reefs, glimmer of topsails on heaving horizons, opal landfalls after weary voyages, pale sands edged with spent foam, wave-worn spars awash in green caves and seaward forests grey with blowing fog.

—from *The Leather Bottle* (1934)

THE HUNGRY OCEAN
Farley Mowat (1921–2014)

The interplay of wind and weather upon the high seas and coastal waters, and their significance for navigation, is frequently the subject of technical writing. Creative writers have taken the analysis a step further by imaginatively capturing the interplay between these forces, and linking them to human fates and character. In the excerpt that follows, Mowat reflects on powerful natural forces and human responses.

The North Atlantic is a hungry ocean, hungry for men and ships, and it knows how to satisfy its appetites. From September through to June a sequence of almost perpetual gales march eastward down the great ditch of the St. Lawrence valley and out to the waiting sea. They are abetted by the hurricanes which spawn in the Caribbean and which drive north-eastward up the coasts as far as Labrador. Only in summer are there periods of relative calm on the eastern approaches to the continent, and even in summer, fierce storms are common.

Gales, and the high seas that accompany them are, of course, the weapons of all oceans; but this unquiet seaboard has two special weapons of its own.

First of all it has the ice—continental masses of it that come sweeping down with the Greenland current to form a great, amoeba-like bulge extending from the coasts of Nova Scotia eastward as much as a thousand miles, and southward five hundred miles from Flemish Cap. The bulge swells and shrinks and throws out new pseudopods from month to month, but there is no season of the year when it or its accompanying icebergs withdraw completely from the shipping lanes.

The second weapon is in many ways the most formidable of all. It is the fog. There is no fog anywhere to compare with the palpable grey shroud which lies almost perpetually across the northern sea approaches, and which often flows far over the land itself. There are not a score of days during any given year when between Labrador and the Gulf of Maine the fog vanishes completely. Even in the rare fine days of summer it remains in wait, a dozen or so miles offshore, ready at any moment to roll in and obliterate the world. It has presence, continuity, and a vitality that verges on the animate. In conjunction with its ready ally, the rock-girt coasts, it is a great killer of men and ships.

The coasts themselves are brutally hard. Newfoundland, Labrador, Nova Scotia, and the Gulf shores appear to have been created for the special purpose of destroying vessels. They are of malignant grey rock that has flung its fragments into the sea with an insane abandon until, in many places, these form an impenetrable *chevaux-de-frise* to which the Newfoundland seamen, out of a perilous familiarity, have given the prophetic name of "sunkers."

The coasts are of tremendous length. Newfoundland alone exposes nearly six thousand miles of rock to the breaking seas. Everywhere the shores are indented with false harbours that offer hope to storm-driven ships and which then repulse them with a multitude of reefs. The names upon those coasts betray their nature. Cape aux Morts, Cape Diable, Rocks of Massacre, Dead Sailor's Rock, Bay of Despair, Malignant Cove, Baie Mauvais, Misery Point, Mistaken Point, False Hope, Confusion Bay, Salvage Point, and a plethora of Wreck Bays, Points and Islands.

Yet by the very nature of their animosity towards seafaring men these coasts have brought out of themselves the matter of their own defeat. Men in these parts have always had to take their living from the sea, or starve; and those who survived the merciless winnowing became a race apart. There are no finer seamen in the world. The best of them come from the outports of Newfoundland and Nova Scotia, and from the islands of Cape Breton and the Magdalens. The best of them are men to ponder over, for they can hold their own no matter how the seas and the fog and ice and rocks may strive against them.

And yet it is also true that these men do not properly belong in our times, for they follow an outmoded creed with undeviating certainty. They believe that man must not attempt to overmaster the primordial and elemental forces and break them to his hand. They believe that he who would survive must learn to be a part of wind and water, rock and soil, nor ever stand in braggarts' opposition to these things.

"Ah, me son," as one old Newfoundland skipper phrases it, "we don't be *takin'* nothin' from the sea. We has to sneak up on what we wants, and wiggle it away."

—from *Grey Seas Under* (1958)

COMING SUDDENLY TO THE SEA
Louis Dudek (1918–2001)

Coming suddenly to the sea in my twenty-eighth year,
to the mother of all things that breathe, of mussels and whales,
I could not see anything but sand at first
and burning bits of mother-of-pearl.
But this was the sea, terrible as a torch
which the winter sun had lit,
flaming in the blue and salt sea-air
under my twenty-eight-year infant eyes.
And then I saw the spray smashing the rocks
and the angry gulls cutting the air,
the heads of fish and the hands of crabs on stones:
the carnivorous sea, sower of life,
battering a granite rock to make it a pebble—
love and pity needless as the ferny froth on its long smooth waves.
The sea, with its border of crinkly weed,
the inverted Atlantic of our unstable planet,
froze me into a circle of marble, sending the icy air out in
    lukewarm waves.
And so I brought home, as an emblem of that day
ending my long blind years, a fistful of blood-red weed in my
    hand.

—from *The Transparent Sea* (1956)

A VIEW FROM SIGNAL HILL
Wayne Johnston (1958–   )

*In Johnson's novel, Joey Smallwood—first premier of Newfoundland—
prepares to leave Newfoundland for the first time. He confronts his fear
of the sea—a vast hostile force that makes a mockery of human endeavour and threatens to change his life forever.*

It occurred to me, for the first time, that I might not come back.

The sea brought out such thoughts in me. My virtual nonexistence in comparison with the eternal sea-scheme of things. I never felt so forlorn, so desolate as I did looking out across the trackless, forever-changing surface of the sea, which, though it registered the passage of time, was suggestive of no beginning and no end, as purposeless, as pointless as eternity.

I had never liked to think of myself as living on an island. I preferred to think of Newfoundland as landlocked in the middle of some otherwise empty continent, for though I had an islander's scorn of the mainland, I could not stand the sea. I was morbidly drawn to read and re-read, as a child, an abridged version of Melville's *Moby Dick,* a book that, though I kept going back to it, gave me nightmares. Ishmael's notion that the sea had some sort of melancholy-dispelling power mystified me. Whenever it was a damp, drizzly November in my soul, the last thing I wanted to look at was the sea. It was not just drowning in it I was afraid of, but the sight of that vast, endless, life-excluding stretch of water. It reminded me of God, not the God of Miss Garrigus and the Bible, whose threats of eternal damnation I did not believe in, but Melville's God, inscrutable, featureless, indifferent, as unimaginable as an eternity of time or an infinity of space, in comparison with which I was nothing. The sight of some little fishing boat heading out to sea like some void-bound soul made me, literally, seasick.

—from *The Colony of Unrequited Dreams* (1998)

THE VIRGIN BERG
Wayne Johnston (1958–   )

Every year, icebergs calved from West Greenland glaciers are carried south in the Labrador Current, and eventually appear along the coast of Newfoundland from March to July. Wayne Johnston's memoir opens with his father's childhood recollection of one particular iceberg that caused great excitement when it appeared off St. John's harbour in 1905.

My father grew up in a house that was blessed with water from an iceberg. A picture of that iceberg hung on the walls in the front rooms of the many houses I grew up in. It was a blown-up photograph that yellowed gradually with age until we could barely make it out. My grandmother, Nan Johnston, said the proper name for the iceberg was Our Lady of the Fjords, but we called it the Virgin Berg.

In 1905, on June 24, the feast day of St. John the Baptist and the day in 1497 of John Cabot's landfall at Cape Bonavista and "discovery" of Newfoundland, an iceberg hundreds of feet high and bearing an undeniable likeness to the Blessed Virgin Mary appeared off St. John's harbour. As word of the apparition spread, thousands of people flocked to Signal Hill to get a glimpse of it. An ever-growing flotilla of fishing boats escorted it along the southern shore as it passed Petty Harbour, Bay Bulls, Tors Cove, Ferryland, where my father's grandparents and his father, Charlie, who was twelve, saw it from a rise of land known as the Gaze.

At first the islands blocked their view and all they could see was the profile of the Virgin. But when it cleared Bois Island, they saw the iceberg whole. It resembled Mary in everything but colour. Mary's colours were blue and white, but the Virgin Berg was uniformly white, a startling white in the sunlight against the blue-green backdrop of the sea. Mary's cowl and shawl and robes were all one colour, the same colour as her face and hands, each feature distinguishable by shape alone. Charlie imagined that, under the water, was the marble pedestal, with its network of veins and cracks. Mary rode without one on the water and there did not extend outwards from her base the usual lighter shade of sea-green sunken ice.

The ice was enfolded like layers of garment that bunched about her feet. Long drapings of ice hung from her arms, which were crossed below her neck, and her head was tilted down as in statues to meet in love and modesty the gaze of supplicants below.

Charlie's mother fell to her knees, and then his father fell to his. Though he wanted to run up the hill to get a better look at the Virgin as some friends of his were doing, his parents made him kneel beside them. His mother reached up and, putting her hand on his shoulder, pulled him down. A convoy of full-masted schooners trailed out behind the iceberg like the tail of some massive kite. It was surrounded at the base by smaller vessels, fishing boats, traps, skiffs, punts. His mother said the Hail Mary over and over and blessed herself repeatedly, while his father stared as though witnessing some end-of-the-world-heralding event, some sight foretold by prophets in the last book of the Bible. Charlie was terrified by the look on his father's face and had to fight back the urge to cry. Everywhere, at staggered heights on the Gaze, people knelt, some side-on to keep their balance, others to avert their eyes, as if to look for too long on such a sight would be a sacrilege.

—from *Baltimore's Mansion* (1999)

A WARTIME SEASCAPE
Alan Easton (1902–2001)

Perhaps no one ever relates to the sea as it actually is, but only as it seems when viewed through a very personal lens—a lens with many facets. One facet might be memory, another culture, and yet another the immediacy of visceral experience. The multifaceted lens through which naval captain Alan Easton contemplated the sea drew on his intimate experience with deep-sea navigation in wartime, as well as upon his reflections on the nature of war, suffering and loss.

The sea itself filled my thoughts as I gazed down at the dark water from the lee wing of the bridge. I marvelled at its phosphorescence and at the strange fascination a phosphorescent sea always held for me. Brilliant like boiling silver on ebony, a million drops of shining metal falling from the bow wave. The sea could be beautiful. It was tonight.

The sea fascinated sometimes. But I hated it. How long had I hated the sea? Why did I? Was it fear? God! I would hate to drown! Yes, that was one fear which had been with me constantly. The prelude to drowning must be terribly lonely. One storm stood out in my memory, one in the Roaring Forties. It came into my mind automatically with the thought of drowning.

I took my hands out of the pockets of my sheepskin and rested my elbows on the rail. No breeze touched me, sheltered there behind the dodger. The ship lifted and leaned imperceptibly, settled quietly and leaned the other way. The noise of water rushing alongside as she forged ahead would have been noticeable only if it had ceased.

There was a time when I had loved being at sea—when I was a boy, a young officer. Those had been carefree days. I had delighted in the rugged life and had wanted to see new places, new things. There was excitement in saying to myself, "Now I'm in Australia." "Is this really China?" "So this is the Land of the Rising Sun on the edge of the Far East." Those had been wonderful times. The Pacific! How lovely that ocean could be. How peaceful the water and verdant the earth; great islands with palms, brilliant flowers, gay birds and natives with their hair dyed blue and yellow and red. But I was not there now. I was on the Atlantic; nor would I wish to be any further from home. The desire to travel had worn thin. Home! That was the only place to travel to now; the one place in the world.

How the Atlantic's grim personality, its wartime personality, brought into sharp focus those who were waiting ashore. How much dearer, more vital, they seemed to become when one was in danger. And this was not selfishness altogether. It would not be easy for them if I were lost, and I pictured with physical distress their shock at getting the news. Yes, this was what made me dislike it. I wanted to be with my family and clear of risks.

Yet there were other reasons too. Maturity had brought a hatred of discomfort. How I loathed being wet; sticky all over with salt. The dreadful jolting and tumbling when you could not take a step without holding on. It had been fun in earlier years, but I had been softened by my years of comfort ashore. I was not really old—barely forty—but old for this job.

Why think of these things? Maybe I did not like the sea; there was no denying I hated the Atlantic, the ugliness of it, the grey dreariness, the eternal whine of the wind in the rigging. But it would not last for ever. One day the war would be over. One day, if I survived,

I would be free again. Meanwhile I knew the sea better than I did the land almost and I was at home in a ship. Home! Damn that word!

Then the porpoises came. Three at first, in echelon, speeding just beneath the surface of the water towards the ship. They turned in perfect formation, like a naval squadron, and cut outward towards the curling bow wave. Then more came, fifty, a hundred, silver streaks woven in the clear black ocean. They fell in with the ship's track but at twice the speed, the young ones following their parents. They veined the water with bubbling phosphorescent pathways. They did not leap. Perhaps they would if I watched them for a while.

—from *50 North: An Atlantic Battleground* (1963)

IT'S IN HOW YOU READ THE WATER
Allan Anderson (1915–1994)

The twenty-minute flight from Vancouver Harbour to Victoria Harbour is always dramatic: from a bird's eye view of distant snow-capped mountains, lush farmlands and the broad expanse of the Fraser River delta, to the ever-changing effects of wind and tide—sometimes even fog—upon the capricious waters of the Salish Sea.

From an interview with Captain Mark Goostrey, pilot

"If you're flying on water you don't have somebody telling you what the wind's doing, or where it's coming from, or which way to land. It's all at your own discretion more or less, and it's your judgment that counts. Like right now. We get some pretty strong winds sometimes in the Twin Otter aircraft. It's a STOL aircraft. In other words, it's good for short take-off and landing. And I've been into Victoria in it blowing, I guess, fifty knots, which is about as good a clip as you want to be landing in because the aircraft starts flying at about sixty knots.

Landing in gusts, well, it's all in how you read the water. You get indication on the water of which way the wind is coming from and what kind of speed it's going, you can see the cat's paws in the water giving an indication of gusts. If it's a big gust you land in it. But if there's a whole bunch of little gusts the aircraft wants to fly and then it doesn't want to fly. So, if you can find an area of calm water where the wind is constant you can try to land in that. That's preferable. If not, look for a big area of wind, a big gust, and set it down right in there.

If you're getting whitecaps in this area, that's just about time to shut it off. We've had occasions in Vancouver Harbour and in Victoria Harbour when it's been just too rough to take off. The wind isn't too strong, but the water conditions will be just too rough on the aircraft with a big load. You could end up breaking fittings and struts and things like that. So I would say about two- or three-foot waves that's breaking is about time to shut it down all right."

—from *Salt Water, Fresh Water* (1979)

TIDAL TEMPEST
Tom Koppel

The Skookumchuck Narrows and Rapids of British Columbia conjure up well-justified awe and apprehension. While the First Nations term "Skookum" now describes a "seaworthy, tautly built and tiddly" sailboat, it originally meant "strong or turbulent." "Chuck" meant salt water. In a classic case of redundancy, coastal sailors now refer to the whole ocean as the "salt chuck." Tucked in behind the Sechelt Peninsula, the Skookumchuck Narrows formed the historical trading route for generations of four major divisions of the Coast Salish tribe—Tuwanek, Skaikos, Kunechin and Tsonai. Today, boaters come in search of challenge and excitement. Those who have dashed through the boiling rapids on a full flood or full ebb 14-knot current can attest to the thrill.

"Skookumchuck" means "place of strong waters" in the Chinook coastal jargon, the traditional lingua franca of the Natives on the northwest coast. And the spot named Skookumchuck Rapids, located along the British Columbia mainland shore north of Vancouver, fully earns that designation. Hiking in from the road with a friend one time, I first noticed a distant rumble pervading the still forest air. Then the wooded trail opened up and we came to a cliff overlooking a raging channel of white water. Off the nearest point of land, jagged standing waves rose some two metres (about six or seven feet) into the air like sharp teeth. In other places, water plunged into deep, gurgling holes. Swirling green bands of turbulence were swept along with the flow and spun off into powerful back eddies where they were deflected by the rocky shoreline.

In mid-channel, the torrent gushed through a gap between small islands and fanned out into a plume of milky rips as it rejoined the main stream. Seagulls wheeled and swooped over the tumult and foam, hunting for fish that had been injured in the natural cataclysm or simply thrust to the surface by the powerful upwellings. It was like an angry river, but the water was salt, not fresh. And rather than plunging down a steep mountainside, it was being propelled by the ebb and flow of the Pacific tides.

Skookumchuck Rapids has some of the fastest tidal currents in the world. It is one of a score of places on the Inside Passage where swift tidal flows put on spectacular displays, create special conditions for wildlife, and give mariners sleepless nights. It is the shallow, constricted entrance to a network of fjords (locally called inlets) that cut deep into the coastal mountains on the eastern side of British Columbia's largest body of sheltered water, the Strait of Georgia, which separates Vancouver Island from the B.C. mainland. Also called Sechelt Rapids, Skookumchuck is like the narrow neck of a very large bottle that is repeatedly filled and emptied as the tides rise and fall.

As the tide floods into the nearby Strait of Georgia, hundreds of billions of gallons pour through the narrow channel into Sechelt, Narrows, and Salmon inlets, and the show begins. After about six hours, the water level inside the nearly eighty kilometres (fifty miles) of inlets has risen as much as three metres (ten feet). The flow slows to a trickle and goes slack. Then, after only ten or fifteen minutes of relative calm, the tide out in the strait ebbs, and all the water in those inlets begins to rush back out again. At peak spring tides, it surges through some places in Skookumchuck at more than sixteen knots.

Skookumchuck is only one of many tidal rapids on the B.C. coast. Farther north along the mainland coast is Nakwakto Rapids, which is the gateway between the open waters of Queen Charlotte Sound and nearly landlocked Seymour and Belize inlets. There, too, the water can race through at around sixteen knots, and a much larger volume of water moves at this high speed than at Skookumchuck, so the display is in some ways even more spectacular. In the middle of Nakwakto is Turret rock, a tiny islet also known as Tremble Island. A government surveyor once decided to sit out a tidal cycle there. The islet shook so violently from the force of the current that he lay face down, clung to the tufts of grass, and stuffed his ears against the roar. Seen from the air when a big tide is running, Tremble Island looks like a ship plowing into turbulent seas. It kicks up a huge white bow wave on the end that is being hit by the tidal flow and leaves a long, swirling wake of turbulence in the other direction. Even the orcas (killer whales) that frequent the region negotiate Nakwakto only near slack tide.

—from *Ebb and Flow: Tides and Life*
on Our Once and Future Planet (2007)

ICE

The ability to differentiate between hard ice and soft ice, and between passable and impassable pack; to recognize weathered floes with their dangerous underwater spurs; to detect lines of weakness and to select the most suitable leads, etc., can only be gained by experience, and no amount of text-book knowledge will stand in its stead. Sea ice is a navigational hazard of the first order, and should be accorded all due respect.

—from *Handling Ships* (1954), Admiralty, B.R. 2092,
for use in the Royal Canadian Navy

ICE
David (Duke) Snider (1957–   )

Operating vessels efficiently and safely in *any* ice regime takes more than theory. It takes understanding of ice physics, growth and degradation, and movement combined with a full understanding of one's own vessel's capability in ice. Hard-earned experience and competence must be combined with careful planning and executing ice passages, and all this must be overlaid on theoretical knowledge. Time and time again, operators without experience and competence have taken on the ice, particularly polar ice, with the added danger of harder old and multi-year ice, and found their voyage either slowed considerably or failed completely.

As the Royal Canadian Navy looks to a future of increased Arctic operations, this hard-earned wisdom must be taken into consideration in developing manning and training.

—from "A Polar Ice Operation: What it takes,"
in *Canadian Naval Review* (2015)

AN ARCHIPELAGO OF ICE
James P. Delgado (1958–   )

Some call it the roof of the world. Others called it *terra incognita,* the unknown land, or *ultima Thule,* the remote north. It is now known as the Arctic. The name comes from the Greek *arktos* (bear), for the region lies beneath the constellation of the Great Bear. An imaginary line, drawn by geographers on the globe at 66°30' north latitude, marks the Arctic Circle; beyond it lies the top of the world. It is also the location of one of the world's longest-sought secrets, the Northwest Passage. Europe's quest for this passage spanned four centuries. Thousands of sailors and more than a hundred ships participated. The ice of the Arctic still holds some of their bones.

The Northwest Passage—or passages, for there are many potential routes—winds through an archipelago of ice, an intricate maze

The remote swarm of a million stars was a tiny, scintillating ball of fuzz against a black velvet backdrop. As I stared at this object in deep space, I realized that my binoculars were a time machine. With their aid I peered 25,000 years back into the long past epoch in which the light from the Hercules Cluster began its journey to reach my eye on this night in Annette Inlet.

I had rediscovered night.

—from *A Dream of Islands* (1988)

Once again with the tide she slips her lines
Turns her head and comes awake
Where she lay so still there at Privateer's Wharf
Now she quickly gathers way
She will range far south from the harbour mouth
And rejoice with every wave
Who will know the *Bluenose* in the sun?

—Stan Rogers, from "The *Bluenose*" (1978)

CHAPTER III
VESSELS

Some vessels displace water and float; others contain it and don't. So much for the difference between a ship and a cooking pot. Or between a seaworthy ship, and one that's sinking. But for purposes of navigation and maritime law we turn to The International Regulations for the Prevention of Collisions at Sea. *They define a vessel as including "every description of water craft actually used or capable of being used as a means of transportation on water." That makes for a wonderfully colourful and imaginative flotilla. And indeed each one of these vessels has at one time or another launched itself from Canadian shores: an imaginative fleet from log rafts to highly technical deep-sea craft. Variously propelled by everything from paddle, oars, wind, gasoline outboards, great diesels or steam-turbines, they have been crafted with a range of skills. Intuition and cunning, as well as scientific marine design and construction, have come into play. The inspiration of builders and designers has sometimes drawn upon a blend of both. Though relatively few craft can be represented in this collection, each vessel, from the early Inuit umiaks and First Nations' canoes, to the schooner* Bluenose *and the experimental naval hydrofoil* Bras d'Or, *bears witness to a distinctive marine tradition. Pride of purpose and achievement, and the exhilaration of success, mark each stage of building. Mariners frequently invest their vessels with human characteristics, and either love them or curse them on a whim.*

THE HAIDA CANOE
Martine J. Reid (1945–   )

The First Nations' canoe, argues Roy MacGregor in his book Canoe Country *(2015), is the foremost unifying symbol of the country. The Haida canoe is a graphic case in point. For the Haida people of the West Coast it was both a seaworthy vessel for commerce and war, and a profound work of art. The canoe expressed spirituality and power, and the role of myth in sustaining community. In the words of acclaimed Haida carver Bill Reid, it was the point of departure for all artistic expression. His widow, Martine J. Reid, recounts her late husband's perspective on the Haida canoe—visually, symbolically and culturally.*

Like other traditional artworks, canoes were vessels of knowledge. They communicated significant information about the individuals and societies that produced them—information that was also expressed in various cultural and spiritual contexts, such as in myths and rituals. Due to their implicit connecting faculty, Northwest Coast canoes were metaphors for different sets of ideas, including wealth and property, exchange and gift, war, marriage and death.

From the time of the Great Flood to the long potlatch journeys of the mid-nineteenth century, the canoe connected the people to the land, the sea, the creatures that inhabit them, other people and the underworld (or spirit world).

In a world where form and spirit fused to create harmonious containers—plank houses, bent-corner chests and boxes, canoe dishes and bowls—the canoe was the ultimate container-conveyor. Made from the land's most revered tree, the giant red cedar, and with the assistance of spirit helpers, it embodied and connected people to Mother Earth. Canoe effigies were at times represented on totem poles as part of their narratives.

In some southern areas of the coast, deceased individuals were buried in canoes on stilts, sometimes with other canoes inverted over them. In other areas, canoes, or canoe effigies, were raised as mortuary poles.

The canoe also connected Northwest Coast peoples to the aquatic world and its wealth, due to which they thrived. Their mythic landscape associated the canoe with copper, the highest symbol of wealth among the indigenous peoples. In a Tlingit myth, copper first appeared in the form of a canoe. Several coastal groups believed in a mighty spirit, the master of the undersea world, who lived at the bottom of the sea. His Tlingit name is Qonagedet, and his Haida name is Goanagada. A powerful shape-shifter, he sometimes emerged... as a large, self-paddling war canoe, also elaborately decorated and painted... In the south, Kwakwaka'wakw mythology portrays a self-paddling copper canoe personified as Gomogwa, the supernatural being and master of ocean riches. He is the donor of wealth as well as of supernatural treasures, and his copper house can be seen arising from the sea. It is located west of the ocean, a destination attained only through death...

Today, First Nations from all along the Northwest Coast have produced hundreds of traditional-style canoes in both wood and fibreglass and have paddled them over long distances to participate in Tribal Journeys. These gatherings allow us a stirring glimpse into the past, when fleets of traditional Northwest Coast canoes navigated the waters of the Salish Sea, the Inside Passage and the open ocean between Northern California and Alaska.

—from *Bill Reid and the Haida Canoe* (2011)

THE STRAIT OF JUAN DE FUCA
Barry Gough (1938–)

The writing of marine history, as Gough confesses, is much more than an intellectual exercise in archival sleuthing. It is about experience. For him the Strait of Juan de Fuca, the Salish Sea's outlet to the Pacific Ocean, has been working its magic since the earliest days of recorded history. Having followed what he calls "Ariadne's thread" through centuries of surmise, myth and the machinations of international politics, Gough affirms Juan de Fuca's claims to have discovered the strait in 1592. In the words that follow he ponders the meaning of this remarkable West Coast seaway.

As for myself, the voyage in the discovery of history continues, seeking always to make sense of the past and, more, to explain it to the reader as best I can. The pleasant work is fuelled by memory as much as it is done to satisfy curiosity. In and out of my local waters had flowed the tides of empires on ceaseless change. The Strait of Juan de Fuca has held the destiny of nations in its ebb and flow. From its portal the waters extend and open out to the ends of the earth.

Visions of the great ships of yesterday pass by my window. One by one they pass through Juan de Fuca's strait. Here she comes now, Vancouver's elegant *Discovery* on exploration, accompanied by Broughton's strangely tubby *Chatham*. They are followed by Alcalá Galiano's remarkably small *Sutil* and Cayetano Valdés' *Mexicana*.

But wait a minute: only forty years or so after, a smoke-belching steamer comes into view, rounding Cape Flattery rather effortlessly, heading purposefully against tides and currents for Puget Sound and Fort Nisqually. This is the Hudson's Bay Company's *Beaver*. Out of the fog bank comes the barque *Harpooner* with supplies and mine workers and men for business and for the land. In 1850 the British paddlewheel sloop *Driver* is seen bringing a young lawyer, Richard Blanshard, to take up the governorship of the young Vancouver Island colony. The *Tynemouth* and other bride-ships will leave from London, and a hundred marriageable women will step onto the settlement's docks. During the Fraser River gold rush and the occupation of the San Juan Islands by the United States Army, the three-decker *Ganges,* a British ship of the line, built in Bombay of teak, enters Esquimalt under sail. This place Rear Admiral Robert Lambert Baynes, echoing its Spanish discoverers, finds glorious and suitable for a naval base, which it becomes, not long afterward—a British anchor of empire in the North Pacific. Captain George Henry Richards, heading a diligent team of six surveyors, has charted the turbulent waters from Cape Flattery right through to the Strait of Georgia on both the Vancouver Island and continental shores, and has even marked the Fraser River for safe navigation up to New Westminster, the newly sited capital of the Colony of British Columbia.

Now the vessels come in increasing number and in greater tonnage. The United States and Royal Navy send some of their largest battleships. The Canadian Pacific Railway develops a trans-Pacific service, and the romance of steam is now in full view as the sleek *Empress of Japan* speeds for Yokohama with mail and passengers and a mixed cargo from the new railhead port of Vancouver. Inbound cargoes of tea and porcelain from the exotic East arrive, and, in the steerage class, Chinese and Japanese on indenture or other permit.

Back and forth, despite the triumph of steam navigation, the sailing ships still pass on their peaceful occasions. There goes the *Ardnamurchan,* a typical steel carrier, working out through the interminably long strait with a cargo of lumber recently loaded at Port Blakely, Washington. And lo and behold, from her Victoria home port, there's the old *Thermopylae,* fastest of the clippers and famous for beating her rival, the *Cutty Sark,* in a race home to London from Shanghai, with tea. There sails HMS *Herald* to western Arctic waters to search for Sir John Franklin. There goes the old whaler *Karluk,* to serve Stefannson in the Canadian Arctic Expedition, and here, inbound, comes the *St. Roch,* fresh from a return transit of the Northwest Passage.

In May 1901 the Indian canoe *Tilikum* is seen working down the strait toward open ocean under sail but driven to the lee shore of Vancouver Island's hard coast. Now out of view, we imagine her finally escaping the clutches of the storms, tides and currents off Cape Flattery with destination London, then home again by curious circumstances on the deck of an ocean tramp. Others are not so lucky: the American steamer *Pacific,* past her prime and loaded with Victoria passengers, sinks with catastrophic losses, and later the British naval corvette *Condor* disappears with all hands.

Now the big ones steam into view. The mighty British battle cruiser *Hood* arrives as an exhibit of British naval might in 1923; in 1940 she will be sunk in the famous action with the *Bismarck* and *Prinz Eugen.* In 1942 the massive liner *Queen Elizabeth* ghosts into Esquimalt Graving Dock for upgrades as a troopship—her existence kept secret, a gang of Victoria High School lads pressed into work parties—then departs urgently on a wartime mission, the fates of democracy hanging in the balance. The British super dreadnought *Warspite*, veteran of Jutland, refitted recently in a Puget Sound yard, heads out to become flagship of the British Eastern Fleet near war's end. There she passes, under tow, the battleship USS *Missouri*, destination Pearl Harbor as the United States Naval Memorial; the signing of the Japanese surrender in 1945 took place on her decks.

The grey, armed ships continue their transits, en route to Korea or Vietnam, taking the military power of the American continent to the Far East, returning battle-hardened. The smart, brightly coloured P & O liners like the *Orsova* and *Oronsay*, links of Empire shipping, come and go and then suddenly disappear from our waters. All the while, and for three generations, Canadian Pacific steamers toil on passage to and from Seattle and Vancouver, sometimes crossing to Port Angeles, and are, sadly, no more. Meantime, the Black Ball Line's MV *Coho* outlives them all and still bridges the strait, linking communities on both sides of the watery divide, a reminder of what we have in common and hold dear.

Acting by stealth and never seen by us, the Trident nuclear-powered submarines of the United States Navy steal out and back from Puget Sound on silent patrol. They are the new bearers of Neptune's trident in an uncertain world. More than half a century ago, in 1958, USS *Nautilus* departs Seattle and exits the strait with a secret destination of the North Pole, under the icecap, then completes a history-making polar transit. Even to Jules Verne this would be heady stuff.

—from *Juan de Fuca's Strait* (2012)

THE HBC'S *NONSUCH*—
WINNIPEG'S DEEP-SEA KETCH
Peter C. Newman (1929–   )

The Arctic voyage of the ketch Nonsuch *in 1668–1669 is unique. Its purpose was not to seek any Northwest Passage to the riches of the Orient, but rather to demonstrate the viability of maritime trade deep into Hudson Bay and southward into present-day Manitoba. The plan cut some fifteen hundred miles off the trade routes that would lead to Quebec City and Montreal. Thus it was that the* Nonsuch *entered Canadian history and linked what is now Central Canada to the rest of the world by sea. A replica of the* Nonsuch, *built in Britain by the Hudson's Bay Company to mark its 300th anniversary, undertook three major voyages of commemoration: in the 1970 and 1971 tours she visited some twenty-eight ports in the St. Lawrence and throughout the Great Lakes, while the 1972 tour took her to ports in British Columbia and Puget Sound. In 1974 she became the centrepiece of the Nonsuch Gallery of the Manitoba Museum in Winnipeg. This is a fitting tribute to a prairie province that boasts a protected habitat for the largest concentration of Beluga whales in the world—in the estuaries of the Churchill, Nelson and Seal Rivers in western Hudson Bay.*

Royal Navy records list the *Nonsuch* as having had a beam of fifteen feet, a draft of six feet six inches and an overall deck length of fifty-three feet. This would be about half the size of the *Mayflower* (1620) and slightly shorter than the sixteen-oared knoors used by the Vikings. In modern terms, the *Nonsuch* was not as long as the twelve-metre sloops in the America's Cup races...

By May 1668 the ships had been outfitted; grocers, chandlers, sailmakers, ropemakers, vintners, butchers, haberdashers, timber merchants and ironmongers furnished the [8-gun ketch] *Eaglet* and [6-gun] *Nonsuch* as floating department stores. Into the little ships were stowed hundreds of items, including hatchets, spears, scrapers, muskets, blunderbusses, pistols, gunpowder, eighteen barrels of shot, paper, quills, ink, thirty-seven pounds of tobacco, compasses, flags, lanterns, ropes, pitch, tar, axes, saws, hammers, anchors;

"shirts, socks and mittens and other slopsellers' wares;" four dozen pairs of shoes; malt for ship's beer, eight gallons of lemon juice to ward off scurvy, five thousand needles; food such as biscuits, raisins, prunes, peas, oatmeal, salt beef and pork; wines and brandy; fifty-six pounds of cork; and a trumpet. Both vessels also carried necklaces of wampum, the standard currency of the Indian trade, consisting of small shell beads that had been brought to England by Groseilliers...

On the misty morning ebb-tide of June 3, 1668, the *Eaglet* and *Nonsuch* were piloted out of the river by Isaac Manychurch for a fee of £5. By evening they had reached the open sea and turned north in a fresh breeze; ten days later they rounded the Orkneys and headed due west towards the New World. Four hundred leagues off Ireland, they were struck by a storm that nearly broached the low-waisted *Eaglet*, forcing her to turn back.

Six weeks later, Gillam sighted the coast of Labrador and turned north, navigating the *Nonsuch* skilfully under clouds of seabirds over the "furious overfall" into Hudson Strait. The tiny ketch sailed past the Belchers and found refuge in the same river mouth where Henry Hudson had wintered more than half a century before. It was promptly named Rupert River, after the expedition's Royal sponsor...

The return of the fur-loaded little ketch caused minimal stir; its cargo, bartered for goods originally purchased for £650, brought in £1,379 on the London fur market, and the ship was resold for £152. Wages of £535 plus the required startup investments, customs duties, the damage to the *Eaglet* and other expenses had failed to make the voyage profitable. But the backers were pleased. The thesis that Radisson and Groseilliers had been expounding for more than a decade had been proved correct: it was entirely practicable to sail into Hudson Bay, winter on its shores and return with a profitable cargo of fur.

—from *Company of Adventurers*, Volume I (1985)

THE SHIPS OF SAINT JOHN
Bliss Carman (1861–1929)

Situated on the north shore of the Bay of Fundy at the mouth of the Saint John River, Saint John is the oldest incorporated city in Canada. Before the construction of the St. Lawrence Seaway in the 1950s made it possible to navigate the river year round, Saint John served as the winter port for Montreal. Until the early twenty-first century, it was the site of Canada's largest shipyard.

Where are the ships I used to know,
That came to port on the Fundy tide
Half a century ago,
In beauty and stately pride?

In they would come past the beacon light,
With the sun on gleaming sail and spar,
Folding their wings like birds in flight
From countries strange and far.

Schooner and brig and barkentine,
I watched them slow as the sails were furled,
And wondered what cities they must have seen
On the other side of the world.

Frenchman and Britisher and Dane,
Yankee, Spaniard and Portugee,
And many a home ship back again
With her stories of the sea.

Calm and victorious, at rest
From the relentless, rough sea-play,
The wild duck on the river's breast
Was not more sure than they.

The creatures of a passing race,
The dark spruce forests made them strong,
The sea's lore gave them magic grace,
The great winds taught them song.

And God endowed them each with life—
His blessing on the craftsman's skill—
To meet the blind unreasoned strife
And dare the risk of ill.

Not mere insensate wood and paint
Obedient to the helm's command,
But often restive as a saint
Beneath the Heavenly hand.

All the beauty and mystery
Of life were there, adventure bold,
Youth, and the glamour of the sea
And all its sorrows old.

And many a time I saw them go
Out on the flood at morning brave,
As the little tugs had them in tow,
And the sunlight danced on the wave.

There all day long you could hear the sound
Of the caulking iron, the ship's bronze bell,
And the clank of the capstan going round
As the great tides rose and fell.

The sailors' songs, the Captain's shout,
The boatswain's whistle piping shrill,
And the roar as the anchor chain runs out,—
I often hear them still.

I can see them still, the sun on their gear,
The shining streak as the hulls careen,
And the flag at the peak unfurling,—clear
As a picture on a screen.

The fog still hangs on the long tide-rips,
The gulls go wavering to and fro,
But where are all the beautiful ships
I knew so long ago?

—from *Later Poems* (1921)

SCHOONER MAGIC
Lou Boudreau (1951–   )

Chester, home of generations of mariners, is often touted as one of the most picturesque towns on Nova Scotia's South Shore. After an adventurous life under sail, a retired mariner remains spellbound by the haunting presence of vessels of an earlier age.

The calm waters of Mahone Bay stretch away to the southeast and a gentle southwesterly breeze blows from over the land. Although the air is still cold, the last of the winter ice has gone and there is the promise of spring in the air. There is a sense of the ocean here. From the granite rocks of Pennant Point to tiny Ironbound Island, this is seafarer country. For so young a country much has gone before. We are now and have always been a sea people, born to a legacy of great schooners... even those of us who claim to be landsmen have an uncle, grandfather, or distant cousin who went to sea from some Nova Scotia port. We were famous schoonermen in days gone by, and when people talked of us the words were spoken with respect. Fine schooners were born on this coast, and our heritage is just as surely steeped in the salty Atlantic as it is rooted in the soil of this land.

I often walk the Chester waterfront in the early mornings, to ponder and take in the beauty. It's a special time for me because I usually have it all to myself, the sea, the sky, the peace, and the magic. They are all mine for those precious dawn moments and I savour the thought of it.

Sometimes I sit on the old wooden bench on the dock facing the sea and after making sure there is no one watching I peer intently into the mist, searching for the ghost I know is there. I can hear the quiet surge of the ocean on the stones at the water's edge and the cries of the gulls. The first whispers of a morning breeze brush my face and I can smell the salt of the ocean. And then my early morning daydream takes me further to the southeast, past the tree-covered islands into the great Atlantic.

There, an ethereal apparition from another time fades in and out of the fog, a lithe and lovely Atlantic siren, come once again to stir the hearts of mortal men. She's the spectre of a tall schooner, silently bound on some mission from a distant land. Tall of spar and long of hull she heels gently, as with canvas taut she reaps the wind. Close-hauled with topsails sheeted tight, the set of her sails is as perfect as her sheerline. The curve of her quarter is as fair as a woman's hip and her stem lovely to behold. Homeward bound, the faint scent of pine forest drifts across her bow, and she knows that she is close. Born here, near the shores of the bay, the thought of seeing her place of birth stirs her spirit. She has voyaged far and although older now, she lifts her bows with the sauciness of a young girl, throwing the spray to leeward.

A smile comes to my lips; could I possibly be hearing the sounds of a schooner at sea? I strain to listen as the breeze plays tricks on my ears. The creak of wooden blocks and the snap of manila rope come and fade. I can almost hear the faint chants and commands crossing her deck as her crew haul on halyard and sheet.

"Together now, again, and again."

Tilting my head slightly I catch the faint whispers of the skipper and mate. "Full and by, make fast."

The image becomes clearer as she closes the land and my schooner comes on under full canvas, leaving a white frothy wake astern, and the graceful curve of her bow wave as it rolls away to leeward makes an angry hiss.

There is the perpetual fog bank off the coast, which she must navigate before making landfall, but there is a familiarity; she knows the rocks and coves and harbours. The first of the sun's rays break the hills to the west and the Nova Scotia schooner glides into the bay. Rounding the point she comes ghosting towards me and even as her fisherman comes gently folding down, her topsails are clewed up. Her catted anchor is unlashed and her sails come down from forward. She glides near to the dock, and I am startled as I hear the command "let go." It takes me a moment to realize that I have voiced the words myself. The chain rattles silently out and the schooner comes to a gentle stop. She has come home and my daydream ends. As I walk back to my house I notice that I have been out for an hour; it is now 7:00 a.m. and the neighbours are stirring.

I've only lived here three years now but in some ways I've been here forever. Born in Baddeck in 1951, I was but a child when my father sailed us away from these shores in a Shelburne-built schooner called the *Dubloon*. What followed was a voyage lasting some thirty-five years. I sailed to South America, Africa, the Mediterranean, and every island between the US mainland and Venezuela. I sailed the oceans and saw the wonders of the world, but despite all this there was always a feeling that I didn't belong, I was always a foreigner, a stranger in strange and often inhospitable lands.

It's different now, the courses I lay are no longer on charts but along the peaceful streets of Chester and the storms I weather are of another nature. I have experienced a wonderful feeling that is new to me, that of belonging. The life of wandering is not a bad or wasteful one but a man needs a home and country. Like the weary schooner that finally returns, I too have come home.

And there is this other secret thing that I have found here, it is not mine alone and so I must share it with you. There is schooner magic all along this coast, and it is free for the taking. The bays and coves are filled with it as are the granite headlands and the rocky shores. It is there for you and I and anyone who would have it. Good for body and soul, this is how to find it. Go quietly at the earliest hint of dawn to the place where you can see and smell the Atlantic. Close your eyes for a moment and face the east and it will come to you.

—reprinted with permission of Capt. Lou Boudreau (2002)

SS *BEAVER*
Norman R. Hacking (1912–1997)

Famous ships develop characters and spawn mythologies. The Hudson's Bay Company's SS Beaver was one of these. Two months after her launch on the Thames on 2 May 1835, the 100-foot vessel built of oak and elm made her way under sail and steam to Victoria via Cape Horn and intermediary stops. The voyage from England to her Canadian station took 225 days. She was the first steamship to operate in the Pacific Northwest, linking isolated communities for trade and commerce, and sometimes aiding the civil power for constabulary duties. In order to honour her prominent role in West Coast history, The Maritime Museum of British Columbia established in 2012 the S.S. Beaver Medal. Presented annually, the prestigious medal recognizes the achievements of individuals who have made outstanding contributions to maritime endeavours in British Columbia.

On the night of July 26, 1888, an old-fashioned, untidy little paddle steamer slowly backed out from the City Wharf in Vancouver Harbour, and churned her way towards the First Narrows and the Gulf of Georgia. She was the *Beaver*, bound for Thurlow Island with logging supplies.

Members of her crew had imbibed a little too freely in waterfront saloons before embarking, and neither seamanship nor discipline was at its best. There was a slight summer mist on the water (later claimed to be a dense fog), and visibility in the Narrows was defective.

Currents were crafty and unreliable, and Captain George Marchant lost control of the vessel. With a barely perceptible grating sound, the little steamer ran high and dry on the beach at what is now called Prospect Point.

The crew were little disturbed by the mishap and stayed aboard for the night. Next morning they rowed back to Vancouver, leaving behind the staunch mortal remains of the first steamboat on the north Pacific coast.

The *Beaver* was fifty-three years old. Her market value for trading purposes was small. Her owner, Henry Saunders of Victoria, had no use for relics or antiques. And since salvage might cost as much as the ship was worth, her fine old oaken timbers were left to disintegrate on the beach, while vandals and curio hunters stripped her of copper sheathings and every movable object. For several years she remained a familiar sight at the entrance of Vancouver Harbour, becoming progressively more forlorn.

The hull was still more or less intact in 1892, but two years later there remained little more than the ribs to show the former hull, and a steam chest high on the end of a protruding pipe.

It seemed fitting that the *Beaver* should end her days in Vancouver Harbour, a city newly born, which marked the beginning of a new age of progress in British Columbia.

The *Beaver* had known old Fort Vancouver on the Columbia River in the days when the word of Dr. John McLoughlin was law on the coast. She had carried James Douglas and Sir George Simpson on tours of inspection to the northern fur posts, and had entertained on her deck the Russian governor of Alaska at Sitka.

She had aided in the development of coal on Vancouver Island, and had seen the growth of Victoria from a wilderness to a capital city. She had been present at the proclamation of the colony of British Columbia, and had carried gold seekers to the Fraser River mines.

She had surveyed much of the BC coastline on behalf of the Admiralty, and she had seen the coming of the first transcontinental railway. She had lived her life to the full, and gave up her proud spirit with the arrival of a new age.

—from *The Princess Story:*
A Century and a Half of West Coast Shipping (1974)

THE SINKING OF RMS *NASCOPIE*

Peter Pitseolak (1902–1973)

Like the ketch Nonsuch *that first sailed into Hudson Bay in the years 1668–1669, the 2,500-ton Royal Mail Ship* Nascopie *was one of the most historic and celebrated ships of the Hudson's Bay Company. Over 285 feet in length, the steamer-icebreaker* Nascopie *was designed and built in Wallsend on Tyne in 1911, and named for First Nations people of Quebec and Labrador. Between 1912 and 1947 she made thirty-four voyages into the Canadian Arctic. Toward the end of summer 1947 she struck an uncharted reef at the entrance to Cape Dorset harbour (Baffin Island), where she remained stranded for over two months. On 25 September she broke in half during a storm. Oral tradition among the Inuit has it that when the ship died that September, the old way of life in the North died with it. In the vernacular of that same oral tradition the Inuit story-teller and photographer Peter Pitseolak extols her place in the history of the North.*

It was sad; that ship helped the Eskimo people. What it carried helped the people before we had the government. When it sank, we were really sorry.

When the *Nascopie* came there was always a lot to eat. The old cook used to feed the Eskimo people.

When the ship arrived we went on and worked for two or three days. Today everyone seems to hate the ships, but then we loved them. The *Nascopie* used to bring all the supplies for the store; if we hadn't had the *Nascopie* there would have been no supplies. As soon as the ship arrived we ate. We ate outside; there was no other place. Those who couldn't work would cook on the shore. They were also paid. The cook fed us. His name was Storekeeper; they used to call out, "Storekeeper!" Ahalona! He gave everything... corn beef, stew... everything. That cook loved to feed the Eskimo people.

In 1946 the old cook was replaced by another. The new cook did not feed the Eskimos. The Eskimo people felt unwanted. With the new cook, the *Nascopie* was changed. There seemed to be nothing to eat on board! I was the only one who could get food. The new cook invited me—but not the others.

The next year there was a new captain also and with the new captain the ship was lost. The Bay manager had radioed the ship's captain that I should go down and meet the ship to pilot it into Cape Dorset. The captain said no. He thought he knew everything. If I had steered the ship, it would never have gone aground. I had been steering the ship for three or four years. The new captain did not want me to meet the ship...

That night, when the tides had risen and the ship had let loose its grip on the rocks, someone sent for me to come and help. Earlier that day my help had been refused; now, when it was too late, I was wanted.

On our way out to the ship we met a big barge full of kadluna [non-Inuit] heading for shore. It was full only of white men and they told us the ship had a big hole. I was the only person who heard this said—my companions missed it because of the noise of the motor. I told the kadluna in my boat that there was a hole in the *Nascopie*. Our boss, the Bay manager, did not want to go to the ship after I told him about the big hole. So I told him, "We must go; there are still people there—they are flashing lights because they want our help." ...

Of all the ships, the *Nascopie* was the most appreciated by the Eskimo people. The *Nascopie's* old cook used to feed the Eskimos, and the *Nascopie* helped the Eskimo people by taking them along where they wanted to go. We were sorry when she sank. She carried many things to buy that were useful and helped us very much. Since the *Nascopie* sank, the ships that come are not so much appreciated. When the *Nascopie* could be seen in the distance, many people were happy.

The *Nascopie* did not wait for the okiak—the "time when everything is frozen." By then she was no longer visible in the water.

—as told to Dorothy Eber in *People from Our Side* (1975)

A Seagoing Work of Art
David Rahn (1946–   )

Norwegian immigrant Ed Wahl and his six sons developed one of the most successful wooden-boat yards on the BC coast. For sixty years, over three generations, as the family's historian Ryan Wahl explains, "the name Wahl became synonymous with efficiency, quality and beauty." Based in Prince Rupert, the family has produced altogether over one thousand boats—trollers, gillnetters and halibut boats alike. But the launching of their 40-foot troller Legacy *in April 1990 marked the end of the era of large-scale wooden-boat building. From then on, metal and fibreglass vessels for both recreation and commerce became the industrial norm. Yet some argued that "tupperware and tin" could never compete with wood.*

In the mid-twentieth century the West Coast fishing industry developed some classic wooden boat designs at a number of legendary boatyards, few of which were more highly esteemed than the Wahl family boatyard in Prince Rupert. Wahl boats set the standard by which fishermen judge all others. On the West Coast there is no higher praise for a commercial wooden boatbuilder than to have his work compared favourably to the Wahls'.

Wahl boats are graceful, lovely riding sea boats, functional as you could wish for; but fishermen love Wahl boats most for their beauty. You *want* to scrape and sand and renew the varnish and paint each season. You feel that you're entrusted with the care of a masterpiece and letting the finish run down to craze and crack cannot be considered. Your rewards are those perfect, endless days riding groundswells on the nearest thing to perfection in wood you and the seabirds will ever see. Brace in the cockpit, sight down the glistening gumwood rail-cap from the checkers to the bow and watch the hull gracefully rise to the waves and fall back gently as it was meant to do, and the memory of those moments will outlast all the fish you'll bring aboard.

These are wonderful ships, perfect for their place and time... a family legacy that lives on in the memories of West Coast fishermen lucky enough to have put to sea in a Wahl boat.

—foreword to Ryan Wahl, *Legacy in Wood:*
The Wahl Family Boat Builders (2008)

LURED BY A DREAM
Philip Teece (1940–   )

The "call of the sea" takes many forms: mentoring by seafaring families, fantasies of foreign travel, and the inexplicable attraction known quite simply as "sea fever." Those who have taken up the sailor's way offer other explanations as well. In the excerpt that follows, the author meditates on the moment when he decided to build the boat of his dreams, and set off to explore wherever winds and tide would take him. The instructive journey along unanticipated courses would take decades—and change his life.

I was standing on a cliff-top on a crisp, lucid April evening in 1966, watching the light change from gold to orange to dull red on the sea at dusk. As I stood lost in my usual daydream about the islands that had become mere shadowy smudges on the horizon, a portent occurred.

From somewhere in the bay behind me, a little sloop came gliding past the promontory, beating her way slowly out to sea against a light and fitful headwind. About eighteen feet in length, and yet obviously a proper seagoing yacht in miniature, she was ineffably perfect. Her seaward progress was graceful, unhurried; the dying breeze was barely sufficient to cause her reddish sails to swell and draw. Her silent, apparition-like presence on that otherwise deserted sea made her appear like an emanation of my own present mood—a fragment of my dream.

As she ghosted slowly past, her tan sails, backlit by the sunset glow, appeared on fire. A wind stirred, riffling the burnished surface of the sea, and the elegant little craft heeled, shouldering aside a tumbling bow wave. The two dark figures who crouched beside her helm were viewed in profile, their faces peering toward the dimming horizon. (Who were those two late-evening sailors of twenty years ago, and where are they now?)

The miniature sloop was, as I have said, perfect. I stood enthralled on the chilly headland, spellbound by the magical glow of her sails and the silent purpose in her long, unhurried outward tacks. Although the distant islands faded now behind a veil of smoke-like dusk, she seemed to continue on toward the blue-grey line upon which they lay.

Gradually the sun dropped further below the horizon, and the little ship's sails dimmed to a pale silhouette. I watched her progress for a very long while, until finally distance and gathering darkness obscured, and eventually swallowed her altogether.

Although I was now very chilly externally, I strolled along the cliff path fired with a sudden sense of purpose, as though some decision had been made. I knew the time had come to lay hands on a quantity of necessary money, somehow, and to give my dream a tangible form. I was certain, too, what that tangible form would be, for the little tan-sailed vessel that had just vanished into the darkening mist had been a perfect vision of my future craft.

—from *A Dream of Islands* (1988)

A MAN AND HIS BOAT
Sam McKinney (1927–   )

Kea was the wooden sailboat in which Sam McKinney—former research associate at the Vancouver Maritime Museum—retraced Captain George Vancouver's 1792 voyage of exploration through the Salish Sea. His justification for buying her is compelling.

Having explained the "why" of my voyage, I now invite you to step aboard my boat, *Kea,* and I will tell you the story of both of us. Pour yourself a cup of tea or a glass of rum, then let your eyes wander around the inside cabin of this 25-foot wooden boat. See how the light from the swinging kerosene lantern is reflected in the varnished mahogany of the cabin sides, curved roof beams and cupboard doors and in the soft glow of brass portholes. Around us, books on tide, navigation, maritime history and ocean voyages line the shelves over each bunk. Tucked away in crannies and drawers are heavy woollen sweaters, socks and gloves. By the companionway hangs rain gear, parkas, pants and wide-brimmed foul-weather hats. In the narrow recess of the fo'c'sle, bagged sails and coils of rope are hung from hooks. Ask me, and I can tell you what lies behind every closed cupboard and drawer: tools, sewing kits, spare blocks, bright shackles, binoculars, a brass foghorn, protractors, dividers and charts. You can tell by what's around us that the boat and I are a matched pair, both of us on the downhill side of our prime and leaning toward the traditional way of things: caulked wooden planks, pine tar, diesel oil, woollen underwear, pipe smoke and Navy rum.

I bought this boat as a present to myself on my 70th birthday, bought it because I needed to break out from under a cloud of uselessness and boredom that hung over me. Such feelings, I found, came naturally with old age, along with the disgust I felt for the skinny, withered torso I would see in the mirror as I stepped from the shower, the fumbling for the wrong key at the front door and the lost hats, gloves and umbrellas I left behind in restaurants and stores. What were my alternatives? I could have joined an exercise class and fought back stiffness. Tied a string to my gloves. Grown a beard to hide the wrinkles. Call the cane a walking stick. Move to that retirement home in a place of sun that would be gated, guarded and gardened. A new career? Impossible. A hobby? How boring. I could have bought a new wardrobe, changed my image from drab sparrow-grey tweeds to something colourful and sporty to go along with the purchase of a red convertible car, one of those flashy imported models. But I am content with my one well-worn old wool jacket and I am determined to get 500,000 miles out of my old Volvo.

Around the house, I was only in her way. I cleaned the cat box, took out the garbage, lifted my feet when she vacuumed the rug and patiently pushed the cart behind her in the grocery store. And yet I led a good life: adored wife of 30 years, comfortable home, reasonable health and financial security. Why, then, that disease of longing for something else when, by all accounts, I should have been content with what I had? The answer was simple: because of who I am and how the person within me likes to live. So I began looking for a sailboat.

—from *Sailing with Vancouver* (2004)

UNION STEAMSHIPS
Beth Hill (1924–2007)

For the lonely settlements and logging camps of British Columbia's Inside Coast, the ships of the Union Steamships provided a life-line with the outside world. Here Beth Hill briefly recalls the shipping company that once played so important a role in these isolated and widely dispersed communities—but was eventually left behind in the face of newer technology and shifting economic realities.

If there is a logo for the Inside Coast during the first half of the twentieth century, it would surely be the black-topped red funnel of the Union Steamships, and the leitmotiv would be the sound of their whistles. They were familiar family friends to the people who used them—*Cutch, Capilano, Comox, Coquitlam, Camosun, Chilkoot, Cassiar, Chelohsin, Chilcotin, Cardena, Catala*—each with her own personality and idiosyncrasies. The glamorous *Cardena*, on the company letterhead and the flagship for a time, was longest in service (1923–1959), with the *Venture* a close second (1911–1946). The *Cassiar* with her big handwheel like an old sailing ship, went into every camp as far as Queen Charlotte Sound. The loggers could wear their caulked boots on the *Cassiar* but not on any other ship. Altogether there were 51 ships in the Union Steamship fleet, at different times.

The company was established in 1889 by a small group of Vancouver businessmen. The first coastal steamer was the *Cutch,* pressed into service while three new steamers were being constructed: the *Capilano,* the *Comox* and the *Coquitlam.* The company survived the hard times of the First World War and had a second expansionist period during the 1920s, when the excursion business was developed... However, as early as 1926 the company's annual report sounded a warning:

"Logging conditions continue uncertain and the company is by no means deriving the amount of revenue from this source as formerly. This is partly due to the fact that log production has been reduced and partly due to the changing conditions of the logging operations. The modern tendency is to mass production at specific points with the result that the scattered camps with the hand-logging system are being gradually eliminated."

Already the life of the coast was beginning to ebb. Lester Peterson's article "British Columbia's Depopulated Coast" describes how increasing centralization of the logging industry was accompanied by the same trend in fishing. As steamship schedules were cut back, the number of homesteaders decreased, for they needed transportation for their vegetables, meats and dairy products. Some could not endure the loneliness. Many of the Indian people were moving to the cities, and the government encouraged isolated bands to join established settlements nearer urban centres, to simplify the provision of services. The thousands of cannery workers no longer moved into the area, a seasonal migration like the fish they once canned. New cargoes—pulp and wood chips—were efficiently moved by barges. Float-planes and new roads further eroded steamboat travel. By 1959 the remaining ships of the Union Steamship Company were sold, bringing to an end 70 years of service.

—from *Upcoast Summers* (1985)

BEHIND THE SCENES
Robert D. Turner (1947–   )

Over nearly a century, the Canadian Pacific operated steamships and motor vessels along the rugged, beautiful and hazardous Pacific Coast. Thousands of skilled, professional mariners, like Chief Engineer Bill Neilson, served on the *Princesses* and took them through some of the most difficult coastal waters in the world. At the same time, passenger services established the standards of their times. Maintaining the consistency of service that was so well remembered on the Coast Service reflected well on the officials of the steamship line and the officers and crew members of every one of the *Princesses.*

The CPR was renowned for its fine food and service; excellent catering was a hallmark of the company. The majority of the cooks who prepared the hundreds of thousands of meals on the *Princesses* were of Chinese decent. For many men, working on the *Princesses* was a lifetime career. Lam Sar Ning, a senior cook, for example, served on the boats for 43 years and Chief Cook John Kung, a native of Victoria, proudly received a gold pass from the company for 50 years of exemplary service. Long ago, that quiet gentleman showed me his pass and we talked about his days on the ships. He recalled starting in 1925 as a mess boy on the new *Kathleen* and later as a junior cook beginning his day at 5:30 a.m., with almost no time off, and his years as chief cook on the *Motor Princess* and later on the *Kathleen* and *Marguerite* when 12- to 13-hour days were still common. And of how he organized a meeting with the other senior cooks and management to negotiate for better working conditions, overtime and shorter shifts.

So many people worked behind the scenes: in purchasing, stores, accounts, or handling baggage; in repairing, painting and maintaining the ships; in coaxing aging boilers and engines along from deep in the bowels of an old *Princess*, or, in the early days, shovelling endless tons of coal in the suffocating heat of the boiler rooms; preparing wonderful meals in the hot kitchens; changing endless linens and cleaning staterooms, or dumping chamber pots; caring for a lost child or a young traveller making a steamship voyage without a parent; chipping ice from the decks; loading cargo at remote ports in the worst of weather; navigating through fog and Pacific storms; and on and on. Endless hours of endless chores.

My sadness is that we cannot remember them all individually. Their achievement was remarkable and the personality and affection that we so often attach to the beautiful steamships is in many ways a reflection of the people who brought them to life.

—from *Those Beautiful Coastal Liners* (2001)

PRAYER FOR A NAVAL SHIP

Seafaring tradition holds that all those who "go down to the sea in ships," to borrow a phrase from Psalm 107 of the King James version of the Bible (1611), have always been God-fearing men. Indeed, this profound respect for the workings of the Divine throughout Creation has often been institutionalized. This was certainly the case in the founding of Canada's navy in 1910, and in its regular use of Christian prayer on formal occasions both ashore and afloat. The Divine Service Book, *from which the following prayer and its title are taken, reflects an ancient naval tradition, which regards a ship as essentially her crew. Hence praying for the crew is the same as praying for the vessel they animate, and which sustains their community.*

A Prayer For the Ship: O Eternal Lord God, who hast united us as shipmates in the bond of fellowship; enable us to be worthy of those who have served before us; and grant us with a willing spirit to fulfil whatever duty may be laid upon us, that when our work on earth is over we may find our rest in thine eternal service, through Jesus Christ our Lord. Amen.

—Department of National Defence, from *Divine Service Book for the Armed Forces* (1950)

RECALLING THE CANADIAN CORVETTE

First conceived as a "Patrol Vessel, Whaler Type" the corvette was designed to meet the urgent needs of wartime navies caught off-guard by the rise of Nazi Germany. The dynamics of the ensuing Battle of the Atlantic in the years 1939–1945 involved rapidly evolving technology, tactics, experimentation and training. The corvette found itself in the eye of this storm. Designed for inshore duties, this highly manoeuvrable ship quickly took on the challenges of high-seas, antisubmarine, convoy-escort duties. Over two-hundred feet in length, and with a top speed of fifteen knots, she carried a variety of armament, and tackled enemy submarines in close-quarters combat. Constantly modified and updated throughout the war, this tough Canadian-built ship is now commemorated by the last remaining corvette, HMCS Sackville, in Halifax, a museum ship in the care of the Canadian Naval Memorial Trust.

The following two excerpts have been written by different authors. The first one shares the reflections of a Quebec barrister who, as a naval reservist, commanded the corvette HMCS Amherst at the height of the Battle of the Atlantic. He focuses on the meaning of the ship for a generation of naval reservists. The second account, by two historians, sets this class of ship into its broader historical context.

Louis Audette (1907–1995)

The corvette was the backbone of the Canadian navy; it was the largest class of ships ever to serve in the Canadian navy and also the largest class of ships ever built in Canadian shipyards.

The Second World War gave rise to an extraordinary expansion in the Canadian navy; of the many thousands of Reserve officers and men who served in the war, few did not owe their early sea time at least in part to a corvette. The ships were marvels of seaworthiness and of personal discomfort; it must be remembered that they were designed before those at the top really gave adequate consideration to the needs of those at the bottom of the ladder.

For sheer worthiness, few ships have ever been better designed. Assigned to fight the U-boat menace, they were barely adequate in speed, their surface armament just met the needs of the moment, their anti-submarine Asdic equipment was barely adequate and their living conditions made heroes of men destined to quite other roles in life.

Whatever their faults and qualities, these fine little ships were productive of an esprit de corps which may not have existed elsewhere. Because the crews were numerically smaller than in frigates, destroyers and bigger ships, they were more closely knit and better known to their officers.

Today there remains only *Sackville* in Halifax to remind the world of a great past. Nevertheless, throughout the land, many men now old will keep in mind the days they spent in corvettes in harsher times.

Ken Macpherson (1926–) and Marc Milner (1954–)

No other warship is so intimately connected with Canada's naval heritage as the ubiquitous corvette of the Second World War. It was, after all, the largest class of vessels ever to serve in the Canadian navy: 123 in various types. It was also the largest class of ships ever constructed in Canadian shipyards: 121 built between 1940 and 1944. These distinctions alone qualify the corvette for special status. It is probably true to say as well—although it has never been determined—that more Canadians went to sea in corvettes than in any other class of ship.

Perhaps more important than mere quantity was the quality of service provided to the nation by its corvettes. Corvettes carried Canada's naval effort through the darkest days of the Second World War. Without them the Battle of the Atlantic, the single most important campaign of the war, might well have gone the other way. As Admiral Sir Dudley Pound, First Sea Lord of the Royal Navy observed, "The Canadian corvettes solved the problem of the Atlantic convoys." In doing so the corvettes carved out for Canada and its navy a major role in the North Atlantic campaign, the only theatre of war ever commanded by a Canadian, and including primary responsibility—by 1944—for the close escort of the main convoys upon which the war effort in Europe depended. No other Canadian service achieved so much during the war, and much of that accomplishment was due to eighty corvettes of the first two building programmes that gave the RCN a central role in the difficult years of 1941–1943.

It is also true that the corvette fleet reflected all the strengths and weaknesses of the Canada of its day. In 1939 Canada had the industrial strength and population to build and man simple auxiliary war vessels in considerable numbers. Rudimentary weapons were available from First World War reserves, or from surplus American and British production. But the war which these ships and men were called upon to fight was a modern, highly sophisticated one. Canada lacked the high-technology industry needed to provide the latest weapons and sensors for modern war. For the most part, though, corvettes did their job just by being there, providing the escorts upon which the whole system of trade defence was built. In the process they laid the foundations of the modern Canadian navy.

—from Ken Macpherson and Marc Milner,
with foreword by Louis Audette,
Corvettes of the Royal Canadian Navy, 1939–1945 (1993)

OIL TANKERS
E. Annie Proulx (1935–)

American writer E. Annie Proulx explores the effect of the discovery of oil on the coast of Newfoundland when the province seemed on the brink of great economic growth. Yet the oil industry also threatened to destroy the old way of life and the ecology of the region. In the fictional newspaper, the Gammy Bird, *journalist Quoyle writes prophetically on the damaging effect of oil tankers. His article, below, is followed by his managing director's rebuttal.*

NOBODY HANGS A PICTURE OF AN OIL TANKER

There is a 1904 photograph on the wall of the Killick-Claw Public Library. It shows eight schooners in Omaloor Bay heading out to the fishing grounds, their sails spread like white wings. They are beautiful beyond compare. It took great skill and sea knowledge to sail them.

Today the most common sight on the marine horizon is the low black profile of an oil tanker. Oil, in crude and refined forms, is—bar none—the number one commodity in international trade.

Another common sight is black oil scum along miles of land-wash, like the shoreline along Cape Despond this week. Hundreds of people watched Monday morning as 14,000 metric tons of crude washed onshore from a ruptured tank of the *Golden Goose*. Thousands of seabirds and fish struggled in the oil, fishing boats and nets were fouled. "This is the end of this place," said Jack Eye, 87, of Little Despond, who, as a young man, was a dory fisherman with the schooner fleet.

Our world runs on oil. More than 3,000 tankers prowl the world's seas. Among them are the largest moving objects ever made by man, the Very Large Crude Carriers, or VLCCs, up to 400 metres in length and over 200,000 deadweight tons. Many of these ships are single hull vessels. Some are old and corroded, structurally weak. One thing is sure. There will be more oil spills, and some will be horrendous.

Nobody hangs a picture of an oil tanker on their wall.

PICTURE OF AN OIL TANKER

More than 3,000 tankers proudly ride the world's seas. These giant tankers, even the biggest, take advantage of Newfoundland's deep-water ports and refineries. Oil and Newfoundland go together like ham and eggs, and like ham and eggs they'll nourish us all in the coming years.

Let's all hang a picture of an oil tanker on our wall.

—from *The Shipping News* (1993)

ROWBOAT
Kenneth Macrae Leighton (1925–1998)

The author described his wooden yacht as a replica of a "jollyboat," or a "ship's boat," such as Captain William Bligh sailed in his epoch-making voyage after the mutiny on the Bounty *in 1789. A finely wrought replica of eighteenth-century craftsmanship, the reproduction was built in the 1990s by naval architect Greg Foster in his boat yard in Whaler Bay, Galiano Island, BC. The author rowed it over five hundred miles from Vancouver to Prince Rupert.*

My boat is made of red and yellow cedar. There is a small foredeck and an absolutely minuscule deck behind the sternsheets. Both give some shelter for my gear but absolutely none for me, of course. There is a single, unstayed mast for a standing lug sail and a tiny jib. If you don't know the lug sail, it is an almost square sail such as the conventional old sailing ships carried in the days of Nelson. It hangs from a pole called the yard and is, as we say, loose-footed. In other words, there is no boom such as you see on a modern, fore- and aft-rigged yacht. Nothing to strike the head of the unwary helmsman. The lug sail is nearly as old as time and is about the safest rig you can think of.

Morag Anne sails well before the wind but rather poorly otherwise which is what you would expect from a boat with neither centreboard nor keel.

For those readers who know the lug sail, this is boring information. I must point out, however, that sailing is pretty much a luxury and a bonus on *Morag Anne*. It's great to get the sail up but it isn't often that the wind, if there is any, is coming from the right direction. That's just a fact of life on this coast. I can't say it bothers me much. I like to row.

When the boat is fully loaded for cruising, I am moving about six or seven hundred pounds. This is the reason that I make no more than two nautical miles an hour in calm conditions. With a following tide or wind I do better than this; when either or both are against me, much less. If the wind is strong from ahead or if the tidal stream against me is more than two knots there is nothing for it but to anchor and wait for things to change. This sort of thing is what makes patience both a virtue and a necessity in small boat cruising. It is, as they say, good for the soul.

I have absolute trust in my boat's seaworthiness. Greg Foster built her with loving care, as he does all his work. I can't count the times I have been asked if I built her myself. Each time my reply is the same. I couldn't possibly build anything that would come close to his standard. He is a master shipwright and a philosopher in wood...

Some description is necessary concerning what may be called the domestic arrangements. During the day the tent lies under the thwart. In preparation for the night it is draped over the mainsail yard which is attached to the mast and points aft, four feet or so above the deck, the free end supported by a line from the masthead. The front of the tent is wrapped around the mast, the after end is open. Spreaders, positioned fore and aft and fastened to the gunwales, hold it taut and away from the sides of the boat. The thwart is removed and I have a living space of five by nine feet. Who could ask for more?

This may seem complicated but a more simple arrangement would be hard to discover. This is not to say that putting up the tent in the rain after a hard day of rowing, in a choppy sea, with wet decks and numb fingers is a piece of cake or a lot of fun. But if something like this bothers you a great deal all I can say is small, open boat cruising may not be for you.

I cook on a small camp stove but, truth to tell, I don't do much more than boil water, for my diet is simple and I am no cook. I am well satisfied with Japanese noodles, Cream of Wheat with added raisins and homemade granola. I drink a lot of tea and coffee which taste better at sea, in the open air, than anywhere else in the world.

The head or toilet is, of course, a bucket.

—from *Oar & Sail: An Odyssey of the West Coast* (1999)

HOME TO REST
F.S. Farrar (1901–1955)

Museum ships are an integral part of Canada's maritime heritage. One thinks of the World War II corvette HMCS Sackville *in Halifax, the wartime destroyer HMCS* Haida *in Hamilton, Ontario, the experimental hydrofoil HMCS* Bras d'Or *at the Musée Maritime du Québec (L'Islet-sur-Mer), and the Cold War era submarine HMCS* Onondaga *at Rimouski (Pointe-au-Père). The Pacific Coast boasts an equally famous ship: the RCMP's legendary* St. Roch, *now housed in the Vancouver Maritime Museum. It was built in 1928 by Burrard Drydock Shipyard of North Vancouver, with an especially strengthened hull for Arctic service. Commanded by Inspector Henry Larsen, she was the first vessel to transit the Northwest Passage from west to east (1940–1942). In 1950 she became the first ship to circumnavigate North America. Her first mate, RCMP Sgt. Ted Farrar, concludes his account of these voyages with a fond farewell to a valiant vessel.*

And now, my tale is ended. So too, have the exploits of a gallant Canadian ship.

No longer will she charge unflinching against the fury of an Arctic gale, beneath a torrent of freezing rain slashing against her ports and cutting into the raw, red faces of the men who loved her. Never again will her rudder be twisted forward by cruel-faced growlers against her squat, round hull. For her, no more lonely nights amid grinding ice floes. And no longer will the men of the North, watching from the shores below their far-flung detachments, see the once familiar sight of the two tall masts and crow's-nests of the little supply boat rounding an ice-bound point for a brief but happy reunion. The *St. Roch* has gone home to rest.

In the fall of 1954 after a 91-day passage she returned via the South to her birthplace, Vancouver. She was accorded a jubilant welcome as she sailed in escorted by a later Arctic victor, HMCS *Labrador.* An honour unique in the history of Canadian ships awaited her.

Through public subscription the good people of Vancouver purchased the *St. Roch* from the Force. She is to be given a permanent berth at Kitsilano Point near the heart of the great western port. There she will be preserved in the tradition of Amundsen's *Gioa,* or even Nelson's *Victory.* In the years to come the *St. Roch* will watch quietly over the waters of English Bay, protected and undisturbed... May the wholesome washing of the timeless sea sweeten her solitude.

—from *Arctic Assignment: The Story of the St. Roch* (1955)

"Look at me, Old Man, that the weather made by you may spare me; and, pray, protect me that no evil may befall me while I am travelling on this sea, Old Man, that I may arrive at the place to which I am going, Great Supernatural One, Old Man."

— Kwakiutl Prayers, Franz Boas,
The Religion of the Kwakiutl Indians (1930)

CHAPTER IV

PASSAGES

Passage-making is the art of conducting a vessel safely between geographical points. It may be a visceral adventure or a lyrical beat upwind. But it is never without its risks. For whether voyaging offshore with only waves and whales for company, or in pilotage waters within sight of a beckoning shore, many factors may impinge on the success of the enterprise. Chief among these are weather and tides, the seaworthiness and equipment of the vessel itself, and the competence of its crew. Yet such is the condition of life at sea on "the Great Common" that seemingly random factors can conspire to impede the passage of even well-found ships and competently led crews. The possibility of human error always lurks in the background. The early explorers faced the special hazard of having to create the very navigational data on which they depended even while making passage into unknown waters; they had to effect repairs "on the run" beyond the reach of shipyards and docks. Harrowing tales of misadventure and marine disaster attest to courage and ingenuity in adversity. Successful passages call the mariner to break with the bonds of shore and venture to sea once again.

VOYAGING: A METAPHOR FOR LIFE
Silver Donald Cameron (1937–　)

Since 1937 the image of the legendary Nova Scotia schooner Bluenose *has been circulating throughout Canada on the 10-cent coin. Launched in 1921,* Bluenose *won the North Atlantic Fishermen's International races between Canada and the United States in her first competition— and held the championship for Canada until the races ended in 1938. Like her rivals, she earned her living as a working schooner fishing for cod on the Grand Banks of Newfoundland. She was lost off Haiti in 1946. In 1963, a replica named* Bluenose II *was launched, and after nearly fifty years of service the replica was completely rebuilt in 2009–2014. In the excerpt below, it is 1983 and the author, signed onto* Bluenose II *as crew for an offshore voyage, ponders the meaning of seafaring.*

Sailing is not so much a job as a calling, a vocation. Voyaging is one of the great metaphors for life itself—life stripped of its fever and fret, focussed on ultimate concerns. The mysterious, tragic quality of the sea echoes the unknowable reaches of the human situation, of our relation to chance and destiny, glory and disaster. Sailing requires a powerful development of crucial human qualities: courage, determination, ingenuity, cooperation, honesty, competence. The sailor daily confronts the possibility of suffering and privation, even of death. Like one or two other ventures—mining and battle, for instance—sailing makes great demands on people and bonds them closely together in the full recognition of their interdependence despite their human frailty. It is understandable, as [historian] Noel Mostert puts it, that "for so many centuries shipwreck struck man as the epitome of irony and despair: the failure of himself at his proven best, within a rope's throw of salvation."

Because his life is founded on risk, the seaman develops attitudes alien to the landsman. Deference, humility, subordination of his own needs to those of the ship—these develop organically, the natural outgrowth of increased understanding. A profound conservatism marks the nautical character, a realization that innovations and bright ideas which work well on the dry and stable foundation of the land may well fail when plunged repeatedly into salt water, buffeted by gales, smashed by expectable accidents. The cost of their failure will not be reckoned in cash or inconvenience but in lives. *Bluenose II* carries modern electronics, but it would be unthinkable to throw away the sextant, the magnetic compass, the chart, and the lead line on the assumption that the electronics will always work. There are old sailors, runs a famous adage, and there are bold sailors, but there are no old, bold sailors.

These habits of mind are really matters of faith—faith in one's own ability, in one's comrades, in the ship. Faith in technology, or in Providence. Superstition and religion are indeed parallel and logical responses to the marine experience. Notwithstanding its semiconductors, *Bluenose II* represents an anthology of ideas which have proven themselves for periods long enough to warrant the faith of seamen. "No designer or builder can have full experience in all things pertaining to vessels," writes the deeply traditional designer R.D. Culler, "but they can and should be very much guided by what worked in the past."

The role of chance, of the gods, is obvious in life at sea. Their role is equally large ashore, but it is easily overlooked amidst the clatter and roar of peripheral matters. Going to sea, in the New England phrase, "centres a man down," and puts his life's concerns into perspective. "Do you realize," said [crew member] Ian Morrison suddenly this afternoon, "that we've heard nothing about the Tory leadership?" Everyone looked pleased at the thought. We sail beyond politics, in a sense, into a region where the soul naturally contemplates its origins and destiny. Hence the power of the voyaging metaphor, casting into sharp relief the essence of all our ventures.

—from *Once Upon a Schooner:*
A Foreign Voyage in Bluenose II (1992)

CABOT AND NAVIGATION
Thomas B. Costain (1885–1965)

In the fifteenth century the mariner had few instruments to guide him on his course. When the weather was clear he could sail with his eye fixed on the North Star; if it was overcast he had to use the compass. The North Atlantic is more likely to provide fogs and grey skies than clear sunshine, and so it was the compass on which John Cabot had to depend. This meant that he did not sail due west, for the compass has its little failings and never points exactly north. In the waters through which Cabot was sailing the variation is west of north, which meant that the tiny *Matthew,* wallowing in the trough of the sea, its lateen sail always damp with the spray, followed a course which inclined slightly southward. This was fortunate. It spared the crew any contact with the icebergs which would have been encountered in great numbers had they sailed due west; and it brought them finally, on June 24, 1497, to land which has been identified since as Cape Breton Island.

The anchor was dropped and the little band went ashore gratefully, their hearts filled with bounding hopes. The new land was warm and green and fertile. Trees grew close to the water's edge. The sea, which abounded with fish, rolled in to a strip of sandy shingle. They saw no trace of natives, but the fact that some of the trees had been felled was evidence that the country was inhabited. All doubts on that score ended when snares for the catching of game were found. Perhaps eyes distended with excitement were watching the newcomers from the safe cover of the trees; but not a sound warned of their surveillance.

John Cabot, raising a high wooden cross with the flag of England and the banner of St. Mark's of Venice (that city having granted him citizenship some years before), had no reservations at all. He was certain he had accomplished his mission. He knew that his feet were planted firmly on the soil of Cathay, that fabulous land of spices and silks and gold. Somewhere hereabouts he would find the great open passage through which ships would sail north of Cathay and so in time girdle the earth.

—from *The White and the Gold* (1954)

CARTIER'S VOYAGES INTO CANADA
Donald Creighton (1902–1979)

Gazing out over the harbour from the top of the ramparts on 20 April 1534, the citizens of St. Malo, France, watched Jacques Cartier set sail on his first voyage to the territory that became known as Canada. Two other voyages followed in 1535–1536 and 1541–1542. Four hundred and fifty years later, a Canadian prime minister, Pierre Trudeau, stood on these same ramparts to commemorate the event. By all accounts, Cartier was the first to document the name "Canada," a word derived from the Iroquois word "Kanata," meaning "village." He was the first to coin the term "Canadiens" to describe those who lived there.

The ships were ready. Charles de Mouy, Seigneur de la Meilleraye and Vice-Admiral of France, had solemnly required the commander, the captains, and the sailors to swear that they would conduct themselves truly and loyally in the service of His Most Christian Majesty, Francis I. The last farewells had been said. The two vessels, each about sixty tons in burden, with their small company of sixty-one souls in all, moved slowly out of the harbour and beyond the jutting promontory on which stood the little town. The narrow, twisting streets, the substantial merchant houses, the walls and great defensive towers of St. Malo receded slowly into the distance. The wind freshened. They were out in the Channel now, heading west. And Jacques Cartier, the Breton master-pilot, who bore the King's commission, stood on deck, shading his eyes against the sun and studying his course...

On May 10th [1534], when Cartier reached the ice-choked waters of Cape Bonavista on the east coast of Newfoundland, he was obviously following a course which fishermen had already made familiar. In a single generation, the Newfoundland fishery had become an industry of major importance for the Atlantic powers in general and for France and Portugal in particular. In France, a large continental country, there was a capacious market; fish, which were required in any case for fast days, were at all times a favourite staple article of diet. Out in the waters off Newfoundland, there were inexhaustible supplies; and the catch, preserved in salt, could be transported without deterioration in the small ships and on the long slow Atlantic voyages of the day. With its sunny, favourable climate, France could readily acquire cheap, copious supplies of the solar salt, produced by the evaporation of sea water, which was used lavishly in the cure. France, in fact, had many advantages. And her fishermen had been pressing them vigorously along the coasts of Newfoundland and Cape Breton Island and into the Strait of Belle Isle.

Other unknown adventurers had preceded Cartier thus far. But, beyond the Strait of Belle Isle, the daring originality of his first voyage began. Leaving Labrador—"the land God gave to Cain" he was inclined to call it—and the rugged, inhospitable, and stormy shores of Newfoundland behind him, Cartier plunged south and west. It was midsummer now, and the days were hot, the skies intensely blue, and the air unbelievably radiant. In a leisurely, inquiring fashion, the French ships skirted the islands and ventured up the deep bays of the Gulf of St. Lawrence. The bright, coloured landscape of northern summer was richly rewarding. Cartier looked admiringly at dense, fragrant pine forests, lush, green meadows, and fields of wild wheat, oats, and peas in flower "as thick and fine as ever I saw in Brittany." And when the French landed, they found strawberries, raspberries, gooseberries, and "Provins roses."

Cartier had found and explored the Gulf of St. Lawrence; but he had missed the great river which drained into it. The St. Lawrence— the "River of Canada" as the French came to call it—was the great central geographical fact in the whole French enterprise in North America; and it was Cartier's happy destiny to complete the discovery which he had begun so promisingly in 1534. Yet the little flotilla of ships—the *Grande Hermine,* the *Petite Hermine,* and the *Emerillon*—which sailed from St. Malo on 19th May 1535, did not at first enjoy the good fortune which had attended the original expedition. They started a month later. They were buffeted and dispersed by violent western gales on the Atlantic; and it was not until late summer was waning into autumn that Cartier began to sail westward up the narrowing Gulf of the St. Lawrence. The information, supplied by his Indian guides, "that one could make one's way so far up the river that they had never heard of anyone reaching the head of it" seemed to end the possibility of an easy, direct passage to the Far East; and Stadacona and Hochelaga, the two Huron-Iroquois villages which he found on the present sites of the port of Quebec and the city of Montreal, were poor, primitive communities which mocked whatever hopes he may have held of cultivated and wealthy native monarchies.

—from *The Story of Canada* (1960)

LANDFALL IN ACADIA, NOVA FRANCIA, 1606
Marc Lescarbot (c. 1570–c. 1642)

In his Histoire de la Nouvelle France *(1609), French lawyer and historian Marc Lescarbot describes in detail his journey to Nova Francia to visit Port Royal and Canso (Port de Campseau) in present-day Nova Scotia. He departed La Rochelle in May 1606, and made landfall in Acadia at the end of July. He returned to France in July 1607 by way of Canso and published his account in 1609. The English translation appeared the same year.*

The 4th day of July our sailors which were appointed for the last quarter watch descried in the morning, very early, everyone being yet a-bed, the Isles of Saint Peter [St. Pierre and Miquelon]. And the Friday the seventh of the said month we discovered, on the larboard, a coast of land high raised up, appearing unto us as long as one's sight could stretch out, which gave us greater cause of joy than yet we had had, wherein God did greatly shew his merciful favour unto us, making this discovery in fair calm weather. Being yet far from it, the boldest of the company went up to the maintop, to the end to see it better, so much were all of us desirous to see this land, true and most delightful habitation of man. Monsieur de Poutrincourt went up thither, and myself also, which we had not yet done. Even our dogs did thrust their noses out of the ship, better to draw and smell the sweet air of the land, not being able to contain themselves from witnessing, by their gestures, the joy they had of it. We drew within a league near unto it, and (the sails being let down) we fell a-fishing of cod, the fishing of the Bank beginning to fail. They which had before us made voyages in those parts did judge us to be at Cape Breton. The night drawing on, we stood off to the seaward. The next day following, being the eighth of the said month of July, as we drew near to the Bay of Campseau, came, about the evening, mists, which did continue eight whole days, during the which we kept us at sea, hulling still, not being able to go forward, being resisted by West and South-West winds. During these eight days, which were from one Saturday to another, God (who hath always guided these voyages, in the which not one man hath been lost by sea) shewed us his special favour in sending unto us, among the thick fogs, a clearing of the sun, which continued but half an hour; and then had we sight of the firm land, and knew that we were ready to be cast away upon the rocks if we had not speedily stood off to sea-ward. A man doth sometimes seek the land as one doth his beloved, which sometimes repulseth her sweetheart very rudely. Finally, upon Saturday, the 15th of July, about two o'clock in the afternoon, the sky began to salute us, as it were, with cannon-shots, shedding tears, as being sorry to have kept us so long in pain. So that, fair weather being come again, we saw coming straight to us (we being four leagues off from the land) two shallops with open sails, in a sea yet wrathed. This thing gave us much content. But, whilst we followed on our course, there came from the land odours incomparable for sweetness, brought with a warm wind so abundantly that all the Orient parts could not procure greater abundance. We did stretch out our hands, as it were to take them, so palpable were they, which I have admired a thousand times since. Then the two shallops did approach, the one manned with savages, who had a stag painted at their sails, the other with Frenchmen of Saint Malo, which made their fishing at the Port of Campseau, but the savages were more diligent, for they arrived first. Having never seen any before, I did admire, at the first sight, their fair shape and form of visage. One of them did excuse himself for that he had not brought his fair beaver gown, because the weather had been foul. He had but one red piece of frieze upon his back, and *matachias* about his neck, at his wrists, above the elbow, and at his girdle. We made them to eat and drink. During that time they told us all that had passed a year before at Port Royal (whither we were bound).

—from *Nova Francia: A Description of Acadia, 1606* (1609)

SINGING THE NORTHWEST PASSAGE
Stan Rogers (1949–1983)

Stan Rogers' "The Northwest Passage" (1981) is perhaps the most famous song in his rich repertoire of folk music. Regarded by many as Canada's second national anthem, it has frequently been quoted by politicians on official occasions. The former governor general Adrienne Clarkson cited it during her inaugural address on 7 October 1999, and again on 23 April 2005 when opening the Canadian Embassy in Berlin. The BBC's World Service programme World Today *mentioned it on 9 October 2007 during a story about Canada's claims for Arctic sovereignty.*

The singer evokes the Northwest Passage—the experience of the sea—as a metaphor for an all-embracing view of Canadian history, as well as for an individual's personal journey through life.

Chorus.
Ah, for just one time I would take the Northwest Passage
To find the hand of Franklin reaching for the Beaufort Sea;
Tracing one warm line through a land so wide and savage
And make a Northwest Passage to the sea.

Westward from the Davis Strait 'tis there 'twas said to lie
The sea route to the Orient for which so many died;
Seeking gold and glory, leaving weathered, broken bones
And a long-forgotten lonely cairn of stones. *(Chorus)*

Three centuries thereafter, I take passage overland
In the footsteps of brave Kelso [Henry Kelsey], where his "sea of
    flowers" began
Watching cities rise before me, then behind me sink again
This tardiest explorer, driving hard across the plain. *(Chorus)*

And through the night, behind the wheel, the mileage clicking west
I think upon Mackenzie, David Thompson and the rest
Who cracked the mountain ramparts and did show a path for me
To race the roaring Fraser to the sea. *(Chorus)*

How then am I so different from the first men through this way?
Like them, I left a settled life, I threw it all away.
To seek a Northwest Passage at the call of many men
To find there but the road back home again. *(Chorus)*

CHARTING DESOLATION SOUND
George Vancouver (1757–1798)

*The journals of Captain George Vancouver provide a unique histori-
cal record of his extraordinary voyages into the northwestern Pacific.
Britain's Admiralty had assigned three major tasks: survey of the west
coast up to sixty degrees north latitude, the search for the Northwest
Passage from the west, and fostering congenial diplomatic relations with
the Spanish explorer Juan Francisco de la Bodega y Quadra and his
officers at Nootka. Among Vancouver's legacy are hundreds of pages of
technical and narrative detail on all that he had experienced, together
with a wealth of remarkably accurate charts. Like the Spaniards, he had
an array of the latest technical resources. These included: magnetic compasses, sextants to determine vertical and horizontal angles, mechanical
chronometers for calculating distance from the Greenwich meridian,
and hand lead-and-line for assessing the depth of water and the character of the seabed. Once having anchored his ships on location, his crew
set off in small open boats to survey each region. His work marks the*

beginnings of what became the Canadian Hydrographic Service, which celebrated its centenary in 2004. In the following excerpt, Vancouver writes of his voyage in June and July 1792 through the Strait of Georgia and into Desolation Sound in the company of the Spanish ships Sutil *and* Mexicana *under Captains Dionisio Galiano (1762–1805) and Cayetano Valdés (1762–1835). The Spaniards were continuing the global expedition of Captain Alejandro Malaspina.*

The night was dark and rainy, and the wind so light and variable, that by the influence of the tides we were driven about as it were blindfolded in this labyrinth, until toward midnight, when we were happily conducted to the north side of an island in this supposed sound, where we anchored in company with the *Chatham* and the Spanish vessels, in 32 fathoms water, rocky bottom. At break of day we found ourselves about half a mile from the shores of a high rocky island, surrounded by a detached and broken country, whose general appearance was very inhospitable...

The infinitely divided appearance of the region into which we had now arrived, promised to furnish ample employment for our boats.

To Lieutenant Puget and Mr. Whidby in the *Discovery*'s launch and cutter, I consigned the examination of the continental shore, from the place where we had lost sight of it the preceding evening. Mr. Johnstone, in the *Chatham*'s cutter, accompanied by Mr. Swaine in her launch, were directed to investigate a branch of this sound leading to the north westward; and Sen[r.] Valdez undertook the survey of the intermediate coast; by which arrangement the whole, or if not of a very considerable extent, would soon be determined. Whilst the boats were equipping, Mr. Broughton went in quest of a more commodious situation for the ships up the sound to the north west.

The weather, which was serene and extremely pleasant, afforded me an opportunity, in company with Sen[r.] Galiano and some of our officers, to visit the shore of the island, near which we were at anchor, and to determine the situation of its west point to be in latitude 50°6', longitude 235°26'. With the former Sen[r.] Galiano's observations agreed, but by his chronometer the longitude was made more westerly. My observations being deduced from the watch, according to its rate [of gain or loss] as settled in Birch Bay, which was not very likely to have yet acquired any material error, inclined me to believe we were probably the most correct.

Early in the afternoon Mr. Broughton returned, having found a more eligible anchorage, though in a situation equally dreary and unpleasant. The several gentlemen in the boats being made acquainted with the station to which the ships were about to resort, departed agreeably to their respective instructions.

The wind that since noon had blown fresh from the SE attended with heavy squalls and much rain, drove us by its increased violence from our anchorage, and almost instantly into 70 and 80 fathoms water. The anchor was immediately hove up, and we steered for the rendezvous Mr. Broughton had pointed out, where about six in the evening we arrived in company with our little squadron. Our situation here was on the northern side of an arm of the sound leading to the north westward, a little more than half a mile wide, presenting as gloomy and dismal an aspect as nature could well be supposed to exhibit, had she not been a little aided by vegetation; which though dull and uninteresting, screened from our sight the dreary rocks and precipices that compose these desolate shores...

Nor was the sea more favourable to our wants, the steep rocky shores prevented the use of the seine, and not a fish at the bottom could be tempted to take the hook.

I had absented myself from the present surveying excursions, in order to procure some observations for the longitude here, and to arrange the charts of the different surveys in the order they had been made. These when so methodized, my third lieutenant Mr. Baker had undertaken to copy and embellish, and who, in point of accuracy, neatness, and such dispatch as circumstances admitted, certainly excelled in a very high degree. To conclude our operations up to the present period some further angles were required. Beside these I was desirous of acquiring some knowledge of the main channel of the gulph we had quitted on monday afternoon, and to which no one of our boats had been directed.

Early the next morning [of 30 June 1792] I set out in the yawl on that pursuit, with a favorable breeze from the NW which shortly shifted to the opposite quarter, and blew a fresh gale, attended with a very heavy rain. Having reached by ten in the forenoon no further than the island under which we had anchored at midnight on the 25th, a prospect of a certain continuance of the unsettled weather obliged me to abandon my design, and return to the ship; where I had the pleasure of hearing the launch and cutter had arrived soon after my departure, after having completed the examination of the continental coast from the place where we had left it, the night we had entered the sound, to about 3 leagues north-westward of our present station, making the land near which we were then at anchor on our northern side, an island, or a cluster of islands of considerable extent. These gentlemen were likewise of opinion, that all the land before us to the westward and NW from its insular appearance, formed an immense archipelago; but knowing Mr. Johnstone was directed to examine that quarter, and coming within sight of the ships, they had returned on board for further instructions.

—George Vancouver, from *A Voyage of Discovery to the North Pacific Ocean, and Round the World,* Vol. I (1798)

COULD I HAVE BEEN ONE OF THEM?
Sam McKinney (1927–   )

In his 25-foot wooden sailboat, retired marine archivist Sam McKinney set himself a daunting challenge—to follow Captain George Vancouver's 1792 journey of exploration through the Inland Sea that separates what is now Vancouver Island from the mainland. While much has changed in two hundred years, the wild, silent beauty of deep inlets, towering peaks and turbulent rapids remain much as Vancouver found them. Significantly, in July 2010, the waters off the south coast of British Columbia—Strait of Georgia, Puget Sound and Strait of Juan de Fuca—were officially renamed the Salish Sea, recognizing the Coast Salish people who populated the area for thousands of years before the Europeans arrived.

In my boat, I encountered the same seas, tides, winds and weather that those explorers confronted. These conditions are ever the same and in encountering them—even though my boat was equipped with an engine and modern electronics—I shared with Vancouver and his men the link of vulnerability that is the ever-present condition of all people who go to sea: fear, boredom and fatigue.

Even so, my relative comfort and security was in sharp contrast to those men in wooden sailing ships and open boats who travelled this uncharted sea of unknown depths, distances, tides, currents, winds and reefs. What, I wondered, were their emotions in the immensity of this great unknown? Their fears? Their sense of time and distance? They ate coarse food, spent long hours rowing and sailing in open boats, camped—wet and cold—on rocky shores, encountered natives of foreign and potentially threatening dispositions. In spite of these adversities, however, and by diligence and determination, they were able to draw a chart of a coastline that was so accurate it was used well into the twentieth century. Then, imagining the hardships, the courage and the dedication of these men, I had to ask these questions:

What kind of men were they who, with so little, accomplished so much? What god, luck, destiny or duty was it that lay behind their indomitable will, perseverance and endurance? For many, of course, it was merely a job to be done, and failure brought the threat of the lash; no romantic, adventurous voyage was this expedition for such men, so how, I wondered, were they able to survive, in both mind and body, the hardships they endured?

And this I asked of myself: Could I have been one of them? To this question, I have no answer, because nothing in my voyage came even close to duplicating any of the conditions endured by the men of the Vancouver expedition. The other question I asked of myself was this: Would I have liked to have been a member of the expedition and, if so, why?

To this question, I give an unqualified yes. The answer to why is because of who I am: a restless person, who has always been on the move toward the edge of what he knows, with the desire to cross over that edge to something unknown where the outcome is in doubt. It is only along the journey toward that edge that I feel alive, no longer a passive spectator of life but a participant at the threshold of something that gives significance to the present moment and a passionate anticipation for the unknown future. That, I think, is the outlook or personality of the explorer, so as an explorer of past and present, I followed in the wake of Vancouver through the Inland Sea.

Compensating for the difficulties of rain, wind and fatigue that I encountered on my own voyage was the pleasurable historical detective work I dealt with in connecting journal entries to the routes taken by Vancouver and his men through these waters. This research gave my cruise an established course of historical significance to follow rather than it being a wandering pleasure voyage of no particular route, destination or purpose. The familiar geography of a well-known harbour or cape was given a historical dimension by knowing something of what happened there, how it was seen in another century, and the reason for the name it was given. In this way, I, too, travelled as an explorer, believing that exploration lies not so much in what is seen but in *how* it is seen. Within that perspective, I discovered along my way messages written for everyone in rock, wave, wind, tide and history.

To follow Vancouver's track, I had a collection of more than 20 charts covering the waters he explored. But for tracing his actual voyage, I had a photographic copy of the single chart he drew of the area of those 20 charts. Titled "A Chart showing part of the Coast of N.W. America with the tracks of His Majesty's Sloop *Discovery* and Armed Tender *Chatham*," it is an exquisite piece of draftsmanship. Its accuracy in defining channels, inlets, headlands and capes is such that I could have thrown out the 20 modern charts I carried and navigated solely with the Vancouver chart and his journal.

—from *Sailing with Vancouver* (2004)

SAILOR WITH A MISSION
J. Lennox Kerr (1899–1963)

Yachtsman and medical doctor Wilfred Grenfell had already marked himself out as a promising medical missionary when, in 1892, the National Mission to Deep Sea Fishermen sent him from the UK to Newfoundland. His voyages to stake out the mission field are legendary. Beginning with a single hospital with two nurses, the visionary doctor expanded his mandate to include an orphanage, cooperatives, as well as social and medical programmes in Newfoundland and Labrador. In doing so he founded the International Grenfell Association. Grenfell himself (1865–1940) was a complex character. People spoke of him as being compassionate, irascible, impulsive, erratic, single-minded and tenacious. Whatever else he might have been, he was certainly a risk-taking seaman.

The Allen Line steamer carrying the new launch and the two nurses arrived, and the nurses were considered much more approvingly than the launch. They were the first fully qualified nurses to visit St. John's and the townspeople asked Grenfell to let them stay in the town. The launch was looked on less favourably by those boat-wise Newfoundlanders. They could see little to admire in this craft. She had been built for river work, and seemed a frail thing to venture among the ice and face the gales of a coast such as the Labrador. She was 45 feet long, but her beam was only 8 feet, and she would roll like a log. Her deck was within 2 feet of the water, most of it occupied by a long cabin-top, with a slender mast forward and a small enclosed shelter for the wheelsman. She could carry a small sail, but would rely almost entirely on a tiny 9-horsepower steam engine. Below decks there was little space. Grenfell's cabin, which would also be hospital and passenger accommodation, was 8 feet by 4 feet, his bed the hard cushions of a side-bench. Altogether the *Princess May* was no sort of craft for the open Atlantic and one of the most dangerous coasts in the world. When Grenfell announced that he intended to steam her to Labrador, with himself as captain, an engineer, and a crew of one, taking [Dr A.R.] Bobardt as a companion, experienced seamen in the port tried to dissuade him. This toy of a boat would never make such a voyage.

The launch had lost her funnel while being shipped, and her propeller shaft was bent. These defects were made good at St John's, and on July 6 the launch was christened. The town made this an occasion to show their admiration for Grenfell. The wharves danced with coloured flags, ships in the harbour dressed overall, as a large crowd gathered to watch Lady O'Brien break a bottle of water over the stem and to hear the Governor make a speech praising Grenfell and thanking the Mission to Deep Sea Fishermen for sending him. The *Albert* [under Captain John Trezisse] had waited for this ceremony, but now, on the same day, she sailed, carrying the two nurses and Dr [Eliot] Curwen. The next morning, at five o'clock, Grenfell steered the *Princess May* out of the harbour for the voyage north.

The voyage of the *Princess May* that year [1893] can be reckoned something of an epic of the sea, or an epic of sheer impertinence. Grenfell was not an experienced seaman. He had sailed small yachts in well-marked and well-charted waters during the summer months, and he had helped fishermen to manage their vessels; but this was no qualification for taking a small and far from able river launch hundreds of miles along a coast he did not know, a coast inadequately charted, and with no navigational aids. Grenfell had not even bothered to check his compass or to give his engines a proper trial before sailing. The *Princess May* was hardly clear of the land before the engine began to give trouble, and the engineer had to adjust and repair with the launch rolling heavily to the Atlantic swell. A course was set, and when a large cliff appeared ahead Grenfell discovered that his compass had an error of two whole points [22½ degrees]. At first he blamed this on the compass binnacle being screwed down with iron nails, but even when these were removed the error was still there. The compass was then taken well forward of the steering position, and it seems, from Grenfell's own story of this voyage, that he had little idea of how to work out his compass error and allow for this when laying his courses. On one leg of the journey along the Newfoundland coast Bobardt, with no sea experience, was at the wheel all day, and steered a course that was two points away from what it should have been. Only a meeting with a fishing-boat told the voyagers where they were. It seems to have been an entirely un-seamanlike and happy-go-lucky adventure, and it is not surprising that when the *Princess May* met bad weather, to roll heavily and take water on board, gear left lying unsecured on deck went overboard.

But Grenfell was happy. At last he was Captain of his own ship and with no sober-faced Trezisse to check his actions. He worked the *Princess May* northward, taking risks that would have made a professional sailor die of fright. He threaded the launch between islands and a fearful collection of submerged rocks, trusting to his own quick reactions and his sure belief that God had work for this vessel and her crew and would see that they reached their goal. He went through fog and pushed against strong winds and heavy seas, sheltering where he could every night and treating the sick who came when they heard that the famous Dr Grenfell was in their harbour. Attempting to cross Belle Isle Strait in bad weather, the launch was driven back to the shelter of the land, but Grenfell wait-ed in the lee of a stranded iceberg until the wind eased and then crossed. Ice in bergs and scattered pans was encountered when the Labrador coast was reached, and had to be avoided, but late one evening Grenfell steered the *Princess May* into the narrow tickle be-tween two islands that is Battle Harbour and made fast alongside the *Albert*. What Captain Trezisse thought when Grenfell described his passage-making is not known, but he must have decided that God kept a long deck-watch when this young man was afloat.

—from *Wilfred Grenfell: His Life and Work* (1959)

GLORY, GROUNDING, AND HOME
William Balfour Macdonald (1870–1937)

A grounding incident in July 1911 dashed Canada's hopes for big-ship training. In the words of the Halifax Herald, *"The Flagship of Canada's Navy was on the rocks of Cape Sable." Indeed, HMCS* Niobe *had sig-nalled she was in "grave peril." Towed to Halifax on 5 August 1911, the ship remained out of service for some sixteen months, until December 1912. But as her captain later reported somewhat condescendingly: "With the ship in the position she was, a gale of wind blowing and dense fog, the Canadian boys behaved fully up to the traditions of the British navy." In other words, the colonials had measured up. A court-martial reprimanded the officer of the watch, severely reprimanded the navigator and dismissed him from the ship. Captain Macdonald's memoir recounts his own perspective on the story.*

Early in 1910, Sir Wilfrid Laurier's government of Canada decided to start a Canadian navy, purchasing the *Niobe* and *Rainbow* as sea-going training ships. The British admiralty asked me to go as captain of the *Niobe,* probably because I was born in Canada. Knowing what happens to naval officers who accept service in "side shows," I did not accept until I had a letter from their lordships stating that they would consider it excellent service, and verbally I was guaranteed my promotion when my turn came. I accepted, but was never promoted.

I was allowed to choose my own officers and 60 active service ratings. The remainder of the crew up to 400 I obtained from the Royal Fleet and Royal Naval Reserve, with some 50 hands who had never been to sea. It was hard but interesting work, not only organizing the crew, but drawing up new regulations, as conditions of service and pay differed from the Royal Navy. The Canadian government wished their ships to fly a blue ensign instead of a white, so I short-circuited them by asking H.M. the Queen to present a white ensign to my ship. This she very graciously did, and the Canadian navy has flown a white ensign ever since [until 1965]...

In 1911, we were sent for a cruise to show the flag at Quebec, Prince Edward Island, and the seaports of Nova Scotia. Towards the end of July, we were at Yarmouth at their home week celebrations, which included a ball given in our honour. All of us went who could be spared, and we lent them our band. At ten that evening I had a message from the ship saying the barometer was falling, and a southwest swell setting into the anchorage.

I left at once, taking the navigator with me; the wind and sea had increased so quickly that I had to board the ship over the stern.

I raised steam, by midnight it was blowing a gale, and the ship dragging, necessitating me to steam to my anchors. Wind and sea abated next day, when I embarked the officers and band left ashore the previous evening, and sailed for another home week celebration at Liverpool, Nova Scotia. I wish I had not. That night was wonderfully calm and clear, we steamed down the Bay of Fundy and headed for the southwest ledge buoy off Sable Island.

Turning over the deck to the officer of the watch, and the navigating to the lieutenant, I went to my bridge cabin to lie down, having been on deck all the previous night; I did not undress or close the cabin door. Shortly before two in the morning the officer of the watch reported that a dense fog had just shut down, but he had sighted the southwest ledge buoy and had heard its automatic whistle. I jumped out onto the bridge, and not wanting to be in that very dangerous locality in thick weather, gave the order "Hard-a-Port" to get sea room. Before the ship answered her helm, with a terrific crash we struck the rocks. There was a long swell running, which lifted our ship off the rocks, only to drop her again with a sickening crash on a new place.

With the greatest difficulty we hoisted out the launch and sailing pinnace, intending to lay an anchor out astern, but both five-inch boat ropes snapped, and boats and 30 men were swept away into the dense fog. I well knew that each crash meant another hole in the bottom. The ship was rapidly filling with water, everywhere below was flooded except, providentially, the boiler room. The rudder, stern post and after part of the keel had gone. The starboard propeller had gone, and half the blades of the port. The port engine room was full of water, and 16 feet in the starboard.

Not knowing how long the poor ship would float, I landed all the Canadian recruits on Sable Island, a long miserable job in that fog. After pumping her out for about four hours, the ship was, suddenly, strangely still. I thought a pinnacle rock had pierced her bottom and was holding her, but our excellent carpenter Mr. Morrel thought she was afloat. We both lay down, right aft, and looked forward along the deck; sure enough, the deck was rising and falling to the swell. We were off. I let go both bower anchors and veered to a clinch, and lowered all boats to within a few feet of the water in case we sank. In spite of both anchors being down, the tide was so strong that we dragged freely during the remainder of the dark hours, in a circle, so that at eight in the morning our stem hit the very reef of rocks that had been our undoing. The capstan engine being flooded, we had to work the cables by hand. To make a long story short, by juggling with our anchors, and what remained of one screw, we managed to go seven miles in 24 hours. Anchoring in Clarks Harbour, with only a foot of water under our keel, I did not care if she sank or not.

I sent a wireless to H.M.S. *Cornwall* asking her assistance. She came all the way from Newfoundland, and exactly a week after our grounding struck a rock two miles from us. Took in 2,000 tons of water, but got off again, took us in tow, and towed us the 190 miles to Halifax. While taking us in tow, she had to pass within a few feet of us, but so dense was the fog that we did not see her until well inside Halifax harbour. Docking revealed very extensive damage. Besides the entire disappearance of the rudder, stern post, an after part of the keel, there were 19 holes in the ship's bottom large enough to drive a car through. It was a marvel she kept afloat.

—from *At Sea and by Land:*
The Reminiscences of William Balfour MacDonald (1983)

SAILING TO YAN
Emily Carr (1871–1945)

On one of her visits to paint in the First Nations villages of the Queen Charlotte Islands (Haida Gwaii) on the Pacific coast, artist Emily Carr was ferried to her destination in a whimsical adaptation of a Haida canoe.

At the appointed time I sat on the beach waiting for the Indian. He did not come and there was no sign of his boat.

An Indian woman came down the bank carrying a heavy not-walking-age child. A slim girl of twelve was with her. She carried a paddle and going to a light canoe that was high on the sand, she began to drag it towards the sea.

The woman put the baby into the canoe and she and the girl grunted and shunted the canoe into the water, then they beckoned to me.

"Go now," said the woman.

"Go where?"

"Yan.—My man tell me come take you go Yan."

"But—the baby—?"

Between Yan and Masset lay ugly waters—I could not—no, I really could not—a tippy little canoe—a woman with her arms full of baby—and a girl child—!

The girl was rigging a ragged flour sack in the canoe for a sail. The pole was already placed, the rag flapped limply around it. The wind and the waves were crisp and sparkling. They were ready, waiting to bulge the sack and toss the canoe.

"How can you manage the canoe and the baby?" I asked the woman and hung back.

Pointing to the bow seat, the woman commanded, "Sit down."

I got in and sat.

The woman waded out holding the canoe and easing it about in the sand until it was afloat. Then she got in and clamped the child between her knees. Her paddle worked without noise among the waves. The wind filled the flour sack beautifully as if it had been a silk sail.

The canoe took the water as a beaver launches himself—with a silent scoot.

The straight young girl with black hair and eyes and the lank print dress that clung to her childish shape, held the sail rope and humoured the whimsical little canoe. The sack now bulged with wind as tight as once it had bulged with flour. The woman's paddle advised the canoe just how to cut each wave.

We streaked across the water and were at Yan before I remembered to be frightened. The canoe grumbled over the pebbly beach and we got out.

We lit a fire on the beach and ate.

The brave old totems stood solemnly round the bay. Behind them were the old houses of Yan, and behind that again was the forest. All around was a blaze of rosy pink fireweed, rioting from the rich black soil and bursting into loose delicate blossoms, each head pointing straight to the sky.

Nobody lived in Yan. Yan's people had moved to the newer village of Masset, where there was a store, an Indian agent and a church.

Sometimes Indians came over to Yan to cultivate a few patches of garden. When they went away again the stare in the empty hollows of the totem eyes followed them across the sea, as the mournful eyes of chained dogs follow their retreating masters.

—from *Klee Wyck* (1941)

OUR MARINE THOROUGHFARE
Pat Wastell Norris (1929–   )

In 1912, Telegraph Cove, on the eastern coast of northern Vancouver Island, served as the northern terminus of a telegraph line that was carried from tree to tree along the Island's east coast. Here the author recalls life in this tiny, sea-bound community in the years between the two world wars.

All along the northeast coast of Vancouver Island, the mountains drop straight into the sea. At the foot of one of them, our small horseshoe-shaped harbour looked out, due north, onto Johnstone Strait. It was a stunning view. Beyond the strait lay the delicate outline of an intricate web of islands; beyond that lay the mainland and the coast mountains. Mount Waddington, the highest peak in the range rose, like Mount Fuji, in the distance.

Johnstone Strait was our thoroughfare, our link with the rest of humanity. In theory, it could have started us on a journey to the ends of the earth, and in practice it sometimes brought us ships from just such places. We travelled Johnstone Strait to shop, to do business, to visit friends, to see a doctor, or just to while away a

Sunday afternoon. On sunny summer mornings when the sea was glassy and rolled away from a boat's bow in oily curves, on bright fall afternoons when the westerlies got up as regularly as clockwork and blew the sea into a blazing blue, or on bleak November days when the southeasters shook the house and turned the sea into an army of great grey rollers smoking with spume; at all these times, in a variety of craft, we emerged into the strait on our errands, be they casual or critical.

A constant stream of marine traffic worked its way up and down the strait: freighters, passenger steamers, tugs and tows, seiners, trollers and yachts. Some of these vessels called in at our little harbour at regular intervals, some simply passed by, and some of them appeared unexpectedly from nowhere, moored for an hour, a week or a summer, and then vanished as completely as if they had never existed.

The most regular of our callers were the Union steamships. Each week, without fail, either the *Cardena* or the *Catala* arrived. Their black hulls, white superstructures and red funnels were familiar to every coastal inhabitant, for they were the north coast's supply line to the city. Each week on "boat day," the ship's radio operator broadcast the estimated time of arrival and then, there they were, rounding the point and blocking the entrance to the harbour with their bulk. Suddenly the air was full of acrid smoke from their funnels, the store was full of fresh food, and the Post Office was full of the mail they delivered.

As children, we made many trips with our mother to and from Vancouver on these ships, and they were always thrilling adventures. Encumbered as we often were by an aged aunt—and sometimes even a canary—we required two staterooms. My sister and I shared one of them, revelling in our independence. However, when it came time to go to bed, we needed help from an adult. Employing some secret procedure that died with them, the stewards on these ships made up the berths so tightly that it took a strong and determined adult to pry the sheets apart. No child was equal to the task. Even when one finally wriggled in under the blankets, it was only those with the general body contours of a postage stamp who could be comfortable.

We were shy country children, and when we descended the broad brass-trimmed stairway to the dining saloon we were always overwhelmed by its magnificence. There were big, round tables with snowy napery, clusters of silver cutlery, glasses tinkling with ice cubes, and stewards in black uniforms and immaculate white shirts. The menu always included the item "celery and olives" and we astonished our adult table-mates by quietly devouring every olive in sight. Travelling thus we had acquired a taste for them and we never, ever, had them at home.

In retrospect, the service that the Union Steamship Company provided was remarkable. They pressed doggedly on through violent winter storms and, perhaps even more remarkably, they kept to their appointed schedules in blankets of fog. Long before radar, these size-able ships negotiated the convoluted channels and narrow passages that formed our difficult coast, and made their regular appearances in the tiniest, most remote settlement. Year after year, with no fanfare and little recognition, their tired-looking captains performed remarkable feats of seamanship.

—from *Time & Tide: A History of Telegraph Cove* (2005)

CHALLENGERS OF THE NORTHWEST PASSAGE
Henry Larsen (1899–1964)

Henry Larsen was a deep-sea Arctic sailor and navigator who became one of the most renowned officers in the RCMP. Known among the indigenous peoples of the Canadian Arctic as "Hanorie Umiarjuag"— Henry with the Big Ship—he skippered the RCMP vessel St. Roch *on daunting and record-breaking northern voyages. Under his command the North Vancouver–built 100-foot wooden vessel became the first ship to transit the Northwest Passage from west to east. It took him two years, from 1940 to 1942. In 1944* St. Roch *became the first ship to transit from east to west in a single season: eighty-six days via the more northerly deep-water route. She later became the first ship to circumnavigate the North American continent. Throughout these arduous voyages, as his memoirs reveal, he remained deeply conscious of the historical dimensions of his undertaking. He loved the people of the North, understood the importance of the northern sea, and pondered its future. In what follows, Larsen recounts a portion of his 1944 passage from east to west, during which he came upon a remarkable cairn. It had been laid by the colourful Quebec mariner Joseph-Elzéar Bernier (1852–1934). As skipper of the Canadian Government Ship* Arctic, *Bernier had, between 1904 and 1911, led many seagoing expeditions into the Arctic and played a pivotal role in laying Canada's territorial claims.*

We ran into more history a bit later when we reached Dealy Island off the southern coast of Melville Island, nearing the eastern approach to McClure Strait. The weather had been bad and continuous snowfall had made navigation rather difficult for several days as both the land and the sun had been obscured. The magnetic compass had been bafflingly unresponsive for days, often with its north point fixed on the ship's head regardless of the direction we were travelling. Then the weather cleared and we spotted a cairn on top of Dealy Island. It was a huge pile of rocks with a large spar surrounded by three barrels and could be seen from a great distance. We anchored close inshore and set out to examine the massive cache which, like the cairn, had been built in the spring of 1853 by Captain Henry Kellett, who had spent the winter there with HMS *Resolute*.

The cache was partially destroyed and its contents had been scattered all over by marauding bears. Originally it had been built in the shape of a house, but only the sturdy stone walls remained, the roof having long since fallen in. At one end were iron tanks of what had been hard, square biscuits. The tanks were rusted through and the biscuits were wet and soggy. By rummaging around, however, we did find a few that were still hard as rock, stamped with a broad arrow, indicating that they were the property of the British Navy. Canned meats and vegetables, stacked up and covered with sod, formed part of one wall, and the centre of the building was a hodge-podge of broken barrels of flour, clothing, coal, rope, salt beef and broken hardwood pulleys for ships' blocks. It was amazing to see the various items left here. Much of it was frozen in ice, but leather sea boots, broken barrels of chocolate, peas and beans and other items were spread around outside. No doubt the bears had had many a good picnic there down through the years. On the beach we found two broken Ross army rifles and some boxes of ammunition, left behind by Captain Bernier...

On the beach we also found an eighteen-foot boat turned bottom-up. It had been left by Captain Bernier, too, and was built of light oak planking. Two steel runners, like those on a sleigh, were fastened to the bottom, and these made the boat useful on the ice as well as in the water. It was far superior to our own skiff or rowboat built for us in Victoria in 1940, which was heavy, clumsy and leaky, so we decided to trade ours for Captain Bernier's.

Regardless of how fascinated we were by all this history we had to push on, as it was already getting late in the season. After a brief examination of Bridport Inlet, a fine harbour on Dealy Island, well protected and seemingly big enough to hold a fleet of ships, we left on August 28. While we had a wide expanse of completely ice-free water along the shore, we could see the ice tightly packed a few miles to the south in Melville Sound. When we passed Cape Bounty, I recalled that Lieut. William Edward Parry, R.N., had passed here too in 1819 with his two sailing-ships, the *Hecla* and the *Griper*. It was he who had named the Cape, and most appropriately, for by reaching that spot on 110th Meridian he won a sum of five thousand pounds. It had been offered by the British Admiralty to the first man to pass that Meridian in the quest of the Northwest Passage...

On Parry Rock we also saw a large copper plate. It carried an inscription of the Union Jack and the Canadian Coat of Arms with the following words: "This memorial is erected today to commemorate taking possession for the Dominion of Canada, of the whole Arctic archipelago, lying to the north of America, from long. 60 W to 141 W, up to lat. 90 North. Winter Hrb. Melville Island, Arctic." July 1st 1909, J. E. Bernier, Commander, J. V. Koenic, sculptor."

Thus, thirty-five years before our visit, on Dominion Day, this doughty and great Canadian skipper recorded Canada's claim to the vast Arctic region north of her mainland to the North Pole. We realized the significance of this declaration and before we left we deposited the record of our call together with various papers and ordinances in a brass cylinder and placed it on top of Parry Rock.

—from *The Big Ship* (1967)

A CASTLE TO CROSS THE SEA
Michael Ondaatje (1943–   )

In his novel The Cat's Table, *Ondaatje hints at autobiographical details in telling of a young boy—also called Michael—who travels on an ocean liner from his home in Colombo, Ceylon (Sri Lanka), to join his mother in London, England. During the three-week journey, he and his new friends share mischievous adventures that weave in and out of the mysterious world of adults. Years later, when Michael looks back on the journey, he realizes that it was a transformative experience in his young life. But for now, his awe at the immensity of the ship and his anxiety that his mother will not be there to meet him at journey's end surely echo the migration experience common to thousands who have left one land in search of another.*

What had there been before such a ship in my life? A dugout canoe on a river journey? A launch in Trincomalee harbour? There were always fishing boats on our horizon. But I could never have imagined the grandeur of this castle that was to cross the sea. The longest journeys I had made were car rides to Nuwara Eliya and Horton Plains, or the train to Jaffna, which we boarded at seven a.m. and disembarked from in the late afternoon. We made that journey with our egg sandwiches, some *thalagulies* [sesame balls], a pack of cards, and a small Boy's Own adventure.

But now it had been arranged I would be travelling to England by ship, and that I would be making the journey alone. No mention was made that this might be an unusual experience or that it could be exciting or dangerous, so I did not approach it with any joy or fear. I was not forewarned that the ship would have seven levels, hold more than six hundred people including a captain, nine cooks, engineers, a veterinarian, and that it would contain a small jail and chlorinated pools that would actually sail with us over two oceans. The departure date was marked casually on the calendar by my aunt, who had notified the school that I would be leaving at the end of the term. The fact of my being at sea for twenty-one days was spoken of as having not much significance, so I was surprised my relatives were even bothering to accompany me to the harbour. I had assumed I would be taking a bus by myself and then change onto another at Borella Junction.

There had been just one attempt to introduce me to the situation of the journey. A lady named Flavia Prins, whose husband knew my uncle, turned out to be making the same journey and was invited to tea one afternoon to meet with me. She would be travelling in First Class but promised to keep an eye on me. I shook her hand carefully, as it was covered with rings and bangles, and she then turned away to continue the conversation I had interrupted. I spent most of the hour listening to a few uncles and counting how many of the trimmed sandwiches they ate.

On my last day, I found an empty school examination booklet, a pencil, a pencil sharpener, a traced map of the world, and put them into my small suitcase. I went outside and said good-bye to the generator, and dug up the pieces of the radio I had once taken apart and, being unable to put them back together, had buried under the lawn. I said good-bye to Narayan, and good-bye to Gunepala.

As I got into the car, it was explained to me that after I'd crossed the Indian Ocean and the Arabian Sea and the Red Sea, and gone through the Suez Canal into the Mediterranean, I would arrive one morning on a small pier in England and my mother would meet me there. It was not the magic or the scale of the journey that was of concern to me, but that detail of how my mother could know when exactly I would arrive in that other country.

And if she would be there.

—from *The Cat's Table* (2011)

CROSSING THE STRAITS
Richard Greene (1961–   )

The Port aux Basques–North Sydney ferry crosses Cabot Strait between southwestern Newfoundland and northern Cape Breton Island, Nova Scotia. Approximately 170 kilometres wide, and named after the fifteenth-century explorer John Cabot, the strait is an important international shipping lane connecting the Gulf of St. Lawrence with the Atlantic Ocean. The name Port aux Basques recalls the whalers from the Pyrenee regions of France and Spain who sheltered and took on fresh water there during the early sixteenth century. By 1857, following the laying of an underwater cable between Newfoundland and Cape Breton Island, Port aux Basques became an important link in the race to complete a transatlantic telegraph cable.

The sea is moving under our passage,
an old year out and a new year in
between Port aux Basques and North Sydney.
The ship rolls in the first breaths of a gale;
it has been so long, ten or twelve years,
since I last sailed, I do not trust my legs
or stomach to hold against the weather,
so lie still as a narrow berth allows,
reminding myself that disaster
is a kind of lottery, and to sink
as hard as winning millions on dry land,
and that sailors, having made profession
of storms, know their work and die old.
In an hour, anxiety drowns in sleep;
the mind, as ever, opposes passage,
and I dream of my flat in Toronto,
its wooden deck stretching across the roof,
a ship remote from this night's turning.
At six I wake and walk through lounges
where some have sat up all night playing cards
or talking, their New Year's revels queasy

and circumspect where the ship's movement
began the hangovers before the drinks.
More have slept in the rows of Lazy-boys
before an almost bloodshot T.V. screen,
its hoarse voice still croaking festively
about the crowds that gathered in Times Square.
The gales have subsided and the sea is calm
less than an hour out of North Sydney;
a heavy breakfast later, I walk along
a deck where snow-crusted lifeboats are hung.
I imagine that in summer this is
the ship's best place, but the air is frigid
this morning, and Newfoundlanders crossing
the Straits see water enough in warmer times
to forego the prospect now, but this moment
of pent chances, between home and home,
is not mine alone, and for most who travel
there is some tear in memory between
the longed for and the given, what they left
and what they are. Nova Scotia looms,
and the purser summons drivers to cars
in the ship's belly, where tractor-trailers
are already roaring for landfall.

—from *Crossing the Straits* (2004)

"They left their punt on the collar, jumped lightly aboard, and loosed the boat from her moorings. Then Eli hoisted the sails while Christopher took the tiller and sent her skimming over the waves between the sunkers straight into the rising sun. And when the first splash of spray struck his tawny cheek the boy laughed and tossed his black hair in the rising breeze and felt like a buccaneer of a younger day, coasting down through the glittering Spanish Main, seeking the isles that lie under the wind."
— Harold Horwood, *Tomorrow Will Be Sunday* (1966)

CHAPTER V

JUST FOR THE JOY OF IT

Build a boat, buy a boat, own a boat, sail a boat: these are among the abiding dreams weaving their way through Canadian nautical folklore and coastal life. Relationships and marriages have been made—and broken—by them. Rich experiences have been gained, and tall tales told. In some respects these nautical ambitions constitute a great escape, either away from, or into, a self-fulfilling reality. Boat names attest to this: Elsewhere, Dawn Treader, Wanderer, Pilgrim, and the arguably more realistic one, Costa Lotta. On good days "yachties" speak euphorically of being "in touch" with nature; they speak of spirituality, zest, vigour and inspiration. On bad days they curse their floating mistress as "that hole in the water" into which they pour all their money. Yet for all that, whether slopping about in the autumn rain, battening down for winter, touching up the brightwork in spring or cresting the waves in summer, they experience yachting as an eminently meaningful preoccupation. It is, after all, a vocation: in answer to the call of the sea.

FAREWELL NOVA SCOTIA
Joshua Slocum (1844–1909)

Nova Scotia–born Joshua Slocum was the first to circumnavigate the world alone. His equally famous vessel is the 37-foot yawl Spray, *which he fully restored from its derelict condition before setting off on the historic voyage in July 1898. His memoir, published in 1900, is a classic: vivid, fast-paced and reflective, always delightfully understated, and frequently opinionated. Here, Slocum departs from Yarmouth, an historic harbour in Acadian territory on the southwest coast of Nova Scotia.*

I now stowed all my goods securely, for the boisterous Atlantic was before me, and I sent the topmast down, knowing that the *Spray* would be the wholesomer with it on deck. Then I gave the lanyards a pull and hitched them afresh, and saw that the gammon [a rope connecting bowsprit to stem] was secure, also that the boat was lashed, for even in summer one may meet with bad weather in the crossing.

In fact, many weeks of bad weather had prevailed. On July 1, however, after a rude gale, the wind came out nor'west and clear, propitious for a good run. On the following day, the head sea having gone down, I sailed from Yarmouth, and let go my last hold on America. The log of my first day on the Atlantic in the *Spray* reads briefly: "9:30 A.M. sailed from Yarmouth. 4:30 P.M. passed Cape Sable; distance, three cables from the land. The sloop making eight knots. Fresh breeze N.W." Before the sun went down I was taking my supper of strawberries and tea in smooth water under the lee of the east-coast land, along which the *Spray* was now leisurely skirting...

On the evening of July 5 the *Spray*, after having steered all day over a lumpy sea, took it into her head to go without the helmsman's aid. I had been steering southeast by south, but the wind hauling forward a bit, she dropped into a smooth lane, heading southeast, and making about eight knots, her very best work. I crowded on sail to cross the track of the liners without loss of time, and to reach as soon as possible the friendly Gulf Stream. The fog lifting before night, I was afforded a look at the sun just as it was touching the sea. I watched it go down and out of sight. Then I turned my face eastward, and there, apparently at the very end of the bowsprit, was the smiling full moon rising out of the sea. Neptune himself coming over the bows could not have startled me more. "Good evening, sir," I cried; "I'm glad to see you." Many a long talk since then I have had with the man in the moon; he had my confidence on the voyage.

About midnight the fog shut down again denser than ever before. One could almost "stand on it." It continued so for a number of days, the wind increasing to a gale. The waves rose high, but I had a good ship. Still, in the dismal fog I felt myself drifting into loneliness, an insect on a straw in the midst of the elements. I lashed the helm, and my vessel held her course, and while she sailed I slept.

During these days a feeling of awe crept over me. My memory worked with startling power. The ominous, the insignificant, the great, the small, the wonderful, the commonplace—all appeared before my mental vision in magical succession. Pages of my history were recalled which had been so long forgotten that they seemed to belong to a previous existence. I heard all the voices of the past laughing, crying, telling what I had heard them tell in many corners of the earth.

The loneliness of my state wore off when the gale was high and I found much work to do. When fine weather returned, then came the sense of solitude, which I could not shake off. I used my voice often, at first giving some order about the affairs of a ship, for I had been told that from disuse I should lose my speech. At the meridian altitude of the sun I called aloud, "Eight bells," after the custom on a ship at sea. Again from my cabin I cried to an imaginary man at the helm, "How does she head, there?" and again, "Is she on her course?" But getting no reply, I was reminded the more palpably of my condition. My voice sounded hollow on the empty air, and I dropped the practice. However, it was not long before the thought came to me that when I was a lad I used to sing: why not try that now, where it would disturb no one? My musical talent had never bred envy in others, but out on the Atlantic, to realize what it meant, you should have heard me sing. You should have seen the porpoises leap when I pitched my voice for the waves and the sea and all that was in it. Old turtles, with large eyes, poked their heads up out of the sea as I sang "Johnny Boker," and "We'll Pay Darby Doyl for his Boots," and the like. But the porpoises were, on the whole, vastly more appreciative than the turtles; they jumped a deal higher. One day when I was humming a favourite chant, I think it was "Babylon's a-Fallin'," a porpoise jumped higher than the bowsprit. Had the *Spray* been going a little faster she would have scooped him in. The sea-birds sailed around rather shy.

July 10, eight days at sea, the *Spray* was twelve hundred miles east of Cape Sable. One hundred and fifty miles a day for so small a vessel must be considered good sailing. It was the greatest run the *Spray* ever made before or since in so few days. On the evening of July 14, in better humor than ever before, all hands cried, "Sail ho!" The sail was a barkentine, three points on the weather bow, hull down. Then came the night. My ship was sailing along now without attention to the helm. The wind was south; she was heading east. Her sails were trimmed like the sails of the nautilus. They drew steadily all night. I went frequently on deck, but found all well. A merry breeze kept on from the south. Early in the morning of the 15th the *Spray* was close aboard the stranger, which proved to be *La Vaguisa* of Vigo, twenty-three days from Philadelphia, bound for Vigo. A lookout from his masthead had spied the *Spray* the evening before. The captain, when I came near enough, threw a line to me and sent a bottle of wine across slung by the neck, and very good wine it was. He also sent his card, which bore the name of Juan Gantes. I think he was a good man, as Spaniards go. But when I asked him to report me "all well" (the *Spray* passing him in a lively manner), he hauled his shoulders much above his head; and when his mate, who knew of my expedition, told him that I was alone, he crossed himself and made for his cabin. I did not see him again. By sundown he was as far astern as he had been ahead the evening before...

The acute pain of solitude experienced at first never returned. I had penetrated a mystery, and, by the way, I had sailed through a fog. I had met Neptune in his wrath, but he found that I had not treated him with contempt, and so he suffered me to go on and explore.

—from *Sailing Alone Around the World* (1900)

REGATTA
Emily Carr (1871–1945)

The sea embraces the port city of Victoria, British Columbia, with tidal water reaching through the harbour and deep inland. Around the end of the nineteenth century, thick bush still encroached upon the small colonial Vancouver Island community. The annual Regatta, held in honour of Queen Victoria's birthday, was a major attraction of the time. Similar events, like the annual Victoria Dragon Boat Festival, continue the regatta tradition today. Here Emily Carr remembers the regattas of her childhood.

The beautiful Gorge waters were smooth as glass once Victoria Harbour had been crossed. The Gorge was an arm of the sea which ran into the land for three miles. Near its head was a narrow rocky pass with a hidden rock in the centre which capsized many a canoe and marooned many a picnic party above the Gorge until long after midnight, for when the tide was running in or out through the pass there was a four-foot fall with foam and great roaring. A bridge ran across from one side of the Gorge to the other, high above the water. The banks on both sides of the Arm were heavily wooded; a few fine homes snuggled among the trees and had gardens running to the water. Most of the other property was public—anyone could picnic on it.

The waters of the Gorge were much warmer than the water of the beaches round Victoria. Jones's Boathouse beside James' Bay Bridge rented out boats and canoes; many people living along the harbour front had boathouses and boats of their own, for regattas and water sports were one of Victoria's chief attractions. Visitors came from Vancouver and from the States on the 24th of May to see them.

The Navy and the Indian tribes up and down the coast took part in the races, the Navy rowing their heavy ships' boats round from Esquimalt Harbour, manned by bluejackets, while smart little pinnaces "pip-pipped" along commanded by young midshipmen. The Indians came from long distances in their slender, racing dugout canoes—ten paddles and a steersman to each canoe.

The harbour was gay with flags. Races started from the Gorge Bridge at 1 P.M. Our family went to the Regatta with Mr. and Mrs. Bales. Mr. Bales had a shipyard just below Point Ellice Bridge, at the beginning of the Arm waters. We got into Mr. Bales's boat at the shipyard where unfinished boats stood all round us just above high tide. They looked as we felt when we shivered in our nightgowns on Beacon Hill beaches waiting for the courage to dip into the sea. But rosy-faced Mr. Bales eased his boats gently into the water; he did not seize and duck them as my big sister did us.

When the picnic was all stowed into Mr. Bales's boat we pushed out into the stream and joined the others—sail boats, canoes, rafts and fish-boats, all nosing their way up the Gorge along with the naval boats and war canoes. There were bands and mouth-organs, concertinas and flags. The Indian families in their big canoes glided very quietly except for an occasional yapping from one of their dogs when he saw a foe in another canoe...

The races started from the Gorge Bridge, came down the Arm, turned round Deadman's Island, an old Indian burial ground, and returned to the bridge.

The Indian canoe races were the most exciting of all the Regatta. Ten paddles dipped as one paddle, ten men bent as one man, while the steersman kept time for them with grunting bows. The men had bright coloured shirts and gay head-bands; some even had painted faces. The Kloochman's was an even grander race than the Indian men's. Solid, earnest women with gay shawls wound round their middles gave every scrap of themselves to the canoe; it came alive and darted through the water like a flash, foam following the paddles. The dips, heaves and grunts of all the women were only one dip, heave and grunt. Watchers from the banks yelled; the Indians watched from their canoes by the shore, with an intent, silent stare.

The Bluejacket Races were fine, too. Each boat was like a stout, brave monster, enduring and reliable—the powerful, measured strokes of the British Navy, sure and unerring as the earth itself, not like the cranky war canoes, flashing through their races like running fire.

—from *The Book of Small* (1942)

RACING FOR THE FISHERMEN'S CUP
Keith McLaren (1950–   )

*The years 1920 to 1938 marked the heyday of the grittiest sailing com-
petitions between fishing schooners from Nova Scotia's Lunenburg area
and the schooners from Gloucester, Massachusetts. Larger-than-life skippers like the redoubtable Angus Walters, master of the* Bluenose, *and
the hard-driving Marty Welsh, skipper of the Gloucesterman* Elsie, *took
centre stage in a contest of strength, skill, experience and endurance.
Featured regularly in the sports page, their exploits triggered lead stories
in papers on both sides of the Canada–US border. In re-creating the
race, McLaren cites witnesses of the day.*

Saturday, October 22, 1921, was crisp and frosty, with a fresh breeze.
It was the perfect day for a race, the northwest wind rising from
twenty to thirty knots as the race progressed over the forty-mile
course off Halifax. Everything that could float was on the water:
Government steamers, cable ships, fishing boats, yachts, tugs and
ferries—all loaded heavily with spectators—wallowed near the start.
At the five-minute gun, both schooners swung into position, the
Elsie easing her sheets and running the line towards McNab's Island,
while all on board hoped for the seconds to pass quickly. The signal
cannon from the breakwater sounded the start and Welsh cranked
over the helm, shooting over the line ten seconds later. With the
Stars and Stripes snapping at the main peak and a twenty-knot
nor'westerly snorting over her starboard quarter, the *Elsie* flew down
the course as if she had an engine in her. She was several boat lengths
ahead of the *Bluenose* at the outset. Observers aboard the steamer
Lady Laurier felt the Nova Scotian had been caught napping and
began to experience that unpleasant "all gone" sensation.

However, it was not long before the *Bluenose* perked up and
fairly smoked after the *Elsie*. A luffing match on the broad reach
for the first mark ended when the *Elsie* crossed over her opponent's
bow and took the weather berth. Walters attempted to pass on her
weather side, but Welsh sheeted in and stood up towards the un-
yielding granite rocks of the western shore, two miles to windward

of the course. Walters put his wheel hard up and swung across the *Elsie's* wake, making for the Inner Automatic Buoy. The *Elsie* followed suit and covered her rival. The two fairly flew across the water, all sails filled in the stiff quartering breeze and hulls rolling heavily in the deep chop. "The end of *Bluenose's* 80-ft. boom was now in the water, now half way up to the masthead as she gained on her rival. The *Elsie* rolled still harder and three times brought her main boom across the *Bluenose's* deck, between the fore and main rigging." It was a constant battle for the weather berth, with members of both crews either handling lines or working aloft or hugging the windward rails. Anyone daring to raise his head above the weather rail on the *Bluenose* caught the edge of Walters's caustic tongue. The skippers strained at the wheels of their vessels, see-sawing back and forth in increasingly heavy seas. Walters finally gave up the fight for the windward berth and managed to shoot past the *Elsie* by coming up under her lee. By this time, both vessels were logging twelve to thirteen knots, the *Elsie* a mere minute and a half astern of the *Bluenose* as she rounded the Inner Automatic Buoy.

As they turned the mark, the wind piped up to twenty-five knots. It was a good fisherman's sea, with plenty of "lop" to it. The competitors eased off on their sheets for the run to the Outer Buoy, just over six miles away. Every kite was flying, booms were off to port and lee rails buried in the boisterous sea. The spray smoked off the crests at each plunge. It must have been a wild ride for the masthead men, whipped around the sky in that cool October wind. The *Elsie* stuck to the stern of her rival and hung on during the run to the second mark. At times, the *Bluenose* would haul ahead and then the *Elsie* would come up on her weather side, her main boom dipping over the stern of her rival. Back and forth they went. As they neared the mark, both doused their staysails and clewed up the fore-topsails, preparing to jibe around the buoy. The big Lunenburger rounded first, followed a mere thirty seconds later by the tough little Gloucesterman. "The great booms swung across the decks and fetched up on the patent gybers with staggering shocks as the crews roused the sheets in for the reach to Shut In Island bell buoy." It was during this leg that the *Bluenose* began to run away from the defender, and she made the nine-mile reach in just forty-two minutes, taking the buoy two minutes ahead of her opponent.

Now began the real test: the thrash to windward. The ability to drag herself off a lee shore in a gale and claw her way to safety proves the real worth of any vessel. When the *Bluenose* rounded the mark and sheeted in hard on a starboard tack for the upwind trial, the wind was cresting at thirty knots. Her staysail and fore-top-sail doused, and a roaring "bone in her teeth," the *Bluenose* began plunging into the heavy sea, burying her lee rail. The *Lady Laurier* observers could see her entire deck as she heeled to an angle of forty degrees. The boat appeared to revel in it, her long body punching through the heavy sea and her crew stuffed up under the windward rail "like bats to a barn rafter," with Walters and his mate at the lee and weather sides of the wheel.

As he passed the mark, Welsh threw his helm over and quickly hoisted his ballooner. The old *Elsie* rolled over onto the starboard tack with every sail aloft. Welsh could not have enjoyed seeing the big Lunenburger flying away from him and desperately raced after her. If carrying more sail alone could win a race, it would have been the *Elsie's*.

In his article for *Yachting* magazine, F.W. Wallace wrote:

Now there is this difference between a fisherman and a skilled yachtsman. The latter knows something about the science of spreading canvas and will forebear to drive his craft under a press of sail when she will make better sailing without too much muslin hung. Not so with the average fishing skipper. He is out to carry the whole patch and nothing gladdens his heart so much as to see his hooker lugging the whole load with her lee rail under and everything bar-taut and trembling under the strain. A roaring bow wave, a boiling wake, and an acre of white water to loo'ard looks good to him, and he often imagines this to be a sign that his vessel is smoking through it at a rate of knots.

Perhaps these skippers lacked the refinement of the yachtsman, but they had far more experience and skill in handling their boats under these rugged conditions. The America's Cup contenders would most certainly have been hunkered down under the lee of Sandy Hook waiting for the weather to settle. This was not the environment for those fined-tuned yachts, but a real fishermen's race that James Connolly later called "the greatest race ever sailed over a measured course."

The combination of wind and too much sail proved to be more than the *Elsie* could bear. First to go was her jib topsail halyard. As a crewman scampered out onto her bowsprit to re-reeve the halyard, the bow plunged deeply into the sea, burying the bowsprit to the third hank of her jib. Moments later, the foremast snapped off at the cap and both jib topsail and staysail came down in a mess of wire stays and rigging. Without missing a beat, the crew set about clearing up the wreckage. The mate and a couple of fishermen headed out on the bowsprit to cut away the jib topsail that was now dragging under the forefoot. "Down into the jumping sea went the bowsprit and the three sailors were plunged under five feet of water. They cut away the sail and brought it in with the crew behind them hauling it inboard thru the green-white smother." Those aloft worked frantically to secure the topmast, assorted wires, blocks and halyards.

Within six minutes the *Elsie,* under forcefully shortened sail, appeared to be making better time than she had before. Angus Walters reacted in the spirit of sportsmanship by immediately dousing his own jib topsail and clewing up his main topsail. Marty Welsh stood inshore on a port tack and raised his main gaff topsail and, by so doing, could have risked losing his main topmast. Once again he was carrying more sail than his rival in the thirty-knot breeze. However, what he needed was more hull in the water, not more sail aloft. *Bluenose* streaked for home "like a kerosened cat through Hades," with her lee rail buried so deep that, according to the press on board the *Lady Laurier*, "we reckoned you could drown a man in her lee scuppers."

After four and a half hours of hard sailing over a distance of about fifty miles, the *Bluenose* ploughed a furrow of white water across the finish. Walters and his crew became instant heroes, arriving home to a chorus of steam whistles and sirens. The valiant *Elsie* followed twelve and a half minutes later.

—from *A Race for Real Sailors* (2006)

THE SQUALL
Milton Acorn (1923–1986)

When the squall comes running down the bay,
It's waves like hounds on slanting leashes of rain
Bugling their way… and you're in it;
If you want more experience at this game
Pull well and slant well. Your aim
Is another helping of life. You've got to win it.

When you're caught in an eight-foot-boat—seaworthy though,
You've got to turn your back, for a man rows backwards
Taking direction from the sting of rain and spray.
How odd, when you think of it, that a man rows backwards!

What experience, deduction and sophistication
There had to be before men dared row backwards
Taking direction from where they'd been
With only quick-snatched glances at where they're going.

Each strongbacked wave bucks under you, alive
Young-muscled, wanting to toss you in orbit
While whitecaps snap like violin-strings
As if to end this scene with a sudden exit.

Fearfulness is a danger. So's fearlessness.
You've got to get that mood which balances you
As if you were a bird in the builder's hand;

For the boat was built in consideration
Not only of storms… of gales too.

Though you might cut the waves with your prow
It'll do no good if you head straight to sea.
You've got to make a nice calculation
Of where you're going, where you want to be,
What you need, and possibility;
Remembering how you've survived many things
To get into the habit of living.

—from *In a Springtime Instant: Selected Poems* (1975)

A Sovereign State of Mind
Silver Donald Cameron (1937–   )

Some nine years a-building, the author's home-made wooden boat became the means for exploring home waters around Cape Breton. But both the building and the subsequent passages under sail proved of greater portent and meaning than the practical experience of craftsmanship and navigation. In this respect, setting forth to sea was perhaps no different for him than it was for other boat builders and sailors in other Canadian waters. Yet, strangely and understandably enough, it was—as for the others—unique.

A ship, said the master shipwright David Stevens, is more like a living thing than anything else a man can build with his hands.

On this brilliant July afternoon, *Silversark* races down the west coast of Cape Breton Island. Her varnished masthead and her tanbark sails trace scallops and swirls on the deep blue of the sky, while foam-crowned waves rolling down from Prince Edward Island slap and gurgle along her black hull.

Silversark is a handsome, muscular 27-foot cutter, but for nearly nine years she was a big project inside a small barn in D'Escousse,

Cape Breton. In 1976, when I shaped her stem and laminated her frames, Lulu was single and living in Denmark, and I was divorced, and Mark Patrick was not even born. In this summer of 1990, Mark is twelve, and Lulu and I have celebrated a decade of marriage.

Today, Lulu sits at the tiller, while Mark lies along the coaming, watching the endless patterns of the wake. There is a certain wonder in this moment. This is the deck which Peter Zimmer spray-painted at Claude Poirier's body shop before we even laid it down. Those are the stanchion bases fabricated by Lulu's brother Terry. Her father and I framed the cockpit where we sit. Lulu painted and varnished almost everything on deck and below.

Small jobs, each of them. How can they add up to a little ship, shouldering her way through the seas of the Gulf of St. Lawrence as though she were indeed a living thing?

Silversark was built to cross oceans, but things have not yet worked out that way. In the meantime, yachts sail into D'Escousse every year from England, France, the United States, even Switzerland. Their crews marvel at Cape Breton's beauty, its clean water, its friendly people, its uncrowded anchorages. Cape Breton, they say, offers some of the finest cruising on earth.

So why not explore it ourselves?

And why not explore its spirit as well as its waterways? When you enter a village under sail, you enter quickly into its life—any village, anywhere. Cruising sailors belong to the freemasonry of the sea, along with the fisherman, the merchant seaman, the ferryboat skipper. The professionals are at the wharf, and you meet them as your lines go ashore. Then the dreamers appear, asking questions and longing to be invited aboard—for cruising people personify a great fantasy: running away to sea, the ultimate dream of freedom.

Admittedly, a voyage around Cape Breton Island in a sailing vessel is hardly a passage in new and uncharted waters. The French trader Nicolas Denys published his description of a voyage around the island in 1672, and his sailing directions can still be followed. The Sieur de la Roque circled the island in 1752 to enumerate its inhabitants for Louis XV. (He found 4,122 of them.) Lieutenant Samuel Holland did a complete survey under sail fifteen years later, and Thomas Chandler Haliburton, the creator of Sam Slick, made a similar tour in the 1820s.

But new eyes see differently. I had lived in Cape Breton for nearly twenty years, and Lulu had been born there, but much of the coast itself would be new to us. Approaching from seaward, we would see a different island.

We sailed from D'Escousse in early July on a voyage of discovery and rediscovery, tacking back into the past even as we reached forward on the summer winds. For Cape Breton is a reality more resonant than it appears to the casual visitor and a voyage takes place not only on the water but also in the mind. Cape Breton has been—still is—an island of dreamers and shamans, of fallen empires and pioneering science, of impassioned music, of sunken treasure, robber barons, gallant soldiers, Communists and cannibals.

A savage, sacred landscape.

A sovereign state of mind.

—from *Wind, Whales and Whisky: A Cape Breton Voyage* (1991)

Sunday Harbour
M. Wylie Blanchet (1891–1962)

Muriel Wylie Blanchet, together with her five children and family dog, set themselves enormous challenges when exploring the BC coast aboard their 25-foot wooden motorboat Caprice *during the 1920s and 1930s. A self-taught boater, navigator and motor mechanic, she learned "on the job" while mentoring her young crew in the ways of the sea. Here she feels the impact of the open ocean past the northern tip of Vancouver Island while making passage almost beyond the limits of many keen yachting folk and their small craft. As the saying goes, she never made mistakes—but she did have memorable educational experiences.*

"What day is it?" asked Jan, looking up from the chart. Sunday, we finally decided, after much thought and calculation—days get lost or found so easily when you have been playing with years and centuries in old Indian villages.

"Well, here's a Sunday Harbour all ready for us!" I looked over her shoulder—a little ring of islands on the fringe of Queen Charlotte Sound. But sure enough, Sunday Harbour was marked with an anchor as shelter and holding ground. I opened the Pilot Book to look it up... British Columbia... Coast Waters... Queen Charlotte Sound... Fog Island... Dusky Cove. Ah! Sunday Harbour. Pilot book says, "Small but sheltered anchorage on south side of Crib Island. Affords refuge for small boats." I didn't altogether like that word "refuge," it sounded like a last extremity. Still, the name was alluring. So, if we need it, Sunday Harbour let it be.

The nine o'clock wind was now flicking at our heels. The mountains had tossed off their comforters and were sticking up their heads to look about them. It does not take much wind, on top of the swell, to make a nasty sea in the sound. I relieved the mate at the wheel— for it depends on the balance on top of a crest whether you make the long slide down the other side safely or not. "I don't quite like the mightn'ts!" said John anxiously. "What mightn'ts?" I asked, as I spun the wheel. "The mightn'ts be able to swim," said John, eyeing the rough waters that curled at our stern.

But even as we were all about to admit that it was much too rough for our liking, we were out of it—for Sunday Harbour opened its arms and we were received into its quiet sabbatical calm. It was low, low tide—which means in this region a drop of twenty-five feet. Islands, rocks and reefs towered above our quiet lagoon; and only in the tall trees, way up, did the wind sing of the rising storm outside.

Low, low tide—primeval ooze, where all life had its beginning. Usually it is hidden with four or five feet of covering water; but at low, low tide it is all exposed and lies naked and defenceless at your feet. Pale-green sea-anemones, looking like exotic asters, opened soft lips and gratefully engulfed our offerings of mussel meat. Then shameful to say, we fed them on stones, which they promptly spat out. We thought uncomfortably of Mrs. Be-done-by-as-you-did, and wandered on in search of abalones on their pale-pink mottled rocks.

Then, blessing of blessings, out came the sun! Sun, whom we hadn't seen for days and days, soothing us, healing us, blessing us. Sunday Harbour? Yes—but it was named for quiet Christian principles and little white churches; and we were worshipping the old god of the day because he shone on us. Sun, O Sun... We slipped off our clothes and joined the sea-beasts in "the ooze of their pasture-grounds."

"Sand-strewn caverns, cool and deep, where the winds are all asleep; where the spent lights quiver and gleam; where the saltweed sways in the stream..." I came up to breathe—Jan and Peter were having a floating competition, Jan was sending up tall spouts of water from her mouth, and the sun was shining on their upturned faces. I looked around for John... there he was doing a dead man's float all by himself—face downwards, only his small behind gleaming on the surface.

Somehow, I mistrusted that word "refuge" from the beginning— it was too suggestive of other things, such as trouble or shipwreck. And then one always forgets that Pilot books, even if they say small vessels, probably mean cruisers as opposed to battleships. All day the place was perfect. We might have been in a land-locked lake, miles and miles from the sea. But as daylight faded, the tide rose. And by and by it rose some more—and gone was our quiet lagoon. We could see the wild ocean over the tops of our island, and the waves drove through gaps that we had not even suspected. The wind, which all day had kept to the tree tops, now swooped and tore at our refuge like a wild frenzied thing... And by and by it rose some more—and the gusts of wind swept our little boat in wide dizzying semi-circles—first one way and then the other. I let out more and more rope, but our anchor started to drag... and it dragged, and the wind blew, and the tide rose; and finally we were blown out of Sunday Harbour, and backwards into Monday Harbour.

—from *The Curve of Time* (1961)

SAND CASTLES
Wayson Choy (1939–   )

From his home in Vancouver's Chinatown, young Wayson Choy is taken by Third Uncle to watch the castle-building contest at English Bay.

By the time Third Uncle and I got off the streetcar and walked down to English Bay, the sculptors were almost all finished their work. It was a cloudy mid-afternoon, but the sun broke through often enough that it made all the sculptures suddenly gleam with texture. Sea creatures rose from the shoreline, mermaids and dragons and fantasy beasts; there was a line of castles beyond these. From my seven-year-old's vantage point, the sculptures were impressive, breathtaking. I began to imagine myself creating something, too. Then the brittle, Toisan accents of my guardian broke into my daydreaming.

"They won't last," Third Uncle said, which I thought was a stick-in-the-mud thing for him to say. "Nothing lasts."

Nearer the incoming tide, groups of older children and adults were creating smaller versions of seascapes and castles by filling wooden boxes, tin buckets and open-ended cans with wet sand. Fists and palms banged on the box and bucket bottoms. Perfect rectangles of sand slipped out. From the tin cans, perfect cylinders.

"Don't get your feet wet," Third Uncle warned, pulling me back. He sniffed the threatening air. "The dampness can make you sick."

Two men and a woman were going around, giving instructions and encouragement. I listened, watched, too shy to participate. Like me, hardly anyone noticed that the sky had darkened.

"Jul lot-sui." Third Uncle said. *"Rain soon."*

The air was moist. On my tongue I could taste the iodine-smell of English Bay. Between the bare legs of adults, their feet carelessly sunk into dangerous wetness, I saw mounds of sand being carved and shaped into seahorses, crabs, lobsters, and turtles with deep-grooved backs. The sun broke through. Their shadows waned and deepened in the sunshine, then disappeared, bringing the sand creatures to life.

"I want to do that," I said to Third Uncle, meaning that I was going to go home and do that in our backyard.

"Only grown-ups do that," he said. "Too dirty for children."

"How come those kids over there are doing that?"

"They're not like you, all dressed up," Third Uncle said. "They don't know better."

One of the castles nearest the water's edge was particularly splendid, and I imagined my tin soldiers climbing those walls, my tanks pushed along those paths; my miniature cowboy horses and Indians scouting about—all of them, tanks and horses included, fighting their usual mixed-up war. There were moats for careless horses to drown in, and little pathways that no tank could navigate. My staring caught Third Uncle's attention.

"Step away from that water," he commanded.

At seven, I was old enough to know that I was never going to go out again with Third Uncle. He was never much fun, a spoilsport. He surveyed the happy scene and saw the coming of doom.

"In a couple of hours, the tide or the rain will wash everything away."

People in swimming suits dashed by us to run down the slope and jump into the water twenty feet away, but I hardly noticed them. I was busy studying how toy shovelfuls of wet sand took shape between slapping hands, how scooped palms of water were splashed onto dry patches, how fistfuls of dark silt adhered to slopes and curves and were carefully recarved with spoons, how creature-eyes were poked with thin sticks, and sagging castle walls were reformed with fragments of wood pulled across their sagging base.

When we got home, I ran into the house and changed into my play clothes as fast as I could. But just as I dashed into the kitchen ready to build my palace in our backyard, the rain began to fall in torrents.

—from *Paper Shadows: A Chinatown Childhood* (1999)

POCKET-CRUISER PASSAGE
Philip Teece (1940–   )

At the age of twenty-five the author built his 18-foot shoal-draft sail-boat Galadriel, *named after a character in Tolkien's* Lord of the Rings. *Tolkien refers to her variously as "the mightiest and fairest of all the Elves that remained in Middle-earth" and again as "the greatest of elven women." Decades later, Teece continues to sail her. Here, he sails in company with another independent sailor in her 20-foot sloop* Aiaia, *named after a mythological island said to be the home of the ancient Greek sorceress Circe. They begin their journey from Vancouver Island, across Georgia Strait, toward Desolation Sound.*

A sailing passage of thirty or forty nautical miles in a fifteen-ton yacht is likely to be pretty quick and easy. In a featherweight pocket cruiser the same trip is a rather different experience; it will typically be far more labour-intensive.

As we tumbled past Protection Island, running north before our bracing morning southeaster, we began to feel what was in store for us. The essential feature of small-craft cruising is motion—quick, unpredictable, violent, bruising motion. Bracing myself continually against my boat's prancing, bucking attempts to fling me overboard, I felt muscles everywhere in my body starting to ache before we had sailed five miles.

Mary, already quite far ahead, was an instructive sight. As always, my view of her boat staggering among the curling ridges gave a more accurate impression of the sea's chaotic state than the sensation of my own motion did. At times *Aiaia* was a flash of white balancing on a watery summit; at other moments she was eclipsed in the trough, showing only her top-rigging above a fence of foam.

Once I snapped up a pair of binoculars and managed to raise them to my eyes long enough for a close glance at Mary. In that instant she was steering with one hand and using the other hand to raise a thermos flask to her lips.

Northward up the Strait of Georgia an almost imaginary mountaintop showed a vague shimmer of itself above a hard, blue horizon.

Chart and compass confirmed that this was Lasqueti Island, a possible destination for us today if our favouring wind held. The nearest point of the island was over thirty-five miles from our morning's starting place among the Flat Tops.

Our real sailing distance would be much longer, thanks to Whiskey Golf. Straddling the direct course between Entrance Island and Lasqueti, Whiskey Golf is a huge wedge of the Strait of Georgia that has been designated a naval weapons testing range. When this military zone is active (on all weekdays), marine traffic must avoid it altogether. Thus our course for the day would be the two long sides of a right angle, close inshore as far as the Ballenas Islands, then eastward to our goal on Lasqueti.

Tossed and buffeted in a rough sea, we would find this a long and exhausting run. Yet on the threshold of such a run there is something that we fear more than strengthening wind and roughening sea: it is far more troublesome for us to discover, miles from our destination, that the wind has suddenly stopped. Our boats are wind-driven ships; we don't try to push them far by outboard power.

Mary was exhilarated by her first crossing of big open water. This I could tell by the style of her sailing. Spreading a sizeable area of canvas wing-on-wing, she was letting *Aiaia* have her head, running much faster than old *Galadriel* could manage. Quickly she shrank to little more than a triangular white dot far ahead.

And then she sailed back!

Rising and falling precariously alongside, she gave me an optimistic thumbs-up sign. Then with a throw of her helm she was off again, enjoying the sport of surfing at hull-speed-plus on the slopes of the northward-marching waves.

We galloped along our way for several hours, with the wind holding steady at about twenty-five knots. *Galadriel* sailed as all short-waterline cruising boats tend to do, rocketing forward at breakneck speed on the crests and wallowing at times to a near stop in the troughs. It is this feature of a very small vessel's heavy weather performance that gives rise to a paradox: some superfast sailing combined with a slower-than-expected overall passage speed. Thirty-five miles of this good fun is hard work!

Although it is difficult for a lone sailor to leave the helm while the boat is corkscrewing over the waves under a press of canvas, sometimes it must be done. When need arises one may heave-to by rounding up into the wind, leaving the headsail sheeted on the windward side to fill in reverse, against the mainsail's forward thrust. This stops the vessel's forward motion but not, of course, her rise and fall on the seas. Getting lunch or using the head in such conditions is like attempting these functions inside an automatic washing machine. When I returned on deck after heaving-to for five minutes, I found that I was displaying a spectacular scrape on my arm, a souvenir of my collision with a drawer in the cabin. Half a mile ahead, *Aiaia* too was momentarily stopped, lying over at a high angle of heel. I kept a prudent watch until Mary re-emerged and cast off her jibsheet to resume sailing.

We ran on. As the afternoon advanced, the hedgehog profile of the southernmost of the Ballenas Islands loomed directly ahead, and the mountains of Lasqueti began to solidify out of the haze. I was starting to feel very weary, but the thrill of our rushing progress continued. Although both Mary and I were carrying headsails too large for the press of wind and swell, the risk seemed justified by our gratifying speed.

—from *A Shimmer on the Horizon* (1999)

PUT HER IN FORWARD
Linden MacIntyre (1943–   )

In MacIntyre's novel the sea forms a backdrop for the dark and painful subject of child abuse in the Church—and boats are the vehicles for exploring human relations. On arriving at his new parish of Creignish on Cape Breton Island, Father Duncan MacAskill befriends the MacKays, Danny Ban and his son, Danny, who sell him a boat, Jacinta. *Here young Danny teaches him how to handle it.*

For a week I'd drive down to the shore and just stare, until I grew conscious of people watching me. Eventually I started the motor, but the thought of untying the ropes and abandoning the land filled me with terror. So I just stood there gunning the diesel engine in ecstasy and fear. There were usually two or three men standing on the far side, watching silently, hands in pockets.

"One of these days," I said as I was leaving.

"For sure," they replied. "No rush." They were smiling. After about ten days, young Danny called and asked about the boat and I told him I thought everything was fine. Engine seemed to be running well. Everything as it should be. "You should really take her out for a run," he said. "Charge up the battery. And before you put her away, maybe change the oil. I'll show you how."

"Put her away?"

"For the winter."

"Right."

"Actually, Dad was saying I should give you a few tips on driving her."

"That would probably be wise."

"What are you doing tomorrow?"...

Young Danny was waiting at the harbour, the engine already running. He released the ropes and shoved us away from the floating dock.

"Okay," he said. "Put her in forward."

I hesitated, shoved the wrong lever. The engine roared, but there was no movement. I imagined crowds at dockside, smirking. Then he was beside me, hauled the throttle back and shoved the gearshift ahead. The boat moved gently forward. I tried to steer, but she balked momentarily, as if aware of a stranger at the controls. Then she grudgingly swung her bow... too far. And we were heading toward the side of someone's large, expensive boat. He gently reached past me again and corrected the wheel then stepped back, arms folded. I was sweating as we moved slowly along the line of docked boats toward what seemed to be an impossibly narrow channel out of the harbour. "You're doing great," he said.

Once outside, I shoved the throttle forward again and my heart accelerated with the diesel. The boat surged.

"Excellent," he said. Then turned and walked toward the stern and just sat there, looking around.

We sailed toward an island that seemed to be about five miles out. "Henry Island," he called out, pointing. The roar in the cab was deafening. The boat was determined not to follow a straight line, and when she'd veer away from the wind she'd pitch violently against the frothing waves. After about half an hour I turned back. The ride became smoother. Danny took the wheel and I went outside, then climbed toward the bow, clinging to a rail above the cab.

I was startled by the near silence there. The wind was icy and my teeth were chattering. Perhaps to reduce my exposure to the chill I lay flat, head over the side, watching the rush of water. Sluicing, foamy furrows fell away cleanly from the flared bow, the sea opening behind like a ploughed field. I thought I heard a strange, sad murmur, a voice I hadn't heard for years. *What are you saying to me?*

Approaching the mouth of the harbour, Danny opened a window and shouted up, asking if I wanted to take her in. I shook my head. I'd hardly got her out; I couldn't imagine manoeuvring my way back in and docking. He managed to do everything at once without hurrying. Turned and tucked the boat smoothly alongside the dock, stepped ashore and secured both lines, then turned off the engine. I just watched.

Ashore, my ears were ringing, my face was on fire. I was chilled to the bone, but I just wanted to laugh.

—from *The Bishop's Man* (2009)

ROWBOAT MEETS CRUISE SHIP
Kenneth Macrae Leighton (1925–1998)

At age sixty-six the author rowed from Vancouver up the west coast to Prince Rupert. Not once in that long journey would he have traded his 14-foot jollyboat for a more comfortable vessel!

It rains hard all night. *Morag Anne* spins at her mooring but I hear no sounds of scraping on rock. All the same, I don't sleep much for the night is filled with strange groaning and moaning. I get up several times, once crawling forward on the foredeck in my pyjamas, trying to trace the source of these peculiar cries. It is black as pitch and very wet.

When dawn comes I am quite disoriented. I think at first that I must have been swept down Hawkins Channel. It takes some time to realize that everything looks different at high water and that the boat has turned completely around. My fears are groundless but there is a momentary frisson of anxiety which sets the tone of the day. The moaning and groaning I had worried about all night comes from kelp wound between the rudder and the hull, like a great, tangled ball of string stretching and relaxing with each wave. It takes more than half an hour and a lot of bad language to get free.

It is still raining hard.

In retrospect you wonder if you really enjoyed all that. How could you? I'm here to tell you that, in spite of everything and even, who knows, because of it, I wouldn't have changed places with anyone.

But it is a gloomy row up Grenville. The channel is nowhere more than a mile wide. When a cruise ship bears down on something the size of *Morag Anne* it seems very large indeed. Sometimes I feel I can reach out and touch the sides of the huge ships that slowly, very slowly and sedately slip up and down the channel. It is surprising how little wash they make. Seiners on the other hand, not all that much bigger than one of the orange lifeboats stacked like toys on the sides of the giant ships, set up a wash that makes rowing very unpleasant.

I feel sorry for the folks on the boats on such a day. They can't see to the tops of the mountainous sides of the channel; for all the view they get they could be sailing along a Dutch canal. The sea is a dull, sullen grey. A gloomy scene indeed and more so, I imagine, if you are paying the earth to see it. If you are standing on deck, hands in the pockets of your parka, woollen hat down around your ears and a drip on the end of your nose, bored out of your mind, full to the gills with breakfast and nothing to look forward to but lunch, you might well be wondering about the cost-benefit ratio. I know I would.

I am better off in *Morag Anne.*

—from *Oar & Sail: An Odyssey of the West Coast* (1999)

"Now welcome, fish, you who have come, brought by the Chief of the World-Above that I see you again, that I come to exert my privilege of being the first to string you, fish. I mean this, that you may have mercy on me that I may see you again next year when you come back to this your happy place, fish."
— Kwakiutl Prayer, "To the Olachen," Franz Boas, in
The Religion of the Kwakiutl Indians (1930)

"There are no cod in the whole frigging ocean."
— Michael Crummey, from "Cod 2"
in *Arguments with Gravity* (1996)

CHAPTER VI
BOUNTY BESTOWED—
BOUNTY BETRAYED

Indigenous oral tradition is rich in tales of oceans once teeming with life, a gift of the Creator. Later stories of John Cabot's arrival on the Banks of Newfoundland in 1497 speak of cod so plentiful that one could walk on their backs. But in the last century stories began to darken: human ignorance, mismanagement and greed intrude, triggering a shift from stewardship to exploitation. The tragic result—depleted fish stocks, closure of fisheries, loss of jobs and dereliction of old communities—is now a matter of public record. Writers weave these themes through their poetry, novels, tales and memoirs.

WALRUS HUNTING
Aua (c. 1870)

Aua, an Iglulik angakok—or shaman—shared this song of his success as a great hunter with his friend, the Greenland explorer and anthropologist Knud Rasmussen, during the latter's renowned Fifth Thule Expedition of 1921–1924.

I could not sleep
For the sea was so smooth
Near at hand.
So I rowed out
And up came a walrus
Close by my kayak.
It was too near to throw,
So I thrust my harpoon into its side
And the bladder-float danced across the waves.
But in a moment it was up again,
Setting its flippers angrily
Like elbows on the surface of the water
And trying to rip up the bladder.
All in vain it wasted strength,
For the skin of an unborn lemming
Was sewn inside as an amulet to guard.
Then snorting viciously it sought to gather strength,
But I rowed up
And ended the struggle.
Hear that, O men from strange creeks and fjords
That were always so ready to praise yourselves;
Now you can fill your lungs with song
Of another man's bold hunting.

—as told to Knud Rasmussen in *Across Arctic America: Narrative of the Fifth Thule Expedition* (1927)

THE WHALERS OF PANGNIRTUNG
Aksaajuuq Etooangat (1902–1973)

Between the 1840s and the 1920s, the area of Pangnirtung, Baffin Island, became part of a lucrative, international whaling industry. Chasing the bowhead whale across the waters of the Eastern Arctic Ocean, whalers from Canada, Scotland and the United States came to rely heavily on their Inuit partners to assist them in the hunt and provide them with food and clothing during the long months of wintering in the ice. After the industry moved offshore, the former whaling station became a Hudson's Bay Company trading post, attracting Inuit families to settle in the area. Today, the hamlet of Pangnirtung has a thriving turbot processing plant and is internationally renowned for its traditional Inuit art.

When I was a child, if the whalers were short of men I was asked to fill in and help them. I actually took part in killing the blue whales even though I was only in my early teens. Every spring, in the month of June, while the floe edge was still a long way from land, the whaling boats would be taken down to the water on big sleds pulled by lots of dogs. The kind of boats I'm talking about had a roof over them, although some were open boats. Once the seal hunting began, the boats would stay out for weeks. Every week a boat would come around the other boats to pick up the catch and take it back to camp, and the other hunters would carry on hunting more seals to fill their boats. The boats would stay in the water until the ice was all gone, which is usually in July. Eventually, each boat would be carrying something: one would be filled with seal meat, another with blubber, etc. Everything was well organized. The *qallunaat* [non-Inuit people]... would take the skins and blubber and the meat would be given to the women for food.

The women would also go seal hunting when there were lots of seals in the springtime. Every spring, they would plan to go hunting while their husbands were whaling. They would be using their husband's harpoons, etc. The men who were still in camp with the women would also help. They would pull the *qamutiks* and women would ride on them. Lots of seals would be killed without using guns. The women would stay beside the seal holes until the seals came up for air; they would kill a lot of seals that way. The men who were still in camp would skin them and take the blubber off the skins.

Regardless of the things that the ships had brought with them, the women would be given cloth free of charge to make dresses. The men would go mainly for the things that they might need for their kayaks or some of the boats. They would take them even though they were all [old] and not fit to be used anymore. And whenever oil or blubber would go bad (yellowish in colour) the men would boil it and when it blackened they would then paint the boats with it, and this thing that we called soot would help to give the boats their colour...

—from Penny Petrone, ed. *Northern Voices: Inuit Writing in English* (1988)

WHALING CAMP
Alice French (1930–2013)

Alice French tells of growing up in the Arctic prior to World War II. She dedicates her book to her children with the words: "Listen, listen my children. / And I'll tell you a story of where I was born / and where I grew up. / About your ancestors and the land we lived on, / About the animals and the birds. / So you can see." Here she recalls her extended family's summer whaling station near Tuktoyaktuk on the Beaufort Sea.

While we were living on the coast we depended on the sea for our food and we had to be very careful not to anger the sea spirit. This meant that we could not work on the skins of land animals. There was rivalry between the sea and land spirits in providing man with his livelihood. Should we be so foolish as to forget this rule, the sea spirit would cause storms to keep us from going out to hunt on the sea. She might also lead all the sea creatures away in her jealousy.

Our whaling trip included all my grandfather's family. There were my uncles Michael, Harry, Colin, and Donald, and my aunts

Olga, Agnes, and Mary. My grandma's married sister and husband were with us, and then there was our own family of six. In all we had five tents. The whaling camp, as a whole, was made up of some thirty to forty families. A freshwater creek flowed into the sea and made a good harbour for our boats.

Once we had settled in, my grandfather went up the hills with his binoculars, and soon sighted some whales. The men launched the boats and headed out to sea. They could be gone a few hours, or all night, so we supplied the boat with enough food to last for two days. When a boat returned we looked at the mast to see how many banners were flying. Our boat had two on the mast when it came in. This meant that they had two whales. Everyone rushed to the beach to help pull the white whales to shore. The children, with their jack-knives and small ulus [Inuit knives], cut bits of muktuk off the tail flipper and ate it raw. Then the women began to work and within an hour the whale was just a skeleton. The meat was sliced into big slabs and hung up on the racks to dry. The blubber was stripped off the hide, sliced into narrow strips and stored in the 45-gallon drums we brought with us. The first layer of the hide was made into muktuk. It was cut into nine-by-nine-inch squares, hung on racks in bunches of ten and dried for two to three days. Then it was cooked and put into the same barrel as the blubber. This preserved it for eating through the winter months. The middle layer of the hide, called ganek, was stretched, dried, and used for shoe leather.

Grandfather was kept busy making ulus and sharpening them. My grandmother's job was to teach us the art of cutting up the whale and making use of every bit of it. She taught us how to make containers from the stomach, but first we had to practise separating the layers of skin on the throat. Until we could do this without putting a hole in the skin, we were not allowed to start the more serious task of container making. There were three layers to the stomach and it took two hours to take them apart. Only the middle layer was used. This was blown up and dried for use as a container for whale oil, dried meat, dried fish and bits of muktuk for the winter. The containers were also used for storing blueberries and cranberries and for floats to mark the position of a harpooned whale.

At the whaling camp the girls learned to make waterproof boots. The top part was made of canvas or of sealskin; the sole of the boot was made from whale skin, crimped with the teeth. I was not good at this, much to my grandmother's dismay. As a result my value as a wife went down. Almost all our clothing was made by hand, so it was important to be good at all these things.

—from *My Name is Masak* (1976)

VICTORIA'S CAPE BRETON SAILORS
Donald MacGillivray (1942–   )

By the 1880s the east coast fisheries and sealing hunt had peaked and fallen into decline. Particularly hard hit were the fleets of Cape Breton Island. Faced with the choice of migrating or working in industries ashore, many chose to sail their ships around Cape Horn to Victoria, BC. Here they experienced great success in the North Pacific seal hunt, and changed the character of the port. Thus while Nova Scotia's sealing fleet dwindled, Victoria's grew. The Cape Bretoners' adventures were the very stuff of popular romance, attracting novelists like Jack London (The Sea-Wolf) and Arthur Hunt Chute (Far Gold).

On a spring day in 1888 the bustling port of Victoria had its cultural mix enhanced with the arrival of three boatloads of Cape Bretoners. At 8:00 a.m. on Tuesday, 24 April the 113-ton schooner *Annie C. Moore* under Captain Charles Hackett arrived, having departed North Sydney 158 days earlier. Thirteen hours later the *Triumph*, a 97-ton schooner under Dan MacLean appeared, after a 128-day passage from Halifax. She was followed within minutes by the *Maggie Mac*, a 196-ton three masted schooner with Captain John Dodd at the helm, having departed Halifax on 9 November. Hackett was from North Sydney; Dodd was a native of Sydney; MacLean was from East Bay. The majority of the crews were also Cape Bretoners, most of them on the West Coast for first time; only Dodd and MacLean had previously sailed out of Victoria. A fourth schooner with a Cape Bretoner at the helm also sailed into James Bay that evening. The *Mary Ellen*, under Alex MacLean, Dan's brother, returned from a nine-week sealing trip along the coast with the largest catch reported to date, entitling the vessel to "carry the broom" as she sailed into port. The most successful schooner would hoist a broom on the main halyard signifying a clean sweep.

That evening the saloons at Tommy Burnes' American Hotel, Erickson's Hotel at the foot of Johnson Street, the Garrick's Head on Bastion Street and other waterfront spots surely rang with a variety of Cape Breton dialects. The Cape Bretoners in Victoria for the first time were probably fascinated with their new home port. It was quite a change from picturesque Arichat, sleepy Sydney or rustic East Bay. The 1880s was Victoria's decade, and as Ivan Doig phrased it, through the lens of diarist James Swan: "Not at all like the dry and dowdy little Queen whose name it wears... the city is in the manner of the youngest daughter of some Edwardian country house family, attractive and passionately self-absorbed and more than a little silly." Maybe a bit risqué as well for the innocent Cape Bretoners, considering the openly advertised opium joints and the Johnson Street brothels. At this time, [wrote historian Charles Lillard] Victoria "had the largest red-light district on the Northwest Coast" and sources suggest that a section of the waterfront was "a miniature Barbary Coast full of sailors and gamblers, whores and drunks... the men were wild and free and the women just as mad."

Most of these Cape Breton mariners were born in the 1850s and 1860s and came of age when the "great days of sail" period was peaking. In 1880 [according to historians Eric Sager and Gerald Panting] Canada had probably "the fourth largest merchant Marine in the world," with almost 75 percent registered in what is now Atlantic Canada. Two decades later local fleets had declined by two-thirds. The "golden age" there had barely lasted a generation. Given the limited economic opportunities for Cape Bretoners, large numbers went down to the sea in coastal vessels, long distance trade and banks fishing, the latter primarily in American schooners from New England ports. With the protective tariff [promoted by Sir John A. Macdonald after becoming Prime Minister in 1878] the

1880s would see significant increases in secondary manufacturing in the region; such land-based economic opportunities help explain the rapid decline in vessel ownership. But few of the new factories located in Cape Breton. Almost 10,000 migrated from the island in the 1880s, twice the rate of the previous decade.

Within a decade there were around 70 sealing schooners based in Victoria; the combined west coast fleet numbered 124. Victoria was fast becoming the world's premier sealing port. This rapid expansion was quite egalitarian, attracting a tough and varied crowd with room for determined newcomers... the largest group was from the Maritimes, and mainland Nova Scotia in particular, contributing at least a dozen well-known captains to the fleet. But there were at least fourteen Cape Breton master mariners involved as well. Part of the explanation for the significant participation of Cape Bretoners was the early successes of Alex and Dan MacLean. In 1886 Alex, in the *Favourite*, brought in the second highest catch of the season. Dan and the *Mary Ellen* returned with a record 4,268 skins. It would be surpassed only once in the history of the fleet. The sealing record of the MacLean brothers in the 1884–87 period was impressive. With an average price in Victoria in the 1880s of $7, they acquired over 18,000 skins, equal to $126,896.

In October 1887 Dan MacLean was in Nova Scotia to acquire a new vessel, and his arrival prompted considerable local interest. The Halifax waterfront was already abuzz with the knowledge that a number of Nova Scotia schooners had recently departed for the trip around Cape Horn. Eight east coast schooners headed to Victoria that year.

The Victoria-based sealers were a feisty, talented bunch and they were soon viewed through a romanticized hue. In a 1903 article "The Romance of Sealing," J. Gordon Smith noted: "They are a varied gathering of sailormen these sealers, but for adventure, or for fun and story, the jolly Cape Breton boys, or the hardy men from Nova Scotia or New Brunswick lead them all... It will be difficult to find a hardier or more daring class of men than these brave fellows who man the sealing fleets."

—Adapted from "Cape Bretoners
in the Victoria Sealing Fleet, and beyond" (2010)

FROM THE SEA
Floris Clark McLaren (1904–1978)

I

Rain, rain in the wind
And the bitter taste of the spray;
The straining eyes that watch
The last sail down the bay.

Rain, rain in the wind,
And the wandering seagulls cry
Over an empty sea,
Under a cloudy sky.

Rain, rain in the wind,
And the watching eyes are dim
Before a sail appears
Over the ocean rim.

Rain, rain in the wind,
And the hungry lines of foam,
The baffled and cheated waves
As the fishing boats come home.

II

Out to the traps, with the wind in our faces,
And a glimpse of a buoy where the mists divide;
Out through the Straits where the black sea races
Eddied and swift with the turning tide.

Home with our catch when the dusk is falling
And the glow in the west has turned to grey;
Home through the Pass with the seagulls calling
And the Dead Man's Light to mark our way.

—from *The Frozen Fire* (1937)

DRAGGING FOR TRAPS
Milton Acorn (1923–1986)

The lobster fishery is a major staple of Prince Edward Island's economy. Although originally shunned by European settlers—and considered fit only for the poor—lobster has long been prized as a delicacy. Today lobsters from the Island are shipped across North America and around the world. But the work can be dangerous. Each year, during the spring and fall lobster seasons, fishermen are at the mercy of wind, tide, fog, shifting sandbar formations and water temperatures for the setting of their traps and the success of their harvest.

When you're hanging to a pendulum
you wouldn't be there unless there's something to do
so mind the swing and mind your job;
like when you're out in a lobster boat
dragging for traps in the swell after the storm.
No time to think: "What am I
doing here, whose mother
loved me along with other fools?"

Turn into the waves and toss,
turn to the side and roll 45 degrees plus,
turn your back to them and mind the splash.
Just don't think you're going to be seasick.
All the time there's traps on the shore
bumped, bruised, broken, tangled with their lines.
Hold on and drag, trying not to be sure
that they're the very traps you're dragging for.

—from *In a Springtime Instant: Selected Poems* (1975)

THE CAPELIN ARE IN!
Wayne Johnston (1958–   )

Capelin (Mallotus villosus) *are a small, saltwater fish related to the freshwater smelt. In June and July they move inshore to spawn along the beaches of Newfoundland where they attract a variety of marine predators—from fish to whales to seabirds. Their arrival is equally anticipated among coastal families who gather them up by the bucketful as both food and fertilizer. Salted, dried and roasted over a fire, capelin have also long been a traditional Newfoundland snack.*

"The capelin are in," my father said excitedly, waking me up one Sunday morning in June after having just got the word from Gordon in Ferryland. They were not in at Bay Bulls or Witless Bay but they were in at Ferryland. The whole family, not bothering with breakfast, piled into the car.

The winter had been cold, spring had come late, but at last the capelin had come ashore to spawn, and with the spawning capelin came the cod; on the beach below the Gaze a mass mating was taking place, the females leaving their eggs buried in the sand where they were insulated from the icy water; once the eggs hatched, they would be carried out to sea with each retreating tide.

The capelin, as if in mass surrender to our species, rolled up on the shore in waves, black waves alive with little fish that, once marooned, flopped about in millions on the sand, olive green on top, silver on the bottom. From a distance, from the height of the house above the sea, it appeared that the water of the coastline had turned black.

By the time we got down to the beach, there were half a dozen stocky, shaggy-maned ponies lined up on the sand at an angle to the water, waiting patiently to serve their purpose, harnessed to carts that had large-spoked wooden wheels. Fishermen wearing rubber kneeboots and tweed sod caps used long-handled dip nets to scoop the capelin from the water and dump them in the carts.

It could have been a scene from a hundred years ago, from June of 1869. The beach swarmed not only with capelin but with children, running about up to their knees in the little fish, each wave being about two parts capelin and one part water. We took off our boots and socks and waded into the capelin. I felt the shock of the icy water on my shins. My feet went numb. I reached down and grabbed two fistfuls of fish, writhing, struggling half-foot-long fish. When I held them to the sun a certain way, I saw, among the olive and silver, iridescent pinks and greens and blues. What a strange bounty it was. I looked about. Dead capelin littered the beach, decaying, drying in the sun, trodden into the wet sand by the horses whose hooves left little craters that filled up with water.

"Mallotus villosus Muller!" my father shouted, chasing my mother down the beach, in one hand a capelin that he said he was going to shove down her dress.

We followed the horses and their carts with their teeming mounds of fish flesh as they plodded down the beach towards the road to the wharf. As they struggled up over the steep incline between beach and road, hoofs slipping, we and several dozen children of Ferryland helped them, pushed the carts, the wooden wheels, cheered when they crested the hill.

We filed along the roadside, a procession of ponies pulling carts of capelin, and fifty or sixty children with dogs trotting along beside us, trying to assert their importance by barking at the ponies who ignored them.

—from *Baltimore's Mansion* (1999)

LOG SALVAGE—WEST COAST STYLE
Ferenc Máté (1945–)

Weathered logs, heaved up by the sea and scattered along the tide lines with flotsam and jetsam, characterize the beaches along the BC coast. New and moist, they can sometimes fetch a price for the ardent salvager. Cast away and rejected, their tortured shapes and often unusual grainings are a treasure trove for woodcarvers. Bleached white through many summers, they lie as wardens of the foreshore, offering shelter and respite to hikers and bathers. Máté's novel of love and adventure conjures up many coastal stories and myths, among them the challenges faced by men who go to sea in tugboats in search of salvageable logs that have broken loose from booms. It highlights the close relationship between logging and seafaring. In this account, the novel's narrator recounts working as a deckhand for a hard-driving, miserly salvager named Henderson and a devil-may-care skipper.

Log salvage is a profession that thrives on the loss of others, a little like grave-robbing except the law is on your side. The International Law of Salvage Rights gives to anyone the right to grab and make his own most of what is wrecked or lost at sea, and villages from Cornwall to Sumatra have eked out a life harvesting the bounty heaven sent with storms. And so did we.

North of us they were felling forests, dragging logs the size of houses to the shore with oxen or steam donkeys, chucking them in the sea, making them into floating booms with chained boom-sticks around them. Then a tug would hook a yoke on, point south, and give her full throttle. And sit there. After a while the booms began to nudge, barely, like a snail. When a storm caught them and smashed a boom or popped loose logs, we'd be there driving eye pegs in them, hauling them behind our rock, fattening up Henderson's pockets and putting a few nickels in our own. Most salvagers wait until the storm dies and the sea calms before heading out, but Henderson wanted us to "get a jump," so out he sent us at the height of gales, into riptides, the darkest nights, because "that, my boys, is when the others hide under the covers, and you alone will harvest the presents from the Lord. And if by His will yea be drowned, well, hell's bells, that's your destiny."...

A mile south of the entrance, a tug dove and bucked, fighting the waves with a three-section log boom behind it. It was dusk. We got ready to go out. We donned sou'westers, tied the cuffs tight with line hoping to keep out at least some of the sea, laid out spikes, eyes, lengths of line, a boom chain, sharpened our knives and marlin spikes, stoked the galley stove under the coffeepot, cranked up the diesel, and cast off from the buoy.

The wind gusted but the sea in the cove stayed a chop; waves could never get in. Eagle Island protected it to the south, leaving a narrow twisting channel to the east and an even narrower opening—a few boats wide—next to the Swede's island to the southwest. There was only one menace in the cove—the wind. The southeast gales would slam into the curve of cliffs and turn and funnel back out with undiminished force past the Swede's island, right into the face of inward-rushing waves. Hell for anyone trying to cross the bar. We headed out at dusk...

The tug reared as she slammed into a wave, and her saw-toothed bow pointed at the clouds. She hung for a moment at the crest, tipped forward, and hurled herself down the back. The propeller lifted clear into the air and its vibrations rattled the iron plates of the stove. I clung to the galley sink and when we hit the bottom of the trough with a bone-jarring thud, the kerosene lamp went out and green water ran a foot deep past the cabin. Then the next wave came and the bow lifted and we surged out of the safety of the cove. Jordan the skipper laughed, loud and self-satisfied. He was still too young to get angry at life, too young to worry about death right there beside him, so he stood cheerfully at the helm in his swaying pilothouse with a smile on his creaseless face. He was never perplexed by the violence of a storm, piloted the tug as if he didn't notice, and in no way felt threatened by the fact that the ocean was trying its best to send us straight to hell. He loved the sea. Loved the creaky tug, loved his dumb but cheery wife, his dough-ball baby daughter, his modest little house under the cedars near Dundarave which he spent every spare moment reshaking, patching, painting, beautifying. He was blessed...

Then we turned west, taking the seas abeam so that we both rolled and plunged. All we had to do was wait and not be blown ashore. The logs were coming; they had to, we knew the winds and currents; we knew our sea. The booms would be breaking up soon and the logs drifting north by northwest, pushed shoreward by the wind, herded by the tide, and they would come like cows home to the stable, toward the jagged bluffs of that nameless bight ahead, where bottom suddenly shoaled and the waves rose up in rage before shattering into foam. But not before hurling everything they had brought: driftwood, floats, nets, lost boats, halfway up the bluff to lodge in crevices and crags.

Jordan had turned the tug bow into the seas, kept the throttle low, and braced himself against the cabinside with his shoulder to have one hand free for his coffee. When he spotted the first log, he eased the tug alongside, and I waited knee-deep in breaking sea with a pike pole. Then harpooned it. I clung to the pole for dear life, waiting for the tug and log to bob in harmony. In that moment of calm at the bottom of a trough, a mere blink of an eye, I yanked an eye spike and lanyard from my belt, threw myself down on my knees to hammer in the spike, yanked out the pike, fed out line, and cleated the bitter end.

By midnight we had done well; we were towing our fifth log toward the safe lee of our rock. The wind still raged, but the moon peeked out and threw shreds of light on the churning sea. Rounding the rock, Jordan slowed. I hauled in the line to prevent it from slacking and fouling the prop, uncleated it, and lashed it to the boom chain that linked the other logs to shore.

—from *Ghost Sea* (2006)

KING SALMON ON THE BC COAST
Edith Iglauer (1917–)

Trolling boats, with their outriggers, paravanes and downriggers, patiently sweep the coastal waters. With multiple combinations of hook-bearing lines, suspended on each side from long slender booms, their spidery image presents an intriguing sight. As Iglauer has written, each year, from spring through fall, these commercial boats appear "like large birds, on the coastal waters of British Columbia. They seem to sit motionless on the surface, but they are moving gently at a speed of around two knots. They are trollers—with a lacework of lines and hooks hanging into the sea from their poles—searching for salmon."

After an hour, there was a familiar sharp tug on the wheel which meant that John was back in the cockpit, in charge of steering again. I went out to join him while he pulled in lines, winding the leaders up and putting them away neatly for the night, with a new pile of salmon in the fish box. He looked at me with a tired smile, rubbing his hands. "It's very bad to keep hitting your hands on the gurdy; it really hurts tonight." He looked around. "I think everybody's gone," he said. "Very few fishermen stay out as long as I do." "Why do you stay out so long?" I asked.

He pushed back his visor. "I suppose because I like it. I love it, as a matter fact. The romance of the thing is so thrilling. The salmon start from six or seven hundred miles up the McGregor River or Skeena River, wandering as fingerlings all the way down through log booms and pulp mills and booming grounds and pollution in the Fraser River until they finally make it to the Gulf of Georgia, out among all the dogfish and seals and every other kind of predator, into the Queen Charlotte Sound; and then they turn around and go back through the trollers, sea lions, seals, gillnetters and sewers, and two hundred thousand sportfishermen in the Gulf of Georgia, up through all the pollution of the Fraser River, into the hundreds of creeks on this coast, to spawn. Think of it! And I've got to outguess the depths they feed at, and when to speed up and slow down, the colour and shape of the lures, the size, type, and weight of the hooks, and the colour of the water. There are some shades of blue where you seem to find coho, but spring salmon are usually in brownish-colour water. I have to remember patterns of runs of various previous years. What I don't know is what's going on under the water." He interrupted himself to nod at a log that was floating by us at a fair distance, with one long-necked cormorant riding on it. "Look, there's a one-seater," he said. "I guess he's a grouchy only child, like me."

John abruptly turned to give his full attention to the line he was pulling in. He unclipped the nearest leader from the mainline, playing his end with subtle grace, as if he were operating a marionette on a single string. I saw a tail flash above the water, creating a great stir of foam, and spied silver glints beneath the surface, which indicated the presence of a very large salmon. The gyrations of the salmon, which was fighting for its life, became more and more frenzied. John stepped back and forth, one minute playing the line off the stern, and the next, as the big fish swung around, moving along the starboard side. John was leaning far out now, grinding his teeth with the effort of holding on to his end of that colourless lifeline of monofilament. Then, as his left hand gripped the line, he reached down with all his strength to bring the salmon's head above water. With a swoop of his long arm, he cracked the frantic salmon on the head with the gaff and, with lightning speed, hooked it into the salmon. Grunting with the effort of lifting the huge fish, he dropped it into the fish box, where its head and tail spilled over both ends. I was dazzled by the iridescent pinks, turquoise, and greens that shimmered among the scales of its powerful long body—as if John had dropped a rainbow onto the shining white boards of the fish box. As I watched, life ebbed away, and minutes later the elegant, glowing creature, which had overflowed its bounds and overwhelmed my senses, was transformed into the lustreless, lifeless fish that was rapidly becoming rigid. I looked back and forth from that aristocrat of the salmon family to John, with awe. "What a battle you two put up!" I said...

It was after six. The afternoon had become grey and cloudy, but now, in early evening, the sun was shining in a clear blue sky. John eviscerated the great spring he had caught, making two little ticks with his long knife at the top of the abdominal cavity and gutting the fish. The first thing he removed was the air sac, which, he explained, was a depth-control mechanism that stores the air the gills take out of the water. He threw it overboard, and the long, pink, tubelike bladder floated away on the surface of the sea, attracting a full quorum of seagulls, whose raucous cries filled the air when he threw the rest of the guts over his shoulder.

I looked at the big, round, sad eyes of the lifeless salmon, at his gaping mouth, and said, "I wish he had gotten away."
—from *Fishing with John* (1988)

SUNDAY MORNING RITUAL
ON THE GOVERNMENT WHARF
Audrey Thomas (1935–   )

The red-painted government wharf is often a gathering place for boaters and fishers around the isolated islands of Canada's west coast. Poignantly, in some places, now-dilapidated red docks are all that remain of abandoned communities whose disillusioned settlers fled the loneliness and poverty of their Pacific isles. Among the vessels regularly converging at these floats were trollers, trawlers and the live-tank cod-boats of this narrative.

Afterward, after they had smelled the yeast and kneaded the dough and made a tiny loaf for Robert in a muffin tin, she covered the bread and left it near the still-warm stove and took the child down to the wharf to watch the fishermen. There were three boats in: the *Trincomali*, the *Sutil* and the *Mary T* and they jostled one another in the slightly choppy water. She looked out toward the other islands for Tom, but couldn't see him. Then carefully she and the little boy went down the ramp to the lower dock, where most of the activity was taking place. A few of the Indians she knew by sight, had seen them along the road or in the little store which served that end of the Island; but most of the ten or so people on the dock or sitting on the decks of boats were strangers to her and she felt suddenly rather presumptuous about coming down at all, like some sightseer—which was, of course, exactly what she was.

"Do you mind if we come down?" she called above the noise of the hysterical gulls and a radio which was blaring in one of the cabins. Two young men in identical red-plaid lumberjackets were drinking beer and taking a break on the deck of the *Mary T*. They looked up at her as she spoke, looked without curiosity, she felt, but simply recognizing her as a fact, like the gulls or the flapping fish, of their Sunday morning.

"Suit yourself, Missus," said an older man who seemed to be in charge.

"But mind you don't slip on them boards."

She looked down. He was right, of course. The main part of the lower dock was, by now, viscous and treacherous with blood and the remains of fish gut. The men in their gumboots stepped carefully. The kill had been going on for at least an hour and the smell of fish and the cry of gulls hung thick in the heavy air. There was an almost palpable curtain of smell and sound and that, with the sight of the gasping fish, made her dizzy for a moment, turned the wharf into an old-fashioned wood-planked roundabout such as she had clung to, in parks, as a child, while she, the little boy, the Indians, the gulls, the small-eyed, gasping fish, the grey and swollen sky spun round and round in a cacophony of sound and smell and pure sensation. She willed herself to stop, but felt slightly sick—as she often had on the actual roundabouts of her childhood—and buried her face in the sweet-smelling hair of her child, as if he were a posy. She breathed deeply, sat up, and smiled. No-one had seen—except perhaps the two young Indians. Everyone else was busy. She smiled and began to enjoy and register what she was seeing.

Everywhere there were fish in various stages of life or death. Live cod swam beneath the decks of the little boats, round and round, bumping into one another as though they were part of some mad children's game, seeking desperately for a way out to the open sea. Then one of the men, with a net, would scoop up a fish, fling it on to the wharf where it would be clubbed by another man and disembowelled swiftly by a third, the guts flung overboard to the raucous gulls. Often the fish were not dead when they were gutted. She could see that, and it should have mattered. The whole thing should have mattered: the clubbing, the disembowelment, the sad stupid faces of the cod with their receding chins and silly Chinamen's beards. Yet instead of bothering, it thrilled her, this strange Sunday morning ritual of death and survival.

The fish were piled haphazardly in garbage cans, crammed in, tails any old way, and carried up the ramp by two of the men to be weighed on the scales at the top. The sole woman, also Indian and quite young, her hair done up in curlers under a pale pink chiffon scarf, carefully wrote down the weights as they were called out. "Ninety-nine." "Seventy-eight." Hundreds of pounds of cod to be packed in ice until the truck came and took them to the city on the evening ferry boat. And at how much a pound, she wondered. Fish was expensive in the city—too expensive, she thought—and wondered how much, in fact, went to these hard-working fishermen. But she dared not ask. Their faces, if not hostile, were closed to her, intent upon the task at hand. There was almost a rhythm to it, and although they did not sing, she felt the instinctual lift and drop and slice of the three who were actually responsible for the kill. If she had been a composer she could have written it down. One question from her and it might all be ruined. For a moment the sun slipped out, and she turned her face upward, feeling very happy and alive just to be there, on this particular morning, watching the hands of these fishermen, hands that glittered with scales, like mica, in the sunlight, listening to the thud of the fish, the creaking and wheeling of the gulls. A year ago, she felt, the whole scene would have sickened her—now, in a strange way, she understood and was part of it. Crab-like, she could feel a new self forming underneath the old, brittle, shell—could feel herself expanding, breaking free.

—from "Kill Day on the Government Wharf" (1967)

CRABBING

Joe Denham (1975–)

The Dungeness crab fishery continues to be one of the most valuable fisheries in the Pacific region, accounting for approximately 34 percent of the total wild shellfish landed in BC. However, the cyclical nature of crab stocks, reduced catches, lower market value and increased costs strain the economic viability of the fishery. Here crab fisherman Francis "Ferris" Wichbaun expresses cynicism toward his hard calling, alluding in passing to his tangled relationship with the two women in his life— his wife, Anna, and his mistress, Jin Su.

There isn't much in the traps. There hasn't been for years now. Still I come out every week and haul up whatever crab might have wandered in over the two-week soak I've given my fifteen-pot strings of gear. Over the years of fishing the Sunshine Coast I've developed a system. The commercial licence I bought with my boat, the *Gulf Prevailer,* allows me to fish 225 traps. So I keep 300 in the water at all times. Because who's ever going to check? I have 150 here in the inlet and 150 in the sandy shallows of Thormanby Island, a small island two and a half nautical miles off the Halfmoon Bay government dock, which is just up the road from our house. So, ten strings on the inside and ten on the outside. Starting Mondays I haul two to four strings a day, weather depending. Each night I hang my catch in old milk crates from the dock and the crab live in there, piled on top of each other as only hearty crustaceans can.

I hate crab. Mostly I think they've been the ruin of me, little private devils that sucked me in with their abundance and commanding market value when I first began fishing, only to all but disappear and sink to an abysmal value the very year I'd finally gathered enough money and gumption to put a down payment on this $450,000 licence and worthless tin can of a boat I've signed my life away to. Of course the reality is they're just crab. I sucked myself in. And despite all Anna's petitioning and tears, I refuse to sell and put the money toward a decent house because I don't know what else I would do with myself. I've found, among other things, that I'm a seaman, through and through...

It's a hard job, crabbing. The traps are a good one hundred pounds empty; the crabs are cantankerous at best; the rotten squid and clam I swap out of the bait cups reeks; and much of the year the weather is changeable and cold. But I work at my own pace, and I work alone. One of the things I've come to realize since meeting Jin Su is that I want and need to spend a fair bit of time alone. Often, once I've nearly finished setting a string out, I shut the engine down and leave the last trap on deck with the end of the float line tied off to the starboard rail. I sit back on deck if the weather is fair, or in my little aft cabin if it's not, and listen. To the birds ruffling and screeching in the wind, water lapping the hull. I like the space the sea affords, the instant openness of casting off from the grid of wires and roads which is the human world.

—from *The Year of Broken Glass* (2011)

WASTING THE SEA
Donna Morrissey (1956–   )

The destruction of the Newfoundland fishery is a matter of historical re-cord. It's a horrific story of human abuse of the environment. Morrissey's novel evokes the human dimension of that "rape of the mother"—the sea—through ignorance, willfulness and malpractice. Here, the fisher-man, Sylvanus, looks on helplessly as "big industry" wantonly squanders irreplaceable resources, and destroys not only fish stock but a whole way of life for outport fishermen. The scene is set in the period spring to fall 1960.

His first day on the water, and he near trembled from the want of it. Yet it was the mother's nervousness that took his mind. He felt it, swear to God, he felt it: her constant shifting, even on the dullest day; her quick leaps from a breeze to a near gale with no warning; her uncalled-for storms up to the end of April; and those long morn-ings of glassy stillness throughout the latter part of May. He knew the wind to be her accomplice, but it were as though the sun and moon held vigil, too, for it was a queer light on the water these days, and he kept searching skyward for a reading of something to come. More precisely, it was what *didn't* come. Two weeks, three weeks, four weeks into the season before a small stream of cod, half the size of four years before, swam wearily to his jiggers.

He near wept. No wonder she was tossing and fretting beneath him. No wonder she was reluctant to yield to his jiggers. He caught sight of a dragger that had crept but a quarter mile sou'west of him, and two more sitting a few miles farther out.

"Bastards!" he spat, watching the one closest to him steaming even closer, two miles farther in than she ought to be by law, the bright orange bobbers of some fisherman's net quickly sinking be-neath its hull. When he thought the beast would swamp him, it cut its engines, engulfing the sea with quiet. The creaking of her winches sounded over the sea, and a mumble of voices as the men aboard milled starboard, leaning over the bulwark. She was raising her net. Lifting his paddles, Sylvanus rowed within a few hundred yards of the mammoth beast, shading his eyes as the iron-shod slabs of wood rose dripping out of the water, thudding heavily against the wooden side of the trawler as the clanging chains winched them upward. The ocean beneath started broiling, foaming white as the net breeched.

"Jeezus!" He knew from talk the size of a trawler's nets, but he'd not seen one, and he stared in awe now, as the thousand-foot netting rose out of the sea, its bulbous shape gushing back water and vibrating with its thousands of fish all crushed together and bulging, strangling, wriggling out through the mesh. The cranking of the winches grew louder as the net rose abreast of the gunnels. A cry cut forth from the men, and Sylvanus stared disbelievingly as the net split dead centre and its cargo of fish—redfish, mostly—started falling, slowly at first, as though the hand of God held it mid-air, but then with a turbulent swoosh, back into the sea.

"Jeezes," and he stared disbelievingly as the mass of redfish floated on the surface like a bloodied stain growing bigger and bigger as the waves took them, spreading them farther and farther outward and toward where he was now standing in his boat. Loud, angry cries grew from the men abandoning the trawler's gunnels. Black smoke spurted out of her stacks, signalling the trawler's return to the open sea, leaving in its wake the drowned redfish spreading like a ruptured sore upon the face of the sea.

Within minutes Sylvanus's boat was encompassed by the fish now drifting on their backs, their eyes bulging out of their sockets like small hen eggs, their stomachs bloating out through their mouths in thin, pink, membrane sacs. Gulls flapped and squawked frenziedly, clutching onto the bellies of the fish, jabbing at the pink sacs till the membranes broke, spilling out the guts. The sea of red broke, and Sylvanus clutched his side sickeningly as he took in the spread of creamy white pods now floating before him. Mother-fish. Thousands of them. A great, speckled gull perched atop one of the pods nearest him, jabbing at her belly, weakening it, rupturing it, till the mother's roe trickled out like spilt milk.

Who, who, Sylvanus silently cried, would accept such sacrifice in the name of hunger? And he sat back, bobbing in his little wooden boat upon the giant expanse of blue ocean, his pitiful few fish at his feet, and he felt his smallness, his minuscule measure against a sphere where thousands of fish can be flung to the gulls thousands of times and count for nothing. He thought of the mother-fish he'd saved from his jiggers over the years, and her sacs of roe, and he drew his eyes now back to the frenzy of the gulls jabbing at her belly, spilling her guts, her unlived life, into the sea, and he weakened, seeing in the mother's fate his own. He rose, churning with anger at the stupidity, the *stupidity* of it, and shook both fists at the pillagers, roaring, "Bastards! You goddamned bastards! You stupid, goddamned bastards!"

—from *Sylvanus Now* (2005)

HALIBUT COVE HARVEST
Kenneth Leslie (1892–1974)

Leslie reflects on the effects that new technology—from dories to steam-driven trawlers—has on the East Coast fishing industry.

The kettle sang the boy to a half-sleep;
and the stir, stir of the kettle's lid
drummed a new age
into the boy's day-dream.
His mind strove with the mind of steam
and conquered it
and pressed it down and shaped it
to the panting giant
whose breath lies heavy on the world.

This is a song of harvest;
the weather thickens with a harsh wind
on this salt-seared coast;
offshore a trawler, smoke-smearing the horizon,
reaps the sea.

Here on the beach
in the cove of the handliner
rain flattens the ungathered dulse
and no cheek reddens to the rain.
From the knock-kneed landing
a faltering path is lost among the rocks
to a door that is closed with a nail.
Seams widen and the paint falls off in curling flakes
from the brave, the bold so little time ago,
the dory high and dry,
anchored in hungry grass.

This is the song of harvest:
the belching trawler raping the sea,
the cobweb ghosts against the window
watching the wilderness uproot the doorsill with a weed.

—from *By Stubborn Stars and Other Poems* (1938)

GOOD-BYE TO ALL THAT
E. Annie Proulx (1935–   )

The following article appears in the Gammy Bird, *American novelist
E. Annie Proulx's imaginary weekly newspaper of a small, fictional town
set on the tip of Newfoundland's Great Northern Peninsula. It depicts
the disastrous effect of dwindling fish stocks on individual fishermen of
Newfoundland.*

There are some days it just doesn't pay to get up. Harold Nightingale
of Port Anguish knows this better than anyone. It's been a disastrous
fishing season for Port Anguish fishermen. Harold Nightingale has
caught exactly nine cod all season long. "Two years ago," he said,
"we took 170,000 pounds of cod off Bumpy Banks. This year—less
than zero. I dunno what I'm going to do. Take in washing, maybe."

To get the nine cod Mr. Nightingale spent $423 on gas, $2,150 on licenses, $4,670 on boat repair and refit, $1,200 on new nets. To make matters worse, he has suffered the worst case of sea-pups in his 31 years of fishing. "Wrists swelled up to my elbows," he said.

Last Friday Harold Nightingale had enough. He told his wife he was going out to haul his traps for the last time. He wrote out an advertisement for his boat and gear and asked her to place it in the *Gammy Bird.*

He and his four-man crew spent the morning hauling traps (all were empty) and were on their way back in when the wind increased slightly. A moderate sea built up and several waves broke over the aft deck. Just outside the entrance of Port Anguish harbour the boat heeled over to starboard and did not recover. Skipper Nightingale and the crew managed to scramble into the dories and abandon the sinking boat. The vessel disappeared beneath the waves and they headed for shore. The boat was not insured.

"The worst of it is that she sank under the weight of empty traps. I would have taken a little comfort if it had been a load of fish." On his arrival at home Mr. Nightingale cancelled his classified ad.

—from *The Shipping News* (1993)

It took the sea a thousand years,
A thousand years to trace
The granite features of this cliff,
In crag and scarp and base.

It took the sea an hour one night,
An hour of storm to place
The sculpture of these granite seams
Upon a woman's face.

— E.J. Pratt, "Erosion"
from *Many Moods* (1932)

CHAPTER VII
PERIL AND LOSS

The twin themes of peril and loss on the sea conjure up dramatic images of storm, shipwreck and human endurance. Seafarers know the experience all too well. For they recognize the ocean not only as a potentially wild and tempestuous place, but as an awe-inspiring power. Since ancient times they have offered prayers and supplications to placate these forces. Even in secular times, invocations and epithets can break forth spontaneously when the chips are down. Current folklore even regards the international distress signal SOS as appealing to a Higher Power to "Save Our Souls." (In fact, it's a quick and unmistakable sequence of letters in Morse code—three dots, three dashes and three dots). News of marine disaster evokes fascination, shock, grief and compassion. Always there exists a tension between those at sea undergoing the experience, and those ashore anxiously awaiting their return—often without knowing what has befallen their loved ones. Well-turned tales pick up this painful irony of memories and anticipations speaking past one another. Rescuers themselves encounter traumatic experiences. The history of attempted rescues is often darkened by tragedy. Poetically, the sea emerges in this context as a grand metaphor incorporating rites of passage, lost innocence, lost relationships and lost faith.

WHALERS LOST
Chief James Wallas (1907–   )

Whaling is deeply rooted in the traditions of the First Nations societies of the west coast of British Columbia. Once a major component of their livelihood, it found expression in cultural and ritual functions. Although highly controversial today, the revival of whaling among First Nations people represents for them a central link with their past: their identity, their physical, mental and spiritual well-being.

The grey whale makes an annual migration of 8,000 kilometres from summer calving in the Bering Sea to the winter feeding grounds off Baja California. Slower and smaller than other whale species, it follows the coast closely, and is therefore a relatively easy target for whalers. Yet, as the Kwakiutl legend reminds us, it would be dangerous for hunters to belittle this powerful and wily whale.

The chief whaler of the village was a man of distinction. He owned his own large canoe dug out of a giant cedar tree.

One day he said, "The food supply of our village is getting low. We must prepare to go whaling."

Several men were anxious to go with him. They packed water in the canoe, but no food. Their equipment was made ready.

The whalers moved down the channel toward the open sea. They looked for the blue, grey or finback whale but would not take the sperm or killer whale that they could not use.

Soon Bulgina, a small grey whale, was spotted. The chief whaler thrust his harpoon and it imbedded itself deep behind the whale's front flipper. The creature blew out a mighty gust of water from his blow hole and started to submerge.

The whale moved off, going deeper and deeper into the water as it went. Sealskin floats had been attached to the line to impede the whale's progress and to prevent him from sinking when he died. They would let the whale tow them until it tired, then finish it off with lances.

But the whale did not seem to tire. It towed them out to the open sea. Although it was pulling a heavy load, it moved very fast.

"It must be the biggest grey I have ever harpooned," exclaimed the chief whaler.

The whale pulled them all day and all night without slowing his pace. The men dreamed about getting home to the feast that would be awaiting them. After the feast each member of their families would receive chunks of whale meat the size of his hand cut to the depth of the whale's backbone. They thought about how good the strips of blubber would taste smoked and boiled.

For four more days the whale pulled them out to sea. It was getting weaker but so were they. Finally they cut the rope because they were afraid they would not be able to find their way back.

They paddled a long, long time in the direction they had come from. Day seemed to blend into night. Then they saw the shore of Vancouver Island.

But they could not find the channel that led to their village. Weakness overcame them. They pulled into shore and got out of the canoe and lay on the ground, where they perished.

—from Pamela Whitaker in *Kwakiutl Legends*,
as told by Chief James Wallas (1981)

LAST SONG
Robin Skelton (1925–1997)

Reaching into
a crack in the rock
to grab the devilfish,
his wrist
was trapped fast
by a great oyster;
none of his kin
could get it out.

Nothing would pry him
loose; no rock

could chip the lip
of the thick shell,
and the tide was rising.
The Spirits of Tide,
he sang to his people,
they are coming!

Look to yourselves!
Bent over, head
bent over, face
turned from the water,
neck straining,
Look to yourselves!
Forced to retreat,
they stood waiting,
listening, learning,
as the sea
surged over
rock and man
and the last of
all last songs,
Spirits of Tide,
they are coming, coming.

—from *One Leaf Shaking* (1996)

FISHIN' IN A DORY
Marq de Villiers (1940–　)

East Coast fishing schooners with their rugged crews and dories worked in all weathers. A fleet of schooners would head offshore and, on reaching the cod banks, would drop off their dories and two-man crew to trawl independently. When fog prevailed, the dorymen could easily become disoriented and find themselves unable to get back to their mothership.

The men described their being lost at sea as "got away," "got astray" or simply being "adrift." In the days without radio or radar, being "astray" like this could mean death.

In winter if a dory goes astray the men might get picked up by another schooner "or they might pull into Seal Island or maybe they'd manage to rig up a drogue with the anchor and oars and other gear—a sea anchor—and ride it out until it clears and a vessel sees them, or maybe they'll capsize or freeze to death or starve. It ain't the first time it happened."

Many a man went missing. "Many a time I've had to haul men off from the bottom of [an overturned] dory," Matt Mitchell remembers, "and I was shipmates with many who were drownded. The very last trip I made that happened. I was never in a dory that was upset myself, but I was into many where we had the divil of a job keeping the water out of her. You'd try to keep her head to, you know, but... sometimes the only thing that would save you was the fish, she was so full of fish the waves didn't have a chance to get down into the dory." Very few fishermen could swim. The water was too cold, and they felt it pointless to learn.

Nobody liked to talk much about the hazards. "It was quite a thing to be in a boat wit' your brothers an' see a dory bottom up an' go an' pick up the dory and couldn't find the men... Back home, you'd be asked, did you have a dirty time, or, how bad was it, but you'll never come home and tell anybody that you have a narrer escape or if you didn't, you didn't tell those things, you forget." It was fate, destiny, just something that happened, luck or ill luck. "There was a dory, overturned. Two fellers and this sea came an' fetched 'er o'er. The one feller couldn't swim—an' the sea drug him away from the dory. An' the other feller—all he could do was hang on. Just an unlucky sea—an unlucky sea come along. An' see this feller he wasn't lookin' you know—he had his head down lookin' in the tub coilin' the trawl. Just an unlucky sea, nobody's fault." ...

For the families, it was very bad: when a man was lost at sea, swept overboard by a heavy sea, or knocked off deck by a boom, or lost in a dory, or in a dory that swamped, the vessel would come back to port with a flag at half mast, as the *Bluenose* did when Bertie "Boodle" Demone drowned in 1922, or Philip Hanhams was swept overboard on a winter trip in 1938. "Ah, there was a lot of scared times for the folks at home," an old man remembered in Lunenburg after the *Bluenose* had gone. "Times that wasn't nice, you [know]. I 'member a boy of 19 once, an' his dory overturned an' he was lost, an' his mother saw the boat come in with the flag at half mast, but she didn't know who." Some of the old sea captains' houses had a flat platform on the roofline that they called the widow's walk, from which the women could see the sea, where they could watch for the boats coming back home, watching for the flag at half mast. There's a house like that on Pelham Street in Lunenburg, built for a sea captain who never came home to live in it, lost at sea when he took to a dory to rescue a boy, his nephew, and never came back. Mostly the body would be missing, but sometimes not, and then they'd put it in the hold where they iced the fish until it was home for burial, but that didn't affect the selling of the fish—what the buyers didn't know couldn't hurt, could it?

Some survived, some didn't. Nobody's fault, as they said.

—from *Witch in the Wind: The True Story
of the Legendary* Bluenose (2007)

THE GROUND SWELL
E.J. Pratt (1882–1964)

A ground swell is a broad and deep surging of the sea, usually caused by a distant storm. Used colloquially, the term describes a growing shift in public opinion. Poetically, however, it intimates an eerie presentiment of some impending tragedy or trauma.

Three times we heard it calling with a low,
Insistent note; at ebb-tide on the noon;
And at the hour of dusk, when the red moon
Was rising and the tide was on the flow;
Then, at the hour of midnight once again,

Though we had entered in and shut the door
And drawn the blinds, it crept up from the shore
And smote upon a bedroom window-pane;
Then passed away as some dull pang that grew
Out of the void before Eternity
Had fashioned out an edge for human grief;
Before the winds of God had learned to strew
His harvest-sweepings on a winter sea
To feed the primal hungers of a reef.

—from *Newfoundland Verse* (1923)

THE SAILOR AND HIS BRIDE
Isabella Valancy Crawford (1850–1887)

"Let out the wet dun sail, my lads,
    The foam is flying fast;
It whistles on the fav'ring gale,
    To-night we'll anchor cast.
What though the storm be loud, my lads,
    And danger on the blast;
Though bursting sail swell round and proud,
    And groan the straining mast;
The storm has wide, strong wings, my lads,
    On them our craft shall ride,
And dear the tempest swift that brings
    The sailor to his bride."

"Fear not the tempest shrill, my heart,
    The tall, white breakers' wrath;
I would not have the wild winds still
    Along the good ship's path.
The ship is staunch and strong, my heart,
    The wind blows to the strand;

Why tremble? for its fiercest song
  But drives the ship to land.
Be still, nor throb so fast, my heart,
  The storm but brings, betide
What may to ship and straining mast,
  My sailor to his bride."

Blow soft and low, and sigh, O gale!
  Sob, sea, upon the bar !
No more o'er thee the ship shall fly
  White-winged as vesper star.
Roll up the shattered mast, O gale!
  Upon the yellow strand,
A dead man's form cast, gently cast,
  Upon the waiting land.
And when again thy breath, O gale!
  Wails o'er the vaulting tide,
Bear not on hurtling wings of death
  A sailor to his bride.

—from *The Collected Poems of Isabella Valancy Crawford* (1905)

RESCUE AT SEA

James Richards (1931–2014) and Marlene Richards (1938–   )
with Eric Hustvedt

*In December 1912 the Nova Scotia–built three-masted schooner,
W.N. Zwicker, under the command of Captain Andy Publicover
(1877–1960), was returning in ballast in heavy winter weather from
New York to home port in Bridgewater, Nova Scotia. En route she undertook a series of daring manoeuvres to rescue the stricken crew of a waterlogged American schooner. The following year this act of great courage
was formally recognized by President Woodrow Wilson and celebrated at
a festive public occasion in Bridgewater.*

A nor'wester started to blow as we left our berth in New York, so all we needed was a tow as far as Flushing Bay, where we let go the hawser at two in the afternoon, December 11. The wind was so strong that all we could carry were our lower sails. We were amazed to find ourselves blown all the way to Pollock Rip Shoal by daylight the next morning. Then it started to blow even harder. We had to take in our spanker and reef our mainsail. Besides the reefed mainsail, all we left on her was the whole foresail, fore staysail and one jib. Even then the vessel nearly capsized at times.

When we got abeam of Cape Cod, I went below to get my first rest of the trip. A few hours later we started to roll deep, so Charles, who was on watch, woke me to ask if we should take in more sail.

I took my glasses (binoculars) on deck for a look around. It was early afternoon. The gale was still blowing and now there were snow squalls. The visibility was poor, but I was able to sight a three-masted schooner about three points on our lee bow about five miles away, heading to the south'ard. I saw that her sails were all blown away, so I ordered the man at the wheel to keep off and run down towards her. I had a couple of the crew go forward to haul down the jib.

As we approached, I saw she was waterlogged. Her decks were level with the water and she was floating on her lumber cargo. When we got close, I could see her crew of seven lashed to the top of her furled up spanker boom. They were getting soaked to the skin by the mountainous seas breaking over the vessel from stem to stern. None of them had oilskins and I knew they couldn't survive the night.

Our own vessel was rolling and pitching so much, I didn't think we could launch a boat, so I manoeuvred the *Zwicker* closer under the lee of the other vessel in the hope the wind and sea would soon go down. We hauled down the forestaysail and hove to, heading to the north. Because we were so light, and the other vessel was so deep in the sea, we drifted faster to leeward. After a couple of hours with no change in the weather, we could just see the other vessel to windward through the snow squalls.

I felt if we lost sight of her I could feel I'd done all I could for her crew. I wasn't sailing away; I was drifting away by the wind and sea.

Also, if I tried to rescue them with a single-hand dory in such a sea, I would be risking the lives of my own crew.

Just before the schooner disappeared from sight, I knew I couldn't leave them to die.

I would have to work fast because it would be dark in about two hours. So, I began to wear ship to get close to the distressed vessel again.

I wanted to go in the dory by myself and keep the crew out of danger. But, as I didn't think I could row against the wind alone, I called for a volunteer. [My brother] Charles stepped forward, but I wouldn't let him go. He was the only other man capable of navigating the *Zwicker* back to land. If we were both lost, our own crew would be doomed, too.

Then a seaman named Fred Richards, the only unmarried member of the crew, called out, "I'll go with you, Captain."

I didn't want his family to hold his death against me or my family in case we were lost, so I said to the rest of the crew, "If this young man loses his life tonight, I want you all to bear witness he volunteered of his own free will, with no pressure from me."

After giving instructions to Charles on our position and the course for Cape Sable, we lashed two thwarts, two pairs of oars, four pairs of tholepins and a bucket into the dory and hove the *Zwicker* around to windward of the water-logged schooner.

Our first task was to get the dory into the water and safely away from our own vessel. It was touch and go, because the *Zwicker* was rolling so deep that the bilge was coming out of the water halfway to her keel. The men had to let go the dory tackles at just the right time or the dory would be drawn under the *Zwicker* as she rolled away to windward, then crushed underneath her when she rolled back again.

The crew waited to drop us down at the very moment the vessel rolled deepest on our side. We let the tackles go at just the right second, but we were still lucky to get away with our lives. Rowing as hard as we could from the moment we hit the water, the dory still got drawn under the *Zwicker*'s quarter as she rolled away. As she was coming back we crouched in the bottom of the boat, waiting for the worst to happen.

Then we began to feel the leeward roll of the *Zwicker* send us back out from under her stern. We could only pray we would be pushed out of harm's way before she slammed down again.

Our prayers were answered, but it was a close call. We felt the quarter of the *Zwicker* scrape against us and feared our bow would be pulled so low the dory would fill. As we scrambled to the oars and tried again to get away, we were relieved to see very little water in the boat. A few moments later we were out of danger from our own vessel and were rowing with the wind and sea toward the waterlogged schooner, a quarter mile away.

Reaching her, we rowed around her stern on the way to her lee side and saw by her nameplate she was the *Henry R. Tilton* out of Maine. Close under her lee, I shouted to the master that I was going to try and save them. I knew that manoeuvring the dory close enough to the *Tilton* for a man to jump into it in stormy winter seas was a difficult and dangerous business, so I told them to follow my instructions exactly.

I had one man unlash himself and come down to the lee rigging. As I instructed, he waited until we were in close enough, then jumped in the stern of our dory and crouched low in the bottom. I had a second man come down and jump in the bow.

Meanwhile, the *Zwicker* had come down around and was hove-to close under the lee of the *Tilton*, so Fred and I were able to row with the wind and the sea back to our own vessel.

My crew were waiting for us with heaving lines, as I'd ordered them. When we were twenty feet away from our own vessel, I told one of the *Tilton*'s crewmen to grab the first line thrown to us, put a boland [bowline] in it and slip it down under his arms. Then he was to jump overboard and let our crew pull him onboard.

I thought this would be the easiest part of the operation, but that seaman almost brought the whole rescue to a sudden end. Once he had the line around himself, he got scared to leave the dory. The crew pulled on the line anyway, bringing the dory in against the side of the *Zwicker* just as she made a deep roll toward us. The crew quickly pulled the man on deck and we just did manage to row far enough away from the *Zwicker*'s hull to keep from getting sucked under her as she rolled away again. The second man jumped in the water when he was supposed to and was pulled onboard the *Zwicker* without mishap.

As each rescued man went onboard our vessel, he would get hot coffee from the cook and warm clothing from the crew, then be taken down to the dining room for a hot meal.

The second trip to the *Tilton* was much harder work than the first one because we had to row against the wind and sea. It seemed to take hours. While we were getting the next pair of shipwrecked sailors in the dory, the *Zwicker* drifted further away, so we were happy to have the help of the wind and sea on the return trip.

When the second pair of seamen were safely onboard the *Zwicker*, we set out for a third trip to the *Tilton*. We were getting tired. It was getting near dark and we had been working at the rescue for nearly two hours. The gale was still blowing, the seas were still high and snow squalls still whirled around us. I decided this would have to be our last trip, even if it meant carrying five men in our small boat.

With the longest and hardest trip, we got the last three men off the doomed schooner. We rowed back with the water up to gunnels, but got the shipwrecked men safely onboard the *Zwicker*. Then our crew threw a line to Fred, who was hauled onboard safely holding onto his oars and thwart. Two lines came out to me. I tied one to myself and the other to the dory painter before I jumped out of the boat with my own oars and thwart. After I made the deck, the crew hauled the dory painter onboard and made it fast to one of the dory tackles. The dory came up onto the deck bow first a short time later.

All we lost was one tholepin.

Fred and I had saved the seven-man crew of a waterlogged vessel from certain death and saved our own rescue boat in the bargain.

We even managed to live through the adventure ourselves.

—from *The Sea in My Blood:*
The Life and Times of Captain Andy Publicover (1986)

The *Titanic*
Gabrielle Roy (1909–1983)

The sinking of the Titanic, *15 April 1912, still resonates from coast to coast in our collective imagination. Gabrielle Roy's story of a childhood social gathering recalls how the raging gale of a Manitoba night brought to mind the horrific loss of that doomed ship some 600 kilometres south of Newfoundland.*

A great ship had been lost at sea, and for a long time, for years even, people talked about it at night gatherings in our Manitoba homes. A mere nothing, perhaps no more than a sharp gust of wind, would bring it back to mind. The raging gale—so vicious that particular night—probably recalled the disaster to us more vividly than usual...

"They were dancing," Monsieur Elie continued, "on board the ship. Dancing," he marvelled, "in mid-ocean!"

"Do they have music to dance to on a boat?"

My uncle Majorique smiled a little at my question, but not to make fun of me. Quite the opposite; my uncle Majorique liked to explain things, and he was good at it, for he had at home a complete set of the *Encyclopaedia Britannica*... So he began telling me about ocean liners: they were equipped with kitchens, pots and pans, libraries, parlours with chandeliers, fresh flowers, games of all sorts for the passengers' recreation, counters at which to settle bills, a small shipboard newspaper, a barber, a masseur, stewards; in short here was a town venturing forth upon the seas... At night it was alive with lights that spilled out over the waves, and there were moments, maybe, when the black water seemed gladdened by them.

And—I know not why—as he kept listing what there was on board the ship, my heart was ill at ease, though I was eager to learn more. When my uncle added that certain completely up-to-date ships even boasted swimming pools, I got a picture at once curious and funny, but one that certainly did not make me laugh; on the contrary, I felt an unknown and terrifying sadness at the thought of people plunging into the water of a swimming pool contained within a vessel itself afloat upon infinite water. My uncle Majorique was answering Monsieur Elie: "True enough, they were dancing, but we must not forget the couples aboard the *Titanic* were almost all newlyweds, Monsieur... on their honeymoons!" ...

I was thinking of those poor people so happy to be together on the ship. Abruptly Monsieur Elie began to scold. He said of them, the folk on the *Titanic,* "Hammerstein! ... Vanderbilt! ... Big bankers from New York! ... Those were the people on the *Titanic!* Millionaires!"

So in fact those poor people were rich!

"Yes," my uncle Majorique agreed, "wealthy couples, handsome, young, happy! ..."

"And they thought their boat proof against all danger," said Monsieur Elie.

"Is there something wrong," I asked them, "about building a sturdy ship?"

Even Monsieur Elie seemed taken aback at my question. He granted that there was nothing wrong about it, probably nothing at all, but it most certainly was wrong to imagine oneself out of the reach of God's wrath. Yet why did he seem so pleased about God's wrath?

"Alas," said my uncle, "the captain had been warned of the presence of icebergs in the neighbourhood. They might still have been saved had only the captain given orders to reduce the vessel's speed. But no; the *Titanic* was cutting through the waves at its normal speed—very fast for those days..."

"An iceberg?" I asked. "What's that?" and I was afraid of the answer.

My uncle Majorique told me how mountains of ice break off from the Labrador ice masses; how unfortunate, even how cruel is our country, since these mountains drift down into the navigation routes... and under water they are seven or eight times larger than what appears on the surface.

So then I had a vivid picture of the graceful, sturdy white ship. With all its portholes brightly aglow, it slipped along our kitchen wall. Then, from Monsieur Elie's side, there moved straight toward the ship the monstrous mountain that had severed itself from

Labrador. And they would meet at a point where the sea was at its worst... Was there no way to warn them once again? ... For surely the ocean is a vast expanse! ...

—from *Street of Riches* (French original 1955,
English translation 1957)

THE *EMPRESS OF IRELAND*
Herbert P. Wood (1899–1995)

The sinking of the 26,000-ton CPR steamship Empress of Ireland *in the St. Lawrence River on 29 May 1914 triggered shock and horror. Proceeding outbound in fog after having dropped the pilot at Pointe au Père near Rimouski, she had been struck by the inbound collier Storstad. Within fourteen minutes, the* Empress *went to the bottom, taking 1,015 passengers and crew to their grave. Among the passengers were 170 members of the Salvation Army, travelling to London with their thirty-nine piece concert band to attend The Third International Congress of the Salvation Army. On departure from Quebec City the previous evening the band had given an impromptu concert on deck, ending with the old hymn "God be with you till we meet again." Salvationist Herbert Wood's long lament, "The Empress," of which a few lines follow, imagines heroic last moments as the ship sinks beneath the waves.*

> Oh, poignant indeed is the scene on that vessel,
> As husband and wife, clasping hands, side by side,
> Look first at the water, then gaze at each other,
> With new understanding at death's rising tide;
> Young comrades, who seldom would think about Heaven—
> With life all before them—expectant and brave,
> Surrender with gladness their means of escaping,
> And fasten their lifebelts on those they would save.

—from "The Empress" in *Till We Meet Again:
The Sinking of the* Empress of Ireland (1982)

DIVING AND DEATH
ON THE *EMPRESS OF IRELAND*
Kevin F. McMurray

The Empress of Ireland *sank on 29 May 1914 after her collision with the collier* Storstad, *taking over a thousand passengers to their death. As McMurray wrote, she "had barely settled into the muddy bottom of the St. Lawrence River when lead-weighted commercial divers hired by the Canadian Pacific Railway began to make their first probes." Commercial diving equipment had changed little since its invention in 1837. The divers—with American Edward Cossaboom among them—had been hired to recover the bodies of the victims, as well as valuable evidence. The ship lay at a depth of some 130 feet, buffeted by strong currents and tides. From the 1960s onward scuba divers have been attracted by adventure and booty. Six divers—one hard-hat and five scuba—have lost their lives searching the wreck. On 15 April 1999 the wreck became a protected historic site. Many artefacts can now be viewed at the Musée de la Mer (Maritime Museum) in Rimouski, near the scene of the sinking.*

Edward Cossaboom was an experienced professional diver from New York who, day after day, descended to the wreck for [American salvor William] Wotherspoon's joint American-Canadian salvage effort. On that morning the hardworking Cossaboom had already retrieved two bodies from inside the ship and returned them to the surface. Then, on another dive, Cossaboom apparently decided to move forward along the flank of the sloping hull, which was exposed to the faint sunlight from above.

Cossaboom's tender aboard the *Marie Josephine* had been lax in keeping taut his charge's umbilical containing his air supply and tether. Unknown to Cossaboom, his lifeline slackened in a lazy arc behind him as he plodded along the hull in his lead-weighted boots. Suddenly a strong current began to buffet the wreck. Before he could scream his predicament over the phone to his tender, Cossaboom lost his footing and slipped over the side of the hull, plummeting another 65 feet to the bottom, at 140 feet.

Cossaboom knew the real dangers that deep diving presented. For every foot farther he descended, an added load of almost half a ton pressed on the surface of his body. At 140 feet down, on the bottom of the St. Lawrence, that load would exert over sixty tons of pressure on him...

This knowledge surely must have flashed through Cossaboom's mind, along with the fate that awaited him as he plummeted to the bottom, frantically trying to stop his fall. But the pressure differential was too sudden and too great. It sent blood flooding into his heart and lungs, quickly exploding these organs before he could stop his plunge or receive an increase of pressure from his tender to compensate for the crushing depths. By the time he hit the bottom, the invading sea pressure had stripped the flesh from his bones. His skin and organs were pile-driven into the only part of his suit that was resistant to the pressure, his copper diving helmet.

Cossaboom's tender signalled the alarm when he lost communication with his diver. By the time the crew and tenders aboard the *Marie Josephine* realized what had happened, there was little to do but send down a search team for his body. Evidently the rescue divers lost the trail of the umbilical line in the dark depths and couldn't find him. No fresh divers were available to continue the search. A Canadian diver [Wilfred Whitehead] aboard HMCS *Essex* [*sic*], anchored nearby, volunteered to take a look around the wreck. On his first dive, he found what was left of Edward Cossaboom. His body was returned to the *Marie Josephine.* The crew later reported that all that remained of the unfortunate diver was "a jellyfish with a copper mantle and dangling canvas tentacles."

—from *Dark Descent: Diving and the Deadly Allure of the* Empress of Ireland (2004)

DEATH ON VANDERBILT REEF
Ken Coates (1956–   ) and Bill Morrison (1942–   )

Nine "Princess" ships were built by Canadian Pacific between 1907 and 1914 for Canada's West Coast trade. Built in Scotland in 1912, the 2,320-ton passenger-freighter Princess Sophia *began her service that same year. Plying between Seattle, Vancouver and Skagway, Alaska, the Princesses formed a vital economic and social link supporting northern development. Their voyages were not without risk, for among other things, ships in those days had no radar. The* Princess May, *for example, had struck Sentinel Reef in Alaska's Lynn Canal in 1912, as did the* Princess Sophia *in 1913. Both ships survived. Now, however, on 23 October 1918, assailed by gales, extremely rough seas and a blinding snowstorm, the* Princess Sophia *struck Vanderbilt Reef, also in the Lynn Canal. She hung on the rock for two days until she sank, taking all 353 passengers and crew to their deaths. Heavy seas prevented rescue ships from helping.*

For whatever reason, by 2:00 a.m. the ship was steaming down the centre of Lynn Canal, when she should have been closer to the east side. Instead of clearing it by hundreds of yards, she was heading straight for Vanderbilt Reef.

At 2:10 the unthinkable happened. The *Princess Sophia,* steaming at her regular cruising speed of 11 or 12 knots, ran directly onto the middle of the reef. Because the reef was so low in the water, the effect was not like that of running directly into a cliff or an iceberg, which would have stopped the ship dead and crumpled its bow; rather, the bow lifted out of the water and, with a horrible grinding and tearing, slid up and onto the rock. The rapid deceleration—from 11 knots to a standstill in a few yards—threw passengers from their bunks and the crew to the deck. Supplies and furniture crashed about, and the men on the bridge were tossed violently into the bulkheads. The turmoil lasted only a few seconds. Then there was silence, followed by commotion as the passengers and crew picked themselves up. For a time the ship's twin screws continued to turn, feebly grasping for water, until the main engines were stopped and their comforting throb was replaced by the ominous howl of the wind.

The *Sophia* hung suspended; the hull, partly afloat in the shallow water, scraped against the rocks, each creak and groan increasing the passengers' alarm. As a precaution, [Captain] Locke ordered the lifeboats swung out on their davits. But it soon became evident that the ship was not going to shift off the reef, and those aboard, reassured for the moment that they were not about to sink into an icy grave, took stock of their situation...

For nearly forty hours the *Princess Sophia* had sat firmly wedged on Vanderbilt Reef, her stern pointing approximately north into the wind and her bow in the general direction of Juneau. Now the wind and waves began to lift the stern off the reef. Under their force the *Sophia* rose, then swung slowly around in a 180-degree turn, as if on a pivot. The weight of the ship as it turned ground the rocks beneath it "white... as smooth as a silver dollar." Now her bow faced up the channel, into the storm, and the *Princess Sophia* began inexorably to move off the reef into deep water. As she began to turn, passengers and crew ran to the lifeboats. Several were launched, others partly lowered, and a number of passengers clambered into them.

Slowly the *Sophia* turned and then, twisting and grinding, slid backwards off the reef. The rocks ripped gaping holes in her hull, tearing out virtually the entire bottom. Heavy bunker oil poured into the sea and frigid water rushed in, flooding the engine and boiler rooms. The boilers exploded, devastating the lower decks. A number of passengers who had sheltered from the storm below decks were killed by the explosion and the flying debris. Portholes were shattered, allowing the sea to enter even faster. The explosion pushed upwards as well, blowing off part of the deck. As the ship settled and began to slide beneath the waves, the wounds in her hull releasing thousands of gallons of oil into the sea, the dark, cold waters of Lynn Canal reached up to claim their victims. In a matter minutes—just long enough for [wireless operator David] Robinson to send his last, panicked message—the water had reached the pilot house. And then the entire ship was engulfed.

The exact sequence of events aboard the *Princess Sophia* that dark afternoon will never be precisely known. Some of the passengers and crew were dressed for an evacuation, and many were wearing life-jackets. Others, however, were in their cabins, some even in bed. Clearly Captain Locke had not called a general alert, for there was no planned abandonment of ship underway at the time she sank. The uneven preparation shows how quickly the final crisis had developed...

Death came quickly for most who jumped. The water was bitterly cold. Jack London, in his most famous story [*The Sea-Wolf*], captured the essence of a plunge in the north Pacific: "The water was cold—so cold that it was painful. The pang, as I plunged into it, was as quick and sharp as that of fire. It bit to the marrow. It was like the grip of death. I gasped with the anguish and shock of it, filling my lungs before the life-preserver popped me to the surface."

This natural gasping reflex filled the mouths and lungs of the victims with oil congealed by the cold. Blown by the spray and the wind, it stuck to clothes, weighing them down. Those who may have made it into the lifeboats were no better off, for as the captains of the rescue ships had predicted, the boats were immediately swamped on the reef, throwing their human cargo into the water. The two wooden lifeboats capsized and floated upside down; the eight steel ones sank. The extra flotation devices—simply hollow rectangular wooden buoys with ropes attached to them—were useless; the idea that people could cling to them until they were rescued was practical in the Caribbean, perhaps, but absurd in the Lynn Canal. One of these devices was later found smashed on the rocks of Lincoln Island with the bodies of four women tied to it. Mercifully, whether by drowning or choking and suffocating on the oil, within a few minutes nearly all were dead. Some were in the steel coffin that the *Sophia* had become; others floated inert in their life-preservers, an oily mass coating their lungs, mouths, and nostrils. The howl of the storm echoed over Vanderbilt Reef. The *Princess Sophia* was gone, only a few feet of its forward mast visible above the water.

—from *The Sinking of the* Princess Sophia*: Taking the North Down with Her* (1991)

THE HALIFAX EXPLOSION
Hugh MacLennan (1907–1990)

Overshadowed by the cataclysmic events on the Western Front of World War I, the Halifax Explosion of 6 December 1917 is nonetheless recognized as one of the major events that shaped the consciousness of Canada. On that day, two ships collided in the constrained waters of Halifax harbour known as "the Narrows:" the inbound Mont Blanc *carrying over three thousand tons of picric acid, TNT and gun cotton, and the outbound* Imo *carrying cargo marked for Belgian Relief. The collision triggered the largest explosion the world had ever seen. It destroyed the city, killed sixteen hundred people and wounded some nine thousand others. MacLennan describes that fateful moment. Although he is an unreliable witness to the technical and professional aspects of ships and shipping, his historical novel, a classic in Canadian literature, captures the explosion's impact on the port.*

Twenty minutes after the collision there was no one along the entire waterfront who was unaware that a ship was on fire in the harbour. The jetties and docks near the Narrows were crowded with people watching the show, and yet no warning of danger was given. At that particular moment there was no adequate centralized authority in Halifax to give a warning, and the few people who knew the nature of the *Mont Blanc*'s cargo had no means of notifying the town or spreading the alarm, and no comfort beyond the thought that trinitrotoluol [TNT] can stand an almost unlimited heat provided there is no fulminate or explosive gas to detonate it...

Then a needle of flaming gas, thin as the mast and of a brilliance unbelievably intense, shot through the deck of the *Mont Blanc* near the funnel and flashed more than two hundred feet toward the sky. The firemen were thrown back and their hoses jumped suddenly out of control and slashed the air with S-shaped designs. There were a few helpless shouts. Then all movement and life about the ship were encompassed in a sound beyond hearing as the *Mont Blanc* opened up.

Three forces were simultaneously created by the energy of the exploding ship, an earthquake, an air-concussion, and a tidal wave.

These forces rushed away from the Narrows with a velocity varying in accordance with the nature of the medium in which they worked. It took only a few seconds for the earthquake to spend itself and three minutes for the air-expansions to slow down to a gale. The tidal wave travelled for hours before the last traces of it were swallowed in the open Atlantic...

The pressure of the exploding chemicals smashed against the town with the rigidity and force of driving steel. Solid and unbreathable, the forced wall of air struck against Fort Needham and Richmond Bluff and shaved them clean, smashed with one gigantic blow the North End of Halifax and destroyed it, telescoping houses or lifting them from their foundations, snapping trees and lampposts, and twisting iron rails into writhing, metal snakes; breaking buildings and sweeping the fragments of their wreckage for hundreds of yards in its course. It advanced two miles southward, shattering every flimsy house in its path, and within thirty seconds encountered the long, shield-like slope of the Citadel which rose before it.

Then, for the first time since it was fortified, the Citadel was able to defend at least a part of the town. The air-wall smote it, and was deflected in three directions. Thus some of its violence shot skyward at a twenty-degree angle and spent itself in space. The rest had to pour around the roots of the hill before closing in on the town for another rush forward. A minute after the detonation, the pressure was advancing through the South End. But now its power was diminished, and its velocity was barely twice that of a tornado. Trees tossed and doors broke inward, windows split into driving arrows of glass which buried themselves deep in interior walls. Here the houses, after swaying and cracking, were still on their foundations when the pressure had passed...

But long before this, the explosion had become manifest in new forms over Halifax. More than two thousand tons of red hot steel, splintered fragments of the *Mont Blanc*, fell like meteors from the sky into which they had been hurled a few seconds before. The ship's anchor soared over the peninsula and descended through a roof on the other side of the Northwest Arm three miles away. For a few seconds the harbour was dotted white with a maze of splashes, and the decks of raddled ships rang with reverberations and clangs as fragments struck them.

Over the North End of Halifax, immediately after the passage of the first pressure, the tormented air was laced with tongues of flame which roared and exploded out of the atmosphere, lashing downward like a myriad blow-torches as millions of cubic feet of gas took fire and exploded. The atmosphere went white-hot. It grew mottled, then fell to the streets like a crimson curtain. Almost before the last fragments of steel had ceased to fall, the wreckage of the wooden houses in the North End had begun to burn. And if there were any ruins which failed to ignite from falling flames, they began to burn from the fires in their own stoves, onto which they had collapsed.

Over this part of the town, rising in the shape of a typhoon from the Narrows and extending five miles into the sky, was poised a cloud formed by the exhausted gases. It hung still for many minutes, white, glossy as an ermine's back, serenely aloof. It cast its shadow over twenty miles of forest land behind Bedford Basin.

—from *Barometer Rising* (1941)

PRAYER WHEN CAST AWAY IN AN OPEN BOAT

The Breton Fisherman's Prayer says it all: "O God, thy sea is so great, and my boat is so small." This "fear of the Lord" became part of Canadian naval tradition with the founding of Canada's navy in 1910. The Armed Forces prayer-book became familiar to generations of Canadian sailors. It has long since fallen into disuse.

O God of all mercies, we call upon Thee in this time of our exposure and great peril. Grant us Thy Presence and Thy help every passing hour of the day or night. Give us the power of endurance; sustain us with patience and hope; preserve us in dangers and privations which we may yet have to face. Guide those who hasten to our rescue and speed them on their mission of mercy. Comfort our sick and wounded comrades and give us all brave hearts to hold on till the time of our deliverance. Amen.

—Department of National Defence, from *Divine Service Book for the Armed Forces* (1950)

NEWFOUNDLAND SEALING DISASTER
Michael Crummey (1965–   )

Each spring sealing ships would set forth from Newfoundland ports on what amounted to an ancestral, commercial ritual—hunting seals. The ships steamed into the vast ice packs that were then drifting down the Labrador coast from the Arctic, and set their men onto the floes to engage in the slaughter. In common parlance, they were working "in the seals." Thus on 31 March 1914, the steel steamer Stephano *(Captain Abram Kean) lay alongside a floe, while some six miles distant, tucked deep in the ice, lay the wooden sealer* Newfoundland, *skippered by his son Westbury. Nothing in the atmosphere suggested the fateful events that followed. Forced by severe weather to spend two days and nights marooned on the ice, seventy-eight of the* Newfoundland's *men perished. There was tragic irony in this, for the men had first sought refuge aboard* Stephano, *but were sent back onto the ice to their own ship as the weather seemed favourable to the hunt. A Commission of Inquiry found no fault, but recommended that in future all sealing vessels carry radios and basic meteorological equipment. Newfoundland poet and writer Michael Crummey recreates the last desperate moments of the crew members who perished.*

Sent to the ice after white coats,
rough outfit slung on coiled rope belts,
they stooped to the slaughter: gaffed pups,
slit them free of their spotless pelts.

The storm came on unexpected.
Stripped clean of bearings, the watch struck
for the waiting ship and missed it.

Hovelled in darkness two nights then,
bent blindly to the sleet's raw work,
bodies muffled close for shelter,
stepping in circles like blinkered mules.
The wind jerking like a halter.

Minds turned by the cold, lured by small
comforts their stubborn hearts rehearsed,
men walked off ice floes to the arms
of phantom children, wives; of fires

laid in imaginary hearths.
Some surrendered movement and fell,
moulting warmth flensed from their faces
as the night and bitter wind doled out

their final, pitiful wages.

—from *Hard Light* (1998)

FROM FLORES
Ethel Wilson (1888–1980)

The small fishboat, Effie Cee, *makes her way southward along the open, unprotected west coast of Vancouver Island, heading for Port Alberni in time for Christmas. On board are her captain, Fin Crabbe; his crewman, Ed; and two passengers—Jason, a young logger hurrying back to Josie, his pregnant girlfriend, and an injured First Nations boy whose parents have entrusted him to the captain's care in hopes of getting him to hospital. En route they encounter a sudden, violent storm during which the* Effie Cee *is lost at sea.*

A few days later the newspaper stated that in the recent storm on the west coast of Vancouver Island the fishboat *Effie Cee* was missing with two men aboard. These men were Findlay Crabbe aged fifty-six and Edward Morgan aged thirty-five, both of Alberni. Planes were continuing the search.

A day or two afterwards the newspapers stated that it was thought that there might have been a third man aboard the *Effie Cee*. He was identified as Jason Black aged twenty-two, employed as a logger up the coast near Flores Island.

On the second morning after the wreck of the *Effie Cee* the skies were a cold blue and the ocean lay sparkling and lazy beneath the sun. Up the Alberni Canal the sea and air were chilly and brilliant but still. Mrs. Crabbe spent the day waiting on the wharf in the cold sunshine. She stood or walked or sat, accompanied by two friends or by the gangling son and daughter, and next day it was the same, and the next. People said to her "But he didn't set a day? When did he *say* he'd be back?"

"He never said what day," she said. "The Captain couldn't ever say what day. He just said the beginning of the week, maybe Monday was what he said." She said "he said, he said, he said" because it seemed to establish him as living. People had to stop asking because they could not bear to speak to Mrs. Crabbe standing and waiting on the busy wharf, paying the exorbitant price of love. They wished she would not wait there because it made them uncomfortable and unhappy to see her.

Because Josie did not read the papers, she did not know that Jason was dead. Days had passed and continued to pass. Distraught, alone, deprived of hope and faith (two sovereign remedies) and without the consolation of love, she took secretly and with terror what she deemed to be the appropriate path.

The Indian, who had fully trusted the man who took his son away, heard nothing more. He waited until steady fine weather came and then took his family in his small boat to Tofino. From there he made his way to Alberni. Here he walked slowly up and down the docks and at last asked someone where the hospital was; but at the hospital no one seemed to know anything about his only son.

—from "From Flores" in *Mrs. Golightly*
and Other Stories (1961)

OIL RIG DISASTER AT SEA
Lisa Moore (1964–   )

On the night of 14–15 February 1982, the Ocean Ranger *sank during a wild storm on the Grand Banks, 267 kilometres east of St. John's, Newfoundland. Built by Mitsubishi, it was the world's largest semi-submersible oil rig. All eighty-four crew members on board perished in the disaster. The Federal-Provincial Royal Commission on the Ocean Ranger Marine Disaster concluded that the rig had design flaws, and that the crew lacked proper safety training, survival suits and equipment. Lisa Moore's novel* February *traces a widow's loss and devastation in the years following the sinking. Fragments of memory return to haunt her as she tries to imagine her husband's last moments. Although Helen is a fictional character, the well-researched novel is based on the facts of the case.*

The phone rang and woke Helen. Telling her to turn on the radio.

Do you have the radio on?

That's the way the families were informed: It's on the radio. Turn on the radio.

Nobody from the oil company called...

The men on the *Seaforth Highlander* saw the men in the water. One is always haunted by something, and that is what haunts Helen. The men on the *Seaforth Highlander* had been close enough to see some of the men in the waves. Close enough to talk. The men were shouting out before they died. Calling out for help. Calling out to God or calling for mercy or confessing their sins. Or just mentioning they were cold. Or they were just screaming. Noises.

The ropes are frozen, the men on board the *Highlander* were telling the men in the water. The men on the *Highlander* were compelled to narrate all their efforts so that the dying men would know unequivocally that they had not been abandoned. And the *Highlander* crew were in danger of being washed over themselves but they stayed out there in the gale on the slippery deck and took the waves in their faces and tried to cling on and did not give in to fear.

They stayed out there because you don't give up while men are in the water, even if it means you might die yourself.

We're cutting the ropes.

Have you got the ropes cut?

Bastard is all iced over.

Hurry up.

And there must have come a moment, Helen thinks, when all this shouting back and forth was no longer about turning the event around, because everybody on both sides knew there would be no turning it around. The men in the water knew they would die and the men on board knew the men in the water would die. But they kept trying anyway.

And then all the shouting was just for company. Because who wants to watch a man being swallowed by a raging ocean without yelling out to him. They had shouted to the men in the water. They had tried to reach the men with grappling hooks. They saw them and then they did not see them. It was as simple as that...

A radio handset caught stray sound floating between neighbouring rigs out on the ocean. A line or two of talk crossed wires. The men on the other vessel, the *Seaforth Highlander,* heard this talk, and they wrote down what they heard. What the men on the *Ocean Ranger* knew was the weather. They knew the waves were thirty-seven feet and the wind had reached eighty or ninety knots. Or the waves were ninety feet and the wind was gathering speed.

On one of the other rigs, a metal shed bolted to the drilling floor blew away.

We're going to need every helicopter they got, someone from the *Ocean Ranger* said. This was the line that came through. Consider the hope in it.

Or the line that came through was: Tell them to send every helicopter they have.

They said: Send everything you have. Someone listening remarked on the calm. It was a calm voice that said about needing helicopters. Of course, there were no helicopters because there was rime ice in the clouds, because of a low ceiling, because helicopters could not fly in that weather, and the men must have known it.

The men on the *Ocean Ranger* sent out a mayday. *We have a list from which we cannot recover.* They gave the coordinates. They said, ASAP. They said eighty-four men.

—from *February* (2009)

DEATH BY DROWNING
Elizabeth Brewster (1922–2012)

Plunging downward through the slimy water
He discovered, as the fear grew worse,
That life, not death, was what he had been after:
Ironic to die in life's symbol and source.

Drowning was not so easy as it looked from shore.
He had thought of sinking down through layers of peace
To depths where mermaids sang. He would be lapped over
By murmuring waves that lulled him into rest.

But all death is a kind of strangulation,
He had been told once and remembered now,
Choking on water like a rope, and coughing
Its bloody taste from his mouth. He had not known
Before how the body struggled to survive
And must be forced, and forced again, to die.

—from *Passage of Summer: Selected Poems* (1969)

FATHERS AND SONS
Michael Falt

On 23 February 2013, five fishermen on an extended halibut fishing trip were lost at sea when their 13.5-metre vessel, Miss Ally, *overturned in heavy seas 129 nautical miles southeast of Halifax. A Lunenburg reader posted the following response to the CBC website.*

I have read several of the comments over the past days since this tragedy has happened and I have decided to put my perspective down. My father was lost at sea several years ago when I was seven years old. He was a lobster fisherman. I remember everything as if it was yesterday. Where I was, how I found out, how I felt, how the community felt and came together for us. I remember the devastating feeling of helplessness, not knowing where he was and holding out hope even when you knew that he had to have died. Praying every day to find his body, I remember my family and I along with people from the community walking the shoreline daily hoping and praying that his body would wash ashore. My mom refused to have a memorial service for him without a body to lay to rest. In those days, all the local fishermen did the search and never gave up—even when hope had gone. Closure is an overused word in today's language but you really do need to have answers to go on with your life. Whenever someone is lost at sea, I am immediately sent back to that day and what I went through. I wish that I could say it got better but it doesn't. Sure, you function and move on, but it doesn't go away and you always think "what if?" My story had a good ending. After months of [our] walking on the shoreline daily, my father's body washed ashore onto a beach and we were able to give him a funeral and get some relief from the pain. My heart goes out to these families and I pray that they do find those bodies to lay to rest. My final thought is that, with all the technology in this world today, I really thought that the bodies would have been found before this, and I stand beside the fishermen that are out there searching in rough waters for their own.

— "Devastating Loss" from *The Chronicle Herald*,
26 February 2013

"Land, bloody land—thanks be to God."
— Sally Armstrong,
from *The Nine Lives of Charlotte Taylor* (2006)

CHAPTER VIII
MIGRATION AND EXILE

A nation built by immigrants on Indigenous land, Canada has become a multicultural, pluralist country. Even its earliest inhabitants likely came to it from other continents. Prior to the 1960s, when aircraft began to predominate on international routes, migrants came primarily by ship into the great sea ports on the Pacific and Atlantic coasts. The sea is therefore an overarching settlers' experience. They came as entrepreneurs in the fur trade, as "daughters of the King" to be brides for the settlers of New France, as indentured workers from China and Japan, as displaced persons and war brides after the European wars. Following World War II, they came in response to successive government policies of immigration that actively recruited workers in a variety of trades and professions. These policies changed over the years: from attempts to preserve the predominance of British and European "whites," to a gradual broadening of "acceptable" nationalities. In time, too, an increasing number of political and economic refugees found new homes in this "promised land," this "land of unlimited opportunities." Yet, Canada's record of dealing with refugee ships has sometimes been harsh. One thinks, for example, of the 1914 expulsion from Vancouver Harbour of the SS Komagata Maru *with her 376 British subjects from the Punjab. Or again, of the*

event in 1939 when an anti-Semitic Canadian government refused to grant sanctuary to the ocean liner MV St. Louis, carrying 930 Jewish refugees fleeing Nazi Germany. Other vessels with asylum seekers followed into the twenty-first century. Whatever the challenges, neither the journey nor the resettlement process has ever been easy: even once having gained a foothold, some migrants may still encounter racism, marginalization, extradition—even exile.

THE VOYAGE OF PAUL LE JEUNE, 1632

Francis Parkman (1823–1893)

The storm-tossed ship that brought Paul Le Jeune, Superior of the Jesuit mission in Canada, to New France in 1632, carried a fervent missionary and educator. He spent seventeen years in the colony, avidly learning various Indigenous languages and teaching, not only among the Hurons, but also among the children of local African slaves. His descriptive anthropological account of the Hurons, and his personal recollections of the cold, hunger and conflicts he endured, are recorded in the Relations.

It was then that Le Jeune had embarked for the New World. He was in his convent at Dieppe when he received the order to depart; and he set forth in haste for Havre, filled, he assures us, with inexpressible joy at the prospect of a living or a dying martyrdom. At Rouen he was joined by De Noüe, with a lay brother named Gilbert; and the three sailed together on the eighteenth of April, 1632. The sea treated them roughly; Le Jeune was wretchedly sea-sick; and the ship nearly foundered in a gale. At length they came in sight of "that miserable country," as the missionary calls the scene of his future labours. It was in the harbor of Tadoussac that he first encountered the objects of his apostolic cares; for, as he sat in the ship's cabin with the master, it was suddenly invaded by ten or twelve Indians, whom he compares to a party of maskers at the Carnival. Some had their cheeks painted black, their noses blue, and the rest of their faces red. Others were decorated with a broad band of black across the eyes; and others, again, with diverging rays of black, red, and blue on both cheeks. Their attire was no less uncouth. Some of them wore shaggy bear-skins, reminding the priest of the pictures of St. John the Baptist.

After a vain attempt to save a number of Iroquois prisoners whom they were preparing to burn alive on shore, Le Jeune and his companions again set sail, and reached Quebec on the fifth of July. Having said mass, as already mentioned, under the roof of Madame Hébert and her delighted family, the Jesuits made their way to the two hovels built by their predecessors on the St. Charles, which had suffered woeful dilapidation at the hands of the English. Here they made their abode, and applied themselves, with such skill as they could command, to repair the shattered tenements and cultivate the waste meadows around.

—from *The Jesuits in North America in the Seventeenth Century* (1897)

THE BITTER TASTE OF FREEDOM
Suzanne Desrochers (1976–   )

Between 1663 and 1673 some nine hundred young women, known as the filles du roi, *arrived in New France as wards of King Louis XIV. Provided with a small dowry, they were sent at state expense to become wives to the bachelors of the colony. Over time, their arrival achieved the desired effect. Whereas in 1663, there had been one woman to every six men, some twenty years later the sexes were about equal in number and the population had burgeoned. In the novel by Desrochers, Laure Beausejour is an indigent woman from the notorious Salpêtrière hospital and prison in Paris.*

Beyond, at some distance into the sea, is the ship they will board for Canada. Laure doesn't know if it is the cold misty air or terror at what lies ahead that makes her shiver. The boat, although one of the largest of its type, looks fragile, almost ridiculous, against the immense backdrop of the ocean. Laure has heard that early summer is the best time to undertake this journey to New France. Attempted too early or too late, their vessel would be shattered on rocks along the coast before they even reached the cruel centre of the North Atlantic...

The passengers are gathered in the hold at dusk for their dinner. The cook's helpers, each carrying an end of the iron cauldron, descend below. One of the Jesuit priests comes out from behind his chamber curtain and heads upstairs for the captain's table. The captain has his apartment and deck that looks out over the water. A few members of the nobility and the clergy, each with their own compartment below deck separated by a curtain from the public area, go up each night to dine with the captain. In the hold, along with the three hundred or so passengers, are the ship's livestock. The animals are separated from the passengers by the boards of their pen, but the dirty straw makes its way through the cracks into the general filth of the ship's bottom, and the smell of the animals permeates the air. A few of the sheep, cattle, and chickens are destined for the colony, but most are to be eaten during the crossing. But the animals are not intended for the indentured servants, ordinary soldiers, and women from the General Hospital. One calf was already killed for the first feast in the captain's chamber. The passengers grumble that they hope the notables will be quick about eating the animals, as they are tired of sleeping with the smells and bleating of a stable.

Between the passenger hold, or the Sainte-Barbe as it is called, and the captain's quarters is the *entrepont* ['tween-decks]. This is where the mail for the colony is kept, including letters from the King to the Intendant and the Governor. These bags are weighed down with cannonballs and are to be thrown overboard if their ship is accosted. In addition, there are religious supplies for the orders of New France, bolts of cloth, wooden furniture, dishes, tools, books, paper, spices, flour, oil, and wine, as well as the passengers' rations for the journey: sea biscuits and lard in barrels, beans, dried cod and herring, olive oil, butter, mustard, vinegar, water, and cider for when the fresh water supply runs out or becomes too putrid to drink. If the passengers wanted additional supplies for the journey, they were responsible for packing them in their luggage. The girls from the Salpêtrière have nothing more with them...

Although they are crowded into a hold that is smaller than any of the dormitories at the hospital, Laure suddenly feels that there is a vast expanse around her. She doesn't mind so much that she has no delicacies to add to her dinner plate. She spoons the monotonous mush into her mouth, savouring the cool thickness of it, because mixed in somewhere with the dry biscuits and fishy stench of her meal is the taste of freedom.

—from *Bride of New France* (2011)

A Hard Chapter in the Book of History
Antonine Maillet (1929–   )

In 1763, the return of peace between the English and the French in North America was followed by a migration of Acadians returning to their homeland from enforced exile in the American colonies. Of the approximately three thousand who returned, most began their lives anew in the unsettled areas of New Brunswick and Nova Scotia; to this day, they represent a strong cultural force in Canada's national fabric. Whereas the deportation had been conducted in overcrowded schooners, individuals generally returned by land. Maillet's fictional widow, Pélagie, piling her cart high with family and belongings, epitomizes the courage and endurance of those who undertook the long trek home from exile. But the memory of the day of deportation is ever with her.

Exile is a hard chapter in the book of history. Unless one turns the page.

Pélagie had heard tell that all along the coast, in the Carolinas, in Maryland, and further north, Acadians from Governor Lawrence's schooners, who, like her, had been dumped off at random in creeks and bays, were little by little resetting their roots in foreign soil.

"Quitters!" she couldn't help shouting up at them from across the Georgia border.

For roots are also one's own dead, and Pélagie had left behind, sown between Grand Pré and the English colonies to the south, father and mother, man and child, who for fifteen years had been calling her every night: "Come on back!"

Come on back!

Fifteen years since that morning of the Great Disruption. She was a young woman then, just twenty, no more, and already with five offspring hanging to her skirts... four to be exact, the fifth on the way. That fateful morning had found her in the fields, where her oldest boy, God rest his soul, had summoned her with his shouts of "Come on back! Come on back!" His cries clung to her eardrums. Come on back... and she saw the flames climbing the sky. The church was on fire. Grand Pré was on fire, and the life she had let run free in her veins until then suddenly boiled up under her skin and Pélagie thought she would burst. She ran, holding her belly, leaping over the furrows, her eyes fixed on her Grand Pré, that flower of the French Bay. They were already piling families into the schooners, pell-mell, throwing LeBlancs in with Héberts and Héberts with Babineaus. Bits of the Cormier brood seeking their mother in the hold, where the Bourgs were calling the Poiriers to look after their little ones. From one ship to another, Richards, Gaudets, Chiassons stretched out their arms toward fragments of their families on other decks, crying, "Take care of yourself! Take care," their cries carried out by the swell to the open sea.

So it is when a people departs into exile.

And she, Pélagie, with the shreds of the family she had managed to save from the Great Disruption, had landed on Hope Island in the north of Georgia. Hope Island! Only the good omen in the name had kept this woman, this widow of Acadie with her four orphans, alive. Hope was a country, a return to the paradise lost.

—from *Pélagie: The Return to Acadie*
(French original, 1979. English translation, 1982)

DO NOT TRUST LARGE BODIES OF WATER
Lawrence Hill (1957–)

Born in eighteenth-century West Africa, Aminata Diallo was abducted from her village and sold into slavery to an American plantation owner. Hill's novel traces her appalling odyssey from Africa to the United States, to supposed "refuge" in racist Canada, and eventually her return to Sierra Leone in a futile bid for freedom on the continent of her birth. In her final years, living in London, sought after by the abolitionists for the eloquence she can bring to their movement, Aminata looks back on her life of abuse, denigration and extraordinary resilience. She reflects on sea voyages she has known, and the horrors they evoke for her.

Let me begin with a caveat to any and all who find these pages. Do not trust large bodies of water, and do not cross them. If you, dear reader, have an African hue and find yourself led toward water with vanishing shores, seize your freedom by any means necessary. And cultivate distrust of the colour pink. Pink is taken as the colour of innocence, the colour of childhood, but as it spills across the water in the light of the dying sun, do not fall into its pretty path. There, right underneath, lies a bottomless graveyard of children, mothers and men. I shudder to imagine all the Africans rocking in the deep. Every time I have sailed the seas, I have had the sense of gliding over the unburied.

Some people call the sunset a creation of extraordinary beauty, and proof of God's existence. But what benevolent force would bewitch the human spirit by choosing pink to light the path of a slave vessel? Do not be fooled by that pretty colour, and do not submit to its beckoning...

Each rising sun saw more people die. We called their names as they were pulled from the hold. *Makeda, of Segu. Salima, of Kambolo.* Down below, at least, I couldn't hear bodies hitting the water. Although the hold was dark and filthy, I no longer wanted to see the water, or to breathe the air above.

After what seemed to be several days, the toubabu [whites] started bringing us back up on deck in small groups. We were given food and a vile drink with bits of fruit in it. We were given tubs and water to wash ourselves. The toubabu burned tar in our sleeping quarters, which made us choke and gag. They tried to make us wash our sleeping planks, but we were too weak. Our ribs were showing, our anuses draining. The toubabu sailors looked just as ill. I saw many dead seamen thrown overboard without ceremony.

After two months at sea, the toubabu brought every one of us up on deck. Naked, we were made to wash. There were only two-thirds of us left. They grabbed those who could not walk and began to throw them overboard, one by one. I shut my eyes and plugged my ears, but could not block out all the shrieking.

Some time after the noise ended, I opened my eyes and looked out at the setting sun. It hovered just over the horizon, casting a long pink path across the still water. We sailed steadily toward the beckoning pink, which hovered forever at arm's length, always close but never with us. *Come this way*, it seemed to be saying. Far ahead in the direction of the sun, I saw something grey and solid. It was barely visible, but it was there. We were moving toward land...

And so it happened that the vessel that had so terrified us in the waters near our homeland saved at least some of us from being buried in the deep. We, the survivors of the crossings, clung to the beast that had stolen us away. Not a soul among us had wanted to board that ship, but once out on open waters, we held on for dear life. The ship became an extension of our own rotting bodies. Those who were cut from the heaving animal sank quickly to their deaths, and we who remained attached wilted more slowly as poison festered in our bellies and bowels. We stayed with the beast until new lands met our feet, and we stumbled down the long planks just before the poison became fatal. Perhaps here in this new land, we would keep living.

—from *The Book of Negroes* (2007)

LAND, BLOODY LAND—THANKS BE TO GOD
Sally Armstrong (1943–   )

Blending history, lore and imagination, Sally Armstrong's novel re-creates the character of her indomitable great-great-great-grandmother, an early settler of New Brunswick's Miramichi Valley. In 1775, strong-willed Charlotte Taylor ran away from her English home with her lover, the family's black butler. Following his untimely death shortly after their arrival in Jamaica, an impoverished Charlotte accepted passage on a ship bound for the Baie des Chaleurs in northern New Brunswick—a land she would claim as her own. In 1980 a granite headstone on Charlotte's grave proclaimed her "The Mother of Tabusintac."

She is on her way back to her cabin when the coast comes into clear view. "Land, bloody land—thanks be to God," Charlotte cries. Soon they steer around the high cliffs of Miscou still being swept by a stiff Atlantic wind and suddenly sail into the calm of the Baie des Chaleurs. Charlotte catches her breath at the sight of a land that captures her soul. A beautiful wilderness lies before her. Forests of fir trees drop off into fields of glistening seagrass that wave over long, sandy beaches. The water around her is teeming with fish. [Able seaman] Will is at her side and tells her the huge marine mammals with the horizontal flukes on their tails are called whales. They move like undersea mountains, riding up to the surface and slipping out of sight again. The smaller ones with tusks are walrus, he says. The cod are so plentiful, she thinks, she could scoop them from the water with her hands. She can hardly believe the long journey from England to the West Indies and now to this place called Nepisiguit is over. Standing in awe at the ship's rail and remembering defiantly what has gone before, she vows, "I will make my own way."

—from *The Nine Lives of Charlotte Taylor* (2007)

AT THE RAIL
Alice Munro (1931–   )

Alice Munro's short story "The View from Castle Rock" is a semifictitious re-telling of the immigration to Canada in the early nineteenth century of her Scottish ancestors. Their long sea journey begins in the harbour of Leith, on the 4th of June, 1818. It evokes the experience of all who left their country of origin to make a new life in this vast land. Marked by birth, death, anxiety, doubt, homesickness and hope, the turbulent crossing is also an emotional divide that looks back to what once was—and is now forever gone—and forward to the unknown.

And on that same day but an hour or so on, there comes a great cry from the port side that there is a last sight of Scotland. Walter and Andrew go over to see that, and Mary with Young James on her hip and many others. Old James and Agnes do not go—she because she objects now to moving herself anywhere, and he on account of perversity. His sons have urged him to go but he has said, "It is nothing to me. I have seen the last of the Ettrick so I have seen the last of Scotland already."

It turns out that the cry to say farewell has been premature—a grey rim of land will remain in place for hours yet. Many will grow tired of looking at it—it is just land, like any other—but some will stay at the rail until the last rag of it fades, with the daylight.

"You should go and say farewell to your native land and the last farewell to your mother and father for you will not be seeing them again," says Old James to Agnes. "And there is worse yet you will have to endure. Aye, but there is. You have the curse of Eve." He says this with the mealy relish of a preacher and Agnes calls him an old shite-bag under her breath, but she has hardly the energy even to scowl.

Old shite-bag. You and your native land.

Walter writes at last a single sentence.

And this night in the year 1818 we lost sight of Scotland.

—from "The View from Castle Rock"
in *The View from Castle Rock* (2006)

LANDFALL IN THE GULF OF ST. LAWRENCE, 1833
William Kilbourn (1926–1995)

Among the many migrants crossing the Atlantic in the early nineteenth century was an ambitious, diminutive Scot who would become one of the most colourful politicians and parliamentarians in Canada: William Lyon Mackenzie (1795–1861). A fiery journalist and businessman with a forceful cast of mind, he had first arrived in Upper Canada in 1820. Here he established The Colonial Advocate, a newspaper advocating reform of political life then dominated by the Family Compact with its grip on privilege, politics and wealth. His advocacy ultimately catapulted him into leading the Rebellion of 1837, an abortive armed revolt against the Canadian establishment. In 1832 he had returned to

England in order to present his supporters' grievances before the imperial government and to visit his native Dundee for the last time. His voyage back to Canada in 1833 matured his thoughts on the experience of migration, and on the political path that lay ahead.

The greater part of the Mackenzies' fellow travellers on the return journey were not now returning British officials or businessmen, but poor emigrant families, crammed into pitching, choleric steerage quarters often occupied by timber or wheat on the eastward voyage, men and women and children who had given up forever the familiar hardships and comfortable custom-bound certainties of a thousand-year-old village for the hope and terror of the unknown. Mackenzie no longer entertained himself with confident hopes and thoughts about the omniscient benevolence of the persons who ruled the Empire, nor was he as certain as he had been at twenty-five on his first adventure on the Atlantic that only a Mackenzie knew how to be loyal. This trip meant committing himself as irrevocably to the New World as the humble folk that travelled with him.

Seven weeks out of port, at length, from the infinity of sky and sea came the land. For the emigrant for whom the village over the next hill meant "far" and the market town, for practical purposes, the end of the world, the first sight of their adopted country, where it did not freeze the senses into incomprehension, must surely have been awesome. Day after day the great shores of the gulf lay aloof from the frail busy society of the small ship, now all but disappearing from sight, now pressing in until the sheer black perpendicular mile of Capes Trinity and Eternity skidded vertiginously above them. How could anyone who knew the Thames or the Dee, who judged rivers by their human, civilized banks, accept the St. Lawrence? Only a few miles from where these others join the sea, kings have ridden on their waters—Saxon Edgar rowed by his thanes; Elizabeth in her royal barge greeted by Leicester; gouty periwigged George saluted by the "Water Music" of his court composer, Mr. Handel. But the coming together of the St. Lawrence and the Atlantic is hooded in the perpetual mists of the sub-Arctic.

Into the high sun of the gulf, the inhuman tallness of the blue and cirrocumulus sky, it is the same. Islands a day's journey in the passing lie like the sleeping form of some species of monster unknown to Greek mythology or some giant never met by the gods of Valhalla. Beyond, on the shore, a forest bleaker by far than the haunted Teutonic woods that scared the Romans so. And the shore itself, the edge of a continental shield that would sternly test the man who believed he was the measure of all things. Gulf, sky, shore, each the infinitely receding and advancing perspective in the brain, the rim of madness, in a land still unthinkably abstract and virgin.

—from *The Firebrand: William Lyon Mackenzie*
and the Rebellion in Upper Canada (1956)

GHOSTS OF HISTORY
Ingrid Peritz

The interweavings of memory, archaeology and forensic sciences can reinforce one's relationship with the sea. Such is the case when relics of a nineteenth-century marine disaster came to light in Gaspé, Quebec, in 2011. The two-masted brig Carricks *had sailed from Ireland in March 1847 carrying emigrants from the Irish estates of Lord Palmerston. On 28 April she ran into a heavy snow-laden storm in the Gulf of St. Lawrence and foundered on the shore near Cap-des-Rosiers. According to a contemporary report, the ship "went to pieces in the course of two hours." Forty-eight of the approximately 176 passengers survived.*

The *Carricks* left Sligo, Ireland, with almost two hundred passengers and crew, completing the transatlantic voyage before foundering off Cap-des-Rosiers. Accounts vary, but most report the deaths of as many as one hundred twenty passengers. The dead—weakened by cold, hunger and exhaustion—were said to be strewn along the beach the following day, then buried, anonymously, in a common grave nearby.

"For a whole day two oxcarts carried the dead to deep trenches near the scene of the disaster," author Margaret Grant MacWhirter wrote in a book [*Treasure Trove in Gaspé and the Baie Des Chaleurs*] published in 1919. "In fall, the heavy storms sweep within sound of the spot. Thus peacefully, with the requiem of the waves and winds, they rest." A half-century after the disaster, the parish of St. Patrick's in Montreal erected a stone marker at Cap-des-Rosiers to the victims whose bodies were recovered and interred. "Sacred to the memory of one hundred eighty seven Irish immigrants from Sligo... eighty-seven are buried here," its inscription reads.

The bones that surfaced in May [2011] were found near the monument, said Michel Queenton, a manager with Parks Canada— Cap-des-Rosiers lies within Forillon National Park. The coastline has been affected by erosion and heavy tides, the forces that exposed the human remains. However, a Parks Canada archaeologist says the precise spot of the *Carricks'* burial ground was never documented, and it's not known if it lies at the monument site. Some accounts say the bodies were interred further up the coast in a church cemetery...

"There is a strong probability the bones come from the communal grave," said Geneviève Guilbault, a spokeswoman for the coroner's office. "We want to be sure it's the case."

That prospect has stirred up the ghosts of history for those touched by the tragedy. Georges Kavanagh grew up within walking distance of the monument to the *Carricks,* and for him it has always been hallowed ground. His ancestors, Patrick Kavanagh and Sarah McDonald, came to the same shores aboard the *Carricks* (also referred to sometimes as the *Carrick* or *Carricks of Whitehaven*). They survived the harrowing transatlantic voyage with their 12-year-old son, but five daughters perished.

Georges Kavanagh, a unilingual francophone, feels a strong pull to the story of his Irish forebears, and he travelled to Sligo last year [in 2010] to connect with his roots. He says local oral history always placed the *Carricks* grave next to the monument, and if the bones prove to be those of the victims, they deserve a proper burial. "I consider that to be something of a sacred site," the 71-year-old said from his home in Gaspé, about fifty kilometres from the monument, which he visits regularly. "To think that so many perished in a shipwreck just a few steps from their promised land. I have great admiration for what they tried to do, leaving everything behind for the hope of better living conditions."

The *Carricks* was one of hundreds of migrant ships bound for the port of Quebec City in 1847, the darkest year of the famine in Ireland. The voyage required a stop at the quarantine station of Grosse-Île, where many refugees met their deaths from disease. Nearly four hundred ships sailed that year toward Quebec, the main immigrant gateway into Canada, filled overwhelmingly with Irish passengers. One in five never made it.

—from "Remains of a 19th-century tragedy?"
in *The Globe and Mail,* 20 July 2011

POINT OF ENTRY
Jane Urquhart (1949–   )

Grosse Île, in the mouth of the St. Lawrence River, served as a quarantine station for the port of Quebec from 1832 to 1937. Its early years witnessed the appalling fate of thousands escaping the Great Irish Famine of 1845–1849. Weakened by malnutrition, disease and filthy overcrowded ships, many who survived the nightmare of the transatlantic crossing died of cholera and typhus at Grosse Île. In 1847, at the height of the famine, over 7,500 were buried in the Irish Cemetery there. Today the Irish Memorial National Historic Site at Grosse Île commemorates the importance of immigration to Canada. Yet in his poem, "Grosse Isle," poet Al Purdy recalls the past horrors of the place: "—a silence here like no mainland silence / at Cholera Bay where the dead bodies / awaited high tide and the rough kindness / of waves sweeping them into the dark." In her novel, Away, *Jane Urquhart writes of one Irish child who survived.*

What the child had forgotten and would not remember until years later were the crowded docks of Larne and the journey there, the suffering, starvation, the desperate throngs on the wharf. He had forgotten the dark belly of the ship where no air stirred and, as the weeks passed, the groans of his neighbours, the unbearable, unspeakable odours, his own father calling for water, and the limp bodies of children he had come to know being hoisted through the hatch on ropes, over and over, until the boy believed this to be the method by which one ascended to heaven. He had forgotten his own sickness which drew a dark curtain over the wet, foul timbers of the ship's wall and the long sleep that had removed him from the ravings of the other passengers until he wakened believing that the shrieked requests for air and light and liquid was the voice of the abominable beast, the ship that was devouring a third of the flesh that had poured into its hold. And after ten weeks crouched on the end of his parents' berth on the *New World*, and six weeks confined to a bed with five other children at the quarantine station at Grosse Isle (some lying dead beside him for half a day), he had forgotten how to recall images, engage in conversation, and how to walk.

      —from *Away* (1993)

THE ALCHEMY OF IMMIGRATION
Derek Lundy (1946–)

Fading photographs, yellowing letters and poignant memoirs are gold for the genealogist. For an immigrant country like Canada in particular, they are life-lines into the past. They help us recapture our identity, grasp our traditions and understand our roots. Emerging from the mists of a lengthy sea voyage these links can gain mythic dimensions. Derek Lundy begins his search for the past by contemplating a photograph of his great-great-uncle Benjamin, taken in 1895 on Salt Spring Island, BC, and tracing Benjamin's journey from Ireland, and around Cape Horn, to British Columbia.

It was quite a journey, when you came to think of it. Immigrants to North America, including members of my own family, did it all the time—it was the quintessential immigrant experience—and that made it seem commonplace. But what an alchemy! The voyage away from the confines of European class, accent, religion, imperial diktat and the claustrophobic "close-togetherness" of everything to the space and light of the New World, its even-handed presentation of the possibility of success and failure. It was like the first true deep breath of a person's life. Although he hadn't followed the immigrant's usual route—at first, perhaps, hadn't even intended to immigrate at all—Benjamin had eventually made that leap too. I wanted to find out more about the man in the photograph, and at least part of the story of his trek from a two-up, two-down workers' house in the Irish Quarter of Carrickfergus, under the shadow of a Norman-English castle in occupied Ireland, to become a landowner on an Edenic island in the Northwest rainforest.

It seemed to me entirely apt that Benjamin's self-displacement from one species of existence to another had been accomplished by means of a sea voyage under sail. He changed his life, made it new, by crossing oceans to a new world. At the same time, his journey of six months on a wind ship, like all such passages, was a sea change in itself...

Each one was unique. From the moment the sailing ship up-anchored or unmoored, or dropped its tow, and began to move under the force of wind on sails alone, everything was thrown into the balance. No one could foretell the incidence or shape of the great things to come: storms, fire, stranding, collision, ice, Cape Horn's disposition, the severity and duration of the inevitable struggle ahead. Nor was it possible to predict from moment to moment what claims, burdens, ultimatums the wind and waves would bring down on the ship and its crew. Every decision to take in or set more sail, each turn of the wheel in heavy seas, the speed and skill with which seamen hauled or furled, spliced or lashed, all the ways of devotion hour by hour, or even minute by minute, by which the ship was continually made able to sail on, or indeed to survive, in the endless chaos of the sea—all these were subject to chance and laden with the possibility of failure or ruin...

Benjamin's passage as a sailor before the mast aboard the *Beara Head* [which he joined in May 1885] is, in part, the mere account of a young man learning the ropes; standing his watches; following orders; enduring cold, exhaustion and danger; helping to save the ship and himself; becoming a seaman. He is also a young man who, in the process of doing all that, learns the eternal lessons of the sea, which is to say that he finds out the sort of man he is, and that he is capable of doing things that, before or even after he did them, seemed almost unimaginably difficult and perilous. And although he is unaware of it, Benjamin is on a voyage freighted with the meanings and burdens of a whole world giving way to another.

—from *The Way of a Ship: A Square-Rigger Voyage
in the Last Days of Sail* (2002)

TOWARDS *GAM SUN*—GOLD MOUNTAIN
Judy Fong Bates (1949–   )

The Chinese Head Tax was imposed on all immigrants from China between 1885 and 1923. Beginning at fifty dollars per person, it was raised to five hundred dollars in 1903—the price of a house in Canada, or the equivalent of two years' salary in China. Despite the financial hardship the tax represented, Chinese men from impoverished villages continued to cross the Pacific under wretched conditions in the hope of a better life in the "Gold Mountain." Ultimately, these dreams were dashed by the Exclusion Act of 1923 which barred all Chinese immigrants from Canada until 1947.

One year later, Hua Fan boarded the large steamship that carried him and dozens of other Chinamen across the Pacific to *Gam Sun*. A tall, pale-faced man with strange orange hair loomed over them, herding the crowd in the right direction. He shouted at them in an odd-sounding language and yanked their long black queues when he wanted their attention. Hua Fan couldn't stop staring. He had never seen a person with so much hair on his face.

For twenty-two days, Hua Fan lived with other Chinamen at the bottom of the boat. Some of the men were returning for the second or third time. A few of them teased him as they looked him up and down.

"What's a skinny fellow like you going to do over there? You think the streets are paved with gold? The *lo fons* treat their dogs better than a Chinaman." But he ignored their taunts. He never complained about the terrible food, the tossing of the ocean, or the mingling stench of unwashed bodies and vomit. Some of the boat uncles though were kind and a few of them taught him how to count to ten in English, to say "yes" and "no," "how much" and "thank you."

When the ship docked in the harbour at Salt Water City [Vancouver], most of the Chinamen stayed there. It was a bustling town, and already the Chinese had established a community. But Hua Fan had to go to the middle of the country, to a small town in northern Ontario, where his uncle operated a small hand laundry.

—from *China Dog and Other Tales*
from a Chinese Laundry (1997)

FAREWELL, MY BANDIT-PRINCESS
Wayson Choy (1939–   )

For Chinese migrants the sea was both a route of hope to the much-touted Gold Mountain, which Canada seemed to promise, as well as the road of peace "homeward" back to China once they had died. According to tradition, the deceased were interred in Canadian soil for seven years, when their bones were disinterred, cleaned and packaged for return by ship. It was not uncommon for an elderly migrant to accompany the bones from Vancouver on this, their final voyage. It was a final farewell to a country whose racist policies and practices since the 1880s had marginalized them and blocked any hope of integration. In Choy's novel, a young girl recounts the departure of her beloved storytelling uncle, Wong Suk, with a shipment of bones. He used to regale her with fairy tales of princes, princesses and their captivating adventures.

We were not allowed to go past the customs landing and departure gates. Everyone started to say goodbye. The dock felt unsteady under my feet; everything smelled like iodine and salt and the sky was bright with light. Father gave a man in a uniform some money to carry Wong Suk's luggage past the gates. I could only look about me, robbed of speech, spellbound. I remember Father lifting me up a little to kiss Wong Suk on his cheek; he seemed unable to kiss me back. His cheek, I remember, had the look of wrinkled documents. He looked secretive, like Poh-Poh, saying nothing. I felt his hand rest a moment on my curls, then a crowd of people began to push by us.

"Hurry," Father said, gently lifting the old man's hand from my head...

The *Empress's* whistle gave a loud, long, last cry, sent seabirds soaring into manic flight; the giant engines roared, churned up colliding waves; the dock shook. The ship began to pull away. I think I saw Wong Suk on the distant deck of the ship. Then, as in a dream, I was standing beside Wong Suk, felt his cloak folding around me under the late afternoon sky. We were travelllng together, as we had promised each other in so many of my games. I wondered how he felt, unbending his neck against the stinging homeward wind.

What wealth should a bandit-prince give his princess? Wong Suk once had asked me, as I turned and turned and his cloak enfolded me, with its dark, imperial wings. And I answered greedily, too quickly, my childish fingers grasping imaginary gold coins, slipping over pearls large enough to choke a dragon, gripping rubies the colour of fire... *everything*... for I did not, then, in the days of our royal friendship, understand how bones must come to rest where they most belong.

—from *The Jade Peony* (1995)

VOYAGE OF THE DAMNED
Irving Abella (1940–) and Harold Troper (1942–)

In May 1939, the SS St. Louis was one of the last passenger ships to sail from Germany on the eve of World War II. Carrying over nine hundred Jewish refugees desperate to escape Nazi persecution, she was refused permission to land, first in Cuba, then in the United States, lastly in

Canada; this left her captain no option but to return to her home port of Hamburg. By allowing bureaucratic indifference and political expediency to trump human decency, Canada effectively used the sea as a defensive moat, thereby condemning asylum seekers to the concentration camps where many of them perished.

On May 15, 1939, nine hundred and seven desperate German Jews set sail from Hamburg on a luxury liner, the *St. Louis*. They had been stripped of their possessions, hounded first out of their homes and businesses and now their country. Like many who had sailed on this ship before, these passengers had once contributed much to their native land; they were distinguished, educated, cultured; many had been well-off but all were now penniless. Their most prized possession was the entrance visa to Cuba each carried on board.

The Jews on the *St. Louis* considered themselves lucky—they were leaving. When they reached Havana on May 30, however, their luck ran out, for the Cuban government refused to recognize their entrance visas. None of these wretched men, women and children were allowed to disembark, even after they threatened mass suicide. The search for a haven now began in earnest. Argentina, Uruguay, Paraguay and Panama were approached, in vain, by various Jewish organizations. Within two days all the countries of Latin America had rejected entreaties to allow these Jews to land, and on June 2 the *St. Louis* was forced to leave Havana harbour. The last hope was Canada or the United States, and the latter, not even bothering to reply to an appeal, sent a gunboat to shadow the ship as it made its way north. The American Coast Guard had been ordered to make certain that the *St. Louis* stayed far enough off shore so that it could not be run aground nor any of its frantic passengers attempt to swim ashore.

The plight of the *St. Louis* had by now touched some influential Canadians; on June 7 several of these, led by [University of Toronto professor] George Wrong and including B. K. Sandwell of *Saturday Night*, Robert Falconer, past-president of the University of Toronto, and Ellsworth Flavelle, a wealthy businessman, sent a telegram to Prime Minister Mackenzie King begging that he show "true Christian charity" and offer the homeless exiles sanctuary in Canada. But Jewish refugees were far from the prime minister's mind. King was in Washington, accompanying the Royal Family on the final leg of its triumphant North American tour. The *St. Louis*, King felt, was not a Canadian problem, but he would, nevertheless, ask [under-secretary of state for External Affairs, O.D.] Skelton to consult on the matter with [minister of justice, Ernest] Lapointe and [director of immigration, Frederick Charles] Blair. Lapointe quickly stated that he was "emphatically opposed" to the admission of the *St. Louis* passengers, while Blair claimed, characteristically, that these refugees did not qualify under immigration laws and that in any case Canada had already done too much for the Jews. No country, Blair added, could "open its doors wide enough to take in the hundreds of thousands of Jewish people who want to leave Europe: the line must be drawn somewhere."

And the line drawn, the voyagers' last flickering hope extinguished, the Jews of the *St. Louis* headed back to Europe, where many would die in the gas chambers and crematoria of the Third Reich.

—from *None Is Too Many:*
Canada and the Jews of Europe, 1933–1948 (1983)

STOLEN BOATS, STOLEN LIVES

Joy Kogawa (1935–   )

In 1942, in the wake of the Japanese attack on Pearl Harbor, the Canadian government forcibly removed some 20,000 Japanese Canadians from the Pacific Coast, and confiscated the fishing boats of all the fishermen among them. These classic vessels were then sold off at bargain prices to "whites." Despite advice from the RCMP that these people posed no threat, racism and war hysteria had triggered the move. The action uprooted families and destroyed a community. Only gradually during the late post-war period have Canadians of Japanese ancestry returned to coastal towns like Steveston at the mouth of the Fraser River, which at one time had boasted forty-nine fish canneries. Today in the municipality of Richmond one of the canneries—and a restored Japanese home—serve as museums. In Kogawa's historical novel Obasan *("Aunt") the narrator ponders family photographs and reflects on the troubling days of the past.*

Grandpa Nakane, "number one boat builder" Uncle used to say, was a son of the sea that tossed and coddled the Nakanes for centuries. The first of my grandparents to come to Canada, he arrived in 1893, wearing a western suit, round black hat, and platformed geta on his feet. When he left his familiar island, he became a stranger, sailing towards an island of strangers. But the sea was his constant companion. He understood its angers, its whisperings, its generosity. The native Songhies of Esquimalt and many Japanese fishermen came to his boat-building shop on Saltspring Island, to barter and to buy. Grandfather prospered. His cousin's widowed wife and her son, Isamu, joined him.

Isamu, my uncle, born in Japan in 1889, was my father's older half-brother. Uncle Isamu—or Uncle Sam, as we called him—and his wife Ayako, my Obasan, married in their thirties and settled in Lulu Island, near Annacis Island where Uncle worked as a boat builder...

One snapshot I remember showed Uncle and Father as young men standing full front beside each other, their toes pointing outwards like Charlie Chaplin's. In the background were pine trees and the side view of Uncle's beautiful house. One of Uncle's hands rested on the hull of an exquisitely detailed craft. It wasn't a fishing vessel or an ordinary yacht, but a sleek boat designed by Father, made over many years and many winter evenings. A work of art.

"What a beauty," the RCMP officer said in 1941, when he saw it. He shouted as he sliced back through the wake, "What a beauty! What a beauty!"

That was the last Uncle saw of the boat. And shortly thereafter, Uncle too was taken away, wearing shirt, jacket, and dungarees. He had no provisions nor did he have any idea where the gunboats were herding him and the other Japanese fishermen in the impounded fishing fleet.

The memories were drowned in a whirlpool of protective silence. Everywhere I could hear the adults, whispering, "Kodomo no tame. For the sake of the children..." Calmness was maintained.

Once, years later on the Barker farm, Uncle was wearily wiping his forehead with the palm of his hand and I heard him saying quietly, "Itsuka, mata itsuka. Someday, someday again." He was waiting for that "some day" when he could go back to the boats. But he never did.

And now? Tonight?

Nen, nen, rest my dead uncle. The sea is severed from your veins. You have been cut loose.

—from *Obasan* (1981)

MY WAR-BRIDE'S TRIP TO CANADA
Janet McGill Zarn, Scottish War Bride (1919–1992)

Following the end of World War II, some 48,000 women—90 percent of them from the British Isles—came to Canada as "war brides." They made the eight-day voyage "across the Pond" aboard liners that had been converted to troopships for wartime service—among them the Aquitania, Britannic, Letitia, Queen Mary, Île de France, Mauretania, Samaria. *On board, the women experienced overcrowding, seasickness and homesickness—offset by camaraderie, "mountains" of good food and a sense of adventure. For many landing at Pier 21 in Halifax, the Atlantic Ocean was a barrier to returning to the "mother country." Yet the eight-day crossing also represented a gateway to new horizons and a role to play in the post-war awakening of a vast land. Recalling the ceremonial singing of "O Canada" as her ship docked in Halifax in January 1947, Gwyneth M. Shirley wrote: "And war brides awaiting sang along / Not sure of the words but liking the song. / Their voices floated across the sea; / Their story passed into history." The Pier 21 Society Resource Centre has archived the war brides' impressions. Today some one million Canadians are descended from them.*

During the night we heard anchors weighed and by morning light saw we were out in the Irish Sea in the middle of a convoy. Those of us from around the Clyde were quite familiar with the underwater boom across the Firth from Cloch Lighthouse to Cowal, Argyll and had seen the freighters file out through the gap between the guard ships for the open sea but beyond that knew nothing except that the navy took over for protection from the subs, based on the French and Norwegian coasts. It was a wondrous sight you could never forget it, all those ships surrounding us in their designated positions travelling in a huge group across the face of the ocean. On a clear day we could count 80 or so vessels, the two passenger ships and as far as we could guess the rest were freighters and tankers, and dimly in the distance you could catch a glimpse of the naval escort. Though separated by a considerable distance we could wave each morning to the crews of the merchantmen, our port and starboard neighbors. We moved south along the Irish coast but after Fastnet it seemed our last link with home had gone for ever, even the gulls finally abandoned us!

On board in daylight hours women, children and servicemen could all mix freely, in fact one girl had her husband aboard and could visit with him during the day until lights out. Blackout was enforced after dark and we were not allowed out on deck; our "boss" was an army man and he was strict, woe betide you if he found that you were not carrying your gas mask, you'd be sent back to your cabin for it, actually no hardship as we'd been doing that for years! Lifeboat drill took place every morning around 9:30 though one morning the alarm did go off at 5:30 and was a bit frightening as we could hear shell-fire; probably a U-boat was around, we'll never know. In a convoy you have no idea where you are in the ocean but we must have traveled south a long way as it turned very warm but we hit very heavy swells and there was a lot of sea-sickness. With only the minimum of medical help aboard we had more or less to take care of ourselves, the children didn't seem to be affected as much as their mothers so it was pretty hard on them but you do recover fast. The crossing took about 8 days then one morning we woke to find the rest of the convoy all gone, just the two passenger ships travelling up the Nova Scotia coast. I suppose the rest went south to New York or maybe to Newfoundland. That morning we sailed into Halifax.

—from *My War-Bride's Trip to Canada – Britannic, April 1945*

BURIAL AT SEA
Nino Ricci (1959–   )

Burials at sea are ancient rituals. In the early days, the remains of those who had died of disease or of battle wounds had to be disposed of quickly. In the best of times, it was done in a variety of ceremonies, some of them conspicuously impromptu. Naval ritual involved two components: military and religious; for civilians, however, prayers and solemn sentences sufficed. Traditionally, one placed the body in a coffin, or wrapped it in sailcloth. Both would be weighted down with lead shot. Nautical lore has it that the final stitch in the body-bag called for a needle through the nose, leaving little doubt that the "dearly beloved" was in fact quite dead. In Ricci's novel, a mother dies in childbirth on her journey to Halifax, leaving her young son to observe her funeral at sea through a grieving child's uncomprehending eyes.

But all these later events happened in a mist. Before the mist set in, though, I was granted a few final moments of clarity—time enough to witness my mother's funeral, which took place the morning after her death, and which I was allowed to attend because no one, not even myself, had noticed that I was burning with fever. The funeral was held at the ship's stern, where the sun deck normally was, though all the chairs had been cleared away now. The sun was just edging above a still sea, the air cold but the sky stubbornly clear; and despite the early hour a small crowd of passengers attended—the ones my mother had befriended, Mr. D'Amico, the grey-eyed German, the honeymoon couple, and several others who I did not recognize, and who stood a ways back as if they were afraid of being turned away. Antonio [the third mate] was there, and the captain, hats in hands, as well as a few of the other officers, the ship's chaplain, Louisa, a sombre and sober Dr. Cosabène. But only Louisa and Mr. D'Amico and the honeymoon couple cried through the service; the others retained a stony silence, stiff and awkward, as if the bright sun and clear sky made them feel unnatural in their mourning.

My mother's body, enclosed in a canvas sack and covered with an Italian flag, lay on a small platform that rose up above the rails and pointed out to sea. After the chaplain had read from his missal Antonio gave the eulogy. But I wasn't following—there had been a mistake, the kind of thing where dead people were not dead or where they could sometimes come back to life again, like that, the way the wheat around Valle del Sole, snow-covered in winter, could suddenly be green again in the spring. In a moment, I was sure, my mother's head would pop out of her sack. "Vittorio," she'd say, eyes all squinty and lips pouting, "look at you, always so serious!" And everyone would laugh.

But now Antonio, his voice hoarse with emotion, was ending his eulogy; and after a long moment of silence a young frail-eyed officer began to play a song on a bugle, while we stood with our heads bowed. When he had finished the chaplain made a sign of the cross, and on a nod from the captain Antonio's hand slipped over a lever beneath the platform that held my mother, hesitated there a moment, then finally wrenched the lever back, hard. The platform tilted sharply towards the sea and the canvas sack slid out suddenly from under the flag; but before I could hear it strike the sea's surface my knees buckled beneath me, and my mind went blank.

—from *Lives of the Saints* (1990)

ONE TIME I CROSSED THE CHINA SEA
Nhung Hoang (1955–   )

From 1975 to the mid-1990s, over three million people fled widespread human rights abuses in Cambodia, Laos and Vietnam. Hundreds of thousands fled by sea in small, often unseaworthy vessels—of these, tens of thousands perished. As the story of the "boat people" unfolded, Canada offered refuge through a vast program of voluntary sponsorship and government assistance. In 1986 the United Nations High Commission for Refugees awarded its prestigious Nansen medal to the Canadian people for welcoming the desperate Southeast Asian refugees. Nhung Hoang's poem captures the terror experienced by the fleeing "boat people." Although the second part of their journey to Canada was by air, it too was filled with the same uneasy mix of apprehension and expectation common throughout history to people seeking a better life in a new place.

One time I crossed
The China Sea,
Full of fear,
In a small boat,
Two typhoons,
High waves
Fierce winds,
Death was so close.

One time I flew
Over the Pacific Ocean,
Full of expectation,
For a new life,
Also full of uncertainty,
For the days in a new country.

—from *Refugee Love* (1993)

"O Eternal Lord God, who alone spreadest out the heavens, and rulest the raging of the sea; who has compassed the waters with bounds until day and night come to an end; Be pleased to receive into thy almighty and most gracious protection the persons of us thy servants, and the Fleet in which we serve. Preserve us from the dangers of the sea, and from the violence of the enemy; that we may be... a security for such as pass on the seas upon their lawful occasions..."

—Excerpt from "The Naval Prayer,"
Divine Service Book for the Armed Forces (1950),
Department of National Defence

CHAPTER IX
A NOISE OF WAR

War on the high seas and the defence of home waters are central to the Canadian experience. Indeed, Canadian naval forces have been shaped by many converging dynamics since the creation of the Royal Canadian Navy in 1910. Not the least of these are geopolitical, domestic, economic, cultural and societal pressures. Arguably, even the navy's early roots in the Battle of Hudson's Bay (1697) and the War of 1812 on the Great Lakes have contributed to its lore. The history of "The Naval Service," as it is affectionately known, is one of a seagoing force that serves the people and legitimate authority, and is underpinned by both nautical and spiritual values.

PROFILE OF A NAVY
Marc Milner (1954–   )

The common perception of a navy is that of a fighting service. In time of war it protects the nation's coasts and trade, and it carries the war to the enemy's shore and attacks his vital maritime interests. But the public perception of navies as armed services designed to wage war belies their more mundane, and more customary, functions. Navies are among the most potent symbols of a state. They represent the extension of national power onto the untamed sea. In times of peace they patrol, assert sovereignty, enforce the rule of law, deter aggression, or show the flag. It is, after all, at sea—what the famous American naval historian and theorist Alfred Thayer Mahan called "the great common"—where the interests of all trading nations converge and overlap. And where, until recently, no globally recognized system except national navies has governed the actions of the unruly—of pirates, poachers, and slavers...

Since its founding in 1910 the Canadian navy has fulfilled all the basic tasks expected of naval forces. It defended hearth and home—and trade—in two major wars and during the Cold War. It has supported peacetime national initiatives, including participation in NATO and United Nations operations, extension of maritime and arctic sovereignty, protection of fisheries, enforcement of international treaties and law, and disaster relief at home and abroad. And, typically, the construction and maintenance of the Canadian navy has also been an important source of government expenditure, of industrial and economic development—and of political largesse.

In the course of its first century the Canadian navy has achieved some noteworthy milestones. During the Second World War, when Canada was, briefly, a great maritime state, its navy became—also briefly—the third largest in the world. In the Cold War the Canadian navy achieved equal international fame for its innovations in anti-submarine warfare. At the end of the twentieth century Canada remains an innovator in modern warship design and construction. In the process the navy staked out a vast area of national interest well beyond the existing territorial waters of the country. In time these areas evolved into Canada's extensive 200-mile coastal economic zones, which included control over the rich Grand and Georges banks.

Sadly, because of the nature of the country, few Canadians ever see their navy and few know much about it. Fewer still, perhaps, would describe Canada as a great maritime state, much less a seapower in the traditional sense. Although Canada was and remains a trading nation, and most of its imports and exports go by ship, the vast majority of Canadians have no contact whatever with the sea that girds their nation on three sides. Moreover, through the twentieth century, Canada has been allied, formally or informally, with the dominant seapower: first Britain, then the United States. The requirement for a navy, if defence of trade and protection from invasion were its primary tasks, has been fleeting at best since 1900.

And yet, since Confederation in 1867, Canada has needed something to protect its off-shore interest. In the early years these concerns consisted of little more than enforcement of fisheries agreements. The assumption of a greater Canadian role in the country's own defence after 1900 and the rising military threat from Germany provided the final impetus for establishing a proper navy only in 1910. Even so, the future of the new Royal Canadian Navy was anything but certain. Before the ink dried on the legislation, Canadians were arguing over what kind of fleet should be built and where, and for what purpose.

Canadians have been arguing about those issues ever since, and with good reason. Navies are expensive to build and maintain, yet they seldom engage in combat. Governments and taxpayers need to be convinced that the heavy, long-term investment fulfils some practical need. In peacetime that need has often been sovereignty, policing offshore areas and protecting marine resources. Navies also fulfil a remarkably useful diplomatic purpose. Warships remain the most moveable manifestations of a sovereign state yet invented. Their good-will visits, a tradition of long standing, carry a cachet unlike any other act—other than a formal state visit. As one recent Canadian ambassador to the Middle East observed: "In two days a visiting Canadian warship accomplished more than I could in two years." Moreover, as the Canadian government discovered as early as 1922, when the fleet was sent to Nicaragua to help settle a debt, or during the turbot dispute with Spain in 1995 when the deployment of Canadian submarines was mooted, navies provide enormous reach and versatility. Perhaps for those reasons, at the end of the twentieth century the Canadian government seems sold on the utility of naval forces.

—from *Canada's Navy: The First Century* (1999)

THE BATTLE OF HUDSON'S BAY
Peter C. Newman (1929–   )

When war between England and France broke out in the 1680s, raiding parties of both countries regularly stormed and captured each other's trading posts. Under the brilliant command of Pierre Le Moyne d'Iberville, the French defeated the British at the Battle of Hudson's Bay (1697) and captured York Factory. The French 44-gun Pélican *faced the 118 guns of the three English ships,* Hampshire, Dering *and* Hudson's Bay—*and won. Since its founding in 1987, the Naval Reserve Division HMCS* D'Iberville, *one of twenty-four such divisions across the country, stands as a memorial to the life and exploits of this remarkable explorer and naval officer.*

Caught between the English-held fort on land and English cannon facing him at sea, d'Iberville had two choices, surrender or fight—and for him that was no choice at all. He ordered the stoppers torn off his guns, sent his batterymen below, had ropes stretched across the slippery decks to provide handholds and aimed his prow at the enemy. As he swept by the *Hampshire*, Captain John Fletcher, its commanding officer, let go a broadside that left most of the *Pélican's* rigging in tatters. At the same time, the two HBC ships poured a stream of grapeshot and musket fire into the Frenchman's unprotected stern.

The battle raged for four hours. The blood of the wounded French sailors bubbled down the clinkerboards through the scuppers into the sea. The ship's superstructure was reduced to a bizarre accumulation of shattered wood; a lucky shot from the *Dering* had blown off the *Pélican*'s prow so that she appeared dead in the water.

In a brief respite, when the two tacking flagships were close enough for the commanding officers to see one another, Fletcher called across from the *Hampshire* demanding d'Iberville's surrender. The Frenchman made an appropriate gesture of refusal, and the English captain paid tribute to his opponent's courage by ordering a steward to bring him a bottle of vintage wine. He proposed a toast across the gap between the two vessels, raising his glass in an exaggerated salute. D'Iberville reciprocated. The ships were so close and the two hulls had so many holes in them that the opposing gun crews could see into each other's smoky quarters. Minutes later, d'Iberville came up on Fletcher's windward quarter and let go with one great broadside, the storm of fire pouring into the English hull, puncturing her right at the waterline. Within three ship's lengths, the *Hampshire* foundered, having struck a shoal, and eventually sank with all hands.

It was barely noon and the desperate splashing of drowning seamen still echoed in the freshening autumn wind as d'Iberville manoeuvred his crippled ship to direct the force of his guns against the *Hudson's Bay*. The Company ship let go one volley and surrendered. During a squall, the *Dering* fled for shelter in the Nelson River. As the *Pélican*'s crew began boarding the vanquished *Hudson's Bay*, a sudden storm came in off the open water, the shrieking wind melding with the screams of the wounded as the rough heaving of the ships battered their bleeding limbs against bulkheads and splintered decks. The *Hudson's Bay* was lucky enough to be driven almost ashore before she sank, so that those aboard could wade to land, but the *Pélican* dragged useless anchors along the bay-bottom silt in the teeth of the hurricane-strength onshore winds. Finally, her rudder broken, she nosed her prow into a sandbar six miles from the nearest bluff. Her lifeboats had been shot away; rescue canoes from shore were swamped as soon as they were launched. The survivors were forced to swim ashore, towing the wounded on a makeshift raft of broken spars. Eighteen more men drowned, and the others stumbled on shore to find the inhospitable land swathed in snow, with nothing but a bonfire and sips of seaweed tea to comfort them.

—from *Company of Adventurers*, Volume I (1985)

PRESS GANGS AND PRIVATEERS
Thomas Raddall (1903–1994)

The American War of Independence (1775–1783) began as a war between Great Britain and thirteen British colonies in North America. However, it soon escalated into a series of international conflicts which placed increasingly heavy demands on Britain's Royal Navy. Impressment, now known as "shanghai-ing," was a violent and often crude way of recruiting for naval service. During this time of upheaval, Halifax served as an important British naval port and fortification—her young men rounded up by dreaded press gangs to serve on British fighting ships.

At frequent intervals the fleet came in, and the Dockyard rang with the labours of shipwrights, calkers, blacksmiths, coppersmiths, riggers, and breamers. These were the days of the press gang, a common feature of Halifax life for half a century. A man-o'-war captain short of seamen was expected by his superiors to pick up his own recruits, and the easiest way was to send his men about the streets of the port seizing every unfortunate youth who fell in their path. These press gangs were armed with cudgels and cutlasses; resistance meant a broken head and later on a taste of the cat-o'-nine-tails to cure the recruit of his stubbornness.

To preserve the form of law it was customary for the admiral to obtain a press warrant from the council, who granted it under pressure from the governor on the ground that the press would rid the town of idle vagabonds. But the vagabonds knew well how to vanish at the first warning cry of "Press!" in the streets, and it was the countryman up to town for the market, the fisherman, the 'prentice boy, the young townsman out for an evening's lark, who fell into the toils. Those with influential friends or employers could count on release later on, but they were few. For two generations of almost incessant war young Haligonians vanished into the lower decks of His Majesty's ships, to die in distant battles, or of the scurvy, the typhus, or the yellow fever which in those days scourged the British service.

—from *Halifax: Warden of the North* (1948)

WAR GAMES
Michael L. Hadley (1936–) and Roger Sarty (1952–)

War gaming has always been an integral part of military and naval operations. It involves imagination, innovation, anticipation, foresight— and sometimes a good sense of humour. It's the old story of trying to anticipate answers to the question "what would happen if?" Perhaps the earliest Canadian war game took place off Halifax, the "Warden of the North," toward the close of the nineteenth century—before Canada even had a navy, and depended upon Britain.

"The Latest Improvements in Scientific Warfare" reached Halifax on 6 July 1881 in what the Halifax *Morning Chronicle* called a "Grand Torpedo Attack." The headlines announced a major test of a new weapon in the fortress town's defences. Military authorities had timed this thrilling event to climax the governor general's visit to the imperial town. Thousands of people thronged the shoreline, from Freshwater to Point Pleasant Park, and the slope up to the summit of the Citadel, with its commanding view of the harbour. Others watched the war game from boats, steamers, and tugs, while some four hundred more held tickets for the governor general's vantage-point on George's Island. How well could Halifax defend itself against assault forces from the sea? The military hoped to provide an answer with a realistic scenario.

The idea of the mock attack was simple. According to the well-briefed press report, "an enemy's squadron, taking advantage of a thick fog, had passed the entrance to the harbour unperceived, and intended to take possession of the Dockyard and the magazines." The defenders had meanwhile seeded the approaches with "torpedoes," or what we now call mines. The lone corvette HMS *Tenedos,* a converted wooden steam sloop with two seven-inch rifled muzzle-loader guns, represented an enemy squadron. On this occasion she enjoyed the brilliant sunshine of a glorious July morning instead of the fog for which the war-game scenario called. The audience watched as *Tenedos* anchored off the first "torpedo" and sent a boat's crew to reconnoitre the dangerous waters. Armed with grappling hooks for tearing the electric cables connecting the mines from their control station on shore, the men probed the channel. This was precisely the method that a secret German memorandum had recommended His German Majesty's Ship (SMS) *Elisabeth* use to combat moored mines in Panama in 1878: either a steam pinnace with trawls or two rowboats moving abreast, with a weighted line suspended between them. But in the British exercise at Halifax the enemy "accidentally" exploded a mine, thereby awakening the garrison to its imminent danger and triggering a withering mock battle between the attacking "squadron" and the artillery ashore.

By all accounts the experiment was a great success. In the *Chronicle's* words: "The roar of the heavy guns to the immediate spectators was perfectly deafening. The simultaneous explosion of... mines was a grand sight, producing novel sensations to those unaccustomed to torpedo displays. The sudden upheaval of large masses of water... carrying with it all kinds of debris, mud and fish... accompanied by the angry rumbling roar of the explosion gave the spectators a faint idea of the grandeur... and horrors of modern warfare." But the tumult had destroyed all the mines. The make-believe enemy slipped through the cleared passage and reached its ultimate target. Halifax faced defeat. But for the moment that did not really seem to matter: the governor general had been "highly delighted and edified" by the operation.

—from *Tin-Pots and Pirate Ships: Canadian Naval Forces and German Sea Raiders 1880–1918* (1991)

Off Coronel
Archibald MacMechan (1862–1933)

On 1 November 1914 Canada lost her first sailors to naval warfare: four midshipmen of the Royal Canadian Navy, from the first class of the Royal Naval College of Canada. The Battle of Coronel took place off the coast of Chile near the city of Coronel where Graf von Spee's powerful East Asia cruiser squadron encountered Britain's much inferior 4th Cruiser Squadron under Rear Admiral Christopher Cradock, RN, in HMS Good Hope. *The Germans handily destroyed their opponents before proceeding to the Falkland Islands, where they themselves were destroyed on 8 December by a British battle-cruiser force. A bronze plaque at the entrance to the Coronel Library in the former Royal Roads Military College (now Royal Roads University) commemorates the deaths of Midshipmen Malcolm Cann, John V.W. Hateway, William A. Palmer and Arthur W. Silver.*

In the stormy Southern sunset, great guns spoke from ship to ship;
Swift destruction, death, and fire leapt from iron lip;
Till two crushed and flaming cruisers vanished dumbly in the
    night,
Sank, nor left a soul behind to tell of that disastrous fight.

In the dark, they died, our comrades, and without a sign they
    passed
But they fought their guns and kept the Old Flag flying to the last.
Death is bitter in lost battle, but they died to shield the Right,
So they swept from that brief darkness into God's eternal light.

—from *Songs of the Maritimes: An Anthology of the Poetry
of the Maritime Provinces of Canada* (1931)

WARTIME SHIPBUILDING
James Pritchard (1939–2015)

The title of the book from which this excerpt is drawn—A Bridge
of Ships*—is a graphic reminder of the vital importance of wartime
shipbuilding. Canadian-built warships and cargo vessels of every description formed massive life-lines across the seas. In shipyards across
the country Canadians not only built these essential warships and
cargo vessels, but repaired and refitted them after their often gruel-
ling voyages. The sites of most of these marine industries are lost to
public memory today: yards like those at Prince Rupert and North
Vancouver (BC), Lauzon (QC), Saint John (NB), Port Arthur (present-day Thunder Bay) and Collingwood (ON). Equally remote seem
the shipyards and boat yards in the Great Lakes which, between 1940
and 1945, produced fifty Flower-class corvettes—the workhorses of
the Battle of the Atlantic—as well as over a hundred minesweepers
and fifty-nine Fairmile motor launches. At the peak of the war effort,
Vancouver's Burrard Shipyards typically employed fourteen thousand
workers, including one thousand women. Welder E.H. Harris remembered those halcyon days in his "Shipbuilder's Ballad": "Each hour we
spend in building, / The more ships can be put to sea; / A giant steel
bridge of freedom / Built in the cause of liberty."*

The history of Canada's shipbuilding industry during the Second
World War is as astonishing as the history of the nation's wartime
navy. The personnel of both expanded by an order of fifty times. Yet,
whereas the story of the Royal Canadian Navy (RCN) is sufficient-
ly well known as to arouse vigorous debates among historians, the
history of Canada's wartime shipbuilding industry remains virtually
unknown...

Wartime shipbuilding had not required Canadian shipyards
to develop an engineering design capacity. In the end, the typical
Canadian yard was a large manufacturing concern without a design and development capability. The industry remained wholly
dependent on what the British wanted built—the simplest ships
possible—and on British naval architects and engineering talent.

With few exceptions, wartime shipbuilding followed British plans and specifications. Little was conceptually new; in fact, the steam technology employed was more than a half-century old. Innovations and reorganization in the yards were limited to increased welding to replace riveting, often over the objections of British marine engineers and naval architects, and sometimes involved brilliant use of new machines such as "Unionmelt" welding on combustion chambers of Scotch boilers. Other improvements occurred outside shipyards among steel fabricators and machinery manufacturers...

Warship production, like other armaments, required a relatively sophisticated engineering industry and a machine-tool industry. Canada lacked both. Little original engineering design was carried out in Canada, which remained wholly reliant upon the United States and the United Kingdom for machine tools until 1942... Although Canada developed and carried out a successful emergency program to construct escort vessels, it failed to develop a capacity to go beyond initial ship specifications. Much of the navy's modernization crisis was due to its failure to learn from combat to modify its own escort ships. All improvements had to wait until they were received from the British Admiralty.

Ironically, the Royal Canadian Navy (RCN), which had been technologically challenged throughout the war, proved to be better positioned for the future than the shipbuilding industry. Since 1943 the navy had been maturing plans for its postwar fleet... Although the RCN still lacked a warship design capacity, at the end of the war it was swiftly acquiring one. These developments and the government's response to the Cold War [1947–1991], rather than any wartime legacy, kept Canadian postwar shipbuilding alive...

Despite its magnificent achievement, Canada's wartime shipbuilding industry left no lasting legacy. The great volume of ship production that Canada achieved was not planned in advance. It was forced upon the country during 1940 and 1941 by the desperate needs of war. Canadian North Sands, Victory, and Canadian types were designed for the sole purpose of providing as many ships as possible in the shortest time possible to move essential war cargos and supplies across the Atlantic faster than the enemy could sink them. That was the task, and it was accomplished.

—from *A Bridge of Ships: Canadian Shipbuilding during the Second World War* (2011)

SEAPOWER
Joseph Schull (1906–1980)

During the crucial years of World War II (1939–1945) Canada's navy served in dangerous waters from the Pacific to the Mediterranean. During the Battle of the Atlantic alone, Canadian warships escorted massive convoys between major ports in North America and Great Britain. As a fighting force, Canada's navy kept the sea lanes open. In doing so it fought pitched battles with enemy forces, especially submarines, losing twenty-four warships to enemy action. Emerging in 1945 as a powerful maritime nation, Canada had owed her seagoing supremacy to an unprecedented confluence of forces: manufacturing and industry, shipbuilding, mobilization of people and supplies—and national will. In writing The Far Distant Ships *as the government's first official history of the navy, Schull aimed not only at providing a riveting account of Canada's war at sea; he also argued for a "big-ship" post-war navy. Ultimately, modern technology and warfare irrevocably changed the old pattern; Canada now has one of the smallest navies in the world—yet one with a global mission.*

"Those far distant, storm-beaten ships upon which the Grand Army never looked, stood between it and the dominion of the world (Alfred Thayer Mahan)." Mahan was writing of the army of Napoleon and the ships of Nelson. Yet his words apply unchanged to the war which began a hundred and thirty-four years after Trafalgar. When Hitler at the summit of his power looked westward from a conquered Europe, the long line of the Atlantic convoy and the grey menace of the Home Fleet rose, invisible and implacable, the barrier he was never to surmount.

Sea power made the conquest of the British Isles an essential for the mastery of Europe and a key to world rule. And sea power made that conquest an impossibility. Dingy, unseen tankers brought in oil for the Spitfires and Hurricanes over seas held open by the Royal Navy. Cargoes of food and supplies, rifles and cannon for the beaten armies returning from Dunkirk, came in by sea. Thereafter sea power—of the United States and Canada and of other nations as well as Britain, sea power moving both on wings and keels—made possible the gathering of mighty resources for the offensive. Sea power bridged the gulf between the old world and the new; linked farms and mines and factories, laboratories and blast furnaces and training camps, with the battlefronts. Sea power was the means of translating strength into accomplishment; the ability to mobilize and concentrate and thrust at the chosen time and at the vital point...

On the Atlantic, throughout the longest and most crucial struggle of the war, Canada's navy grew to be a major factor. In almost every other naval campaign her ships or men were represented; playing frequently an obscure, sometimes a brilliant part. Their work was a share—and no more than a share—of the national effort. The men of the merchant ships wrote an epic which will not be forgotten while the nation remembers its past; and men toiling ashore performed daily impossibilities.

—from *The Far Distant Ships: An Official Account of Canadian Naval Operations in the Second World War* (1950)

THE MAPLE LEAF SQUADRON
Author unknown

Sea shanties and nautical folk songs colour and communicate the seafarers' life. In the nautical world, group singing accompanied many seamen's tasks such as weighing anchor, rowing dories and whalers, and hauling sails. In the process, verses were added or dropped at will, and frequently shaped and re-shaped in order to deal with local circumstances. Such "occupational ballads" serve not only to bond a team of workers, but to create their characteristic mythologies. *The zest of the performance— whether fantasizing on battle, rejecting authority and routine, or boasting of sexual prowess—captures youthful attitudes to lives that in wartime can be bitter and brief. Gallows humour frequently prevails. Such was certainly the case when depicting the life of convoy escorts during the Battle of the Atlantic. (1939–1945).*

Then here's to the lads of the Maple Leaf Squadron,
At hunting the U-Boat it's seldom they fail;
Though they've come from the mine and the farm and the
    workshop,
The bank and the college and maybe from jail.

Chorus:
We'll zig and we'll zag all over the ocean,
Ride herd on our convoy by night and by day.
Till we take up our soundings on the shores of old Ireland,
From Newfy to Derry's a bloody long way.

We're out from grey Newfy and off for green Derry,
Or swinging back westward while tall waters climb;
The grey seas roll round us, but never confound us;
We'll be soon making port and there'll be a high time.

So we're off to the wars where there's death in the making,
Survival or sacrifice, fortune or fame;
And our eyes go ahead to the next wave that's breaking,
It's the luck that's before us adds zest to the game.

—Traditional

DOWN THE GANGPLANK INTO
THE EUROPEAN THEATRE OF WAR
Earle Birney (1904–1995)

*Some 368,000 Canadian troops served in Europe during World War II.
They were transported overseas in scores of ships that had been converted
from commercial liners in order to increase their carrying capacity. Some
of them were as large as the 81,000-ton Cunard liner* Queen Mary
*which reached speeds of 28.5 knots. When she sailed from Halifax with
Winston Churchill on 27 August 1943 she carried 15,116 troops. While
most ships sailed in convoy under naval escort, these "Monsters" as they
were called in code, sailed independently. Given their high speed and
manoeuvrability, and their secretly planned zigzag courses, they could
outrun enemy submarines. Troops on board were never informed where
they were going, nor by which route. It is in such a situation that Earle
Birney sets his n'er-do-well, accident-prone, quixotic hero. Birney's pi-
caresque novel* Turvey *won the Stephen Leacock Memorial Medal for
Humour in 1949.*

At last the order raced through the camp and they were stuffed into
another train and shunted into Halifax. There was a long day of
standing in an embarkation shed rumbling with trucks and echoing
with officers. Then with his overcoat buttoned by command to the
neck, and his respirator on his left side and his water bottle full of
coca-cola on his right, and his haversack slung on his left, and his
rifle on his right, and his pack on his back, and his tin helmet jog-
gling on his head, and ammo pouches full of chocolate bars across
his chest, and his dunnage bag in his left hand, and a berth card and
a mess card and a tag and an extra roll of issue toilet paper in his
right, Turvey boarded the grey transport. Though the thought came
to him that the Atlantic was even deeper than the transit camp, he
descended into the ship's bowels, smelling already of kippers and
boiled cabbage, and struggled to the top of a four-tier bunk, with
something like relief.

The Atlantic, it is true, proved even more monotonous than
their waterlogged barracks: six days of zigzagging in a putty-coloured

waste of waters, six days of life-boat drill and kit inspection and lining up for meals, seven queasy nights of rolling on an emaciated mattress in a man-packed hold. Since they were not in convoy, there was nothing to look at but the salt-chuck, of which Turvey thought there was far too much and all the same. Nor was he comforted by the ship's name, *Andes*. It was such a heavy name, much heavier than water.

But somehow the *Andes* buoyed Turvey's body safely, while his spirits, never easy to douse at any time, were sustained by his fairly consistent winnings at black jack and by the thought that he was approaching every moment nearer a glamorous new world...

And then with the seventh morning came sunlight on a bright green headland, and Catalinas in the air.

"Africa, like I said," McQua muttered.

"Nerts. I bet it's Greenland. Taint Nova Scotia anyway," said a Haligonian.

"I see a castle," Turvey shouted. "Maybe it's Spain!"

"Why don't you chaps get wise to yawselves. That's Iahland dopes," drawled the veteran Tank Sergeant.

Ireland it was, green as a pool table. And, in a few hours, the rockier coast of Scotland, real wrecks on English sandbars, destroyers circling a convoy, and the bombed docks of Liverpool. Turvey had arrived in a land where, if the tales of the Tank Sergeant and the warnings of the Security Officers were true, training schemes were conducted with live mines and honest-to-god shells, enemy spies listened in every restaurant, you didn't dare scratch a match except behind blackout curtains, the ale was terrific, and the girls all blonde and all lonely. Britain, land of air-raids and thatched-roofed beer parlours—and Mac and the Kootenay Highlanders. A new land and a new Turvey, his crime-sheet cancelled in Halifax, and a shiny new pay book in his pocket in which the adjutant had forgotten to stamp any of his O-scores. Turvey straightened his helmet and marched down the gangplank into the European Theatre of War.

—from *Turvey* (1949)

U-69 SINKS THE FERRY *CARIBOU* IN CABOT STRAIT
Michael L. Hadley (1936–)

Among the major losses of the war years was the 266-foot, 2,222-ton Newfoundland ferry Caribou *during her regular nightly crossing of the Cabot Strait. Her route ran the 110-mile stretch of open water between the Canadian National Railway's railhead in North Sydney, Nova Scotia, and Port aux Basques, the western terminus of the Newfoundland Railway. Her courses cut across the convoy routes at a critical choke-point in the Battle of the Atlantic.*

On the dark night of 13 October 1942 German submarine U-69 was lurking about for targets of opportunity in Cabot Strait. Its skipper knew that Canadian naval patrols and escorts faced heavy challenges: a harsh climate with its fog and gales; ice-choked passages in winter, and the severe oceanographic conditions that always seemed to favour the submarine. For here the fresh water of the St. Lawrence River mingled with the salt water of the sea, and produced protective layers under which a submarine could hide with impunity from probing sonar.

Ferries had been making regular runs between Sydney, Nova Scotia, and Port aux Basques, Newfoundland, since 1898. Whole families depended on the company. Sons followed fathers to sea in its ships. Perhaps more than anything else, this aspect of coastal life brought the realities of war at sea painfully home to the peaceful Gulf coast communities. Up to now they had felt relatively secure from the threat of the German submarine fleet. But with *Caribou's* regularly scheduled run, crews no longer asked *whether* the U-boats might strike, but simply *when.*

The SS *Caribou* departed North Sydney on schedule at 7 pm that evening and exercised Life Boat Stations. Of the 237 persons aboard, scarcely a hundred would survive the crossing. Wartime conditions required the darkened ship to steer an evasive route. This evening she steamed at ten knots northward from Sydney towards Cape North before curving toward Port aux Basques with her single naval escort. U-69, commanded by 27-year-old Kapitänleutnant Ulrich Gräf, lay waiting.

Shortly before midnight local time, with relatively calm sea, very good visibility, and weak aurora borealis, Gräf sighted his target. He identified it as a large passenger freighter belching thick black smoke, followed by what he thought was a two-stack destroyer. He erred on both counts. The "destroyer" was a minesweeper, and the ferry was small. Both ships—*Caribou* and HMCS *Grandmère*—were running blind, for neither had radar.

SS *Caribou* was just 40 miles southwest of her destination at 2:21 am when the surfaced U-69 fired a single torpedo from a range of 650 metres. Forty-three seconds later the torpedo struck home, exploding the ship's boilers. Her bottom torn out, the ferry sank in just four minutes. Shocked into wakefulness by the attack, and jolted from their bunks, passengers sought out family members under chaotic conditions before gaining access to the upper deck. Many became separated in the confusion. The submarine had dived, and could now hear the loud wracking noises of *Caribou*'s bulkheads breaking up as she sank to the bottom.

Meanwhile, scantily clad passengers scrambling along sloping decks, or in search of family members in the cabins below, had little time for reflection. Water was rushing into darkened cabins and passageways, passengers groped for lifebelts and hastened to safety. Some survivors reported the sheer terror, panic, and "indescribable chaos" before the ship went down. They told of passengers clutching for lifeboats and rafts, many of which had been shattered by the explosion; they spoke of a woman "in a frenzy of terror" who threw her baby overboard and then jumped after it to her death; they recounted the tale of 15-month-old Leonard Shiers of Halifax who was lost at sea three times—only to be saved each time by a different rescuer. He was the only one of fifteen children aboard to survive. In all, the situation was confused and desperate.

The swift destruction of the *Caribou* left survivors to a night of quiet desperation, debilitating hypothermia, and sometimes a lonely death. Exhausted and terrified as many were, the spiritual heritage of generations of seafaring Newfoundlanders gave them strength.

Throughout the night one could hear praying and the singing of hymns. Clutching debris, an upturned boat, or huddled in overcrowded rafts for up to five hours, many survivors bore witness to selfless courage. Typical of this spirit was Nursing Sister Margaret Martha Brooke, RCNVR, of Ardath, Saskatchewan, who struggled all night long in the vain attempt to save her companion, Nursing Sister Agnes Wilkie, RCNVR, of Carmen and Winnipeg.

News of *Caribou's* fate reached the Canadian public three days after the event. *The Ottawa Journal* proclaimed "Caribou Sinking Proves Hideousness of Nazi Warfare;" the *Halifax Herald* headlined "Women, Children among Victims as Torpedo Strikes." It claimed the loss as the "Greatest Marine Disaster of War in Waters Fringing the Canadian Coast." When the *Caribou* death-toll of 137 persons was finally established, the press could assert with little exaggeration that many families had been "wiped out." Eye-witness accounts emphasized the viciousness of the attack; they highlighted the courage and stamina of those who survived, and the human dignity of those who succumbed. For the first time, Minister for the Navy Macdonald preached in a style he had not previously adopted: "The sinking of the SS *Caribou* brings the war to Canada with tragic emphasis. If anything were needed to prove the hideousness of Nazi warfare, surely this is it. Canada can never forget the SS *Caribou*."

In 1945, Nursing Sister Brooke won the Order of the British Empire for her gallantry and courage on that fateful night. In 2015—when she was one-hundred years old—the navy named an arctic patrol vessel after her.

—adapted from *U-Boats against Canada:
German Submarines in Canadian Waters* (1985)

CONVOY TO TOBRUK

Osmond Borradaile (1898–1999) and
Anita Borradaile Hadley (1938–   )

The eight-month Siege of Tobruk, the strategically vital port on Libya's eastern Mediterranean coast, was the scene of a number of running battles between Allied and Axis forces in World War II. Libya had begun the war as a colony of Italy, but as the Siege opened in 1941, had fallen under British control. Serving under special assignment with the British Army, Canadian cinematographer Osmond Borradaile was aboard the British minelayer HMS Latona *proceeding from Alexandria to resupply the besieged port of Tobruk. En route,* Latona *and her convoy experienced a devastating attack by German aircraft. The state-of-the art* Latona *blew up and sank, thus ending her brief five-month career.*

That evening I was enjoying a drink in the wardroom with some of the officers when action stations sounded. Grabbing my camera, I rushed onto the deck. A glaring sun hovered just above the horizon, and we were heading right into it. Planes suddenly appeared overhead out of the dazzling brightness. Once again we took evasive action. A low-flying plane, only fifty feet or so above the water, shot out of the sun and headed straight for us. The *Latona* swerved sharply as the aircraft dropped a torpedo and veered away. Just as I caught the plane in my camera finder, our pom-poms opened up right on target. A flash and cloud of smoke followed the steady thump of shells and the water below sprang to life as the disintegrating plane hit the surface.

The enemy attack slowed down sporadically, only to pick up again with added fury as reinforcements closed in. It was getting quite dark when a concentrated attack opened up on us. In the course of the ensuing action I think the Axis threw everything they possessed at us: torpedoes, bombs from both high-level and dive-bombing planes, flare after flare. All this together with our own guns made a spectacular display and provided me with enough light to get something really worthwhile. I had scarcely exposed three rolls when a heavy bomb landed by our four-inch gun turret. Knocked unconscious by the explosion, I saw no more of HMS *Latona*'s desperate fight for survival.

Eye-witness accounts allowed me to piece the story together. The bomb that had knocked me out had crippled the ship's steering gear. Ablaze, she had become a sitting target. As the crew assembled on deck to abandon ship, two officers ordered batches of men to jump onto the deck of HMS *Encounter* as she passed close by. By the time the last group of men had jumped to safety, the section of the ship where they had been standing had become a mass of flames and the two officers were too late to make the jump themselves. They made their way to the stern to signal one of the destroyers to come back for them. A pile of land mines caught fire as they waited. The intense heat forced the decision to jump into the water and swim to the destroyer, when a body fell onto them from atop another stack of mines. Although badly burned, it seemed to move, and those two valiant officers decided not to desert it. Instead of leaping into the sea, they waited for HMS *Encounter* to make one final pass across the stern. Grabbing the unconscious bulk by the ankles and wrists, they tossed it to the passing deck before jumping to safety. I owe my life to those two brave men, for I was the dead weight they saved. Minutes later, the *Latona* blew up in a huge ball of flames and sank almost immediately, taking thirty-eight of our men with her.

I regained consciousness around midnight in the wardroom of HMS *Encounter* where the doctor was attending the wounded. I had second-degree burns from my neck up: my lips, ears, and scalp were crisp. These the doctor plastered with tannic acid jelly. But what grieved me more than my wounds was to learn that my cameras and negatives had gone down with the ship. Indeed, my precious Newman Sinclair camera must have acted as a shield, for it saved my face from severe lacerations. It possibly even saved my life.

—from *Life Through a Lens: Memoirs of a Cinematographer* (2001)

THE LAST SIEGE OF MALTA
Gordon W. Stead (1913–1995)

Many Canadians served with British forces during the two world wars. The seas on which they served shaped them as much as did the Forces with which they sailed. Whether going to sea in capital ships in the North Sea, motor torpedo boats in the Channel, or Fairmiles in the Mediterranean, their lives were irrevocably changed. Seafaring triggered self-reflection, and frequent meditation on human conflict and purpose. One such mariner was Gordon Stead, a naval reservist who fought in coastal craft in the Mediterranean against Germany and Italy at the height of the Siege of Malta. This was one of the most crucial theatres of war. Powered by two gasoline engines, the motor launches reached a top speed of 21 knots, but had a range of some 1,500 miles when cruising at 12 knots. They were floating "powder kegs," for they carried 5,000 gallons of high-octane fuel.

In June of 1942, midway through the second year of the latest siege of Malta, one of the smallest ships to wear the proud White Ensign of the Royal Navy was at sea off the beleaguered isle, attended by a harbour craft. The sun was almost at its zenith in a cloudless sky, its glow rebounding from the serene blue water. In the near distance through the light haze loomed the pale gold margin of the land. No other vessels marred the even surface of the sea, and all that day no aircraft scarred the sky.

I was the captain of this little ship and this day stands out in my memory because it was so peaceful and because we were so alone. We—my ship, her crew, and I—were quite used to being alone at sea outside our fortress. Our striking forces had all been driven out to safer havens. But it was unnatural that we were not threatened from the air. Five days before, three front line German fighters had roared in upon us out of the sun and filled our wooden, petrol-driven vessel full of holes. For months the "blitz" had been continuous, and the rain of bombs had laid waste the dockyard and much of the surrounding built-up area. On this one day, although there were no friendly fighters anywhere nearby, we were left in peace.

The action was to westwards and to eastwards where two convoys fought to reach our Island a day's sail away. While we prepared for their arrival at the focal point, the blitz descended on our approaching friends and left us be. Gerry had no time for us. Remnants of one convoy only made it into Malta, but that relief staved off surrender for lack of food and fuel. With the convoy there came also modest reinforcements. This was the turning point, although that could be no more than a premonition on that strangely tranquil day.

How came this small craft to be in this exposed position? How came I to be her captain? We were as far into this hostile sea as it was possible to get—a thousand miles from the nearest friendly base at either end—without starting to go out again. We had flouted this hostility to get here three months before, since when our larger colleagues all had left. We were now the very, very tip of British seapower in this historic sea. We would go on to continue as the leading edge of the naval thrust that cleared the Mediterranean...

While my own tale, it is as much the story of the ship, for I commanded her throughout her operational career and when I left she died—poignantly symbolic of the naval usage that a captain and his ship are one. Tossed by the winds of war, we, too, were like "a leaf upon the sea" an allusion reinforced by the maple leaf badge we wore upon our bridge front to assert that her commander was Canadian.

The context of this story is the most murderously destructive war that has yet been fought. More horrendous wars have been invented, but they have not so far been let loose upon the world.

However, my war differs from the current popular conception of a global conflict. It was not fought by people in front of radar screens pushing buttons to launch missiles at some target half a world away. Rather it was a deadly game of contact and manoeuvre and team play wherein one might see his adversary or at least his vehicle. Being personal, there was room for initiative and daring.

Moreover, my time was served at sea, and the sea imposes terms that are quite different from those permitted by the land. Mariners must first learn to live with every mood and hazard of a temperamental element. The menace of the enemy is just one more reason for being sharp. When the enemy appears, he comes in small packages—an aircraft or a ship—and the object of the exercise is to put the threatening package out of action. Once that is done, the people from the package become survivors to be rescued, since they no longer bear upon the outcome. For officers and crew, sea fights mean standing on an open bridge or manning armament or engines—it is the ship that does the running as though the adrenalin were flowing in her veins.

Scenarios like these mean lengthy periods of tension, sudden shocks of fear, and instants of high excitement—albeit tempered by the joys and challenges of being at sea—but they do not inflame the blood. There are no mass charges by wild hordes sticking bayonets into fellow humans. There can be pain and suffering, but no vast scenes of carnage. And, ordinarily, there is no call for hatred.

—from *A Leaf Upon the Sea:*
A Small Ship in the Mediterranean, 1941–1943 (1988)

THE SEA IS MY ENEMY
Hugh Garner (1913–1979)

During World War II—from 1939 to 1945—Canada's navy had to draw on many young and inexperienced personnel. In response to the demands of war the naval force grew from four ships and some nineteen hundred personnel to over four hundred ships and ninety thousand personnel. Under such conditions, recruits unfamiliar with the ways of the sea—and who had perhaps never even seen it before— became professional seamen in astonishingly short order. They had to in order to survive. Wartime service in the Naval Reserve was a rite of passage. In Garner's novel one such recruit sets off to sea in 1943 aboard a Flower Class corvette on his first tour of convoy duty across the Atlantic.

The pre-dawn air was chill with the wind which swept off the blue-glass ice shelf of Greenland a few hundred miles to the north-west, and the cold black sea was raised into sullen, turgid ridges, its fringe of white petit-point blown away with each gust of wind.

Ordinary Seaman Clark, nineteen years old, Royal Canadian Naval Volunteer Reserve, stepped quickly through the sliding door of the wheel-house, shutting it behind him, and stood in the darkness on the narrow platform staring out at the noisy, heaving sea. He looked up into the darkened sky, catching a glimpse now and again of a patch of star-studded heaven as it dipped and curtsied behind and between the wider ceiling of scudding clouds. The whole cosmos revolved around an axis formed by the jutting bow and fo'castlehead of the small ship, and the whistle of the wind through the struts and halyards accompanied the pirouette of the fading night.

As he stood still, fastening the top toggle of his woolen duffle coat against the wind, he became aware of the dark, dreadful loneliness of the sea. He was suddenly afraid, and he tuned his ears to the more familiar sounds of the ship and his fellows. From below him came the clatter of pans in the galley as the assistant cook, who had been baking his nightly batch of bread, cleaned up before his mate arrived to prepare breakfast. Up ahead the four-inch gun strained at its lashings with every rise and fall of the gun deck, and the shells clanked mournfully in their racks. There was the sound of feet being stamped on the boards above his head as the port look-out changed his position on the wing of the bridge. The noises from aft were swept away with the wind.

The sounds of the ship only accentuated the noisy quietude of the limitless expanse of the sea, so that the boy shivered, and his hands gripped the railing beside him. Suddenly he was afraid of losing his grip on this heaving thing which was his only connection with security, and he feared to be cast away into the sea which hissed and foamed as it reached with white-nailed fingers upon the freeboard below.

Standing there he realized that the sea cannot be loved; it is an enemy upon which men sail their puny craft—an alien thing armed with a multitude of claws ready to pull them beneath it with scarcely a ripple or a trace. It is too vast and too black and too uncomprehending to be loved. It gives neither succor nor hope nor life to those who must depend upon it. It is beautiful and terrifying, and gigantic and insatiable; a desert of water over which men travel through necessity.

He no longer thought of submarines and torpedoes, for now his fears were those which have followed men from the dawn of time; the primeval fears of the elements: of wind, of lightning, of the sea.

He strained his eyes aft to try to catch a glimpse of the look-out on the ack-ack platform; to find another human being with whom to share his terror; but the man could not be seen; he was alone. He fought with himself against the dread which rose through his fibres like a scream. With a desperate urgency he stumbled down the steep steps of the ladder, his heavy coat buckling around his thighs and his hands sliding down the wet railings, not allowing himself to look at the water, his eyes fixed on the swiftly falling stern of the ship. Half-way to the bottom his rubber sea-boot slipped from the serrated step, and his hands lost their grip upon the rails. With a soft thud, and an imperceptible swoosh of clothing, he fell the remainder of the way to the steel deck, and lay there, one arm doubled behind him, and his terrified eyes hidden behind their curtained lids. To his unhearing ears came the slap of the stoical sea as the tips of its tentacles caressed him through the drains along the scuppers.

—from *Storm Below* (1949)

A Memory of the Merchant Marine
Alan Easton (1902–2001)

Having served in both the Merchant Marine and the wartime Canadian navy, Alan Easton well knew the character of seafarers and the challenges they faced. From his own perspective of having commanded warships throughout the Battle of the Atlantic (1939–1945) he ponders the courage of those seamen who manned the cumbersome, often unarmed merchant ships that he had escorted across enemy-infested seas.

I finished this voyage with the sober realization that it was the merchant seamen who took the real onslaught of the enemy at sea. Their ships could hardly fight back against the elusive submarine and, due to their ponderous bulk, could not manoeuvre quickly to avoid their attacker. They always presented the best targets.

The men who lived in these ships could not have been unaware of their vulnerability. They pushed their ships along, never knowing when they would be singled out for extinction. In convoy they had little knowledge of how the enemy was deployed, and not much more when travelling alone. They lived, as it were, on the edge of a volcano. The constant suspense must have been awful.

These men may have tramped from Cape Town to Rio alone and unprotected save for an old heavy gun, crossing an ocean where powerful German surface raiders roamed. Up the Brazilian coast and through the Indies, still alone, to North America, where soon there was to be such devastation that upwards of a hundred ships (half a million tons) a month would be lost. Then in convoy across their familiar Western Ocean where their lives were in constant jeopardy, not only from the enemy but from the perils of the sea. On the coasts of the United Kingdom they would be haunted by torpedo-firing E-boats and hidden mines, and hunted by the bombers of the *Luftwaffe* who might well bring to an abrupt end, under the very lee of their home port, their ten thousand mile voyage.

In the semi-silence of war few people knew of the colossal tasks these unsung, un-uniformed and unnoticed heroes achieved. If any became known, too often they were overshadowed by the epics of the fighting men who had done no more and probably less. None but their families really knew how dangerous were their missions. If they came home—which 30,000 British merchant sailors failed to do— they soon had to turn again and face the same onerous conditions.

We who served under the White Ensign did not go through the torments they went through, nor did the other fighting services. A merchant seaman could fortify himself with nothing but hope and courage. Most of them must have been very afraid, not for days and nights but for months and years. Who is the greater hero, the man who performs great deeds by swift action against odds which he hardly has time to recognize or greatly fear, or the man who lives for long periods in constant, nagging fear of death, yet has the fortitude and endurance to face it indefinitely and carry on?

There was a motto in my old boyhood training ship: "Quit ye like men, be strong." It may have helped those who had been weaned to the sea by this foster mother and who could still remember it.

—from *50 North: An Atlantic Battleground* (1963)

FINALE
George Whalley (1915–1983)

Narratives about war at sea often indulge in a kind of romanticism untenable on land. For in land wars, the debris of mortal combat scars the earth. Not so at sea where the bloody battles between ships on the high seas leaves neither trace of carnage nor sites for national shrines. George Whalley's poem "Battle Pattern," of which this excerpt forms part of the seventh and final canto, puts the lie to that notion. Written to mark the sinking of Germany's battleship Bismarck *by Allied forces on 27 May 1941, the poem is marked by its realism and mythic dimension. This reflects Whalley's own experience of war at sea as a Canadian naval reserve officer.*

There is not elegy enough in all
the winds and waves of the world to sing the ships,
to sing the seamen to their rest, down
through the slow shimmering drift of crepuscule,
sinking through emerald green, through opal dimness
to darkness. Not all laving of all the world's
oceans, loving moonwash of warm
tropic seas can ever heal the hearts
smashed to fragments of desolated darkness.
Sink now, life ended, down through the haunts
of trumpetfish and shark and spermwhale, down
to the still siltless floor of the ocean where

A Noise of War / 291

no light sifts or spills through the liquid drifting
of darkness, where no eye sees the delicate
dark-wrought flowers that open to no moon.

—from *The Collected Poems of George Whalley* (1986)

The old men I saw in my drives around the bay, sitting side-on to their windows, looking out across the water that was often separated from them by nothing more than a stretch of beach, there and not there depending on the tide—I fancied that I understood them now. Each putting-out to sea you could imagine was the start of some journey that, though endless, was not pointless, the point being simply to go and keep on going. They sat, these men, looking out at the sea they were now too old to fish or even venture out onto. But still they were held fast, sea-spellbound.

— Wayne Johnston,
from *The Colony of Unrequited Dreams* (1998)

CHAPTER X

PORTRAITS

The art of portraiture aims at capturing the defining character of persons, and often the situations in which they find themselves. Whether with deft brush strokes on a broad canvas, in the fine lines of a pencil sketch or in a well-crafted poem, portraiture captures fleeting moments—a gesture, a cast of mind, some deeply personal hint at an inner world. It ponders facial features which, according to convention, lead through the eyes to the soul. There are many faces in the nautical world: the face of "those who go down to the sea in ships," the face of those they leave behind and the face of the deep itself. Significantly, the tools of literary portraiture—the use of figures of speech, for example—function the same way as the painter's brush. Here, the sea often emerges as a metaphor for what contemplatives call the interior life. Whether playfully, wistfully or in its darker moods, the sea resonates with the most primal intuitions of the human mind.

I Was Born by the Sea

Una H. Morris MacKinnon (1853–1947)

I was born by the sea!
My cradle song
Was sung by the waves to me,
The old song,
The low song,
The song of the ancient sea;
Over and over they sang to me
Their sweet, soft, drowsy melody;
Sweetly I slept without a fear,
Dear was the song to my infant ear;—
The old song,
The low song,
The song of the ancient sea.

I was born by the sea!
My fairy tales
By each roving wave were told;—
Wild tales,
Weird tales,
Tales of the brave and bold;—
Tales of the seas by winds distressed,
Of coral caves where sailors rest;
Tales of the maids with sea-green hair,
Singing the songs that lured them there.
Wild tales,
Weird tales,
Tales of the brave and bold.

—from *The Tides of the Missiquash* (1928)

OLD SLOCUM
Pierre Berton (1920–2004)

Attracted to the sea and seafaring very early in life, the legendary Joshua Slocum was born on 20 February 1844 in Annapolis County, Nova Scotia. Gaining experience in a range of vessels from cabin-boy on a fishing schooner to captain of a commercial freighter, he sailed what were then known as the Seven Seas. At the age of fifty-four he became the first to circumnavigate the world alone. After restoring the once derelict 37-foot yawl Spray, *he had departed Nova Scotia in July 1898. Then, in November 1909, he set sail once again on one of his regular winter cruises and was lost at sea.*

Old Slocum sits hidden in his book-lined cabin aboard the *Spray*, totally alone, as he has been since he departed Yarmouth, Nova Scotia, the previous July. Old? Actually he is fifty-two. It is just that his face is leathered by the sea and the winds—the skin nut brown and crinkled, the chin and ears a little grizzled—that his hands are gnarled and knobby, that his body is all bone and muscle, and that he has already lived a lifetime and more. Supple as a bobcat, agile as a monkey, he is the most experienced saltwater man of his age, but also an anachronism—a committed sailor in a world that has done with sail. The days of the clippers have ended. The bustling ports of Saint John, Lunenburg and Halifax have wound down. The big rafts of squared timbers have all but vanished from the Ottawa River and life is beginning to speed up...

He is acutely aware of being alone—alone with the vastness of the horizons, the play of the winds, the wells and currents of the sea, the moving sun and the wheeling stars. The very coral reefs, he will write, keep him company. His living companions are the flying fish that slap onto the glistening deck each night, the whales that cruise majestically past, the sharks, whom he calls "the tigers of the sea," and the birds: the men o'war soaring high above him, the red-billed tropic birds wheeling and arcing in the sky, the gulls and boobies screeching in his wake and settling on his mast.

With the sun rising astern and the Southern Cross abeam every night, he sprawls out in his cabin (for the *Spray*, which he has fashioned with his own hands, miraculously steers herself), reading his way through his library (Lamb, Addison, Gibbon, Coleridge, Cervantes, Darwin, Burns, Longfellow and his two greatest favourites, Robert Louis Stevenson and Mark Twain), poking about in his galley (trying his hand at fish stew and hot biscuits to lighten his regular diet of potatoes and salt cod) and occasionally (very occasionally) digging out his sextant to check his latitude.

Carried forward as if on a vast, mysterious stream, he is at one with his surroundings, feeling "the buoyancy of His hand who made all the worlds"—Old Slocum, veteran of a hundred sea adventures, survivor of a dozen murderous encounters, master of the ocean's finest sailing vessels (gone, now, every last one of them, sunk, beached, stove in, ravished, abandoned to the rot); Old Slocum on the greatest adventure of all, an adventure no one else has dared; Old Slocum, owner, master, mate and crew of a cockleshell, sailing all by himself around the world. Forty-six thousand miles. Three full years. Another lifetime...

So here he is, all alone as he prefers to be—Joshua Slocum, a Bay of Fundy boy from Annapolis County, Nova Scotia, born in 1844 into the age of the clipper ships: a seaman at sixteen, a first mate at eighteen, master of his own ship at twenty-five and at thirty-seven, captain of the *Northern Light,* the finest sailing vessel afloat. Joshua Slocum, master mariner, washed up at fifty, stubbornly refusing to come to any accommodation with steam power or iron hulls, preferring to work as a carpenter in a shipyard but forced out of that, too, for want of a fifty-dollar union fee. Joshua Slocum, picking up odd jobs on Boston harbour boats and hating it, dreaming of the great days of canvas, when he was king of the ocean, dreaming and hating his work until, on one black day, an entire load of coal mixed with dirt ("Cape Horn berries" they call it) half-buries him. In that moment, Slocum, casting his mind back to the *Northern Light* (two thousand tons, three decks, 233 feet long, full-rigged), can stand it no more. He quits his job and determines to return to the sea. He will make the longest possible voyage in the smallest possible craft and he will do it all alone.

—from *My Country: The Remarkable Past* (1976)

CHARLOTTETOWN HARBOUR
Milton Acorn (1923–1986)

An old docker with gutted cheeks
time arrested in the used-up-knuckled hands
crossed on his lap, sits
in a spell of the glinting water.

He dreams of times in the cider sunlight
when masts stood up like stubble;
but now a gull cries, lights
flounces its wings ornately, folds them
and the waves slop among the weed-grown piles.

—from *In a Springtime Instant:*
Selected Poems (1975)

EASTERN SHORE
Charles Bruce (1906–1971)

He stands and walks as if his knees were tensed
To a pitching dory. When he looks far off
You think of trawl-kegs rolling in the trough
Of swaying waves. He wears a cap against
The sun on water, but his face is brown
As an old mainsail, from the eyebrows down.

He has grown old as something used and known
Grows old with custom; each small fading scar
Engrained by use and wear in plank and spar,
In weathered wood and iron, and flesh and bone.
But youth lurks in the squinting eyes, and in
The laughter wrinkles in the tanbark skin.

You know his story when you see him climb
The lookout hill. You know that age can be
A hill of looking; and the swaying sea
A lifetime marching with the waves of time.
Listen—the ceaseless cadence, deep and slow.
Tomorrow. Now. And years and years ago.

—from *The Mulgrave Road* (1951)

SNAPSHOTS OF A *BLUENOSE* SKIPPER
Keith McLaren (1950–   )

Angus J. Walters (1881–1968) was a consummate deep-sea fisherman and tough-minded captain. As skipper of the famous fishing schooner Bluenose *during the International Fishermen's Cup races from 1920–1938 he gained renown as a feisty and cagy racing tactician. Tales of his sailing prowess are among the most gripping in schooner lore.*

Walters had a formidable reputation himself. He had been only thirteen in 1895 when he had first gone fishing and was still in his early twenties when he became master of his first ship. He was known as a "driver," a no-nonsense, hard-nosed skipper with a flinty character and a caustic edge to his tongue. He was blessed with a remarkable ability to carry sail and a sixth sense when it came to fishing; his vessel was always amongst the top boats when the biggest catches of the season were reckoned...

The master of a fishing schooner had to have the confidence and skill to be able to sail miles from shore in variable sea conditions, tidal currents and poor visibility. A crew's livelihood and safety depended on his being able to pinpoint a prime fishing spot, sometimes hundreds of miles from the home port, and make landfall safely after the trip was finished. There were no radars, radios or electronic navigation aids of any kind. A few skippers could use a sextant to perform celestial sights, but most were content with the basic navigational tools: a compass, a chart, a lead line and the confidence that comes from years of experience and local knowledge...

Walters has been seen as hero or villain, depending on the side of the Canada-United States border. Although he was known for his caustic tongue and for playing hard and fast with the rules [of sailing races], even his worst critics could not fault his superior seamanship. The American maritime historian Howard Chapelle later called him "an aggressive, unsportsmanlike, and abusive man," but acknowledged him as "a prime sailor." North of the border, Walters was a champion who contributed greatly to a spirit of nationhood in a young country so often overshadowed by her neighbour to the south. This was especially true during the depths of the Great Depression, when Canada desperately needed larger-than-life heroes who were tough and resourceful. The *Bluenose* became a national icon, her image appearing on everything from soft drinks to underwear. Today, her likeness remains engraved on the Canadian 10-cent coin.

—from *A Race for Real Sailors: The* Bluenose
and the International Fishermen's Cup, 1920–1938 (2006)

THE LIGHTHOUSE KEEPER'S DAUGHTER
Floris Clark McLaren (1904–1978)

I never look out of the windows any more;
All there is to see is sand and water.
I think I would give my soul to see a mountain,
Or willows over a brook, or a forest of redwood.
Twenty-eight years I've looked at sand and water;
I used to dream about going away to the city
But it would have broken Dad's heart if I ever had left him,
So for twenty-eight years I've kept my dreams a secret,
And helped Dad to tend the light,
And watched the steamers that passed us.

Twice a month a boat stops here with the mail;
Once two girls from the city came out here "to see the
　　lighthouse";
They thought it was beautiful here,
The white tower and the endless blue water...
I suppose prison walls might be beautiful
To those outside of the prison.

I used to dream too of some day finding a lover,
But now I know that no lover will ever come to the lighthouse;
Just the old men on the boat,
And George, The Lightkeeper's Assistant.
Dad doesn't know that I don't like George
Because his neck is thick and his hands are hairy;
He wants me to marry George, "a steady dependable fellow";
I think a mother might understand, but I don't remember my
　　mother.

I used to struggle and fret and fight against things,
But I'm tired of that, and besides it's no use to struggle.
I'll marry George, and live here or at some other lighthouse,
And die there some day, I suppose, but that will not matter
Because I have never lived.

—from *The Frozen Fire* (1937)

PORTRAIT OF ELIAS PALLISHER
Harold Horwood (1923–2006)

Memorable characters populate the pages of much historically based nautical fiction. The character of Newfoundlander Elias Pallisher is a case in point—a fisherman marked by rugged independence, deep sense of community and a simple faith. In adversity he reveals a stubborn inability to grasp that others weaker than he cannot emulate his stoic virtues.

A fish failure such as that which hit the bay shore that year is one of the regular hazards faced by inshore fishermen who can travel in their small boats only to the nearby fishing grounds. The ocean currents and the climate vary greatly from year to year. The bait fish—caplin and squid and herring—come and go with the currents, seeking waters where their own food, the tiny plankton, can multiply. When the waters happen to be right the bait fish crowd toward shore in countless billions, some coming to feed, some to spawn, and the codfish crowd toward shore behind them until they are "eating the rocks" and the net traps at the headland berths are full to bursting every morning. But some years the water is too cold, or a titanic disaster overtakes the bait fish offshore, or the squid reach the bottom of their eight-year cycle. And some years—once or twice in each generation—all these things happen at once. Those are the years of famine for the men and women and children who live out of the cod traps. Day after day they rise before dawn, eat bread and tea by lamplight, don oilskins, and coax tiny engines into life, heading out through the murk to their trap berths, hoping that the fish may have struck in. Day after day they haul the huge, box-shaped hempen traps, only to find them empty save for the strings of kelp and rockweed tangled in their leaders by the force of the tide.

Elias Pallisher was, year after year, the most successful fisherman in the Bight. A tall, thin man, very dark, his hair showing a touch of gray, his face sharply cut and unemotional, but deeply lined from squinting into sun and wind, he was a trap owner with a big investment in gear and four share men working with him. Though most years he cured hundreds of quintals of fish (each quintal representing a hundred and twelve pounds dry weight) as shares for himself and his traps, he cured only twenty-eight—a little over three thousand pounds—the year of the fish failure. Even at that, he was more fortunate than the other fishermen. Some had five or six quintals, some literally nothing.

Elias was inclined to blame those who had nothing—the weak and the improvident among his neighbors.

"Warn't never a year a man couldn' scrape enough to feed hisself and 'e's family, do 'e work at it," he said to his wife and sons. "I 'lows anyone kin get fish enough fer 'e's own use, with a jigger if 'e got nought else, no matter how bad it be. An' 'e can raise spuds too, in the gaps betwix the rock, allowin' 'e've a mind. Ain't never knowed a year when ye couldn' pick berries neither, bein' as ye ain't too lazy t' bend yer back. But o' course there be those as expects God's gifts to drop straight into their hands."

"Hush, Elias," Martha Pallisher scolded. "It ain't fer we to judge. If some poor 'angshore be brought low be 'is own foolishness, maybe that be a cross an' affliction 'e can't help. An' it ain't the fault of 'e's wife an' children, surely."

"'Tis God's law," Elias stated flatly, "that a man suffer fer 'e's sins, kin 'e help 'em or no—an' that 'e's wife an' children suffer along with 'im. It be written that way, an' ye can't get around it."

—from *Tomorrow Will Be Sunday* (1966)

NORTH SHORE, PEI
Anne Compton (1947–   )

There is a sense of eternity that is accessible where sea meets land—a place synonymous with the meeting of eternal time and everyday life. The poet's use of the word "(vocal)" in the final stanza suggests that the women's voices and the sea's voice are one and the same.

Who knows? Perhaps they walk the beaches in their
    long-belted dresses,
the Island women of long ago.
Possibly, we will see them, in a lucent spell of light,
    tidal pacing leisurely,
an assemblage through the surf.
Their hair come loose from its combs—though it's whipped
    by the wind—is left unattended
as they perambulate the coast.

They're absorbed in telling over lives lived inland past the
    dunes.
Doubtless, it's of the fields that they're speaking
or a cairn that stood there once.
And the men whose fieldwork's finished
sleep on: solaced by the sea-sounding speech of women naming
    men.
It's not for the living
they slow-step through the swell with their heads bent together
and their skirts stiff with salt.
Every birth begins a story and the story as they tell it defies
the tumbled silence of stone.

If we saw, could we hear, in the interval of the wave, what ghost
tells to ghost
so coolly now passion's past.

What they know must be as limitless as the sea (vocal)
that rolls to Europe
off the Island's North Shore.

—from *Opening the Island* (2002)

JOHN ANTLE: SKIPPER-PASTOR
Michael L. Hadley (1936–   )

*"When the maverick missionary pioneer John Antle founded the seagoing
Columbia Coast Mission in 1904, he set events in motion that helped
change the face of British Columbia's coastal society in remarkable ways.
A deep-sea navigator and yachtsman, the crusty Newfoundlander priest
took up the threads of the Grenfell Mission of Labrador and wove them
into a unique pattern specially adapted to the needs of Canada's Pacific
Coast." Thus begins the history of a medical-mission that served isolated
settlements with its colourful array of some twenty ships and boats until*

*well into the mid-1970s when aircraft and changes in industry spelled
its demise. His watchword "church service, not Church Services" encap-
sulated his approach.*

Seafaring was the obvious choice of profession for the coastal men of
Newfoundland where the founder of the Columbia Coast Mission
grew up. John Antle had known boats from his earliest days. Born
in 1865, he had watched square-rigged sealing vessels from many
countries working their way in and out of ice-strewn harbours. He
eventually sailed before the mast with his father, who skippered a
barquentine out of Harbour Grace. Antle's father intended his son to
follow this tradition, and planned to send him to the nautical school
in St. John's. From the family's point of view, this would have been
natural, perhaps even providential. But young John had a mind of
his own and refused to go to sea on his father's terms. "What, then,
are you going to do?" his father asked. "I'm going to teach school
and then I hope to enter the ministry." "Who's going to pay for all
this?" the father testily enquired. "Not you," retorted young John.

Abrupt, direct and uncompromising, Antle displayed a self-
determination that at first seemed ill considered. Yet his approach
revealed the beginnings of both a vision and a leadership style rooted
in a profound compassion. At age seventeen, he resolved to place no
further burden on his father for training and education; he regarded himself a man and would see to matters on his own. Although
he did go to sea as his father wished, he did so in response to a call
much deeper and more spiritual than hunting seal and catching fish.
While taking up the profession of seafaring, he was becoming, in the
biblical phrase, "a fisher of men."

The rough notes of John Antle's unpublished memoirs reveal a
reflective, tough-minded man who enjoyed the challenges of life.
Before his eighteenth birthday, he had taken a job as teacher and cat-
echist on the northern coast of Newfoundland. Of that early period
he later wrote: "I learned the hard way to stand on my own feet and
make my own decisions." He always sought new tasks, even launching himself into a sailing mission along some forty miles of the Strait
of Belle Isle to visit his charges. Bleak, barren and sparsely populated,

the region offered little solace. From there he moved to Conception Bay as teacher and lay reader. Throughout his life he felt indebted to the friends and families of Christ Church, Newfoundland, for "rubbing off the hard corners of my character and manners, and otherwise perfecting the groundwork fitting me for the high calling" of pastor. It was not so much the intellectual challenge of theological study that attracted him; he had little patience with abstractions. Nor did he have much patience with those who saw the ministry as a sinecure. What mattered was the Social Gospel that sought practical solutions to human problems. Time and again he touches these themes in his memoirs: his work during the smallpox epidemic at the town of Island Cove; his caring for the diphtheria victims in Harbour Grace, before returning to theological studies at St. John's College in the provincial capital; his polite disdain of expatriated English candidates for the priesthood who seemed ill suited and ill motivated for their tasks.

—from *God's Little Ships* (1995)

MORNING LABRADOR COAST
Michael Crummey (1965–   )

Morning Labrador coast
my father is thirteen
no, younger still
eleven maybe twelve
shivering to warm himself in the dark

The rustle of surf behind him
the passiveness of it at this hour
the grumble of men waking early
in the shacks
the steady muffle of piss
smacking a low mound of moss at his feet

He's almost given up on childhood
works a full share on the crew
smokes dried rock-moss rolled in
brown paper out of sight of his father

Each morning he makes fists to work the stiffness
out of his hands and wrists
the skin cracked by sea salt
the joints swollen by sleep after hours of work
he soaks them in the warm salve
of his urine
shakes them dry in the cold air
and turning back to the shacks
he sees stars disappearing in the blue
first light breaking out over the water,
the dories overturned on the grey beach
waiting

—from *Arguments with Gravity* (1996)

A COD-FISHER'S LIFE
Farley Mowat (1921–2014)

The cod fishery was once the nautical gold of the Atlantic. But since those days, overfishing and environmental devastation by foreign factory ships and "draggers" overtook fishing by deep-sea schooner and dory. The Canadian government declared a moratorium on cod fishing in 1992, and banned fishing one year later. In 1967 Mowat caught a glimpse of what it had once been like.

Our first trap was set in nine fathoms off Bois Island and we reached it just at dawn. While the rest of us leaned over the side of the skiff, staring into the dark waters, our skipper tested the trap with a jigger—a six-inch leaden fish equipped with two great hooks, hung on the end of a heavy line. He lowered the jigger into the trap and hauled sharply back. On the first try he hooked a fine fat cod and pulled it, shimmering, aboard.

"Good enough!" he said. "Let's haul her, byes."

So haul we did. Closing the trap mouth and then manhandling the tremendous weight of twine and rope took the best efforts of the five of us and it was half an hour before the trap began to "bag," with its floats upon the surface. As we passed armloads of tar-reeking, icy twine across the gunwales, the bag grew smaller and the water within it began to roil. We had a good haul. The trap held twenty or thirty quintals [one quintal = 112 pounds] of prime cod seething helplessly against the meshes.

One of our number, a young man just entering his twenties, was working alongside the skiff from a pitching dory. He was having a hard time holding his position because of a big swell running in from seaward. An unexpected heave on the twine threw him off balance, and his right arm slipped between the dory and the skiff just as they rolled together. The crack of breaking bones was clearly audible. He sat back heavily on the thwart of his dory and held his arm up for inspection. It was already streaming with blood. A wristwatch, just purchased and much treasured, had been completely crushed and driven into the flesh.

The injured youth lost hold of the net and his dory was fast driving away from us on the tide rip. Our skipper cried out to us to let go of the trap while he started the engine, but the young man in the drifting dory stopped us.

"Don't ye be so foolish!" he shouted. "I'se able to care for myself! Don't ye free them fish!"

Using his good arm, he swung an oar over the side and hooked an end of the header rope with it, then with one hand and his teeth he pulled himself and the dory back to the skiff along the rope. We took him on board, but he would not let us leave the trap until every last cod had been dip-netted out of it and the skiff was loaded down almost to her gunwales. During all this time, perhaps twenty minutes, he sat on the engine hatch watching us and grinning, as the blood soaked the sleeve of his heavy sweater and ran down his oilskin trousers.

When we got back to the stage it was ten o'clock and the sun was high and hot. Pat Morry met us with a truck and we took the lad away to the doctor who set the bones and took sixteen stitches to close the wound. I went along and as we left the doctor's little office the young man said to me: "Skipper, I hopes I never spiled yer marnin'!"

—from *The Boat Who Wouldn't Float* (1969)

BOXING THE COMPASS
Richard Greene (1961–   )

Boxing the compass is a lost art from the days of the magnetic compass. It was a teaching technique to make young seamen thoroughly conversant with this primary aid to navigation. In those days, the compass rose was marked off in "points" moving clockwise from north through east, south, west and back around to north again. These were known as the "cardinal points." A candidate had to be able to recite the sequence both clockwise and anticlockwise—with all the intermediate points and "quarter points" in between. Whereas today one might want to order the helmsman to steer a specific number of degrees on the gyro, the helmsman once had to respond to such orders as "steer north-east by east a quarter east." The expression "to box the compass," is now used in the sense of "to get one's bearings," or to "make sense of one's life." In the following sonnet, it becomes a metaphor for meditating on the approaching death of the narrator's father.

Remember when you breathed so easily,
lit a pipe behind cupped hands when the wind blew?
Trees you planted bending every way from true,
grey water hove up as breakers out to sea,
baffling gales turned round in their weatherly
boxing of the compass, all thirty-two

points of tumult bearing on Baccalieu
or Bell Island? And things I could not see—
'Whales,' you said, 'Out there, dozens of whales.'
An hour later, we watched through streaming glass
but I could not tell a pothead from a wave.
Forty years on, I lie through a night of gales
in your emptied house and see them pass,
blow, plunge in waters deeper than a grave.

—from *Boxing the Compass* (2009)

THE FISH PLANT
Donna Morrissey (1956–   )

In the mid-twentieth century, the advent of the frozen fish industry in Newfoundland put an end to the traditional ways of small fishing communities. Men went to work on company-owned trawlers, while women left the back-breaking work of spreading salt fish to dry on the flakes and found new jobs in processing plants. Despite poor pay, shift work and multiple health hazards, women gained a degree of financial independence they had not known before. Yet the passing of the old way of life was painful, if inevitable. In Morrissey's book, a fisherman, Manny, tries to convince his brother to let go of the past: "The whole goddamn thing's turned around. They don't need we salting fish no more, not with the factory freezers on board. And you can't help but see the truth of it. Might not be what we wants, but it's a better way, simple as that. Freezing fish is a better way of keeping them than salting. Bigger boats is a better way of catching them. Simple as that. And if we don't go along with it, we're out in the cold."

Change! From what into what? thought Adelaide dismally as the second buzzer rang, sending fifty or sixty workers jostling around her, assailing her nostrils with the stringent smell of tobacco and black tea as coats and caps got swapped for aprons and hairnets, and dozens of bodies pushed her along, fighting for a dip in the disinfectant water filling the trough before heading onto the floor. Marching past nine work stations laid out side by side before a long conveyor belt, Adelaide stood at the tenth and last, all thoughts about *change* evaporating as she fixed her hairnet in place, tied on the stiffly bibbed rubber apron that hung to her knees, pulled her filleting knife out of her rubber boot, and hauled a pan of fillets off the conveyor belt rumbling along in front of her. Slapping an ice-cold fish from the pan onto the piece of acrylic that marked her workplace, she slit the V-bone from the fillet, trimmed the tail, and hacked apart the flesh too soft or bruised, then flicked each section into a pan designated for different grading. One of the belts rumbling out of the holding room at the back of the plant started a low moaning that quickly accelerated into a shrill screech, sending her clamping her hands over her ears as the sound shivered through her teeth.

"Shut it down, shut it down" hollered somebody. "Sweet Jesus, shut it down!" The demonic sound subsided, and Adelaide let go her breath with relief. Four weeks! Four weeks she'd been standing here, and never had her nerves been more jagged. Hell is what this plant was, bloody hell with its ten stations to each side of the conveyer belt, and another belt rumbling behind her with another twenty stations, making for forty stations and forty women, arguing, cackling, and shrieking over the belts rattling along its pans of fish from the filleters to the skinners to the trimmers (of which she was one), and then on to the packers where it was wrapped in five-, ten-, twenty-pound boxes and nailed shut and jammed into freezers, steel plates clanging, doors slamming, steam hissing from the web of pipes snaking barely a foot over the tallest head. And despite its being the loudest, the station closest to the skinners and the holding door was the one she chose to work at, sparing herself the added aggravation of having to shout back at Suze or Gert or her mother or a dozen others all working around her, bellowing to each other over the ruckus of the machinery.

Most mornings she worked three hours steady, up to break time, without a word, without looking up. Yet, hellish as it was, she rested assured she'd never have to scrape another maggoty fish, for not even a mosquito ventured into this low, oblong cell of harsh overhead lights, of walls shaking from the clanging, vibrating generators, of air putrid with gut and gurry, and fishers out-shouting each other over the clanging of the motors and winches as they tied up at the wharf in their longliners and skiffs and motorboats and punts, unloading their thousands of pounds of fish into the holding station.

Yet, despite the growing complaints of those working around her for more air, longer tea breaks, and a place to sit and have lunch, she liked it just fine to stand straight-backed, not hunched; to have her world reduced to a piece of acrylic with a light beneath it and five pans in an arc around it; to have her daily wardrobe consist of an oversized rubber apron dragging past her knees and a hairnet that rendered her and the rest of them—men and women alike—to caricatures of old women. What need to expend five minutes of caressing the yellowy petals of a buttercup, of gazing through the honeyed haze of the sun, of feeling last evening's raindrops slide coolly down one's cheek—of what use was anything when most of daylight's hours were spent standing imbecilic amongst the maniac roar of machinery, hacking apart flesh already eating itself?

—from *Sylvanus Now* (2005)

THIS IS THE OLD TIMER
Norman Hadley (1964–2016)

In his collection of dramatic dialogues and monologues known as Salty Dips, *Hadley created a fictional character ideally suited to radio broadcast. Desperately trying to bridge his loneliness in the waters off Victoria, BC, the character, Old Timer, tries to engage other boaters in conversation. In so doing, he absent-mindedly hogs Channel 16—the distress channel restricted by law to emergencies and to making initial contact with another vessel. Typically, boaters in the scenarios do not want to answer this lonely caller, for they know that once contact is made, they will never get rid of him. Instead of making contact, the Old Timer broadcasts largely to himself.*

"This is the Old Timer. Uh, I'm looking for a radio check. Over."
"Loud and clear, Old Timer. Out."
"Roger that. You read me loud and clear. Uh, over."
(Pause... radio static)
"Old Timer again. Uh, roger your last. Much appreciated. And I read you loud and clear also. Over." (Pause)
"This is the Old Timer... again. I did not catch the name of your vessel. Over." (Pause)
Silence. Crackling in radio.
"Uh, Get any bites today?... young fella? Over."
Lengthy pause.
"Just getting started. Out."
"Roger that. Hope you have a splendid one. I'm just off Fleming Bay. Over." (Pause)
"Old Timer again. I'm just on my own here. Let me know if you find the fish. Over."
"Will do. Out."
"My wife... bless her, passed away, five years gone now. Rest her soul. She used to pack my lunch on fishing days. Always a thick slice of cheese and some Melton Mowbray pie. Over." (Pause)
"Mel-ton Mow-bray. Over." (Pause)
"I miss her terribly. Over." (Pause)
"Are you near Albert Head? Over." (Pause)
"I grew up as a boy hearing the sound of the fog horn on Trial Island. Staines Point. Over." (Pause)
"What do they call it? A diaphone?" (Pause)
"As a lad I used to lie in bed listening to it. I imagined it was calling me out to sea. Used to frighten me so. Waaaarren. Waaaarren. Over." (Pause)
"My name is Warren you see. Uh. Old Timer over." (Pause)
Time passes....
"Well, I've had no luck. Best I get in before it gets dark. Over." (Pause)
"My wife used to have my tea ready for me when I'd come home. God love her. Over." (Pause)
"Hope you land the big one young fella.

[....]

Old Timer, this is Victoria Coast Guard Radio. This is the international distress and calling frequency. Please move to a working frequency. Out.

"This is the Old Timer. Roger. Thank you Sir. And a good day to you. Out."

(Pause)

"You fellas do a damn fine job..."

(Pause)

"Old Timer heading for home. Out"

—from "A Boatload of Salty Dips" (2013)

MY GOD, THAT'S A WOMAN!
Allan Anderson (1915–1994)

From an interview with Doreen Noseworthy, Portugal Cove, Newfoundland.

"I'd go down with the rest of the men dressed up in oilskins, just like the rest of the guys, and all with their long rubbers on, you know. And I'd go down to go out in the boat and next you could hear somebody: 'My God, that's a woman, there's a woman there!' And it's just breaking day, right early in the morning, and they couldn't get over it, the older fishermen that would be getting ready to go out on the water, they really couldn't get over it. They'd say, 'Look, there's a woman.'

Now my husband has had the most fish down there, and the fishermen say that: 'Well, he must have his charm aboard'—this is what they refer to me as, his charm. Last year, I stayed home a couple of days, and the two days I stayed home they had no fish. So the next day I went down and they had eighteen thousand pounds. So all of the men joked and said: 'I'm takin' you tomorrow.' They all wanted me to go out with them the next day, like.

Our boat is well equipped, and any real heavy work like hauling the main ropes and stuff like this is mostly done by a gurdy. So I haul the ropes along with them, I don't mind. But there is work now that really is too heavy for a woman to do, like when you start haulin' the trap first, to picking up the main ropes and gettin' them across the boat and stuff like this. Well, there is women in Newfoundland could do it, but as you see, I'm not that big. I'm not even five foot tall. I'm four eleven."

—from *Salt Water, Fresh Water* (1979)

PORTRAIT OF A COMMUNITY—
THE ESCUMINAC VICTIMS AND SURVIVORS
Compiled from various public records

A CBC report expressed it this way: "June 19, 1959: a fierce hurricane lashes the Gulf of St. Lawrence, wreaking awesome damage and disaster on the New Brunswick coast. The storm devastates the small port of Escuminac, as 130 km/h winds and 15-metre waves sink 22 fishing boats and drown 35 men in the deadliest hurricane in Canadian history. The tragedy leaves 19 widows and 83 fatherless children, a catastrophic loss to a town of just 600 people."

An impressive stone sculpture by Acadian artist Claude Roussel now stands over two metres tall on Escuminac Wharf. Entitled Les Pêcheurs—The Fishermen, *it bears the names of the victims. Unveiled on 19 June 1969, and visible both from sea and from shore, the memorial is a stark and sombre reminder of the perils of the sea.*

Chapman, John, 16. Bay du Vin. He was the main support for his parents and his eleven brothers and sisters.

Chiasson, Albert, 50. Baie Ste. Anne. Survived by his wife, Eva, and twelve children aged 15 years to six months.

Chiasson, Alphonse, 17. Baie Ste. Anne. Son of Albert.

Chiasson, William, 47. Baie Ste. Anne. Survived by his wife, Lozia, 37.

Chiasson, Adrien, 20. Baie Ste. Anne. Son of William.

Chiasson, Robert, 16. Baie Ste. Anne. Son of William.

Cook, Fraser, 60. Howard's Cove. P.E.I. His son, Edward, survived.

Daigle, Edgar, 32. Baie Ste. Anne. Survived by his wife, Leocade, and five children from two months to eleven years.

Gauvin, Charles, 53. Lameque. Survived by his wife, Emma, and seven children.

Kelly, Arthur, 27. Kouchibouguac. Survived by his wife, Annetta, and five children from six years to two months.

Kelly, Hector, 19. Richibucto. Son of Hugh.

Kelly, Hugh, 50. Richibucto. Survived by wife Josephine.

Kingston, Clifford, 54. Bay du Vin. Survived by his wife, Fern, 51, and two sons aged sixteen and seventeen.

Kingston, Windsor, 34. Bay du Vin. Son of Clifford. Survived by his wife, Violet, 31, and eight children from nine years to a baby.

MacLenaghan, Alfred, 30. Bay du Vin. Single, but supported his parents and family.

Manuel, Amon, 43. Manuel's Post Office. Survived by mother, wife and two daughters.

Manuel, William G., 70. Manuel's Post Office. Sole supporter of his wife Rose, 67, and his sixteen-year-old grandson.

Martin, Alonzo, 23. Baie Ste. Anne. Survived by his parents, whom he supported.

Martin, André, 39. Baie Ste. Anne. Survived by his wife, Dorcas, 26, and their three children, aged three years, twenty months, and three months.

Martin, Rémi, 19. Baie Ste. Anne. Survived by his mother and her five other children, ranging from two months to seventeen years, all of whom he supported.

McLeod, George, 39. Bay du Vin. Helped support both his parents.

Mills, Allan, 47. Black River. Survived by his wife, Annie, 45, and six children aged two years to twenty-four years.

Mills, Andrew, 21. Black River. Son of Allan. Survived by his wife, Rita. They were expecting their first-born the following month.

Richard, Geoffrey, 60. Baie Ste. Anne. Survived by his wife, Mary, 64.

Richard, Jean-Louis, 26. Baie Ste. Anne. Son of Geoffrey.

Richard, Lionel, 29. Baie Ste. Anne. Son of Geoffrey.

Robichaud, Raphael, 42. Manuel's Post Office. Survived by his wife, Caroline, 45, a 15-year-old, and his widowed mother, 82.

Robichaud, Victor, 42. Manuel's Post Office. Survived by his wife, Rose Anna, and eight children, the eldest of which was twelve.

Roy, Leo Joseph, 29. St. Margaret's. Survived by his pregnant wife, Julia, 22, and two-year-old child.

Taylor, Harold, 20. Bay du Vin. Survived by his mother and her seven other children, the eldest of which was eighteen.

Williston, Cunard, 49. Bay du Vin. Sole supporter of his widowed mother and his sisters.

Williston, Eric, 13. Bay du Vin.

Williston, Haley, 19. Bay du Vin. Survived by his father and mother, whom he helped support.

Williston, Haynes, 40. Bay du Vin. Survived by his wife, Agnes, who was expecting a child.

Williston, Oswald 'Ossie,' 40. Single.

Thirty-five years later, one re-married widow reflected:

"Sometimes I think I had it hard, and then I look around and think there are people having it worse. I think I took my spite out on the Lord for a while, but I guess I must have a lot of faith or I wouldn't be able to go through what I did. I know I have a lot to be thankful for—a good husband and eight good children. They have a memorial every year—but I can't take it."

BEST CHEF
Wayson Choy (1939–   )

The blatant racism that lay behind the enactment of Canada's notorious anti-Chinese legislation—from the Head Tax of 1885 to the Chinese Exclusion Act of 1923—reveals itself in the experience of Choy's father as a cook on the Canadian Pacific Steamship Line.

When I was old enough to listen at last to Father's stories about his labours on the CPR ships, I came to understand better his bouts of drinking and his roving eye.

The combination of twelve- to fourteen-hour shifts, cramped working conditions and the superior attitudes of his white supervisors created in him a bursting rage that he had to struggle hard to contain. There were a dozen daily humiliations that he had no chance to dispute. Chinese crew must leave last, always stand aside for others, take the worst bunks and sleeping cabins, and never be taught any other duties beyond those fit for no-class, half-salaried labourers. Every day, Father had to swallow his bitter frustrations. He came home with a hair-trigger temper.

Father was not entirely helpless. His pride often saw him through unjust situations and won him some respect. One of his favourite stories, typical of his instinct to fight back, he repeated over and over.

"Captain complain every morning his breakfast cold!" Father shook his head with renewed anger every time he began this story. "Captain just come two weeks to ship. New captain. Don't know I best chef!"

Father was a perfect chef, the kind who challenged everyone else to keep up to his standards. He took immense pleasure in his skills as a chef; he enjoyed the spontaneous compliments of the crew, who fed off his table, and remembered every guest who'd sent a note to thank him for his attention to their orders. Each day, when the last round of cooking was done, Father and his assistants left the galley spotless. The bottoms of hanging pots and pans shone like mirrors. Before the former captain had left the ship, he had shaken Father's hand and told him, "I wish I could take you with me, Toy."

Father was proud to be recognized by his first name.

But the new captain was displeased.

Blunt typewritten notes arrived every day by two p.m., just before Father's two-hour break; day after day, the notes came, written for a simpleton to comprehend.

"Porridge cold!!!" read one note, the three exclamation marks, like daggers, underscoring the captain's displeasure. "Coffee—ice!!!"

Father recounted the paper litany of complaints that the captain sent for his attention. "Eggs and bacon cold. Toast cold. Coffee like goddamn ice!"

By the second week, the complaints turned into reprimands too insulting for Father to bear. Father began to read them aloud to the crew. A war had been declared between Captain and Chef.

"What the hell's going on in that galley?" one note read.

There was, of course, a reason for the chilly breakfast trays that eventually made their way to the captain's private cabin. As the new executive officer, the captain had changed the way things worked. He didn't want Father's lowly assistant, a shuffling galley Chinese, to be seen anywhere near the officers' quarters. Father's helper was now commanded to deliver the breakfast tray to the captain's chief officer or, if he was not available, to find his assistant, one deck below. In turn, and in full uniform, the assistant officer would ascend to the captain's cabin, knock on the door, wait five seconds, enter, and leave behind the full tray.

Father was furious. But his galley status did not allow him an opportunity to respond, and it was no use waiting for the captain to drop in for any explanation. Except for his first visit to announce who he was, it was clear from his pompous, nose-above-the-smells attitude that the new captain would not be caught dead among the lowest-paid crew, the Chinamen.

"I fix Captain," Father told his crew. "I fix him good."

Father spent an evening heating up a series of dinner plates and coffee cups in the oven. When he had figured out how long a plate and cup would hold heat without glowing or cracking, he gave the mate specific instructions about delivering the captain's breakfast.

Father knew the captain always went for a morning walk on deck before he returned—promptly at 7:15 a.m.—to his waiting breakfast.

One morning, on Father's strict instructions, the mate bypassed the First Officer and his assistant, slipped into the captain's quarters and laid out the full breakfast tray. The mate told Father he had, with oven mitts, carefully put the main dishes on the woven table mat, and everything looked fine. Father went on with the business of the galley, cooking, and ordering others to follow his schedule of breakfasts for the crew and guests. In the midst of a humming galley, everyone was astonished to see the new captain blundering through the swinging double doors, bellowing for Father.

"Where the hell is Choy!"

Father stepped up, wiped his hands on his long apron, tilted back his chef's headgear, and looked the red-cheeked captain in the eye. The man's eyes blazed back at him.

"The plate singed my fingers!" he yelled. "I almost scalded my tongue with the goddamn coffee!"

"You want hot!" Father said. "I give you hot!"

"Damn it, Choy—" the captain started, but Father took over, his fists hitting the stainless-steel surface of the galley counter.

"Every morning—*bang!*—breakfast leave my stove hot!" Father pointed to the eggs sizzling in the pan. "You breakfast leave my stove hot, yes? Egg from stove hot, yes?—*bang!*—Toast hot, coffee hot—*bang, bang!*—Leave hot." Father paused, rested his fists on the counter, then quietly finished: "... and you get cold." Father looked at his crew, then back at the broad face before him. "*Who* you blame?"

Whenever he recalled the look on the captain's face, Father roared with laughter.

"After that," Father repeatedly told me, "no more shit-you noise from captain."

—from *Paper Shadows: A Chinatown Childhood* (1999)

ACKNOWLEDGEMENTS

We have been assisted, encouraged and inspired by many people both in Canada and abroad. All of them kept our spirits up in various ways as the project developed. Although they are too numerous to list individually, we owe them our deepest thanks and appreciation.

We especially acknowledge the enthusiasm and practical insight of the late Jim Munro, founder of Munro's Books, Victoria, BC, who immediately saw the potential of an early idea and opened the way toward publication.

Without the creative imagination of writers and poets, our book could not have been. The names of our contributors are in our Permissions section, but their enrichment of the fabric of Canadian life surpasses a mere word of appreciation. We honour them and give thanks for their vision. Similarly, we are grateful to all those associated with authors' estates who have generously given permission to reprint.

All of the publishers listed in Permissions graciously gave their consent, without which our book would not have been possible. At the outset, we particularly appreciated the wise counsel of Philip Cercone (McGill-Queen's University Press). Later, as we navigated the complexities of Canadian copyright law, publishers and their indefatigable agents were generous and supportive in granting permissions and issuing licences.

Libraries, museums and archives were fathomless treasure troves. Among those whose assistance was invaluable were Lee Edgar (Vancouver Maritime Museum), Jennifer Hevenor (Canadian Museum of Immigration at Pier 21), Lesley Read (Robinson College Library, Cambridge, UK), Joan Ritcey (Association of

Newfoundland and Labrador Archives) and the staff of University of Victoria Libraries, Interlibrary Loans and Special Collections.

For the sheer volume of sleuthing involved in tracking down copyright status and—where requisite—permissions, we offer our deep appreciation for the infinite patience of Liv Albert (Penguin Random House Canada), Jessica Luet (Access Copyright) and Patrick Osborne (Library and Archives Canada).

Friends and family too numerous to list have plied us with suggestions and patiently put up with our singlemindedness. Among them, Sel and Joan Caradus hosted a generous celebration in honour of *Spindrift*, while Matthew Wolferstan put everything aside to create his illustrations in record time. Our thanks to all of them.

Finally, our appreciation to the wonderful team at Douglas & McIntyre: project editor Peter Robson, managing editor and cover designer Anna Comfort O'Keeffe, contracts coordinator Nicola Goshulak, proofreader Lucy Kenward, designer Mary White, editorial assistant Brianna Cerkiewicz, ebook designer Shed Simas and to our copy editor Patricia Wolfe.

PERMISSIONS

Abella, Irving, and Harold Troper. *None Is Too Many: Canada and the Jews of Europe, 1933–1948*, © 1983, 2000, 2012 Irving Abella and Harold Troper, published by University of Toronto Press. Toronto. Reprinted with permission of the publisher.

Acorn, Milton. "Dragging for Traps," "The Squall" and "Charlottetown Harbour" from *In a Springtime Instant: Selected Poems* (Mosaic Press, Oakville, ON: 2012, 2015) edited by James Deahl, reprinted by permission of Mosaic Press on behalf of the Estate of Milton Acorn.

Admiralty, Navigation and Direction Department. *Handling Ships.* London: Admiralty, 1954. Public domain.

Anderson, Allan. *Salt Water, Fresh Water.* Toronto: The Macmillan Company of Canada Limited, 1979. © Copyright Allan Anderson 1979. This work is protected by copyright and the making of this copy was with the permission of Access Copyright. Any alteration of its content or further copying in any form whatsoever is strictly prohibited unless otherwise permitted by law.

Armstrong, Sally. *The Nine Lives of Charlotte Taylor.* Toronto: Random House Canada, 2007. Copyright 2007 Sally Armstrong. Reprinted by permission of Penguin Canada, a division of Penguin Random House Canada Limited.

Aua. See Rasmussen, Knud.

Audette, Louis C. See Macpherson, Ken.

Bates, Judy Fong. *China Dog and Other Tales from a Chinese Laundry.* Toronto: Sister Vision, 1997. Copyright © 1997 Judy Fong Bates. Reprinted by permission of McClelland and Stewart, a division of Penguin Random House Canada Limited.

Berton, Pierre. *My Country: The Remarkable Past*. Toronto: McClelland and Stewart, 1976. Copyright 1976. Reprinted by permission of Doubleday Canada, a division of Penguin Random House Canada Limited.

Bilby, Julian W. *Nanook of the North*. London: George W. Newnes Ltd., 1925. Source: Library and Archives Canada, AMICUS 21772752.

Birney, Earle. *Turvey*. Copyright 1949, 1951 McClelland and Stewart Ltd. Reprinted by permission of McClelland and Stewart, a division of Penguin Random House Canada Limited.

Bissoondath, Neil. The excerpt "The Imprisoning Sea" is taken from the novel *A Casual Brutality*, originally published by Macmillan of Canada, subsequently re-issued by Cormorant Books, Toronto. Copyright © 1988, 2002 Neil Bissoondath. Used with the permission of the publisher.

Blanchet, M. Wylie. *The Curve of Time*. 50th Anniversary Edition. North Vancouver: Whitecap Books Ltd., 2011. Reprinted with permission of Tara Blanchet.

Boas, Franz. From *The Religion of the Kwakiutl Indians*. New York: Columbia University Press, 1930. Reprinted with permission of the publisher.

Borradaile, Osmond, and Anita Borradaile Hadley. *Life Through a Lens: Memoirs of a Cinematographer*. Montreal and Kingston: McGill-Queen's University Press, 2001. Extract "Convoy to Tobruk," with permission of the publisher.

Boudreau, Lou. 2002. Reprinted with permission of Capt. Lou Boudreau.

Bowman, Louise Morey. "Sea Sand," from *Moonlight and Common Day*. Toronto: Macmillan, 1922. Source: Library and Archives Canada, AMICUS 6218916.

Brewster, Elizabeth. *Passage of Summer: Selected Poems*. Toronto: The Ryerson Press, 1969. With permission of the University of Saskatchewan.

Bruce, Charles. *The Mulgrave Road*. Toronto: Macmillan, 1951. Reprinted with the permission of Harry Bruce.

Bruce, Charles. *The Mulgrave Road: Selected Poems of Charles Bruce*. Edited by Andy Wainwright and Lesley Choyce. Porters Lake: Pottersfield Press, 1985. Reprinted with the permission of Harry Bruce.

Cameron, Silver Donald. *Once Upon a Schooner: A Foreign Voyage in Bluenose II*. Halifax: Formac Publishing Limited, 1992. Reprinted with permission of the author.

Cameron, Silver Donald. *Wind, Whales and Whisky: A Cape Breton Voyage*. Toronto: Macmillan Canada, 1991. Reprinted with permission of the author.

Carman, Bliss. *Later Poems*. Toronto: McClelland & Stewart, 1921. Source: Library and Archives Canada, AMICUS 5485641.

Carr, Emily. *Klee Wyck*. Toronto, Vancouver: Clarke, Irwin & Company Limited, 1941. Public domain.

Carr, Emily. *The Book of Small*. [1942] Vancouver: Douglas & McIntyre Ltd., 2004. Reprinted with the permission of the publisher.

Choy, Wayson. *The Jade Peony*, 1995. Douglas & McIntyre. Reprinted with the permission of the publisher.

Choy, Wayson. *Paper Shadows: Chinatown Childhood*. Penguin Books Canada Ltd., 1999. Copyright 1999 Wayson Choy. Reprinted by permission of Penguin Canada, a division of Penguin Random House Canada Limited.

Coates, Ken, and Bill Morrison. *The Sinking of the Princess Sophia: Taking the North Down with Her*. Fairbanks, Alaska: University of Alaska Press, 1991. With permission of Ken Coates.

Cochkanoff, Greg, and Bob Chaulk. SS *Atlantic: The White Star Line's First Disaster at Sea*. Fredericton, NB: Goose Lane Editions, 2009. Copyright 2009 by Greg Cochkanoff and Bob Chaulk. Reprinted with permission of Goose Lane Editions.

Compton, Anne. *Opening the Island*. Markham, ON: Fitzhenry & Whiteside, 2002. The poem "North Shore, PEI" is reprinted with permission of the publisher and Anne Compton.

Costain, Thomas B. *The White and the Gold: The French Regime in Canada*. New York: Doubleday & Company Inc. 1954. Copyright © 1954 by Thomas B. Costain. Copyright renewed © 1982 by Molly Costain Haycroft and Dora C. Steinmetz. Used by permission of Doubleday, an imprint of the Knopf Doubleday Publishing Group, a division of Penguin Random House LLC. All rights reserved.

Crawford, Isabella Valancy. *Collected Poems* [ed. J.W. Garvin, 1905]. Introduced by James Reaney. Toronto: University of Toronto Press, 1972. Reprinted with permission of the publisher.

Creighton, Donald. *The Story of Canada*. Toronto: The Macmillan Company of Canada Limited, 1960. Reprinted with permission of the Creighton estate.

Crummey, Michael. *Arguments with Gravity*. Kingston, Ontario: Quarry Press Inc., 1996. With permission of Michael Crummey.

Crummey, Michael. *Hard Light*. London, ON: Brick Books Classics 5, 2005. With permission of Michael Crummey and Brick Books.

Day, Frank Parker. *Rockbound*. © University of Toronto Press 1989. Originally published by Doubleday, Doran & Company in 1928. Published by the University of Toronto Press in 1973. Public domain.

Delgado, James P. *Across the Top of the World: The Quest for the Northwest Passage.* Douglas & McIntyre, 2009. Reprinted with the permission of the publisher.

Delgado, James P. *Waterfront: The Illustrated Maritime History of Greater Vancouver.* Vancouver, BC: Stanton Atkins & Dosil Publishers, [2005] Second Edition, 2010. Excerpt reprinted with permission of the publisher.

Denham, Joe. *The Year of Broken Glass.* Nightwood Editions, 2011. "In on the Tide" and "Crabbing" reprinted with permission of the publisher.

Department of National Defence. *Divine Service Book for the Armed Forces.* Toronto: Ryerson Press, 1950. Source: Library and Archives Canada, AMICUS 7846163.

Desrochers, Suzanne. *Bride of New France.* Toronto: Penguin Canada, 2011. Copyright © 2011 Suzanne Desrochers. Reprinted by permission of Penguin Canada, a division of Penguin Random House Canada Limited.

de Villiers, Marq. *Witch in the Wind: The True Story of the Legendary Bluenose.* Toronto: Thomas Allen Publishers, 2007. Reprinted with permission of Dundurn Press and Marq de Villiers.

Dudek, Louis. *The Transparent Sea.* Toronto: Contact Press, 1956. Reprinted with permission of Gregory Dudek.

Dudek, Louis. *The Poetry of Louis Dudek: Definitive Edition.* Ottawa: The Golden Dog, 1998. Reprinted with permission of Gregory Dudek.

Easton, Alan. *50 North: An Atlantic Battleground.* Toronto: Ryerson Press, 1963. Markham, ON: Paperjacks, 1980. © 1963 Alan Easton. This work is protected by copyright and the making of this copy was with the permission of Access Copyright. Any alteration of its content or further copying in any form whatsoever is strictly prohibited unless otherwise permitted by law.

Eber, Dorothy. *People from Our Side, a life story with photographs by Peter Pitseolak and oral biography by Dorothy Eber.* Edmonton: Hurtig Publishers, 1975. Eber, Pitseolak and Eber, Dorothy Harley. "Modern Times." *People from Our Side.* MQUP, 1993.

Etooangat, Aksaajuuq. "The Whalers of Pangnirtung." In Penny Petrone, ed., *Northern Voices: Inuit Writing in English.* Toronto: University of Toronto Press, 1988. Reprinted with the permission of Pudloo Timothy Etuangat and Tommy Etuangat.

Falt, Michael. "Devastating Loss" from *The Chronicle Herald,* 26 February 2013. Available online at http://thechronicleherald.ca/letters/788013-reader-s-corner-devastating-loss. Reprinted with the permission of the author.

Farrar, F.S. *Arctic Assignment: The Story of the St. Roch.* Illustrated by Vernon Mould. Edited by Barrett Bonnezen. Toronto: The Macmillan

Company of Canada, 1955. With the assistance of Access Copyright, and the permission of Vernon Mould.

Fong, Judy. See Bates.

French, Alice. *My Name is Masak.* Winnipeg: Peguis Publishers Limited, 1976. Reprinted with the permission of Dominic French.

Garner, Hugh. *Storm Below.* Toronto: Collins, 1949. Markham, ON: Paperjacks, 1984. Extract reprinted with permission of the Hugh Garner Estate, and Barbara Wong.

Gough, Barry. *Juan de Fuca's Strait: Voyages in the Waterway of Forgotten Dreams.* Madeira Park, BC: Harbour Publishing, 2012. Excerpted and re-printed with the permission of the publisher and the author.

Greene, Richard. *Crossing the Straits.* Toronto: St. Thomas Poetry Series, 2004. With permission of the publisher and Richard Greene.

Greene, Richard. *Boxing the Compass.* Québec: Véhicule Press, 2009. The excerpt from the poem "Boxing the Compass" is used by permission of the author and Signal Editions/Véhicule Press.

Hacking, Norman R., and W. Kaye Lamb. *The Princess Story: A Century and a Half of West Coast Shipping.* Vancouver, BC: Mitchell Press Limited, 1974. Reprinted with permission of the publisher.

Hadley, Anita Borradaile. See Borradaile.

Hadley, Michael L. *God's Little Ships: A History of the Columbia Coast Mission.* Madeira Park, BC: Harbour Publishing, 1995. By permission of the publisher and the author.

Hadley, Michael L. *U-Boats against Canada: German Submarines in Canadian Waters.* Montreal and Kingston: McGill-Queen's University Press, 1985. Reprinted by permission of the publisher and author.

Hadley, Michael L., and Roger Sarty. *Tin-Pots & Pirate Ships: Canadian Naval Forces & German Sea Raiders 1880–1918.* Montreal and Kingston: McGill-Queen's University Press, 1991. Reprinted with permission of the publisher and authors.

Hadley, Norman. "A Boatload of Salty Dips." Unpublished manu-script. Printed with permission of the Estate of Norman Hadley.

Hill, Beth. Excerpt from *Upcoast Summers.* Horsdal & Schubart Publishers Ltd. 1985. Copyright © 1985 by Beth Hill. Reprinted with permission of TouchWood Editions.

Hill, Lawrence. *The Book of Negroes.* Toronto: HarperCollins Publishers Ltd., 2007. Excerpt from *The Book of Negroes* © 2007 by Lawrence Hill. Published by HarperCollins Ltd. All rights reserved.

Hoang, Nhung. "One Time I Crossed the China Sea," in *Refugee Love,* Ottawa: self-published, 1993. With permission of Nhung Hoang.

Horwood, Harold. *Tomorrow Will Be Sunday.* Garden City, New York: Doubleday & Company, Inc., 1966. Excerpt reprinted by permission of Andrew Horwood.

Horwood, Harold. *White Eskimo: A Novel of Labrador.* Toronto: Doubleday Canada, 1972. By permission of Andrew Horwood.

Iglauer, Edith. *Fishing with John.* Madeira Park, BC: Harbour Publishing, 1992. With permission of the publisher.

Jackman, S.W. ed. *At Sea and By Land: The Reminiscences of William Balfour Macdonald, RN.* Victoria, BC: Sono Nis Press, 1983. Reprinted with permission of the publisher.

Johnson, E. Pauline (Tekahionwake). *Legends of Vancouver.* Vancouver: David Spencer Limited, 1911. Vancouver/Toronto: Douglas & McIntyre, 1997. Reprinted with the permission of the publisher.

Johnston, Wayne. *Baltimore's Mansion: A Memoir.* Toronto: Alfred A. Knopf Canada, 1999. Copyright © 1999 1310945 Ontario Inc. Reprinted by permission of Alfred A. Knopf Canada, a division of Penguin Random House Canada Limited.

Johnston, Wayne. *The Colony of Unrequited Dreams.* Toronto: Vintage Books, 1998. Copyright © 1998 1310945 Ontario Inc. Reprinted by permission of Alfred A. Knopf Canada, a division of Penguin Random House Canada Limited.

Kerr, J. Lennox. *Wilfred Grenfell: His Life and Work.* London and Toronto: George. G. Harrap & Co., 1959. Reprinted with permission of Adam J. Kerr.

Kilbourn, William. *The Firebrand: William Lyon Mackenzie and the Rebellion in Upper Canada.* Toronto: Clarke, Irwin & Company Limited, 1956. Reprinted with permission of the Dundurn Group.

Kogawa, Joy. *Obasan.* Toronto: Lester & Orpen Dennys, 1981. Toronto: Penguin Canada 1983. Reprinted with permission of the publisher and Joy Kogawa.

Koppel, Tom. *Ebb and Flow: Tides and Life on Our Once and Future Planet.* Toronto: The Dundurn Group, 2007. Reprinted with permission of the publisher and Tom Koppel.

Larsen, Henry, with Frank R. Sheer and Edvard Omholt-Jensen. *The Big Ship.* Toronto and Montreal: McClelland and Stewart Limited, 1967. Reprinted with permission of Doreen Larsen Riedel.

Leighton, Kenneth Macrae. *Oar & Sail: An Odyssey of the West Coast.* Smithers, BC: Creekstone Press Ltd., 1999. Reprinted with permission of the publisher and the Leighton Estate.

Lescarbot, Marc. *Nova Francia: A Description of Acadia, 1609.* Trans. P. Erondelle, 1609. New York & London: Harper & Brothers, 1928. Source: Library and Archives Canada, AMICUS 4528552.

Leslie, Kenneth. *By Stubborn Stars and Other Poems.* Toronto: The Ryerson Press, 1938. Reprinted with permission of Rosaleen Leslie Dickson.

Lowry, Malcolm. *The Collected Poetry of Malcolm Lowry.* Edited and introduced by Kathleen Scherf. Vancouver: © University of British Columbia Press, 1992. All rights reserved by the publisher. Reprinted with permission of the publisher.

Lowry, Malcolm. *October Ferry to Gabriola.* Vancouver: Douglas & McIntyre, 1970. Reprinted with the permission of the publisher.

Lundy, Derek. *The Way of a Ship: A Square-Rigger Voyage in the Last Days of Sail.* New York: HarperCollins, 2002. Copyright © 2002 Beara Inc. Reprinted by permission of Alfred A. Knopf Canada, a division of Penguin Random House Canada Limited.

Macdonald, William Balfour. See Jackman, S.W.

MacGillivray, Don. "Cape Bretoners in the Victoria Sealing Fleet, and beyond." *The Northern Mariner / Le Marin du Nord.* Vol. 20, no. 3. July 2010, 239–242, 244–45. Reprinted with permission of the editors.

MacIntyre, Linden. *The Bishop's Man.* Toronto: Random House Canada, 2009. Copyright © 2009 Linden MacIntyre. Reprinted by permission of Random House Canada, a division of Penguin Random House Canada Limited.

MacKinnon, Una H. Morris. *The Tides of the Missiquash,* in Eliza Ritchie, ed., *The Songs of the Maritimes.* Toronto: McClelland & Stewart, Limited, 1931. Public domain. With assistance from Access Copyright.

MacLennan, Hugh. *Barometer Rising.* [First edition William Collins Sons & Co., 1941; New Canadian Library edition 1989.] Toronto: McClelland & Stewart Ltd., 1989. Reprinted with permission of Blanche C. Gregory Inc.

MacMechan, Archibald. "Off Coronel," in Eliza Ritchie, ed., *Songs of the Maritimes.* Toronto: McClelland & Stewart, Limited, 1931. Source: Library and Archives Canada, AMICUS 2274515.

Macpherson, Ken, and Marc Milner. *Corvettes of the Royal Canadian Navy 1939–1945.* Foreword by Louis C. Audette. St. Catharines, ON: Vanwell Publishing Ltd., 1993. Reprinted with permission of the publisher.

Maillet, Antonine. *Pélagie: The Return to Acadie.* [*Pélagie-la-Charette,* Montréal: Leméac Éditeur Inc., 1979.] Copyright © 2004 by Antonine Maillet, translated by Philip Stratford. Fredericton: Goose Lane Editions, 2004. Reprinted by permission of Goose Lane Editions.

Martel, Yann, *Life of Pi*. Toronto: Vintage Canada, 2001. Copyright © 2001 Yann Martel. Reprinted by permission of Alfred A. Knopf Canada, a division of Penguin Random House Canada Limited.

Máté, Ferenc. *Ghost Sea*. New York: W.W. Norton, 2006. With permission of the author and Albatross Books/W.W. Norton.

McKinney, Sam. Excerpt from *Sailing with Vancouver: A modern sea dog, antique charts and a voyage through time*. Victoria: TouchWood Editions, 2004. Reprinted with permission of TouchWood Editions.

McLaren, Floris Clark. *The Frozen Fire*. Toronto: The Macmillan Company of Canada Limited, 1937. Reprinted by permission of Diane McLaren.

McLaren, Keith. *A Race for Real Sailors: The Bluenose and The International Fisherman's Cup, 1920–1938*. Vancouver and Toronto: Douglas & McIntyre, 2006. Reprinted with the permission of the author and the publisher.

McMurray, Kevin F. *Dark Descent: Diving and the Deadly Allure of the Empress of Ireland*. Camden, Maine: McGraw-Hill / International Marine, 2004. Reprinted with permission of the publisher.

Milner, Marc. *Canada's Navy: The First Century*. © Toronto: University of Toronto Press, 1999. Reprinted with permission of the publisher and the author.

Montgomery, L.M. *Anne's House of Dreams*. Toronto: McClelland & Stewart Limited, 1920. With permission. L.M. Montgomery is a trademark of Heirs of L.M. Montgomery Inc.

Montgomery, L.M. *Anne of Ingleside*. Toronto: McClelland & Stewart Inc., 1939. With permission. L.M. Montgomery is a trademark of Heirs of L.M. Montgomery Inc.

Moore, Lisa. *February*. Toronto: House of Anansi Press Inc., 2009. Selection from *February* copyright 2009 by Lisa Moore. Reprinted by permission of House of Anansi Press Inc. Toronto. www.houseofanansi.com.

Morrissey, Donna. *Sylvanus Now*. Toronto: Penguin Canada, 2005. Copyright © 2005 Donna Morrissey. Reprinted by permission of Penguin Canada, a division of Penguin Random House Canada Limited.

Mowat, Farley. *The Boat Who Wouldn't Float*. [1969] Toronto: McClelland & Stewart, 2009. Copyright © 1969 Farley Mowat. Revised text copyright © 1974 Farley Mowat. Reprinted by permission of McClelland & Stewart, a division of Penguin Random House Canada Limited.

Mowat, Farley. *Grey Seas Under*. An Atlantic Monthly Press Book. Boston and Toronto: Little, Brown and Company, 1958. With permission of the Farley Mowat Estate.

Munro, Alice. *The View from Castle Rock*. Toronto: A Douglas Gibson Book, McClelland & Stewart Ltd., 2006. Copyright © 2006 Alice Munro. Reprinted by permission of McClelland & Stewart, a division of Penguin Random House Canada Limited.

Newman, Peter C. *Company of Adventurers,* Volume I. Markham, ON: Viking, Penguin Books Canada Ltd., 1985. Copyright © 1985 Power Reporting Ltd. Reprinted by permission of the author and Penguin Canada, a division of Penguin Random House Canada Limited.

Norris, Pat Wastell. "Time & Tide: A History of Telegraph Cove." in Howard White, ed., *Raincoast Chronicles Four/Five*. Madeira Park, BC: Harbour Publishing, 2005, 43–52. Reprinted with the permission of the publisher.

Ondaatje, Michael. *The Cat's Table.* Toronto: McClelland & Stewart Ltd., 2011. Copyright © 2011 Michael Ondaatje. Reprinted by permission of McClelland & Stewart, a division of Penguin Random House Canada Limited.

Parkman, Francis. *The Jesuits in North America,* Part Second. [1897]. Williamstown, Massachusetts: Corner House Publishers, 1970. Public domain.

Peritz, Ingrid. "Bones found on Gaspé coast could be of 1847 shipwreck victims." *The Globe and Mail,* 19 July 2011, A4. Extract by permission of Ingrid Peritz and *The Globe and Mail.*

Petrone, Penny. See Etooangat, Aksaajuuq.

Pitseolak, Peter. See Eber, Dorothy.

Poole, Michael. *Ragged Islands: A Journey by Canoe Through the Inside Passage.* Douglas & McIntyre, 2010. Reprinted with the permission of the publisher.

Pratt, E.J. *Newfoundland Verse.* Toronto: Ryerson Press, 1923. Public domain. With assistance from Access Copyright.

Pratt, E.J. *Many Moods.* Toronto: Macmillan Company of Canada, 1932. Public domain.

Pritchard, James. *A Bridge of Ships: Canadian Shipbuilding during the Second World War.* Montreal & Kingston: McGill-Queen's University Press, 2011. Excerpt reprinted with permission of the author and the publisher.

Proulx, E. Annie. *The Shipping News.* New York: Simon & Schuster Inc., Scribner Paperback Fiction, 1993. With permission of the publisher.

Pryde, Duncan. *Nunaga: My Land, My Country.* Edmonton: M.G. Hurtig Ltd., 1971. Published 1985 by Eland Publishing Ltd., UK. Reprinted with permission Eland Publishing Ltd. © 1971 Duncan Pryde.

Purdy, Al. *Beyond Remembering: The Collected Poems of Al Purdy.* Madeira Park, BC: Harbour Publishing, 2000. Reprinted with the permission of the publisher.

Raddall, Thomas H. *Halifax: Warden of the North.* Toronto: McClelland and Stewart Limited, [1948] revised edition 1971. With permission of Dalhousie University, the copyright holder.

Raddall, Thomas H. *The Nymph and the Lamp.* Halifax: Toronto: McClelland and Stewart Limited, 1950. With permission of Dalhousie University, the copyright holder.

Rahn, David. See Wahl, Ryan.

Rasmussen, Knud. *Across Arctic America: Narrative of the Fifth Thule Expedition.* New York: Greenwood Press Publishers, 1969. With permission of University of Alaska Press.

Reid, Martine J. *Bill Reid and the Haida Canoe,* edited by Martine J. Reid. Madeira Park, BC: Harbour Publishing, 2011. Reprinted with the permission of the publisher.

Ricci, Nino. The excerpt "Burial at Sea" is taken from the novel *Lives of the Saints.* Published by Cormorant Books, Toronto. Copyright © 1990 Nino Ricci. Used with permission of the publisher.

Richards, James, and Marlene Richards, with Eric Hustvedt. *The Sea in My Blood: The Life and Times of Captain Andy Publicover.* Hantsport, NS: Lancelot Press Limited, 1986. With permission of Captain James Richards and Marlene Richards.

Ritchie, Eliza. See MacMechan, Archibald.

Roberts, Theodore Goodridge. *The Leather Bottle.* Toronto: The Ryerson Press, 1934. Source: Library and Archives Canada, AMICUS 6264475.

Rogers, Stan. "The Bluenose," Dundas, ON: Fogarty's Cove Music, Inc., 1981. With permission of Ariel Rogers, Fogarty's Cove Music, Inc.

Rogers, Stan. "The Northwest Passage," Dundas, ON: Fogarty's Cove Music, Inc., 1981. With permission of Ariel Rogers, Fogarty's Cove Music, Inc.

Roy, Gabrielle. *Street of Riches.* Translated from the French (*Rue Deschambault,* Paris: Flammarion, 1955) by Harry Binsse. Toronto: McClelland and Stewart, Limited, 1957. Reprinted with permission of Gabrielle Roy Fonds.

Sarty, Roger. See Hadley, Michael. *Tin-Pots and Pirate Ships.*

Schull, Joseph. *The Far Distant Ships: An Official Account of Canadian Naval Operations in the Second World War.* Ottawa: Queen's Printer, 1950. Source: Library and Archives Canada/AMICUS 2482226/pages vii–viii.

Shirley, Gwyneth M. *Ballad of the Brides.* Canadian Museum of Immigration at Pier 21 (S2012.2275.1) www.pier21.ca. With permission of Gwyneth M. Shirley.

Skelton, Robin. *One Leaf Shaking.* Victoria, BC: Beach Holme Publishers, A Porcépic Book, 1996. With permission of Alison and Brigid Skelton.

Slocum, Joshua. *Sailing Alone Around the World.* [First published in 1900.] New York: Dover Publications, Inc., 1956. Public domain.

Snider, David (Duke). "A Polar Ice Operation: What it takes," in *Canadian Naval Review* (vol. 11, no. 1, 2015). With permission of the publisher.

Snively, Gloria. *Exploring the Seashore in British Columbia, Washington and Oregon: A Guide to Shorebirds and Intertidal Plants and Animals.* West Vancouver: Gordon Soules Book Publishers Ltd., 1978. With permission of the author and the publisher.

Stead, Gordon W. *A Leaf Upon the Sea: A Small Ship in the Mediterranean, 1941–1943.* Vancouver: © The University of British Columbia Press, 1988. All rights reserved by the Publisher. Reprinted with permission of the publisher.

Teece, Philip. *A Dream of Islands.* Victoria, BC: Orca Book Publishers, 1988. Reprinted with permission of the publisher and Philip Teece.

Teece, Philip. *A Shimmer on the Horizon.* Victoria, BC: Orca Book Publishers, 1999. Reprinted with permission of the publisher and Philip Teece.

Thomas, Audrey. Excerpted from *Ladies and Escorts.* Ottawa: Oberon Press, 1977. With permission of Audrey Thomas.

Turner, Robert D. *Those Beautiful Coastal Liners: The Canadian Pacific's Princesses.* Victoria: Sono Nis Press, 2001. Reprinted with permission of the publisher.

Urquhart, Jane. *Away.* Toronto: McClelland & Stewart Inc., 1993. Copyright © 1993 Jane Urquhart. Reprinted by permission of McClelland & Stewart, a division of Penguin Random House Canada Limited.

Vancouver, George. *A Voyage of Discovery to the North Pacific Ocean and Round the World.* 3 vols. John Vancouver, ed. London: G.G. and J. Robinson and J. Edwards, 1798. Source: Library and Archives Canada, AMICUS 9548291.

Wahl, Ryan. *Legacy in Wood: The Wahl Family Boat Builders.* Preface by David Rahn, Madeira Park, BC: Harbour Publishing, 2008. Reprinted with the permission of the publisher and the author of the preface.

Wainwright, Andy, and Lesley Choyce, See Bruce, Charles. *The Mulgrave Road.*

Wallas, James. See Whitaker, Pamela.

Whalley, George. *The Collected Poems of George Whalley.* Edited with an Introduction by George Johnston. Kingston, ON: Quarry Press, 1986. With the permission of Emily Whalley.

Whitaker, Pamela. *Kwakiutl Legends.* As told by Chief James Wallas. North Vancouver: Hancock House Publishers Ltd., 1981. With permission of the publisher.

Wiebe, Rudy. Excerpt from *Playing Dead: A contemplation concerning the Arctic.* Copyright © 1989, Edmonton, AB: NeWest Press Ltd., 1989, 2003 by Jackpine House Limited. Reprinted by permission of NeWest Press. All rights reserved.

Williams, Glyn. *Arctic Labyrinth: The Quest for the Northwest Passage.* Toronto: Viking Canada, 2009. Copyright © Glyn Williams. Reprinted by permission of Penguin Canada, a division of Penguin Random House Limited.

Wilson, Ethel. Excerpted from *Mrs. Golightly and Other Stories.* Toronto: The Macmillan Company of Canada Limited, 1961. Copyright © 1990 University of British Columbia Library. Reprinted by permission of McClelland & Stewart, a division of Penguin Random House Canada Limited.

Wood, Herbert P. *Till We Meet Again: The Sinking of the Empress of Ireland.* Toronto: Image Publishing Inc., 1982. With the permission of Glen Herbert Wood.

Yorath, Chris. *A Measure of Value: the Story of the D'Arcy Island Leper Colony.* Victoria/Surrey: TouchWood Editions. An imprint of Horsdal & Schubart Publishers Ltd., 2000. Copyright © 2000 by Chris Yorath. Reprinted with permission of TouchWood Editions.

Zarn, Janet McGill. "My War-Bride's Trip to Canada—Britannic, April 1945." Janet Zarn arrived from Scotland as a War Bride, 1945. Canadian Museum of Immigration at Pier 21 (S2012.2275.1) www.pier21.ca. With permission of the Museum.